Prefa

Because this book heavily features a play
Shakespeare), I think it is only fair to prov
so that I don't accidentally assign you sup
stand what is going on.

Here are the characters you ought to know, and a brief summary of the play
itself:

Leontes – King of Sicily, and a right bastard of a man who accuses his wife of
infidelity and has her imprisoned for it.
Hermione – pregnant wife of Leontes; innocent of said infidelity.
Paulina – a noblewoman; ride or die for Hermione.
Perdita – Princess of Sicily, abandoned in Bohemia as an infant because Leon-
tes doubts her paternity. Raised by a shepherd, and in love with Florizel.
Florizel – Prince of Bohemia, in love with Perdita.
Polixenes – King of Bohemia, Florizel's father, once besties with Leontes.
Mamillius – son of Leontes and Hermione; dies in act three.
Antigonus – Paulina's husband. Killed by a bear in act three, as he abandons
the infant Perdita on Leontes' orders.

The play begins with Leontes suspecting that Hermione is conducting an affair with his close friend, Polixenes, the King of Bohemia. He thinks the child
she is carrying is not his own, and has her imprisoned for it. Polixenes flees
back to Bohemia to escape his wrath.

Hermione gives birth in prison. Paulina pleads with Leontes to
acknowledge his child, but it comes to nothing. He sends away for a message
from an oracle to give him the truth, which will be revealed at Hermione's
trial, and in the meantime sends the infant Perdita with Antigonus into the
wilds of Bohemia to be abandoned. Shortly after abandoning Perdita, Antigonus is killed, and his death is noted with one of Shakespeare's most famous
stage directions: [exit, pursued by a bear].

At Hermione's trial, she swears her innocence but Leontes still does not
believe her. The message returned from the oracle reveals her innocence—
and says that Leontes will never have an heir if Perdita is not recovered.

Hermione faints, and it is revealed that she has died soon after, and so has their son, Mamillius. Now Leontes repents, but of course it is too late.

Sixteen years pass. Perdita has been raised by a shepherd who has grown wealthy, and she is in love with Florizel, the son of Polixenes. Polixenes does not approve of his son's choice of bride, and so the two lovers flee to Sicily, where Florizel and Perdita intend to prevail upon the hospitality of Florizel's father's childhood best friend, Leontes.

They are pursued by Polixenes and the shepherd who raised Perdita as his own, who shares the tokens with which she was found that testify to her royal birth.

Perdita is reunited with her father, and, being now known to be a princess, she and Florizel are free to marry. Paulina reveals she has had a statue made of Hermione, and as they gaze upon it, the statue at last comes to life—and Leontes, Hermione, and Perdita are all together again.

Chapter One

London, England
November, 1824

When first Lydia Alcott had imagined herself upon the stage, her mind had conjured up such fanciful notions: the whisper of the curtain drawing; the reverent hush that would sweep over the crowd; the incandescent joy of moving an audience to laughter—or to tears.

In the years that had followed, that whimsical notion had been crushed to splinters. The curtain drawing inspired no such reverence from the audience, who always seemed to pay half attention at best. If there had ever been silence, it would have heralded only empty seats, for the crowd rarely achieved anything beneath a dull roar. And the only thing remotely incandescent was the flare of the gaslights, which burned into her eyes at each performance.

The nobles were the worst of the lot. At least in the lower theatres in which she had played, those attending had been determined to get their money's worth of each performance, but the aristocracy—they had more money than sense, and the theatre, for them, was not something to be attended for the *art* of it, for the purpose of being swept away into the grandeur of the tale playing out before their eyes, but something of a social event that one attended if one were at loose ends.

In fact, the stage and its actors were little more than window dressing to the true dramatists of the evening, which was to say, those who had come out dressed to the nines, to see and be seen, to chat, to visit, and largely to ignore the performance which they had all paid for the privilege to attend.

She supposed she ought not judge them too severely. *The Winter's Tale* had never been amongst her favorites, either. But it was an effort to make herself heard over the buzz of voices for the few people—perhaps six or seven at the very most, amongst a crowd of hundreds, *thousands*, even—who *were* being properly attentive.

The air was stifling. Thick with cloying perfumes, with the attendant heat of so many bodies crammed together. It was always stuffy, but tonight it seemed even more so. As if the air itself were weighted with something momentous.

A bead of sweat trickled down the back of her neck, disappearing beneath the low neckline of her gown. The role of Perdita wasn't a large one, but it held a certain prestige nonetheless, even if she had only a handful of lines and didn't truly make an appearance until the fourth act.

But here was the beauty of theatre: with the donning of the Bohemian shepherdess costume and the cosmetics and the wreath of dried flowers upon her head, she could, for too brief a time, pretend she was someone else entirely.

Perdita, loved by the faithful Florizel who had cast off father and country in pursuit of that love. The play carried a message as old as time itself—that love transcended every obstacle.

What utter rubbish. Perhaps that might be the case, *if* one happened to be a long-lost princess. Otherwise she had little doubt that eventually Perdita would find herself abandoned, with only her sheep for company.

Thank *God* Perdita had so few lines; there was something in the air that pressed Lydia to distraction, some aura of menace that settled at the back of her neck, rather like eyes boring into her skin. Like the queer current that pervaded the air just before a bolt of lightning struck the earth, she could *sense* something amiss.

She stumbled over her last lines, drawing a brief, concerned look from Giles Montgomery—playing King Leontes—and hoped it would be interpreted by the audience as only a daughter's nerves to be reunited with her father.

Giles would no doubt have *words* for her this evening. Unprintable ones, and a great number of them.

At last the play wound down to its ostensibly happy conclusion; a family reunited, young lovers free at last to marry. The applause should have felt like a victory and yet it hit her ears like a death knell. Her knees shook as she took her bow, surreptitiously scanning the crowd, searching for the threat she had felt, seeking the direction from which the aura of malice had originated.

There—in a box at the right; the cold, dark eyes that had haunted her for the last five years. She would have known them anywhere.

Marcus Beaumont, Baron Newhaven.

He had to have arrived late. She would have seen him so much earlier otherwise. It had become a habit of hers, in the years since last they had met, to search him out. Not out of any misguided leftover love, but out of self-preservation. Even now, she could hear the echo of his last words to her ringing in her head: *Leave London. Should you ever think to return, I will make you regret it.*

Well. She *had* returned, and after too long an absence. The days when she could be cowed by such a threat had long since passed. She was not the foolish young girl she had once been; she was not the friendless, pitiful waif whom he had cast off as easily as breathing.

Though she had hoped never to lay eyes upon him again, had hoped that time and distance had driven her from his mind as she had sought to drive him from hers, still she was the consummate actress that she had forged herself into over the last years.

As the company turned to depart the stage, as the curtain on its strings began to drift closed once more, Lydia swept a graceful curtsey, turned her face full toward the baron's box, and blew him a kiss.

There, she thought as she exited the stage at last. *Make of that what you will, my faithless lord.*

Giles was waiting for her in the wings, his brows furrowed and cheeks hollowed in that peculiar way that heralded a coming storm. He had them, from time to time, whenever one of the members of the acting company he owned had failed to live up to his exacting standards. They tended to blow over quickly, so long as he felt he had been understood and heeded.

Lydia had never had much patience for them, and that, strangely, had earned her his respect over the long years of their friendship and working relationship.

"What the devil was *that*?" he said. "You've never flubbed a line in your life."

Lydia snatched the flower crown from her head, thrusting it at him. "I'm too old to play Perdita," she said. "Give me Hermione; I can make do with her."

"Oh, truly?" Kitty—who had got the role of Hermione—asked. "If you want it, it's yours. I'll take Perdita, and happily."

Giles summoned forth a black look that encompassed the both of them. "All the cosmetics in the world couldn't make you sixteen again, Kitty."

"Well!" Kitty stabbed the tip of her pointed nose in the air, crossing her arms over her chest in a fit of pique.

"And you." Giles jabbed his finger at Lydia. "You haven't got the tragedy in you for Hermione any longer."

"I've played Hermione dozens of times; I know the lines backwards and forwards again. *You've* given me Hermione before!" Her fingers tangled in the braid of her hair as she worked to unknot it, shaking out the twists as she went.

"Yes, and when I did, you *were* tragic. You haven't the stomach for it any longer." Giles pressed the tips of his fingers to his forehead, rubbing away the lines imprinted there by his scowl. "You're good—but you might be great, if only you could find yourself within the character rather than the character within yourself. If you can draw only from what you are, then you will never be anything more than *good*."

Stung, Lydia turned on her heel and began to walk toward the rear of the theatre and the dressing room. It was perhaps ten seconds before Giles fell into step beside her.

"I can't give you Hermione, even if Kitty wants to give up the part," he said. "But perhaps Paulina."

"*Paulina!*"

"It's all I've got. Meg had decided to leave the company, and that will leave the role vacant." He said the words with an irritable grumble, but she knew that only masked his worry. Meg was not the first to leave, and unless the company could scrape up the funds to pay better, she would not be the last.

"We need a patron," she said; a repetition of the same old argument they'd had dozens of times before.

"I've told you; I won't compromise my integrity for a handful of coins." His hand sliced through the air as if he could skewer her words with just the tips of his fingers. "Paulina," he said again, decisively. "You've got the fury for it. Which you will leave on the stage—if you wish to remain with this company."

Lydia gave a snort. It was not the first time Giles had threatened her career, but she had long grown accustomed to his bluster. She slammed through the dressing room door.

"It's a good role," Giles snapped as he followed behind her. "Richer than Perdita by half. You know that."

"I want Hermione." Lydia snatched up a cloth, dunked it into the bowl of water that had been set upon a counter top, and began to swab the layer of cosmetics from her face.

Giles tossed Perdita's flower crown atop a stack of discarded costumes and cast himself into a chair. "You can't have Hermione. My God, only listen to yourself—I can't have a tragic queen spitting her lines with such venom upon my stage! You'd make me a laughingstock." He thrust his fingers through his powdered hair, and a shower of white rained down upon the floor.

"Yes, well, perhaps poor Hermione has earned the right to a little venom." Oughtn't the much-maligned queen, so unfairly accused of infidelity, be at least a *little* angry at the turn of fate?

"No, pet," Giles laughed. "She's the true tragedy of the piece. She needs must retain her saintly suffering absent the anger she deserves."

"I beg your pardon. Mamillius dies without the comfort of his mother by his side. Antigonus is torn to shreds by a bear!" Slapping the cloth down, Lydia wrenched at the laces binding her within the bodice of her gown.

"You're just angry that Leontes gets his happy ending."

Slanting Giles a severe look from beneath her lashes, Lydia hissed, "Your pardon, then, for wondering why Leontes should deserve one."

"All's well that ends well?" Giles suggested, which earned him a glare.

"It doesn't!" The laces snared in her fingers, and Lydia cast up her hands again with a gesture of aggravation. "Good God, I do loathe this play. Half tragedy, half farce—but all is well, so long as Leontes suffers not for his crimes."

"He's a *king.* Who is there to force him to it?" Giles stretched out his legs, crossing one ankle over the other. "Perdita gets her happy ending," he wheedled. "And so does Hermione."

"Sixteen years late!" And Hermione's happy ending had come at the cost of her son's life and nearly two decades of separation from husband and daughter.

"Better late than never."

"*Hah.*" The plait of her hair came loose at last. "Leontes should have suffered longer."

11

"Vicious." Giles crooked a finger. "Here; come. I'll loose your laces for you."

Good. All her laces had been done up so tightly she'd struggled to wheeze her lines through the cinch of them. Pulling her unbound hair over her shoulder, Lydia gave Giles her back. "Leontes doesn't deserve his happy ending," she muttered sullenly.

"You're making much ado about nothing."

"Oh, *stop*." She cast a glare over her shoulder through the curtain of her hair.

In the mirror, the mischievous slant of Giles' mouth told her that he had not quite done making sport of her. "It's meant to be a comedy, when all is said and done. There's no sense in love's labors lost for a comedy," he said.

"*Giles.*"

"Hold. You'll be able to dredge up ever so much more anger when you can breathe properly." There was a tug at the strings of her stays, and at last she drew a breath unencumbered. She let the gown drift free of her arms even as she reached for the hairbrush resting upon the vanity.

"There you are; free at last," Giles said as he stepped away, edging toward the door as he caught sight of the brush within the tight clench of her fist. "I daresay *Paulina* would have the wherewithal to threaten bodily harm."

"All right," Lydia cast out caustically, lifting the brush in threat. "If I can't have Hermione, then I'll have Paulina."

Giles snickered, one hand on the frame of the door. "As you like it," he said.

The brush struck the door just as it closed behind him—precisely where his head would have been had he remained. The sharp *smack* of it had failed to blunt the sharp edge of her anger, and she sank down into the chair at her vanity, sliding her fingers into the tangles of her hair to massage away the tension that had gathered near her temples.

Giles had not asked—since he never did—what, exactly, had caused her to stumble on stage. He cared only that his precious productions met with acclaim, however it had to be done. Her personal life was of no concern to him whatsoever provided it did not affect her performance. Once, she had loved him for his indifference to such matters, but just now...

Just now, she wished him more friend than employer. Just this once, she would have liked a handful of commiseration, of sympathy. But he never could manage that much so fresh off a performance.

And, too, he had never much been the victim of matters of the heart.

Lydia shoved the gown, which had fallen to her waist, off at last. No doubt Sybil—the costumer—would fume at the wrinkles she'd pressed into the fabric with her carelessness, but then they were meant to be pressed each morning for the evening's performance, and would want only a little extra attention for it.

She dragged her fingers through her hair, gently pulling at knots and tangles, regretting for a handful of moments that she had chosen the hairbrush to throw—but still her knees trembled beneath the light cotton of her chemise, and she did not yet trust herself to rise.

Paulina. She could do Paulina. She had before. Giles had been right, blast him to perdition—she *did* have the anger within her; the righteous indignation necessary to play the role of the incensed noblewoman defending the honor of a beloved queen. She could taunt Leontes with his faithlessness, with his callous disregard for the innocent Hermione. She could bring all of the spite, all of the vengeance denied her to the fore and heap it like burning coals upon his wretched head.

But it was not Giles' blond head she envisioned in her mind's eye, thrashing in agony beneath the crown of coals. It was hair black as night; black as the malice sheltered within a treacherous heart. Crisp and sleek strands that had been cool beneath her fingers when once she had stroked them, outward beauty masking such inner perfidy.

Eyes every bit as dark promising retribution for a crime she'd not committed.

She shuddered despite herself. Five years, and that fury burned still so brightly behind his eyes. As if he had stewed in it—lived it, breathed it, and *nurtured* it all this time. Why? She had left, as he had commanded. She had *left*, and she had suffered, and somehow, despite the shattering pain, she had survived.

She dashed at her eyes with the back of her hand, rubbing away the sting that had gathered just at the corners. There in the mirror of the vanity, staring back at her—*there* was Hermione. The tragedy of it all writ fresh upon her face as if it had only just happened.

With a scathing sound, her hand clamped upon a puff still laden with this evening's leftover powder and she cast it at her reflection, obscuring the hateful image beneath a thin coat of dust.

"Temper, temper."

The icy bite of that voice sheared her straight through, and it took every ounce of skill that she had cultivated over the last five years to let it wash over her as if it hadn't affected her in the least. To her relief, Hermione had been vanquished by that fine dusting of powder, and as her nails dug crescents into the soft flesh of her palms, she found Paulina within her.

"Get out of the dressing room." She did not bother to look in his direction, did not intend to dignify his presence with more attention than he was due. The shadowy image of him in the mirror, largely concealed beneath the coat of powder, was more than she wished to see of him besides—and still her eyes tracked his movements behind her. Like the snake he had proved himself to be, he might strike at any time and it would be wisest to keep him in her sights however she had to manage it.

A low laugh; his distorted image in the mirror grew as slow footsteps sounded upon the floor behind her. The hair at the nape of her neck lifted at the sound of them, which contained a menace of their own. Like a predator stalking prey, he *prowled* toward her. "What, no greeting?" The silky smooth tenor of his voice could not begin to mask the spite underpinning the words. "And after all that we have been to one another."

Lydia managed a tight smile over teeth that were clenched to the molars. "A pity that I do not recall our time together quite so fondly as you, my lord." The steadiness of her voice surprised her. A little high, perhaps, a touch raspy, as if she had just shaken a nasty head cold—but *steady*. "I'm in my underthings. I demand you absent yourself at once."

"I've seen you in less."

He'd seen her in nothing at all. But she had been young, then, and so foolish. All the stars of the heavens had lived within her eyes, and each of them had shone only for him. "Never again." She extended one arm, rolled her wrist until her fingers curled gracefully toward the door from which he had entered. "Get *out*, before I must have you removed. How embarrassing that would be for the both of us." He had not the stomach for scandal. She had learned that before.

"Oh, I think not." A fingertip just there at the nape of her neck, tracing the skin down toward the neckline of her chemise. "I have never much been a patron of the arts," he said. "But after this evening…I find myself inspired."

Vindictive, more like. She sensed him hovering over her shoulder, and kept her gaze firmly fixed ahead, drifting over the tiny bottles of perfume that sat upon the vanity, as if she had nothing more pressing to attend to than to spend a leisurely few minutes selecting a scent.

A slight tug as he caught a lock of her hair between his fingertips. "I told you what would happen if you chose to return to London," he said, and his voice seethed with that cold rage.

"Yes," she said on a sigh, endeavoring to sound bored. "You'd make me regret it."

His warm breath wafted over her shoulder. His voice, a snap of cold that whisked away the heat, rumbled at her ear: "I would so hate to make a liar of myself."

Lydia let her lids drift closed. No, not a liar—but he would delight in making a mockery of everything they had once been to one another. Everything she had *thought*, in the terrible foolishness of youth, that they had been. "You don't own London, my lord, for all that you would lay claim to it."

That wretched laugh, as sour as if it had long rotted in his chest all these years. "No? Best you take your leave of it anyway, or I swear to you, Lydia—I will own *you*."

Chapter Two

Not *this* again."

Marcus scowled over his glass of brandy as his brother's voice split the silence in which he had been stewing. "Damn it all—I *told* Bayberry not to admit you." But the room spun as he tried to rise from his chair, and he only narrowly avoided spilling the remaining contents of his glass across the floor in his efforts to set it safely aside upon the table near his seat.

"Bayberry would rather risk your wrath than mine, so it would seem." There was the strain of leather and of aged wood as Rafe took up the seat across from his own and stretched his legs out. "I heard you attended the theatre this evening. Was that wise?"

Wise? No. But necessary? Beyond measure. Marcus pressed his shoulders back into the supple leather of his chair and gave an idle flip of his fingers. "She's returned to London. I could not let such a trespass go unanswered."

"There are better ways to send a message." Rafe stretched his arm out, securing the bottle of brandy for himself lest Marcus decide to make use of it once again. "I'll admit I was…curious. I saw her a few nights past. Perdita, was it not? She was good."

Of *course* she was bloody good. She lied with her eyes, with her lips, with her body. She lied with every syllable she breathed, every sigh, every tremble. She was a liar born and bred; she had mastered artifice like art. She had been made to tread the boards—and she had been made to drive men mad.

"*Perdita.*" The name left his lips with a scornful sound. "It's an offense against all mankind to give her such a role."

"I thought she played it well enough. Did you see her, after?"

Marcus turned his head, let his hard gaze speak for him.

"And how was she, then?"

Beautiful. Marcus scrubbed his fingers over his eyes, feeling his jaw clench. "Older," he said at last. "Older, and—" Still beautiful. Her long blond hair trailing down her back like sun-touched silk. Would her eyes be still as green? She hadn't even *looked* at him. Did not she owe him that much,

16

at least?

That much, and more.

"I must have caught her between clients," he said at last, and thank *God* for that much, for he'd had little enough control of his ferocious temper as it was. If he had caught her with another man, he doubted he'd have maintained it. "She was at her toilette. Half-clothed at best." She'd smelled of powder, sweat, and still that sweet, underlying fragrance that he remembered so well. Jasmine, just at the nape of her neck. And her hair—as soft as he'd recalled, twining about his fingers.

The great pretender she was, she had sounded so unaffected by his presence, his touch, and that alone had infuriated him...until he'd seen the leap of her pulse in her throat. *Liar.* Every bit as much the liar he'd thought her.

Rafe heaved a sigh. "She's been in London, what? A sennight? How many clients could she have possibly acquired in that time?"

"Father would say cats and whores land upon their feet," Marcus said. And she was *still* so bloody beautiful. "No doubt she's scraped together at least a handful. She's accustomed to the finer things, after all."

He had accustomed her to them, years ago. For a few months, before he had learned what she was, she had been his mistress—and one, shamefully, he had been determined to marry her. He could only thank his lucky stars that he had not had the opportunity to wed her before he'd uncovered her perfidy, or he might be well and truly trapped to the brazen, scheming witch.

"Have done with her," Rafe advised, his voice pitched low. "I would not see you lose yourself again."

Rafe had not seen him lose himself the first time, much to his relief. A younger son had lesser responsibilities, but also fewer options. He had taken up a commission years before and had still been away on the continent for the duration of Marcus' affair with Lydia—and he had only returned after the damage had been done. After Marcus had been humiliated before all of London. After he had already become a wreck of his former self.

He had become what she had made him: a cold, callous man, impervious to the machinations of the female sex. Reclusive, hardhearted, indifferent. These were the gifts that Lydia had left to him. Gifts he'd return to her a hundredfold ere they were done.

She had escaped London unscathed five years ago, wisely taking him at his word. And if she had *stayed* gone, he might have found a measure of peace—

No. That was a lie. He'd found not a shred of it in her absence. She had killed his heart, murdered any hope of happiness. That she sought to return *now* was an offense of the highest order, and one that could not go unpunished.

"I'll see her ruined," he rasped. "As she ruined me."

Nothing else would suffice. Only then—when she was truly shamed, when she prostrated herself in all the humiliation she deserved to bear, when she *begged* for the tatters of her derelict life—would he be at last appeased.

Lydia stood outside the dressing room, wishing desperately that she could erase the filthy sounds emanating from therein from her mind. A banging sound, rhythmic, gradually increasing in frequency. No doubt the knocking of a chair's legs against the floor.

"Oh, my lord!" Clara's breathy whimper; Lydia would have recognized the feigned throes of passion anywhere. Clara was not one of the better actresses amongst the company. It was why she had largely been relegated to the ensemble cast.

A heave. A grunt. A rasped curse. And then a renewed knocking. *Christ.* Lydia clasped Paulina's costume in her fist, no doubt wrinkling it something awful.

"Why the hell aren't you on stage? I want to see your Paulina before tonight's show."

Lydia half-turned at the advent of Giles' voice, slanting him a flat look. "The dressing room is presently occupied," she said.

A well-timed shriek of affected pleasure seared her ears.

Giles' brows lifted. "Emily?"

"Clara."

"Lord Rathbone, then." Giles shook his head in consternation. "They'll be a while. Come; you can avail yourself of my office."

"I wish they would find some place more private to conduct their affairs," Lydia sniffed as she followed dutifully behind him.

"I'll have a word with her about finding a more opportune time and place," Giles said. "But you know as well as I what the theatre pays. I don't begrudge her the desire for a little extra coin in her pocket. God knows London is too expensive by half." He slipped the key from his pocket, and opening the door for her.

There was scarcely space to turn around amidst the cluttered furniture and stacks and stacks of papers. "My laces?" Lydia turned her back to Giles. "I was hoping Clara would help me with them, but—well, you know."

Obligingly, Giles took his fingers to her laces. "You've had offers, you know. You could reach so high as a marquess, if you had a mind."

Offers? As if Giles were her procurer? "No, I thank you. I won't be owned." Never again. Once had been quite enough. *Too* much, in point of fact.

Giles stifled a sigh as he wrenched the costume from her hands and shook it out. "Pride makes a poor meal," he said. "A quick tumble would pay you twice what I do for an entire production. For God's sake, Lydia, you live hand-to-mouth as it is—"

"I have all I need." Which wasn't much, when it came down to it. A rented room in an unsavory part of town, but still it was all her own, for the duration of her time in London. There was nothing more precious to her now than pride, for if she surrendered that—

If she surrendered that, she would have nothing at all.

She stepped out of the puff of skirts that had fallen to her knees, let Giles lift Paulina's costume over her head and drape it down. Once more his fingers were on her laces. "Not so tightly, please. I could hardly draw breath last evening."

The silence that settled in her ears was thick and tense. Halfway through the laces, Giles was moved at last to break it. "The gentleman from evening last—ought I be concerned?"

"Concerned?" Lydia echoed. "Whatever for?"

"One hears whispers."

One hears *gossip*. Her teeth clenched against the sharp retort.

"He's the one," he said. "He was your lover." It had not been a question.

"Once." Her lungs expanded on a breath, and there—she could breathe well enough. "Years ago. Why do you ask? You never have before."

"It didn't matter before," Giles said. "So long as your past had no adverse effect upon my productions." He scrubbed his fingers through his hair, heaving a sigh.

Well, *really*. He had been content enough to capitalize upon her unhappiness so many years ago.

"A baron," he said. "And a damned influential one at that. I don't want trouble in my company."

"I've not made trouble for you."

"*Yet.*" A scowl tugged at the corners of his lips. "But you taunted him last eve, Lydia. It's flying about London as we speak. The whole of the theatre saw it. For God's sake, *I* saw it. I wouldn't have cared, but for the gossip." His hand flattened upon the corner of the desk. "We can't afford enemies."

It was years and years too late for that. "His enmity is reserved for me. You need not concern yourself with it," she said. God, she hoped it was the truth. "He came only to deliver a message." *Leave London.*

"Which was?"

"Immaterial, and soon to be superfluous." They had only a month-long engagement. In fact, they had gotten it only through a rare turn of luck, since some calamity or another had befallen the usual players that had most recently occupied the Theatre Royal Drury Lane. Soon enough they would be off again. But she would *not* leave London at *his* bidding. "I can handle myself, Giles. I have done for some years now."

Uncertainty flickered across Giles' face. "But can you handle Newhaven?"

"Do you doubt me?" She let a sly smile creep across her lips, lowering her lashes. "Have you known me to overstate my talents?"

The corner of his lips twitched; a mirthless, wry expression. The slight censure within his blue eyes scorched her to her very soul. "No," he said, at last, "But I *do* know that you're not as good an actress as you think you are."

God, Marcus hated watching Lydia flit about the stage, hated watching the bastard playing Florizel make calf's eyes at her. He oughtn't to have come again to the theatre, but she had weighed too heavily upon his mind for Marcus to keep his distance.

The whispers had followed him up to his box, though he'd arrived late as he had the evening before. Still there had been enough people milling about to make it clear that her trespass of the previous evening had been noted well enough. Probably it had made its way into a few of the more salacious scandal rags.

In the brief break between the fourth and fifth acts, he had near been moved to violence when one of the visitors to his box—out of courtesy, or curiosity—had made an offhanded remark, flavored with the ribald.

"A pretty piece; I'll give her that. One need not wonder what it is you saw in her, Newhaven. If fortune favors me, perhaps I'll see *myself* in her."

How strange, how infuriating it was that the first emotion that had risen within him had been *offense* at the implication. Marcus had been able to offer nothing more than a sharp, dire stare, which contained such enmity that the offender had taken himself off at last in a state of discomfort, leaving Marcus to stew in his unrelieved fury.

She had not glanced even once in his direction, though she had to know he had come. All of London knew it. And yet, as the curtain closed, there was not even the briefest acknowledgement of his presence.

Last evening she'd blown him a kiss—a scathing, mocking tribute. This evening, he had been banished from her thoughts so completely that he might as well never have existed at all. She dared much.

Well, she would *eat* her indifference.

The halls were lined with gentlemen eager to make themselves known to whichever actress they favored, and Marcus swept past the lot of them just as he had the night before. The man situated at the entrance to the private areas behind the stage was more bridge troll than guard; his palm wanted only the grease of a coin placed into it, and then Marcus was amidst the thick of the actors and stage hands, who paid him little enough attention in their haste to relieve themselves of their costumes and to set the scenery aright once more.

The dressing room, where he'd found her last eve—he started toward it, dodging the people milling about him. As his hand fell upon the handle, he paused at the sounds emanating from within.

Masculine grunts. Feminine sighs. Unmistakable sounds of passion.

A pure, frothing rage swept over him. The door crashed open, the violence in the doing startling a screech out of the woman within—*not* Lydia.

"For Christ's sake," the man said, tucking himself back within the fall of his trousers, his disheveled hair obscuring his eyes. "A knock would have been polite."

The woman, a petite redhead, covered herself once more with a dressing gown of dubious opacity, wrought of some fine gauzy linen, which concealed not half of her charms. "Ye'll 'ave to wait yer turn," she said, with a haughty lift of her chin. "I don't do two at once."

"I don't want *you*," Marcus snarled. "Where the hell is Lydia?"

"Gone already." A clipped voice from behind him. Marcus turned to level a glare at the interloper; a blond man with eyes like chips of ice, who was

21

now looking past his shoulder. "Clara, I've told you. Not in the damned dressing room. You're not the only one that must make use of it."

"Yes, Mr. Montgomery," Clara said, sullenly. "I mean, *no*, sir." But her hand stroked down her paramour's chest in a suggestive manner.

"Get you gone," the blond man snapped. "And if you monopolize the dressing room again, you'll be out of this company." As the couple sauntered past—no doubt to resume their amorous interlude somewhere else—Marcus once again merited the man's attention. "Lord Newhaven, no? Lydia's gone home already, and she wouldn't wish to see you besides, so I'll thank you to take yourself back the way you've come."

The pointed turn of phrase might as well have been a knife slipping between his ribs. "But she'll see others?"

"What business is it of yours? You threw her over some years ago, did you not?" That cool, assessing gaze had judged him a fool already.

"Is that what she told you?" Marcus inquired icily.

"To be frank, Lord Newhaven, she's told me little enough. But what I have gleaned speaks not well of you."

"Then you're as much a fool as she is a liar." Marcus elbowed past Mr. Montgomery, his gaze sweeping the halls—just in case the man liked Lydia well enough to lie for her. "You're the manager, then?"

"I own the company. What do you want with Lydia?"

"That's none of your affair." Marcus felt a sneer curl his lip. She'd escaped cleanly, then. At least *this* evening. "She entertains at her home, then?"

"That's none of *yours*."

Wheeling about, Marcus jabbed one finger to the man's chest. "You do not come between her and me," he said. "*Ever.*"

Montgomery's brows lifted in interest. "Wouldn't dream of it."

"I'll have her address."

"You damned well will not. I haven't got it myself, and wouldn't give it to you if I did." A queer expression had tucked itself into the curve of Montgomery's mouth, something that might have approached amusement if he had given it leave to spread itself out. "Planning to scare off her clients at her home?"

So she *had* got them there! He wrapped his fist round Montgomery's cravat and pulled. "*Names*," he snarled.

Though he was no doubt half-strangled by the tightening of the cravat about his throat, Montgomery heaved a sigh of acute indifference. "I don't pay attention to such things so long as they do not affect the workings of my company," he said. "Why should you *care*, my lord, if you don't—" A hesitation; an incredulous chuckle. "By God, you *do* want her still. Oh, this is rich indeed; a farce to warm a winter's night. Good meat for an actor, this."

"Oh, I *want* her." Marcus released his hold upon Montgomery, freeing the man to rub one hand to his tender throat. "I want her *miserable*. Crawling, begging, *pleading* for a crumb of mercy." Which he would deny her. Naturally.

"You *want* to run off her paramours."

It was fitting that she lack for company, as she'd ruined his taste for it these five years past. "I want her to feel the pinch of poverty," he said. "I know well enough how actresses supplement their income."

"Pay me," Montgomery said baldly.

"I beg your pardon?"

"*Pay* me," Montgomery repeated. "I'll make certain none get near her for the foreseeable future." He adjusted the knot of his cravat, doing his best to brush out the wrinkles that Marcus' fingers had carved into the linen. "Acting pays not well, it's true—even to the owner of the company. I'd like to live more comfortably than I do, but, alas, my services are not in such high demand. Besides, I find my actresses perform the better when their minds are not polluted with carnality."

"How much?" The inquiry left his lips before he was aware of speaking the words—a tacit agreement; admitting more than Marcus had intended Montgomery to know.

And well did Montgomery know it. "One hundred pounds ought to see me through."

A pittance to him, but a fortune, probably, to an actor. He would bargain for better. "One hundred pounds—and I'll have run of the theatre as I please."

Montgomery choked out a laugh. "For all the good it will do you, aye. I'm an *actor*, my lord, not a procurer. I won't sell you Lydia's company." A wry twist of his lips. "There's a thin line between love and hate, I think."

"Then thinking ill becomes you. I don't want her." Even to Marcus' ears, it had the pitch of a lie.

"And yet no one else may have her. Playing at the dog in the manger ill becomes *you*, my lord." With an indolent gesture of his hand, Montgomery indicated the theatre at large. "Do as you will; it'll avail you nothing with Lydia. You may deliver your payment to me here tomorrow morning." Off he went, shaking his head with barely disguised mirth.

And Marcus was left wondering if he hadn't come out the loser.

Chapter Three

Lydia found that she had missed London perhaps more than it had deserved. It was cold, dirty, and barren this time of year, and the breeze nipped straight through the thin fabric of her gown. She had had coin enough in her pocket to purchase a pasty on her walk home to St. Giles, but only just.

Once, all too briefly, she had lived within a small townhouse in Mayfair. When she had been Marcus' mistress.

She hadn't liked to think of herself as such—and indeed, he had never said as much, at least in her hearing. But what else did one call a woman who enjoyed a man's attentions without benefit of marriage? Who lived upon his largesse?

She would have sworn he had loved her. And he *had* promised to marry her—as soon as he could accustom his parents to the idea.

Even then, she ought to have known it for the lie it had been. Men did not marry their mistresses. And lords especially did not marry nobodies born of common stock. She had had no dowry, no connections. But she had let herself be swept away by a lord's promises and a beautiful dream, and she had lived quite happily for some months, until it had all come crumbling down.

And then she had had nothing at all; just a handful of broken promises to go along with her broken heart. A reputation in tatters, so infamous then that she could not even secure her former position as a seamstress. She had met Giles while serving ale to rowdy dockworkers, since it had been the only job she had been able to find.

Marcus had left her with less than that with which he had found her.

Even now she was not sure when or what, precisely, had changed between them. One day they had been happy, and the next—

The next he had accused her of unfaithfulness, and cast her out into the streets as if she meant nothing to him at all. And that had been *it*; the *end*. No amount of tears or denials could have convinced him otherwise. He had hissed those hateful words to her, and she had believed he had meant them. All his love—or what she had imagined to be love—had turned to contempt in a moment. It had happened so swiftly that she had been left feeling as if she had been struck by a runaway carriage. The whole of her life had changed in an instant.

She had grieved. Mourned his loss as if he had died. It had been that very anguish that had attracted Giles, and Hermione had been her very first role. In had, in fact, been not so much a role she had played but her grief expressed upon the stage. In the theatre there was a sort of catharsis, and she had healed herself through it—to a point. Until her grief had at last shifted to anger, and then she had lost Hermione.

She did not intend to lose anything else at Marcus' hands.

In the crisp November air, she climbed the steps and rapped upon the door of Mrs. Hawkins' boarding house. This late in the evening the door would be locked, and she had been in such a haste to flee the theatre that she had left her key upon the dressing table. But Mrs. Hawkins could be relied upon to answer, provided the hour had not yet reached midnight.

The door creaked open, and Mrs. Hawkins peered out into the evening, blinking owlishly behind gold-rimmed spectacles. "Miss Alcott?"

"Good evening, Mrs. Hawkins. I'm afraid I left my key at the theatre this evening." Lydia offered an apologetic smile.

A frown tugged at the corners of the woman's lips, the weight of judgment settling there. "I don't approve of the theatre."

Or *any* entertainment, really. Reading polluted the mind. Dancing was one step away from sin. Thank God the woman did not read the papers, either, or Lydia suspected she would find herself tossed out on her arse.

"I know, Mrs. Hawkins." But her wretched theatre pay spent as well as any other coin, and Mrs. Hawkins had been desperate to let the room that Lydia had taken—though she'd charged a premium for so short a term.

"I know what you theatre girls are like. I run a *good* home, Miss Alcott. An *honest* home. A *respectable* home."

"I know, Mrs. Hawkins," Lydia repeated. "May I come in?"

With a sniff, the woman cracked the door far enough to allow Lydia to slip inside. "What production did you say you it was?"

She hadn't, for Lydia hadn't fancied another lecture on the evils of theatre. And yet she answered anyway: "*The Winter's Tale.*"

Another sniff, which made Mrs. Hawkins sound as if she were beginning to come down with pneumonia. "I don't approve of Shakespeare."

Well, *really*. Who didn't approve of *Shakespeare*?

"And your role?"

"Perdita, for now." Just until the end of the week, when Meg intended to resign her role of Paulina. She'd caught herself a lord as a protector, and that role paid far better than the theatre.

"I don't approve of Perdita, either. Bold as brass, Perdita is." Mrs. Hawkins took up the candle she had placed upon the table in the hall. "You may see yourself up to your room, Miss Alcott. And mind you don't forget your key again."

Lydia held in her sigh until Mrs. Hawkins had retreated once more to her room, snapping the door shut behind her. Just three more weeks. She could bear Mrs. Hawkins' condescension just a little further.

A storm was brewing. Marcus could sense it roiling beneath the surface. Tension furrowed his father's brow, pushing a scowl into the lines of his face, which he hid behind the pages of his paper. Mother was distressingly quiet, lingering over her breakfast past the point that her drinking chocolate had gone cold.

He hadn't lived at home in years, but he took breakfast with his family a few times a week and had since he had taken up his own bachelor lodgings some years ago. It was a torturous endeavor, to say the least. He endured it only for Diana; his younger sister, who would have borne the brunt of Father's nastiness all on her own otherwise.

"Out with it," Marcus said at last, through a mouthful of toast. "If you've something to say, you might as well."

Mother drew in a quavering breath—but then she had always been the sensitive sort, no doubt owing to Father's abrasive, unnecessarily critical nature. Her lips trembled, and her watery eyes dropped once more to her plate.

Father made a deep sound of perturbation in his throat, his mouth firming beneath the greying hair of his mustache. "I do read the paper, Marcus. We are aware that you have been spending an inordinate amount of time at the theatre. *That woman*—"

"Is of no concern to anyone." He hadn't discussed Lydia with them five years ago, and he did not intend to begin now. He had not discussed Lydia with *anyone*. Mistresses were common enough, but they were not fit for public consumption, and he—he had kept her discreetly, knowing well enough what

Father's opinion would be. At least until the scandal of their parting. *That* had been impossible to keep quiet. There had been such a lot of shouting—mostly his—on the very public street that he had thrown her out into. Had he been thinking clearly at the time, he might have exercised a bit more discretion in it, but that had not been possible for him then.

He had, however, kept his feelings close to his chest since. Thank *God* he had not told them that he had planned to wed her before the truth of her infidelity had been made public. He could not have borne their further disappointment.

Father folded his paper in half and set it aside upon the table. "For God's sake, tell me you have not become involved with her again."

Marcus sliced through a sautéed mushroom. "Define involved."

"*Marcus.*" Father slammed down his napkin in what would have been a grand display of temper, had not the delicate linen landed upon the table with little more than a whisk of sound. "Have you nothing else to say?"

Marcus considered the question, canting his head. "Cook's gone a bit heavy with the salt on the eggs this morning."

Mother made the sort of simpering, placating sound that had been the hallmark of his childhood, her delicate hands fluttering like the wings of an agitated bird. "Now, darling," she said, in that halting, quavering voice, as her eyes darted between Marcus and Father, whose face had darkened with the coming storm. "You must know we only want what's best for you."

What was best for the family, more like. Even as a very young child, he had been treated like the noble scion of the Beaumont family that he had been expected to be. Little wonder he'd never gotten round to informing them of his intentions to marry Lydia. Father would have been horrified. Ashamed, even, that Marcus would have lowered himself to wed a woman who hadn't even a hint of aristocratic blood in her veins.

"What is *best* for him is to be *married*," Father said gruffly, his voice heavy-laden with scorn. "He's avoided his responsibilities too long already." His mustache twitched over his lips; a portent of an impending outburst. Marcus had learned the signs well enough by now. It had become something of a sport—between him and his younger siblings—to see who could provoke one the quickest.

"I'll marry when I'm ready," he said, and was rewarded with another twitch.

"You're three and thirty already," Father blustered. "If you are not yet ready, you never will be. You have obligations—"

Marcus scoffed. "Rafe can fulfill them as easily as I."

"*Rafe is not my heir!*" The roar echoed round the dining room, the booming resonance of it ricocheting between the crystal drops adorning the chandelier hanging above.

Only two twitches before the explosion, Marcus reflected. Father *was* in a state.

"Good heavens, whatever can be the matter so early?" Diana swanned into the room in the wake of Father's below, nearly colliding with a footman. "Papa, you'll push yourself into apoplexy."

"My children are a plague upon my house," Father grumbled, casting a narrow-eyed glance at Mother, as if she held the sole responsibility for those children. "My daughter, still unmarried—my heir striving to push me into an early grave." He rubbed one hand over his chest as if his heart troubled him.

Marcus had not missed the high flush that burned across Diana's cheeks at the censure. "Father, that's hardly fair. Diana bears no blame for it." She had been affianced practically from the cradle to the son of a marquess, who had absconded from England early in Diana's very first Season, and had not since returned.

"*Hmph.*" The scathing sound suggested that not only *could* Father place the blame for her unmarried state squarely upon Diana's shoulders, but that he intended to do so with relish.

Ducking her head, Diana sank into the seat next to Marcus and fumbled for her silverware.

Marcus muttered, "You'd do better with your spectacles." She was nearly blind as a bat without them, but—

"Those accursed things. She doesn't need them," Father huffed.

"Now, Harold," Mother soothed. "They're really quite pretty. Such lovely filigree upon the earpieces."

"They make her look like a bluestocking, or perhaps a governess." Father carved up a bite of bacon and chewed viciously. "*Common*, that is to say."

Common was the absolute worst thing a person could be, in Father's estimation. He'd had such grand plans for his children, none of which had come anywhere close to fruition. They were disappointments, all, and they had never been allowed to forget it.

At least Rafe had had the good sense to stay clear of the family for the most part—but then, he was only the spare, largely unnecessary. Marcus had, as a child, longed to be in Rafe's position: mostly ignored, rarely called out onto the carpet for any sort of misbehavior, simply because his position had been of little consequence.

When Rafe had purchased his commission, it had taken Father nearly six weeks even to notice he was gone, whereas Marcus and Father had been at odds almost the whole of his life.

Father cleared his throat. "Marcus, I am told Diana has got an engagement this evening—a dinner party, or some such nonsense. You will escort her. And for God's sake, you will *look for a wife*."

Marcus slid a glance toward Mother, who looked as if one more row might put her off of her breakfast entirely, and found from somewhere deep inside him a molecule of pity. Though he had no intention of honoring Father's dictatorial decrees, still he said, "Of course, Father." *But first,* he thought, *the theatre.*

The purse landed at the edge of Giles' desk with a heavy *clink*. "For you," he said, with a magnanimous wave of his hand.

"Me? Whatever for?" Lydia weighed the purse in her palm, tugged the strings, peered within, and nearly choked. "Good Lord—how did you come by this?"

"Newhaven, if you must know." Giles propped his feet upon his desk as he reclined in his chair, disturbing a small stack of papers. Bills that had come due, most likely.

Her eyes narrowed in suspicion, Lydia began, "You didn't—"

"No; I've no talent for thievery, so set your mind at ease." His shoulders lifted and fell in a short shrug. "Or rather, don't. You might have preferred the thievery."

"Giles," Lydia said in a warning tone, though her hand curled round the purse. "What have you done?"

"It's more of what *he's* done," Giles said, endeavoring to look innocent—a look he did not accomplish well, even for the seasoned actor he was. "Damn near broke the dressing room door from its hinges last eve. Looking for you."

A queer tightness settled in her throat. She had suspected as much. Which was why she had absented herself from the theatre so quickly after the

29

performance.

"Clara took no note of my request to find a better place to conduct her liaisons," Giles said. "Newhaven caught her going at it with her lord. I suppose he must've thought he was to catch *you*."

Lydia's breath stalled in her lungs. "Why should that have mattered?"

"Hell if I know, but I tell you it *did*." The way that Giles watched her face, searching for any hint of betraying emotion, troubled her. "And since it troubled him so, I thought—why not profit from it?" He favored her with a sly smile.

"Profit?" Lydia echoed uncertainly, eyeing the purse in her hand.

"I told him I'd drive away your suitors if he paid me for the purpose," he said. "And there—that was delivered round this morning, as promised."

"But I have no suitors," Lydia said. At least, none she'd accepted.

"Let's keep that between us, shall we? There's no reason he ought to know he's paid for a privilege that has gone unexercised until now. Since I cannot pay you what you deserve, I felt you might as well subsidize your income in this manner, as you will not do as the other girls. And Newhaven can hardly think any worse of you."

It was true, but still it stung. Paid to whore, or *not* to—it would make little difference in his mind. And yet, she held a fortune in her hands which she had earned for nothing that she was not already doing.

She held the purse out to him. "Here," she said. "You ought to have some, at least." Since he had been the one to finagle it out of Marcus to begin with.

"Already took my cut. Fair's fair, after all. Twenty percent extortionist's fee." A grin flashed across his mouth, which swiftly faded. "Lydia, I think it only fair to warn you…whether he hates you or no, the man is obsessed. I've rarely seen the like."

The shiver that slipped down her spine was surely just a remnant of the chill that had settled over London, and nothing more. She wished she had a proper cloak to blunt it. "Whatever he feels is no concern of mine," she said.

"Oh, I think it must be. Rather, I think he will *make* it your concern. He was prepared to pay a great deal for your chastity," Giles said, and paused to mull his words over in his mind a moment. "There is a power in that, you know. He will use you, do you let him. Rather, I think you would be better served to tip the scales in your favor and use him instead."

Use him. How sweet those words sounded. Lydia savored the promise of vengeance like a fine wine trickling upon her tongue. *Use him*, as she had before been sorely used in turn.

"A woman's wiles are lost upon me," Giles said, with a shrug. "You know that well enough. But Newhaven—I think he's the perfect victim for yours. Had you the mind for it, you could turn his hatred to passion in a heartbeat."

"Say rather the *stomach* for it." The words came out as bitter and cold as her heart had become. "You said we could not afford to have him as an enemy."

"Did I? How shortsighted of me. I ought to have said we cannot afford him as an enemy during our London engagement. Surely you can seduce him just enough for that."

"And when the company moves on?" Lydia inquired.

"Break his heart, darling. Be proper vicious about it, if it suits you." Giles leveled a speaking look at her. "I'll admit, he pricked my temper last evening. The arrogance of the aristocracy knows no bounds. He thought to come into *my* theatre and make demands of me—well, he will learn better. Squeeze the life's blood from his beating heart, my girl, and get a little of your own back from him."

"Had he one to speak of, I might be tempted to do just that," Lydia said savagely.

Giles chuckled. "If you might only have seen him last evening, you would know he *has* got one indeed—and it isn't buried so far down as either of you imagine. He wears it here," he said, with a gesture of one hand. "Just upon his sleeve. Yours for the taking."

Or, perhaps, for the *breaking*.

Chapter Four

No one's looking," Marcus said. "You can put on your spectacles if you like."

Diana grumbled something beneath her breath, but began rooting around in her reticule to withdraw a small pair of silver-framed spectacles. "I suppose I might as well," she muttered. "I've missed the first three acts already. Or enough of them at least." Darting a glance around—as if it would avail her anything—at last she eased the spectacles over her eyes.

"You ought to wear them more often," Marcus chided. "You've accidentally snubbed at least three people."

"I haven't!" Diana gasped, horrified at the accusation.

"You have." Marcus nodded to a box across the theatre. "I think it was Miss Emerson who was trying so desperately to get your attention." And who was now turned resolutely away, her nose turned up.

"Oh, dear. You ought to have told me!"

"If you had worn your spectacles, you would have seen for yourself."

Diana's fingers threaded together in her lap. "They don't suit me," she said. "Papa says so."

"Father says a great many things that aren't worth the attention it would require to listen." Marcus hadn't made a habit of paying much of any in years; there was no reason Diana ought to do so herself. Not when she, like he and Rafe, would fail to measure up to Father's exacting, impossible standards.

"Well, I shall have to make my apologies to Miss Emerson, I suppose," Diana said. And then, lightly, "I hadn't thought you cared so much for *The Winter's Tale*."

"I don't count it amongst my favorites," Marcus replied.

She turned to him, her dark brows lifted above the rim of her spectacles. "But to come *three* times? I dare say there should have been someone to whom you might have lent your box, instead. There's always someone—" She broke off with a gasp, peering down upon the stage. "Oh, Marcus. Is that—"

He gave a short, tight nod.

"I thought you had—that is to say—" Her shoulders slumped. Weakly, she said, "She plays Perdita well."

"Better than she has any right to do."

Silence settled between them—or as much silence as could be had in the theatre, which was not much. Marcus watched Florizel twirl Perdita across the stage, swearing a devotion Lydia certainly did not deserve. A nameless rage bubbled up within him at the sight of someone else's hands upon her hips, holding her too closely.

"I liked her enormously," Diana admitted softly. "I would never have suspected unfaithfulness of her."

No. Nor would Marcus have done. "It seems she was an actress even when she was a seamstress. Perhaps some women make every venue their stage." Every crowd their audience. Every man their prey. He'd fallen in love with a pretty face and a false heart. More fool, him. "It was no fault of yours," he said to Diana as she squirmed a little in her seat.

"Wasn't it, though?" Her lips pursed. "Even just a little? When you met her because of me?"

That much was true; he had escorted Diana to her appointment that fateful day to be fitted for a number of gowns that she had needed for her first Season. It was at the shop that Diana had favored that he had first encountered Lydia.

There had been something between them immediately. Something undeniable and grand; strange and wonderful. She had blushed and stammered and he—he had liked the fact that she had been so obviously affected simply by his presence.

Always the actress, Lydia.

But he had been just as affected by hers. Enough so that at the conclusion of Diana's fitting, when he had conducted her once more back home, he'd returned to the shop. To *her*. And he had been unable—and unwilling—to stay away. She had seduced him without effort; as captivating then as she was now.

"She was very kind to me," Diana said, her voice faltering. "I suppose I thought—I hoped—that you would marry her. So that we could be friends, since—well, you know." She gave a little shrug. "I couldn't have been friends with your mistress."

No; a mistress was not a fit companion for a lady. But if he had made her his baroness, well...the application of a title forgave a multitude of sins. He shifted uncomfortably. "I wasn't aware you knew of that. *Then*, at least."

Of course, the whole of London had known—eventually. But he had thought he had been discreet enough to have evaded notice before then.

"Marcus, *everyone* knew. Papa had some dreadful fits about it, I can tell you that much. Why, he swore he would cut you off if you did not dismiss her—but I suppose he hadn't the time to make good on his threat before you did." Diana let out a sigh, her shoulders sinking.

Dreadful fits? No one had whispered a word of it in his hearing. Not that such threats would have swayed his mind regardless; he'd had money enough of his own by then, investments prudent enough to see him more than comfortable for the rest of his days, and had never been much the spendthrift. "But he never said as much to me." He had thought they had learned, as everyone else had, with the scandal of a scene he'd made once their affair had come to an abrupt end.

"No? Well, you *do* tend to dig in your heels when it comes to Papa." Diana issued a small sigh. "I don't suppose you've spoken with her?"

"Once. Just once." To reissue his threat; to make clear to her what she risked if she stayed. "I told her to leave. Warned her that if she stayed, I would"—*own her*—"ruin her."

"Yes, well, I think you've done that well enough once already," Diana said softly.

Marcus felt his brows draw together. "What the hell is that supposed to mean?"

"Haven't you any idea of what happens to ruined women? Truly?" she asked. "No; I suppose men don't concern themselves much with such things. Once, she had a respectable career. Not *lucrative*, mind you, but *respectable*. Of course, there wasn't a reputable shop in London that would take her on thereafter, nor would she have managed to find another protector." She leveled him a look wise beyond her years, and twice as cynical. "It's my understanding that gentlemen who offer their protection to a woman generally expect services rendered only unto *them*. You had accused her—quite publicly— of questionable honor in that regard."

"A pretty way of phrasing it," Marcus sneered.

"I beg to differ. It's all quite ugly, when one peels away the veneer of civility that we paper over it with." Diana issued a little sigh. "The truth is, Marcus, that she lost ever so much more than you did. Respectability is a currency more valuable than coin. Actresses have less than none."

It was a simple fact, distasteful as it was. The seats and boxes of the theatre were filled with the upper echelons of society, and yet the actors and actresses they had come to see perform merited none of their respect for their art or their talent.

And there was Lydia as Perdita, having once more won her prince and reclaimed her birthright, taking in the applause of the audience comprised of ladies who would shun her and men who would seek to purchase her favors—for all the good it would do them now.

He suspected that as he and Diana watched her take her bow below, they saw very different things.

"I must say, I never expected you to be possessed of so very many opinions," Marcus said at last.

"Men never do." The slight lift of the corner of her lips was sharper than it had had any reason to be. "I suppose I know just as well as she must the futility of waiting upon a man's convenience. That to a woman a promise is precious as rubies, but too often to a man it is a string of sweet words without much weight behind them."

And she *would* know, he thought. Four and twenty, now, and still waiting upon the man who had scurried away from his obligations to her. "She made promises, too," he said, a touch defensively. Fidelity had been amongst them, and love. Both betrayed.

"Yes, I suppose she must have done. But I have often wondered—when she had surrendered so much of herself to the security of your promise, why would she give cause for you to break it? Such a foolish thing to do…and Lydia never struck me as a fool."

Lydia had not looked at him even once, though his eyes had followed her all evening. He could resent her for that, as well. "Perhaps she thought she could reach higher than a baron," he said.

"Rubbish. You'll be a marquess one day. If you *had* married her—"

"I'd planned to," he admitted. "I'd promised to." He had got the ring already; purchased new because Father had been unlikely to open the estate jewels to him to wed a woman of no breeding, no consequence, no wealth, and no connections.

Diana let her fingers flex in her lap. "I've never understood it," she said again, her voice laden with her confusion. "I tell you, there is no sense in it, not an ounce. She had nothing at all to gain of it."

Those words rang within his head like the clang of a bell, and then—the curtain swooped closed, obscuring the actors upon the stage. *No.* He was not ready, yet, to be done with her for the evening.

Marcus surged to his feet. "Stay here," he said. "I'll return shortly."

"Marcus? What!" Diana scrambled to her feet, but it was too late—Marcus let the door to the box shut in his wake.

After all, he had been promised run of the theatre.

"Lord Newhaven," Lydia said, allowing a frosty note to creep across the crisp syllables she uttered. "You are making an unfortunate habit of bursting in on me in my underthings." It was truth and lie at once; he *had* burst in upon her in her underthings, but she had contrived for him to do so. It had seemed to her a better option than running the risk of him catching a glimpse of her gown, so out of date now and patched over more than was reasonable.

She had also…wondered if there might be truth to put to Giles' assertion of his *obsession*. If appearing before him less than fully clothed might bring whatever lurked within him to the fore. Two birds; one stone—and only a bit of skin to win it. An actress rarely had the luxury of privacy, and whatever had remained of modesty in her had been smothered years ago, besides.

He shoved the door closed behind him, right in the face of a chorus girl, who shouted some coarse words through it. "I've paid enough for the privilege."

"You've not coin enough in your coffers to purchase *that*." Lydia poured all the honeyed sweetness she could summon into the words.

"Oh? Once you were bought rather cheaply, if I recall." The sharp report of his heels upon the floor. She supposed it was meant to make her feel stalked, threatened. But there was always someone waiting nearby. More than once, one of the girls had taken on a patron who had got too rough; she had no fear at all for her safety.

"Judgment looks poorly on you," she said lightly, letting her shoulders lift in a nonchalant shrug and watching his eyes track the motion in the mirror. "How very like a man to make a woman his mistress and then to hold her in contempt for it. I am what you *made* me."

A muscle tightened in his jaw. "Should you think to ply that particular trade in London, you'll find that avenue closed to you."

"So Giles said." She blotted at her face with a wet cloth, rubbing away the powder, the rouge. "Unfair, my lord, to play such games with a woman's income." But less unfair, now that she had a purse full of his coin to sustain her.

"I told you I would ruin you." His voice had lowered, roughened. And his eyes—they followed the slow strokes of the cloth down her throat, to the valley between her breasts.

"You told me you would *own* me," she purred. "Better men than you have tried."

Those dark eyes jerked up, held hers captive within the mirror. "Which men?" he rasped, and his fists clenched at his sides.

"Any; all. They are all better than you." She rather enjoyed the flare of fury there in his eyes. But beneath it—yes; that was *desire.*

Her heart gave a vicious pulse in her chest, skipping through a few harried beats. Exultation; that was all it was. The strains of a victorious melody swelling within her. For all of his venom, for all of his jabs and slights, he wanted her still.

She could almost see it there, his heart upon his sleeve. She would not have called it *love*, what passion lived within him. But hate and obsession both? Those she could use. Was she not owed *her* pound of flesh from him? He had taken his already, and so much more than that.

The strength that coursed through her was lent to her from all those wicked women who had come before her: Delilah, Jezebel, Eve. She found them, all, within her as she cast aside the cloth and rose to her feet.

It had been easier to look at him within the mirror. Safer; as if they had been separated by more than the reflection of the glass. He had not much changed with the last five years, except that any propensity to smile had been relieved from his face. But she—she *had* changed.

He eyed her as if she were the Serpent in the Garden, and his hands flexed as if he had imagined wrapping his fingers round her throat and squeezing the life out of her. But she would not stay her steps, and he would not retreat from them.

"I could have you, if I wanted you," Lydia declared. Her hand breached the space yet between them, and she laid the very tip of one finger upon his chest. "I could have you in a moment—half of one, even."

"No," Marcus said, but his chest heaved with it, with a deep, frenetic breath. *No*, but it had come out half defiance, half uncertainty. His fingers flexed again. To grab for her? To strangle her? It didn't matter which; still she had *won* something of him.

"*Yes*," she crowed. "With only a snap of my fingers."

A growl rumbled within his chest. "Not if you were the last woman on earth."

She laughed, and in it trilled her delight, the joy of the mockery she made of him.

She snapped her fingers.

Marcus lunged. Like a beast of the wilds, his hands were claws snarling in the drape of her hair down her back, fingers tangling, pulling. Her back hit the wall behind her hard enough to startle a fresh laugh from her lungs.

Lydia breathed in triumph alongside the heady scent of shaving soap. He'd trapped her arms between them, but she would not give him the satisfaction of a struggle. Instead she lifted herself onto her toes, though the motion pulled at the hair caught in his fist. "Whenever I please," she whispered, and her breath feathered over his lips.

She saw the battle that raged within the depths of his eyes, saw desire at last win out over fury. "Damn you," he said, his voice low and guttural, an instant before his lips crashed down over hers.

Chapter Five

The merry ring of her laughter still rang in his ears; an affront against his honor. Which she had also made mockery of, without care or thought, as if it were of no more consequence than a gnat.

She was not laughing *now*. Nor *could* she have done, even had she wished to do so. Kissing her had been one way to still her tongue. The best? Likely not. He had played right into her hands, too easily baited. The regret for that would come, and the rage with it, sometime in the not-too-distant future.

For the moment, there was nothing but the pleasure of having her in his arms once again. He had missed the taste of her, the feel of her. The warm satin of her skin; the silk of her hair twined around his fingers. The hauteur that had kept her spine straight and stiff as steel left her one moment at a time, as if each of her muscles relieved themselves of it individually. It translated to a strange, erratic relaxing of the tension she had held, in fits and bursts.

First her heels had sunk back onto the floor. Then her hands had loosened between them. At last her head fell back against the cup of his hand, vivid green eyes closing as her long, inky lashes fluttered across her cheeks.

Just as much a victim of passion as he, for all that she had taunted him with it. Two could play at that game; he could feel the peaks of her nipples even through his coat, the tremble that slipped down her spine.

With some effort, she managed to pull her mouth from the cover of his, gasping for the air she gained. "I wonder what it says of you, my lord," she whispered, the icy bite of her voice a stunning contrast to the heat of her body against his own, "that you cannot keep your hands from me despite your professed dislike."

He let her feel the sting of his teeth against the side of her throat, leaving behind a small mark that would remain with her even after he had gone. *Ownership*, in some small way. "Dislike," he said roughly. "That's too tame a word."

She rolled her hips to his, finding the evidence of his arousal that he would have denied her if he had known she would seek it out. "Do you call *that* hatred, then?"

He called it *stupidity*, and the inevitable result of years of celibacy. His cock didn't know the difference; it answered to the call of a lush, female body in his arms. And all the better if she smelled of jasmine and tasted sweet as sugar despite the tartness of the tongue she wielded against him otherwise.

Which he would have again. She had made the critical error of turning her face toward him anew, her chin notched up, pride scored into every line of her face. Pride, and victory. She counted herself the winner of this battle? Well, he would not be the one to cry off.

His thumb found the lush pillow of her lower lip, slightly bruised. "I *will* own you. I promise you that."

Her teeth snapped. "You had such a chance before; you'll not get a second."

A laugh dredged itself up from somewhere deep in his lungs. "By God, I am going to *enjoy* making you eat those words." When had he last mustered up even the slightest approximation of enjoyment? Of *anything*?

But this—this he would *savor.*

He let his hand fall, gathering up a fistful of her shift until he could slide his palm up her leg, toward the juncture of her thighs. A heaven he hadn't touched, hadn't tasted in years, mere inches from his fingertips. Her breath came faster as his hand coasted up the smooth skin of her inner thigh. "Open," he murmured against her parted lips. "Just a bit more—"

"Marcus?" The door creaked. "We are going to be dreadfully—*oh.*"

Lydia's every muscle locked tight, her hands fisting between them. "L-Lady Diana," she croaked, her cheeks flushing hot with humiliation. "Let me go, you oaf," she hissed to Marcus, in a vicious whisper.

He did not. "I told you to stay in the box," he cast over his shoulder.

"I'm not a child to be ordered about," Diana said, though a brief glance over his shoulder had revealed that she had shaded her eyes with her hand—cognizant enough at least to understand she had stumbled across a scene she had never been meant to witness.

Lydia ground the heel of her foot into the toe of his boot. "Your sister! Are you *mad?*"

Perhaps a little. *More* than a little—she made him a step beyond mad. "Stop wiggling, for God's sake. I couldn't have known she would follow me down," he said. To Diana, he asked, "How the hell did you even come to be here?"

"Mr. Montgomery fetched me down," she said, weakly. "He said my presence had become necessary, which, in retrospect, I can see was not at all the truth. Miss Alcott, would you care for something to cover yourself?"

"No," Marcus snapped. *Damn* Montgomery for his interference. Hadn't he paid for better?

"*Yes*," Lydia gasped. "My dressing gown. It's just there, behind the door." She managed to wriggle one arm free, extending her hand in Diana's direction. "Thank you," she said, as her hand closed around the fabric.

"You're quite welcome." Diana edged away once again, drifting toward the door. In a tone of mild surprise mingled with embarrassment, she said, "Marcus, I do believe you'd better let Miss Alcott go."

"Go back to the damned box, Diana," Marcus gritted out between clenched teeth. "I'll retrieve you when I am through—"

"Oh, you're *through*, Lord Newhaven. Quite through." Montgomery's voice was an unwelcome addition to an already crowded conversation. "For what it is worth, Lady Diana, your presence *was* necessary. There's nothing like the company of one's sister to cool the fires of ardor." Fortunately, he had been proved correct. What lust had only moments ago clouded his head had faded enough that Marcus would not embarrass himself did he turn to face their audience of two.

"Lydia, do you require assistance?" Montgomery inquired.

"No, Giles, I thank you." She jabbed Marcus in the stomach with the point of her elbow, and he at last allowed her a step of breathing room in which to don her dressing gown, which she did in all haste, smoothing down the rumpled fabric like a small bird settling its ruffled feathers.

Marcus stabbed his fingers through his hair. "Run of the theatre," he snarled, casting a poisonous look at Montgomery, who could not have looked less interested. "You promised me—"

"Run of the theatre does not include monopolizing the dressing room," Montgomery said, his tone inflected with boredom as he crossed his arms over his chest. "I've got half a dozen actors eager to change their costumes and be about their business. Don't, I beg you, make yourself more tedious than already you are."

Tedious! "Bloody damned *actors*," he spat caustically, jerking at the knot of his cravat, which felt overly tight.

"Sour grapes," Montgomery chided, a smirk settled there at the right-hand corner of his mouth. "*Out*, Newhaven. We should all like to go home."

And where *was* home, exactly? The question settled on the tip of his tongue, but he knew that Lydia, standing so cool and remote with one hand resting upon the flat surface of the vanity table and the other holding together the edges of her dressing gown, looking every bit as if ice would not have melted in her mouth, would not answer if he asked.

"I will not ask again," Montgomery said.

He hadn't asked the first time, but Marcus threw up his hands in aggravation. "Come, Diana. We're leaving." And he pushed past Diana and Montgomery both, the harsh thud of his footsteps revealing the depths of his fury.

Lydia let out her breath on a sigh, closing her eyes and locking her elbow to support herself when every muscle in her body wanted only to wilt.

"All right?" Giles asked.

She nodded. "All right. But thank you nonetheless."

"Ah, that was my pleasure. Lady Diana, my apologies for embroiling you within your brother's affairs."

Lydia's eyes flashed open once more. Diana had remained behind?

Lady Diana offered a tentative smile, like she wasn't certain whether or not that much familiarity was appropriate. "He's in a state," she said. "It will take him a few minutes, I think, to notice I have not followed." She sucked in a breath, her gaze falling on Giles. "He wouldn't have hurt her."

"You need not defend him to me."

"But it's true," Diana said in a rush. "Marcus is—well, he's a quite a lot of things, really, but he truly isn't the sort that would ever hurt a woman."

Well. Not *physically*, at least, Lydia thought. But emotionally? He could be devastating. *Had* been devastating.

"You've mistaken my meaning, my lady," Giles said. "If I had thought he posed a risk of any physical harm, you may be certain he would never have gotten within a stone's throw of Lydia."

"Oh. Well." Diana chewed her lower lip uncertainly, her eyes darting once more toward Lydia, then shying away once more. "I hope you will not think me ill-mannered," she said. "But I have always wanted to ask. And now that I've the opportunity, I think I must."

The terrible weight of the coming judgment sat like a leaden ball inside Lydia's stomach. It had been there for years, really. She ought to have become accustomed to it. And still she heard herself say, "Ask, then. I will answer."

"Did you do it? Did you do what—what he thought you had done?"

Surprised by the sudden upwelling of tears that burned behind her eyes, Lydia felt her whole body give a strange, violent tremble. She sat heavily upon the chair at the vanity, her hands falling into her lap. And she shook her head. Just once.

"I knew it," Diana whispered. "*I knew it.*"

There was a sob there, somewhere deep in Lydia's throat; some tiny bit of anguish that had ignited itself once more. With some effort she swallowed it back, her fingers tensing upon the fabric of her dressing gown. "You had better go, my lady. You will be missed."

"Oh," Diana said, her brows drawing together. "But, Marcus—"

"Will never believe otherwise," Lydia said, though the words cracked as they emerged, brittle and fragile as glass. "Save your breath for more useful causes, my lady."

For a moment, Diana vacillated. "But he should *know*."

"For what purpose?"

"Because—I thought—" Diana stammered over the words. "You were engaged for a time, no?"

"He made certain promises," Lydia allowed. "Which I permitted myself to believe were genuine well past the point it had become clear they were not." She knitted her hands in her lap. "I let that dream die long ago. There was a time I would have cared whether or not he believed in me, but that time passed years ago, and it is dead and rotting in the ground."

Diana ducked her head. "Then I am sad for both of you," she said.

For a long moment, neither of them spoke—but Lydia had an odd sort of feeling deep in her chest; a nameless longing for a time that had once nestled in the palm of her hand for so short a duration before it had finally fluttered away past the tips of her fingers. But she had never *caught* it; never *owned* it. In another life, a different one, this woman might have become her sister by marriage. Perhaps they would have been friends.

But it could never be. She drew in a deep, steadying breath. "My lady, you had best go." Quickly, and before she was missed in truth. Before Marcus returned for her.

"Yes," Diana said haltingly, and at last her feet turned toward the door. "I suppose I should do. I wish—" But her voice faded away into an awkward, stilted silence. "Good evening to you, Miss Alcott."

"And to you, Lady Diana." And that was that, and nothing else. Wisely,

Diana slipped back through the door and down the hall.

Lydia managed to hold out until Diana's footsteps had faded to lash out with one arm, sweeping everything from her vanity with a cascading, discordant crash.

"Feel any better?" Giles asked.

"No. Not even a little." A brutal, bitter laugh slipped from her lungs, and she swiped the back of her hand across her eyes to stem the flow of stupid, silly tears. "Do you know, she is the first person to ask me that. The *very* first. Not *why*," she clarified, with a little flip of her wrist. "*If.*" Her narrowed gaze sliced across him. "*You* never even asked."

"I didn't care," Giles said. "It made no difference to me whether you had or had not. But I had suspected as much, at least. You played the wrongly-accused Hermione all too well for it to be solely affectation." He bent to retrieve the box of powder, which, thankfully, had not opened when it had crashed to the floor with the sweep of her arm. "You act best," he said, "when you are not acting at all."

Lydia sniffled. "Thank you, I suppose."

He made a rough sound in his throat. "It's not a compliment. Makes it damned difficult to place you in roles. At any moment, by the turn of your emotions, you could lose it. Still, I've never seen a better Hermione."

Her fingers wrapped around the powder box as he handed it back to her, knuckles whitening. "I can play Paulina just as well."

"I'm certain you will." Giles' lips flattened into a grim smile. "I imagine, if nothing else, Newhaven will see to that much."

Tedious. The word had yet to leave Marcus' brain, drowning out the gentle hum of conversation that drifted around him. *Tedious.* Montgomery did not know the first thing about tedium. *This* was tedium—this aimless, pointless process of gathering after dinner and making witless remarks about the weather and everyone's opinions thereof.

"Marcus, you're scowling," Diana whispered from her position beside him on the couch as she lifted her cup of tea to her lips.

"I beg your pardon." It came out more gruffly than he had intended. "I simply don't see the point in any of this."

A tiny smile slid over Diana's mouth. "There isn't one," she said. "At least, not one that I have ever been able to discern."

"Then why did you choose to attend?"

"Because I should be at loose ends otherwise, and the only thing worse than being a spinster is to be a spinster left to her own devices in perpetuity."

"You're not a spinster. You're engaged."

"Yes; to a man I've not clapped eyes on since childhood," she sighed. "You should count yourself lucky that it is only a dinner party and not a ball. No one ever asks me to dance, and one can only sit at the side of a room for so many hours at a time before one's temper grows quite foul." She reached for the tiny plate of biscuits she'd commandeered and hidden between them, her teeth snapping clean through a crisp wafer. "At least there is no dancing to be left out of this evening. Have you given thought to Papa's demand?"

Demand? Oh, right—Father wanted him married. He'd been saying as much for years, though Marcus had never humored him. "No," he said honestly. "I've no interest in it."

"Oh, to be a man and to cast off the mere thought of marriage with such a cavalier air," Diana sniffed, as she squinted in the low light. "Who is present this evening?"

Marcus smothered a laugh behind his palm. "You would know if you wore your spectacles."

"I think I like guessing better," Diana said. "I should be so bored otherwise. Who, though, Marcus?"

He tipped his head toward the fireplace, where two young women stood. "That is Miss Smythe, I think, there conversing with Lady Esther."

"Hm. Not Lady Esther," Diana said. "She's got too much a fondness for cats."

"I can't abide cats."

"Curiously, neither can Lady Esther," Diana said. "They make her sneeze something dreadful—but she loves them anyway. I think she had six at last count."

"*Six?*"

"Yes; and all named after English kings, if you can imagine. Even the girls." She disguised a laugh with another bite of biscuit. "Miss Smythe is quite pleasant. Everyone likes her, but no one had yet offered for her."

He wasn't going to be the first, but at least this game of speculation was keeping Diana occupied and in a good humor. "She's a bit short."

"Well, one can hardly hold that against her. I daresay she'd prefer to be taller, had she the choice of it. So would I. Who else?"

"The Framingham chit," Marcus said, stifling a laugh as Diana cast him a censorious glare at the rude address.

"Miss Framingham is lovely," she said. "Well-educated. I think she reads in several languages, including Greek. You should never be bored."

"She's too blond," Marcus said.

"Too blond?" Diana rounded on him, agog. "*Too* blond? I beg you tell me, how can one be *too* blond?"

Marcus shrugged. "Her hair's too pale," he said. "Makes her look washed out. Sickly, almost."

"It's quite fashionable!" Diana protested with a huff. "I wish I had hair like hers. Black is never in fashion, I tell you." Over the rim of her tea cup, she muttered, "*Too blond*, indeed."

Marcus snickered, settling his cup upon his knee. "There's Miss Too-good," he said. "One of them at least. The youngest?"

"No; Susannah has married already. It must be Phoebe, and I wouldn't inflict you upon her."

"I beg your pardon. *Inflict* me?"

"She's a friend, after a fashion," Diana said. "Quite frequently we end up together, sitting with the dowagers. She isn't much asked to dance, either. And do you know, I think she prefers it."

"It's just as well," Marcus said. "I don't favor blue eyes."

"Oh? And what color *do* you favor?"

"Green," Marcus said, absently, as he stirred a second lump of sugar into his tea.

"Ah," Diana said, her voice dropping to a murmur. "I believe I take your meaning."

Marcus frowned, slanting her a sidelong glance. "What meaning?"

"She must not be too short," she said slyly. "Or too blond. Her eyes should be green, if possible, since you do not favor blue. Had I asked, would you say also that your preferences ran not toward redheads?"

Suspicion narrowed his eyes. "I'd not given it much consideration."

"But they don't," Diana said, her mouth curling. "I suppose Miss Framingham would be too tall? But then she *is* quite slender."

"As a reed," Marcus said.

"Which you also don't favor."

His jaw clenched. "Why should that matter?"

"Because, dear brother," Diana said sweetly, in a voice that would not carry, "your ideal woman, as you have thus described, is *Lydia*."

"She isn't." Marcus bit back a foul word, conscious of their location. "Blast. I should never have exposed you to her—"

"Between the two of you this evening," Diana interjected dryly, "yours was the worse behavior. Besides, women are never as ignorant of such things as men would like to believe. Had you noticed her dressing gown?"

"No. Why should I have done?"

"It's old. Quite old, I should say." Her fingers danced along the edge of the plate, seeking another biscuit. "One wonders that she should be so ill-clothed."

"She's an actress. Her salary cannot be much." But if she had been supplementing her income with prostitution, if she had had a protector of any sort... "How old, do you think?"

"Years and years. It'd been patched over in a few spots. Worn nearly threadbare in places." A delicate shrug of her shoulders. "I imagine she must treat it carefully, because otherwise it would fall apart at the seams."

"It makes no difference to me what she wears," he said. "I only want her to *leave*."

"Oh? That is a surprise, given how reluctant you were to let her go. One wonders what might have occurred had I not walked in when I did." Diana let a smirk linger about the corners of her lips. "Or what I might have witnessed had I arrived just a few minutes later."

"Unmarried ladies certainly do not wonder such things," Marcus growled.

"Oh, I *promise* you they do."

"One does not discuss such things with one's sister, besides." His hand tightened upon the fragile handle of the tea cup. "It was a mistake to take you with me this evening. I won't make it again."

"But you will *go* again." All certainty there in her voice. Sometimes a man forgot a sister could be as maddening as any other female.

"It's none of your concern. Put her from your mind; I'll see that you do not cross paths with her in the future."

"How ought I put her from my mind, when *you* have not these past five years?" Diana said, her voice vaguely accusatory. "Marcus, she said she had not."

"Had not what?"

"Done it. Betrayed you." Diana's hand settled over his own, squeezing lightly. "I believed her."

Of its own accord, a scathing sound eked from his mouth, drawing more than one befuddled stare. And he waited, stewing silently, until notice fell away from them before he muttered, "She's an actress. She's meant to make you believe things that are not true. If she has prevailed upon you to tell me such lies—"

"In fact, she advised me not to," Diana said, her voice threaded through with disappointment. "I asked, and she answered, and that is all. She said there would be no point in saying as much to you—"

"She had the right of it there," Marcus bit off.

"—and now I see why. You truly cannot even consider it." Her hand released his, and she settled back into her seat, resigned to suffering through the rest of the evening.

"There is nothing to consider. She gambled and lost. She will not get her claws into me again."

"Careful, Marcus," Diana chided. "The only claws I witnessed this evening belonged to you."

Chapter Six

I want you to follow her," Marcus said over a light supper to his brother at their club.

Rafe's knife scraped sharply over his plate, eliciting several hard stares from the men at neighboring tables. He did not pretend to misunderstand Marcus' meaning. "Have you lost your damned mind?" he hissed.

Yes. Yes, he had, rather. It was a sorry state of affairs, but it was what it was, and he wasn't going to waste the time or the energy in self-flagellation. "I'll pay you. Handsomely," Marcus said.

"I'm not in need of funds." Rafe's eyes had narrowed considerably. "God's teeth, Marcus. You think that just because I took up a commission, that I am perpetually in want of money? I've coin enough to feed my habits, and more besides. I don't need yours."

"Then why do *I* always end up paying for our meals?" Marcus inquired.

"Because you're my elder brother. You're meant to do such things. Even if I've got money, *you've* got more," Rafe said, flashing a disarming grin for a fraction of a second, before his expression wavered. "Marcus, it's been five years. This obsession will destroy you. Let it go, for your own peace of mind."

Peace of mind was not something to which Marcus had been able to lay claim for some time. And his mind had only grown more muddled with Lydia's return. "I need this," he said. "*For* my peace of mind. I would not ask otherwise." Scrubbing one hand over his mouth, at last he admitted in a low voice, "I paid Montgomery—the company owner—to foil any liaisons she might undertake. But he claims not to know where she resides, and I can't—"

I can't bear to think of some other man's hands upon her. Holding her. Touching her. Kissing her.

"Marcus—"

"I *need* this," he repeated. "Please, Rafe."

Rafe chewed, swallowed, and washed the bite down with a swig of ale. "It's a mistake," he said. "You're bound to learn something you don't like."

"I've done that already," Marcus said tightly. "She's been warned. If she

49

has elected not to listen, then that is *her* mistake." And she'd pay for it. She'd pay, and pay, and pay, until at last his wounded pride, his fury, his honor, were satisfied. And when he'd had all he wanted of her, then *she* would be the one left devastated.

Rafe bit out a sigh. "This evening, I assume? From the theatre?"

"Yes. It must be this evening. There's no performance tomorrow." A whole day in which she would slip the leash he'd meant for her if he did not discover her whereabouts, and quickly. "She might take a hack. You should be prepared."

With a low sound, something like aggravation, Rafe said, "I'll find her. Don't concern yourself with it." He jabbed the tines of his fork at the lump of meat upon his plate. "What then, when you've driven her out of London for good? Will you acquiesce to Father's demand and marry?" He delivered a sharp smile with this, like any respectable younger brother. "Diana told me," he said.

"Diana would do well to mind her business," Marcus muttered.

"Why should she, when it's ever so much more entertaining to mind *yours*?"

Marcus returned the slice of Rafe's taunting grin to him. "Then prepare to do your own duty, Rafe, for I've no intention of folding to Father's demands. And when he realizes it at last, it'll be *your* bollocks he'll be twisting to get his heirs."

"*Hell*," Rafe grunted, as if he'd just found himself punched in the stomach. "I suppose I have Miss Alcott to thank for that."

The worst of it was that he wasn't wrong. Lydia had destroyed any capacity to love, to *trust*, that ever had existed within him. With her defection, she had twisted the course of fate for more than just himself. If she had not betrayed him—

If she had not betrayed him, he'd have married her. Probably they'd have had two or three children by now. Father would be placated, if not in his choice of bride, then at least in the security of the line of succession. And Rafe could go merrily along, playing the scapegrace younger brother, without overmuch responsibility.

"Not to worry," he said lightly, though even he heard the undertone of menace in his words. "She'll pay for that, too."

Blast and damn, and damn again.

Lydia scowled down at the box of powder which had failed to remove the mark that Marcus had left upon her neck. It simply wasn't opaque enough to conceal it, and if she *did* somehow manage to do so, she'd be so pale that she would be appearing on stage this evening as the *ghost* of Perdita instead.

Perhaps she could arrange her hair to cover it? Carefully she tugged at a few pins, sliding loose a cluster of curls. No—now she looked merely deranged and disheveled. She tilted her neck, easing closer to the mirror to see the mark better. Probably it was too small, too subtle, to be seen by anyone but the other actors.

But *she* knew it was there, and that was enough to want to erase it.

She had arrived late to the theatre, but that hardly mattered, given that she didn't come on until the fourth act. Tomorrow, she would read for Paulina again, and next week she would take up the role in earnest.

Giles had ribbed her mercilessly about the mark on her throat, since Perdita's costume would not cover it. But Paulina's would. Provided she did not acquire more of them, at least.

Thank God the dressing room was deserted already. There was no one to see her blush like the innocent young girl she hadn't been in years. How humiliating. She had thought herself immune to such things, beyond them. Since Marcus had thrown her out on her arse, she'd been kissed, fondled, ogled—and not one look, one kiss, one touch had elicited anything other than indifference at best or disgust at worst.

She had assumed she had lost the taste for such things. That the passion in her had died along with her heart.

Only for it to come alive again once more, the moment that Marcus had touched her. Sizzling in her veins, and heady as opium smoke. She had thought to taunt him with it, to tease and mock him with his own desire, only to have her own trap turned round on her.

A bitter pill to swallow, that.

They were like poison to one another now, and each encounter sliced one more piece from the heart that he had already left battered and broken. She could only hope her venom was the more potent. That if they killed one another in this dance of revenge, she outlived him even if only by a moment.

A pyrrhic victory was still a victory. Wasn't it?

Yes. She closed her eyes, inhaled, and held her breath deep in her lungs. It was just *acting*. A game of pretend. Child's play, really. She had only to hold the iciness of her heart in her eyes, to turn her mind from the warmth of his fingers upon her skin. The weight of his body on hers.

"Woolgathering? You're meant to be on stage in ten minutes, give or take."

She did not betray her surprise with even the tiniest quiver. Instead, she released her breath slowly, deliberately. Her fingers curled around the handle of her comb. "If you insist upon invading my privacy," she said, as she extended it to Marcus, who had appeared just behind her, "do be good and make yourself useful, my lord."

There—he could not conceal his expressions so easily as she. She had caught him off guard with the demand, and his hand reached out for the comb as if it were an unfamiliar thing; a tool he had not used in some time. His fingers brushed hers as he took the comb from her hand, and he might as well have scorched her.

"You've got pins in." He eyed them like they were weapons, as if at any moment one might leap to life and bite him.

Deliberately, she smiled. Sharp. Dangerous. "I won't need your help to replace them." He was a disaster at it anyway. But the brushing? He'd been adept enough at that.

She watched him weigh his options, staring at the comb in his hand as if it contained an unsprung trap just waiting to catch him unawares. That delightful indecision; the jump and pull of a muscle in his cheek. The teeth clenched behind the arrogant jut of his jaw. *Wonderful.*

And then that dark gaze turned upon her hair, and for a moment there was a raw sort of longing there. His fingers twitched as if he desired nothing so much as to bury them in the clinging curls. The lure proved too powerful to resist. With the fingers of his free hand, he began to pull pins free one at a time.

He had always loved her hair.

That, it seemed, had not changed. The coil of it came loose a piece at a time, tumbling over her shoulders. The pins clattered to the surface of the counter beside her elbow. He held the comb like a weapon; perhaps a dagger to plunge into her heart, and then—

The teeth touched her scalp, burrowing between strands, and passing lightly through the unbound length of it. A slow, smooth stroke, straight down her back. "You couldn't do this yourself?"

"I could, but I'd prefer to put an interfering baron to some good use." The satisfaction in her voice had drawn an ireful glance from him, and she swallowed back a chuckle as she reached for a pot of rouge.

"You don't need that," he said, with a man's overconfident opinion of cosmetics.

"In fact, I do. The gaslight makes me look quite sallow." It was twice as harsh as candlelight, in fact, and could burn a person's eyes if they looked at it too long. She rubbed twin spots of rouge into her cheeks. The rosy hue was glaring so close up, but would be softened with the distance between herself and the audience. His hand had paused in its strokes through her hair as he considered her face in the mirror. "The comb," she prompted, with a careless flick of her hand. "And do be quick about it, if you please."

Oh, he had *not* liked being so ordered. Men were so predictable, so easy to manipulate.

He laid the comb aside, job half-finished at best. "You'll not find it quite so simple to control me now," he said, as his fingers gathered up a handful of her hair, rubbing it between them.

But she already had. He simply did not understand it.

"I? Control *you*?" She let out a light, airy laugh. "I wouldn't dream of it, my lord."

"Liar." His fingers cupped the back of her neck, trapping her hair within them. "My God, you lie as easily as you breathe."

The accusation stung, though she would never let him see it. "I did not request your presence, my lord. *You* came to *me*." Here. Now. When all action was directed upon the stage; when the chances of discovery were so much lower. A deliberate choice.

"I paid for the privilege," he reminded her.

"So that is what this is? The protection of your investment?" The sharpness of her voice warred with the softness of her face. "Whatever you paid Giles, it is business only between the two of you. You haven't coin enough to purchase *me*."

He knelt, slowly, until she could see his face there in the mirror just beside her. "Ah, Lydia. I think we both know I won't need coin." His cheek scraped hers, a light abrasion that sent a shiver careening down her spine.

Blast. A dimple had carved itself into his cheek, his teeth sharp in his smile. Lydia closed her eyes against it. But she was not the only one so affect-

53

ed, and she reassured herself with that thought—that only last evening he had snarled at his sister rather than release her.

Those same hungry hands slid over her shoulders, which were barely covered in Perdita's Bohemian garb. Little licks of fire trailed in the wake of his hands. The tip of his tongue touched her neck, there, just over the mark she'd tried—and failed—to conceal with powder. "You don't cover this," he said, and his voice rumbled along her skin.

Her eyes flashed open. "Or what?" she demanded, and let her hand fall upon his chest, watching his pupils dilate with the motion.

"Or I'll give you more than you can cover," he said. His palm flattened upon her cheek, trapping her face there, facing him. He breathed against the corner of her mouth. "You're going to lose, Lydia."

She had already lost. She had lost everything to him already. What remained of her was so much *less* than she had once been; just the scraps and tatters of a pride that had been savaged. The best she could hope was to break him just as thoroughly. "I wouldn't place a wager upon it," she said, and nipped his lower lip.

The legs of her chair rocked as he seized her chin, slanting his mouth over hers. Unbalanced just as physically as emotionally. Her tongue parried the thrust of his, her hand fisting in his hair.

That low groan he gave into her mouth tasted a bit like surrender, and she smiled. Whatever his intention, that sword sliced both ways. Desire matched against desire, until she could not determine whose was the greater. Perhaps they would both perish to the fire of it.

But she had miscalculated. He had come dressed as one did to the theatre; all buttoned into starchy fabric, with only his gloves gone wanting. And she—she was in Perdita's shepherdess costume, the linen thin and light to move breezily about the stage. His hand cupped her thigh, a burning reminder of that same abbreviated touch last eve.

Only now there was none to stay it. His thumb stirred the crisp curls between her thighs.

She gasped, "*Marcus.*"

He sipped his name from her lips. "Let me," he crooned. It was a bitter sweetness in his voice; a false tenderness. But the helpless passion that wore his breathing ragged? That could not be feigned at least. He seduced himself even as he seduced her. What was there to be lost in taking her pleasure of him?

She eased her thighs apart, relishing the low sound he made in the back of his throat as the tips of his fingers found her at last. Wet, wanting, as she hadn't in years. A soft stroke, lingering against her slick flesh, seeking a deeper connection.

There was nothing contrived in the hot fan of her breath against the side of his neck just above the collar of his shirt. She rubbed her lips against the salty flesh there, luxuriating in the scent of desire that lay thick upon his skin. His thumb rubbed the bead of her clitoris, and she felt the spark of that sensation slide sweetly through her veins. Only a moment more she could allow herself, but she might well have sold whatever was left of her soul for half a dozen.

He sank his longest finger inside her just as she sank her teeth into his skin. "*Christ*, Lydia."

Enough. She braced her feet upon the floor, shoved away from him. The legs of the chair scraped against the wood floor; a jarring sound. And she stood, even if her legs trembled beneath the fabric of her costume. There was no time to replace her pins; she would simply have to leave her hair down.

There on his knees he looked like a supplicant to a goddess' shrine. *Hers.* That was right, she thought. He *ought* to have worshiped her. If he were wise, he would have done.

Even as his chest heaved in frenzied breaths, he tried to bargain: "Five minutes more."

"I haven't even one for you." She snatched at Perdita's flower crown and laid it atop her head. The whole of her body hummed with unrelieved tension, with the promise of satisfaction denied. She watched the realization come over him at last. That he had timed his arrival poorly in the grand scheme of things; that he had been the architect of his own undoing in it. She was called away by the stage.

He climbed to his feet once more, his hands flexing. "I'll return later. We are not done here."

Lydia cast him a self-satisfied smile. "*I* am done here, my lord. Do enjoy the remainder of the play." And she enjoyed the slack-jawed shock that slid over his face as she slipped out the door and made once more for the stage.

A point scored against an arrogant lord. If only all victories felt so delicious.

Christ, Marcus could still feel her there, so soft upon his fingers. All luscious wet heat and delicate female flesh. And now could only watch her make such simpering expressions to Florizel, when just an hour ago the slick nectar of her body had coated *his* fingers.

She wouldn't meet him backstage this evening; he knew it in his bones. A few simple touches, a brief kiss that had rocked him to his core, and she— she had walked away from him so *easily*. Left him with the taste of her upon his lips, her soft jasmine scent embedded into his brain. Hungry as he'd not been in years.

"Go," Marcus growled to Rafe, who occupied the seat beside him. The play would conclude with the next scene, and someone had to be ready to catch her as she fled the theatre.

"You're not yourself this evening," Rafe said, his voice awash in a wondering tone. "What has she done to you?"

Marcus might have laughed, had he the ability. "Nothing," he said, and that much was true enough. Nothing—except to twist the trap he'd meant for her back onto him. Probably it spoke not well of either of them.

"You look like hell," Rafe said as he rose to his feet.

Fitting enough. He felt like it, as well. "*Go*, damn you."

Rafe heaved a sigh, heading for the door of the box. Only to pause, hand curled around the handle. "There is a saying that has been on my mind lately," he said, "It goes something like, 'Before you embark on a journey of revenge, dig two graves.'"

"What the devil do you mean by *that*?"

"I mean you ought to take care," Rafe said, "that you don't bury yourself in your efforts to bury *her*." His cool gaze raked Marcus from head to toe, a flash of judgment in it. "Every action you take is one more shovelful of dirt. But whose grave is it you're digging? Because from where I stand, it looks like yours."

Marcus narrowed his eyes. "And you would know?"

"I have eyes, Marcus," Rafe said as he wrenched the door open. "And you—you've got a love bite on your neck." With one hand, he indicated a spot just above Marcus' collar. "Just there," he said. "I wonder from whom you received it."

The door closing in his wake was just one more sting to Marcus' wounded pride.

Chapter Seven

I didn't hold supper for you," Mrs. Hawkins sniffed, crossing her thin arms over her chest as she came into the kitchen, where Lydia had been preparing a pot of tea.

Lydia had never expected that she would. She hadn't, even once. "That's quite all right, Mrs. Hawkins. I purchased something on my way home," she said as she stripped off her gloves and tucked them into her pocket. There was a grease stain just there, on the tip of the right index finger, from the meat pie she'd eaten. Probably wouldn't come out in the wash, but then the gloves were old anyway, the fabric stiff with their years.

Mrs. Hawkins blinked behind her spectacles. "If you want supper, you'll have to be on time for it."

She *had* paid for the privilege of an evening meal; it was part of the cost of letting the room. "I'm afraid the theatre doesn't let out until half ten at least," she said. "So it simply isn't possible."

"Ghastly business, the theatre," Mrs. Hawkins clucked. "Simply *ghastly*." She drew her shawl down further over her shoulders and performed a shudder which Lydia thought was a touch too melodramatic. "Filled with women of loose morals. No better than they ought to be, I expect."

You should see the men. Lydia strove to keep her smile painted to her face. "The world we live in, Mrs. Hawkins, can be so unkind to a woman alone. I try not to judge too harshly, for I would not want that same judgment directed upon me."

"And *are* you alone, Miss Alcott? Have you no family?"

"I have some, ma'am. Just in Whitechapel." The kettle began to boil, and Lydia removed it from the heat and poured its contents carefully into the tea pot, which had been prepared with just enough tea leaves to produce the weak tea Mrs. Hawkins preferred. A habit born of pinching pennies until they shrieked, Lydia suspected. There was neither sugar nor milk, but Lydia was more concerned with warming her cold hands from the chill of the winter air. "My father is a butcher," she said. "My mother helps him round the shop.

And my older sister, Lavinia, works in a factory that makes the most beautiful silks. Would you care for a cup of tea?"

"I suppose so." The assent was issued somewhat resentfully, as if she were leery of sharing a table with an actress. "Do you see them often?"

"No, ma'am." Rather, it was *they* who would not see *her.* Even Lavinia, with whom she corresponded occasionally, she had not seen in years. "They also disapprove of the theatre," she hedged. The theatre had not been the cause of their rift—*that* had been her short-lived affair with Marcus—but it certainly had not endeared her to them any further. It had hurt, to be ignored. And worse still to have no one to whom to turn when their predictions had become reality.

She knew, in the way of a daughter who had once been so very cossetted and coddled, that they still loved her. It was just that the shame had run deeper than that love. And now—well, too many years had passed already. She had thought, now and then, about paying a visit. But the prospect of a door slammed in her face had seemed too large a risk to bear.

"I send them money. Whatever I can spare from my wages," she said. It had not been terribly much in the past, even though she lived simply. But she had got enough from the money that Giles had wheeled out of Marcus that she could send over a sum that ought to see them through the winter comfortably. "Papa is getting up in years. Lavinia says his joints plague him whenever there is a hard rain." Which was often in London.

Mrs. Hawkins retrieved two cups from a cupboard and set them upon the table. "There is so little filial piety left in the young," she said, and there might have been the tiniest flicker of approval in her watery blue eyes. "And you *are* still young. You could find a more respectable vocation."

True. She had never aspired to be an actress; it had simply been an opportunity she had seized on for want of anything else. Probably now the scandal she had found herself embroiled within so many years ago had died down enough that her sins, while not *forgiven*, would have been considered an ancient matter too far distant to be worth much dredging up. She hadn't loved being a seamstress, either, but she was quick with her hands and quicker with a needle. It was what had kept her clothing from falling apart at the seams so far past their seasons.

Acting had been a crutch of sorts, when she had been left broken and bleeding. It had held her up when she might have crumpled beneath the weight of her grief. She had not loved tearing her heart out of her chest and holding it up for a captivated audience to gawk at each night upon the stage, but it had served her far better *out* of her than bottled up within. Perhaps it had saved her, after a fashion.

She sipped her tea in silence for a moment, considering. "I know your opinion of the theatre, Mrs. Hawkins. But we actresses are all just women, doing what we can to eke out a living. There are so few occupations that allow a woman to be self-supporting."

"Then perhaps you ought to turn your talents toward catching a husband instead," Mrs. Hawkins advised.

Lydia wondered what Mrs. Hawkins would say if she knew that her first and only attempt at *that* was what had led to her notorious career. "No; I thank you. If I have learned nothing else, it is that the last thing upon which a woman can depend is the fickle affections of a man."

"A lesson I suspect many women in your profession take too long to learn," Mrs. Hawkins said, but it did not have the sharp tang of censure to which Lydia had become accustomed.

It was perhaps the most civil conversation they had ever had, all things considered. She did not think that she had much swayed Mrs. Hawkins' mind, but perhaps they could live amicably for the remainder of her time in London.

Lydia collected the cups once the pot had been drained and took them to the sink. "I'll do the washing up," she said.

Mrs. Hawkins winced as she stood. "Kind of you," she acknowledged, with a little nod. "These old bones do struggle at times. I'll go up, then. Perhaps I'll hold supper for you tomorrow after all."

Lydia acknowledged that with a small nod of her own, and just as she was drying her hands upon a bit of toweling, a fierce rap sounded upon the front door, echoing through the silent halls of the house.

Mrs. Hawkins pulled a frown. "A visitor? At this hour?"

"Perhaps another resident has forgotten their key," Lydia suggested.

Mrs. Hawkins waved that away. "No, my dear, you are the only one given to such foolishness. Besides, the other girls were present all for dinner, and none has gone out, to my knowledge. Not many are brave enough to walk St. Giles after dark."

St. Giles was not half so bad as some of the places she had, however briefly, called home. "Shall I accompany you to the door?"

"If you please." But the words had been issued in such a tone that suggested that she would be dearly grateful for the additional body. "I reassure myself that burglars rarely offer the civility of knocking, but—" But she was

59

just a frail old woman, and she would not well manage anyone with nefarious intent.

The shadows in the hall seemed to collect around them as they went together to the door, where Lydia hung back just out of sight, prepared to spring forward and shove the door closed should such an action prove itself necessary.

Mrs. Hawkins called through the door, "Who is it?"

Muffled by the sturdy wood, a masculine voice returned, "I beg your pardon for calling so late. I have an…appointment with Miss Lydia Alcott."

Offended fury crackled up Lydia's spine, snapping it straight as a board. "No, he hasn't!" she hissed to Mrs. Hawkins, who had turned to level a searching stare at her, which she could feel even in the thick of the darkness. "I swear to you, he hasn't." Oh, lord. Had an admirer followed her home? She had had to shake persistent suitors in the past, but never had one been so bold as *this*.

"I run a *respectable* home, Miss Alcott." From only the sibilance of the words, Lydia understood that she had lost much of the good will she had gained in only a handful of seconds.

"I know, Mrs. Hawkins," she said, aware of the note of a plea in her voice. "Whatever he claims is a lie."

Mrs. Hawkins turned the lock and cracked the door open. "She denies you, sir," she said through the crack. "This is a respectable boarding house. There's been no men to pass through this door in more years than you've been alive."

"A…boarding house?" The words were uttered in a tone of confusion. "This is a boarding house?"

Lydia pulled herself from the shadows, creeping forward to peek at the caller. The voice she had not recognized at all…but that midnight black hair, and eyes nearly as dark—they *had* to be a family trait. She thought she recognized Marcus' angular jawline in his face, the same breadth of shoulder.

Oh, good God. The *brother*.

She had never met him, had quite forgotten that he had even existed. And now he was *here*, at her very door—or at Mrs. Hawkins' door, which was arguably worse. How had he even found her? *Why?*

No doubt at Marcus' behest. A shudder slipped down her spine—he could make trouble for her. And it would take little more than a whisper to do it. Already he had roused Mrs. Hawkins once more to suspicion. And if word got around where she was residing…

Mrs. Hawkins would not take kindly to a parade of men coming to call, even if Lydia had no intention of accepting any of them. Her respectable boarding house would be subject to rampant speculation, to gossip.

"Miss Alcott?" Mrs. Hawkins prodded. "Have you anything to say?" The subtext nestled within that brief question suggested that if she knew what was good for her, she had *better*.

Her voice snarled in her throat, arrested by the possibilities that swam around within her head. It was all she could do to stare, and to fret over how she would prove she had made no such appointment, that she had certainly not invited this man to call upon her here.

A short, tense silence reigned before at last the man—*Rafe*, she thought he was called—was at last moved to break it. "My mistake," he said, and his eyes swept over her with a cold speculation, as if he could see straight through to her soul. "There's been a misunderstanding. Your pardon for pre-vailing upon you so late."

His fingers touched the brim of his hat—a brief, respectful gesture—and at last he turned to go. Mrs. Hawkins half-turned as the door shut smoothly. "A mistake?" she asked.

"I swear upon all I hold dear, I have never seen him before this moment," Lydia said in a rush.

By the low, critical sound that Mrs. Hawkins made in her throat as she turned once more for the stairs, Lydia guessed that she had not much been believed. She could almost feel the wafer-thin ice upon which she tread cracking beneath her feet.

Marcus held the strings of her temporary home within the palm of his hand. Only the tiniest tug would wrest it from her.

"A *what*?"

"A boarding house," Rafe repeated as he reached out and snagged the bottle of brandy from its resting place upon the table between them to set it at the side of his chair, where Marcus could not reach it. "You've had enough this evening, I think."

The brandy was the last thing on his mind, for all that he'd poured enough of it down his throat already. "In *St. Giles*?"

"Yes, St. Giles. It's only a short walk from the theatre. Ten minutes; possibly less."

A damned *walk*. No doubt a *gauntlet* peppered with pickpockets and prostitutes. Marcus passed one hand over his face, smothering the breath that shuddered out of lungs that felt too strained by half. She could almost certainly afford better than St. Giles, though probably not by much. But a damned *boarding house*? A tiny rented room in a place like that? And it *would* be tiny— St. Giles was packed to the gills with those less fortunate, riddled with rookeries. He couldn't imagine that a room she had let there would be anything but a place to rest her head.

"You're certain?" he heard himself ask, the tremor of hope in his voice astounding him. Perhaps there had been some mistake. Perhaps Rafe had followed the wrong woman.

"As certain as I can be," Rafe replied. He swirled the amber liquid in his glass, letting the firelight sparkle over it. "I thought you might ask, so—well, it's quite possible I've caused problems for her."

"How do you mean?"

"I mean I knocked upon the door and asked for her by name. I led the proprietress to the assumption that we had arranged an assignation." Rafe slanted him a regretful grin. "Just in the happenstance that it was *that* sort of place, you understand."

Marcus' fingers tightened upon his glass, which had come up empty all of a sudden. "And?"

"She denied me, of course." Rafe swallowed back the last of his brandy and set his glass aside. "The old bat that runs the place was all in a snit over the mere implication of it. But Lydia *was* there—there's no question of that."

Marcus ran his fingers through his hair in a futile attempt to pull away the dark thoughts cluttering his brain. "So her lovers—she sees them elsewhere, then."

"If there are, then she surely must," he said. "But—" Rafe hesitated, lips pinned.

"No; out with it." Marcus waved one hand.

"I don't think there are," Rafe said in a rush. "She'd be living better than she does if there were. She'd be better dressed, that's certain enough."

"Better dressed?"

"I've seen shop girls with clothes in better style," Rafe said. "Her gown was years out of date, and she hadn't even a pelisse to go over it. If I had to guess at it," he said, and his voice had lowered to a reflective murmur. "If I had to guess at it, I'd say she's living hand to mouth. Probably St. Giles *is* the best she can afford. Probably a rented room is all she can manage."

"She might have seen you. Misled you intentionally." It had the sound of a plea within it.

"I don't see how she could have done. She couldn't have known she would be followed, and it would have required an admirable amount of foresight to dress as she had only to mislead." Rafe made a rough sound in his throat. "She couldn't have expected me," he said. "I saw her just briefly through the door, and I would swear that she was as much surprised as she was horrified."

"She's an *actress*." God, but he'd had to repeat that a few too many times of late.

"Well, then, her skills are to be commended," Rafe said. "Because I've never seen a performance quite so convincing." He blew out a breath, shaking his head. "You said you had paid off her employer to ensure she had no patrons, hm?"

"One hundred pounds," Marcus confirmed.

"Then you've been had," Rafe said, with a shrug. "Because from the state of her dress alone, I'd say it's been years since last she had one."

Years. Marcus rubbed one hand over his mouth. It could not be so. "She's a beautiful woman," he said. "It's not likely."

"I can only give you my opinion," Rafe said. "I've no familiarity with the wench myself."

No, but he might have, if circumstances had arranged themselves differently. And there it was again in his chest; that terrible sense of loss that tugged at the strings of his heart—or where it once had been, before Lydia had ripped it, still beating, out of his very chest. "I was going to marry her," he said, feeling himself sinking into that very same maudlin sentimentality that had plagued him so long after Lydia's defection.

"I remember," Rafe mused. "Your letters were filled with nothing but her. I felt like I knew her already. I was—sorry to hear that it had ended badly." He filled his glass anew, keeping the bottle at his side like he suspected that Marcus might snatch for it. "Still, I wonder why she threw you over. Even as your mistress—"

"She wasn't my mistress," Marcus snapped.

Rafe smothered an incredulous laugh. "She lived in a house you paid for, did she not? You purchased her clothes, her food? Provided an allowance, perhaps?"

Of course he had done. What could she had provided, on the salary of a seamstress? "It wasn't like that. I *loved* her. There was never any—anything *legal* brought into it." He hadn't wanted the stain of contracts brought upon their relationship, as if she had traded her affections for the baubles he had purchased for her.

"Then she was a fool," Rafe said. "To have so ill-guarded her reputation, without the surety of better."

All she had needed—or so he had thought—was the surety of his promise. "I only needed time," he said. "To accustom Father to the idea." But he had not been willing to honorably wait for it. He had pressed her for more than conversation, more than infrequent visits. He had wanted her at his convenience, in his bed, in his arms.

"Then *you* were the fool to think you ever could have done," Rafe said ruthlessly. "I suppose that must have been why. When the bloom had faded from the rose, when she realized the precariousness of her position, she must have lost faith in you."

"I was careful with her reputation," Marcus protested, but—hadn't Diana suggested otherwise? He had thought himself so clever to keep her quietly, safeguarding her reputation as much as possible before they were married. But if *Diana* had known...

"You can't have your cake and eat it, Marcus," Rafe said. "*Nothing* remains secret in London for long. Surely you must have known that. It was always bound to come to a bad end."

He had, in a vague sort of way. But he simply hadn't cared overmuch. He *had* planned to marry her, after all, and when that had been accomplished—well, she would have been the Baroness of Newhaven, and the wife of the heir to a marquessate. Whatever she had once been would have been immaterial. She would have derived her respectability from the power of his name.

"She wasn't my mistress," he repeated sullenly. "I never meant to make one of her." She had been meant to be his *wife*.

"But you did," Rafe insisted. "Even if you would call it something else. How long had you thought you could keep her in that role? Because if you had been waiting upon Father's approval, you'd have died before earning it." He made a scathing sound in his throat. "It's possible she was looking for a way out before she became saddled with the inevitable results of such a liaison. Can you imagine how much worse it might have been for her had she conceived? My God, without a contract to support her, you'd have owed nothing even to your child."

In point of truth, it had been a *relief* at the time that he had owed her nothing. She had owned not even the clothes upon her back, nor any interest in the little house they had shared. He had only wanted to be rid of her then, and he had nursed his anger through the worst of the heartbreak and regretted that he had not had the chance to inflict worse.

"Hell," he said, slouching in his chair in a manner that would have horrified his mother to the very tips of her toes.

"If it's revenge you're after," Rafe said, his voice leaving little doubt that he had already leapt to that assumption, "I doubt there's much more you could find to take from her."

If Rafe had drawn the correct conclusions, then he was right—she had no reputation, no money. Nothing tangible or otherwise that could be stolen.

Why, then, did the thought bring him no comfort?

Chapter Eight

Lydia had hardly slept. Which was not to say that sleep had ever been easy to come by—but last evening had been worse than most, with her mind too full of every evil possibility that might befall her to do more than close her eyes on occasion and catch at sleep in only the briefest of snags.

Dawn had risen and peeped through the thin curtains lining her solitary window when at last she had given up the attempt altogether. It was too early to rise, given that she'd spend the majority of her day in the theatre, rehearsing until Giles was satisfied with her portrayal of Paulina, but there was nothing to be gained from lazing about.

She dressed in her second-best gown—which was not saying much— and crept down the stairs, eager to be free of the house and the oppressive gaze of Mrs. Hawkins, who she was certain would turn it upon her as if she might see straight into Lydia's stained soul to determine which sins she ought to be castigated for this morning. Probably she could have dredged up an even dozen which might merit her attention, but Lydia had not the patience to sit quietly and to have them cast up before her again.

Especially those which she had not committed.

But in the flurry of kitchen activity which had commandeered Mrs. Hawkins' attention for the time being, Lydia made it safely down the stairs and to the door without being spotted—only to have the sigh of relief that had collected in her lungs turn to a squawk of surprise upon turning from the door once she had made it through that gauntlet.

Marcus stood there, at the bottom of the steps, lying in wait, his hair ruffled by the brisk wind that shimmied down the street. He had a scarf wrapped round his neck, and he was buttoned up to it in a thick coat, his hat held in one hand. He looked exactly like what he was—a man with far more money than sense, standing on the street where any enterprising thief might make an example of him.

"What the *hell* are you doing?" she hissed, before she could think better of it. "Do you *know* what sort of neighborhood this is?"

"Do *you*?" he countered, and beneath the unshaven line of his jaw she could see that muscle twitch and pull, as if his teeth were clenched all the way to the molars. "And you've been *walking* home?"

He hadn't any right at all to criticize her for it! "You set your damned brother upon me," she accused. "Do you know what my landlady thought of me? I thought she would turn me out in the middle of the night!"

"She damned well ought to," he snarled back. "You cannot mean to stay *here*."

"It is no business of yours where I stay." Her clipped, crisp syllables were frostier than the November air. "It is no business of yours at all." *She* was no business of his. He could go hang, for all she cared. Resolutely she turned away, only to find herself stayed by the pressure of his fingers wrapped around her upper arm.

It was in her head, just briefly, to scream. But that would do her no good at all in St. Giles, where folk tended to mind their business unless they had some good reason to mind someone else's. Worse still, for all that Mrs. Hawkins' sight was none too great, she had ears like a fox—and an insatiable nosiness. If Lydia brought so much as a whiff of scandal to her door, well then—

She'd be out. Immediately.

"You are not staying here," he said, his breath coming out in a puff of white and full of barely-harnessed fury. "I am not *asking*, Lydia. I am telling you what will—and will *not*—happen. You're damned lucky I elected not to beat the damned door down and pull you out."

She drew an infuriated breath, swallowed it down, and managed to grit out. "I will not discuss my place of residence with you."

"Good. I hadn't planned to have any such conversation, since there is nothing you could say that would sway my mind." His fingers slid down her arm to tighten on her wrist, reeling her closer like a fish snared on a hook. "I have been standing out here since before daybreak," he said. "Do *not* test me."

Test him? She opened her mouth to lambaste him as he so richly deserved.

"Lydia." It was just her name, only one word, but it cut straight through the icy morning air, taking the breath straight from her lungs with it. "Do *not*."

Abruptly she recalled that she was meant to be *seducing* him, to twist that obsession, as Giles had so named it, and him with it round her little finger until he danced to her tune and she could repay him for the wounds he'd inflicted upon her. Against all odds, it seemed she might be…succeeding. She had been so furious, so full of righteous indignation for what he might have cost her, that she had never stopped to consider what, exactly, had brought him to her very doorstep before dawn, when she had never known him to rise before ten if it could at all be avoided.

Fear. Worry. Anxiety. They were all there, stark and shimmering beneath the masking shroud of fury that had painted itself across his features. For *her*. There was no reason at all that he ought to concern himself with her, with her safety—except that perhaps he could not help himself.

The scales had shifted, however subtly, in her favor.

How far could she push him? How far *ought* she? She flexed the fingers of the hand he held still within his grip. "I won't leave London on your command," she said, tipping up her chin. "You'll not be rid of me so easily, my lord."

"Yesterday I was Marcus." The shred of a sly smile eased through his anger, and still he did not release her. "Do you remember it?"

She stamped upon his foot, digging in her heels when he would have pulled her nearer. "Yesterday, you had not sent your *brother* to inform upon me!"

"And thank God I did," he countered. "*Anything* might have happened to you. *St. Giles!* What in hell were you thinking?"

"That it's near enough to the theatre to walk," she said, knowing full well that such an answer would only provoke him further.

It worked far better than she could have hoped. He breathed in tiny surges, as if he had to force each breath between the terrible clench of his teeth. The words came out with yet more effort; a short, sharp, staccato demand. "You. Are not. Staying. Here."

She laughed, a contrived tinkling sound, like that of the tiny silver bells she'd seen strung up in shop windows. "The days when you might have commanded me are gone, my lord."

"For God's sake, Lydia—if you are to be at anyone's mercy, it will damned well be *my own*."

Oh. Well, wasn't that just fascinating?

His face flushed a vivid red, like he'd been set afire by the heat of his own fury. "You can afford better than this," he said, and she fancied she heard half a question in it. Uncertainty, at least.

"I really cannot." Not true, exactly, but then she did not owe him truth. She had funds enough tucked away in a purse beneath the underthings packed within a dresser in her room—funds that had come from him, after Giles had bilked them from him. And she could have likely afforded the let of a small townhouse, if she could have found one available only for a month, and if she had been willing to cull the coin from that which she typically sent on to her family. Which she had not.

Another wrathful exhale. "Your patrons must pay you twice over again what you earn in wages."

He was attempting, in a roundabout fashion, to pry an admission from her. She didn't see the purpose in it, since he would not have believed a truthful answer, did she wish to give one. "Must they, then?"

"*Damn* it all, Lydia—"

"*All?* I should say not." She summoned a sweet smile, the sort she might have given him once, so many years ago now. "Only you." She relished the inarticulate sound of rage that curled up his throat and out into the winter air. "My lord, I would remind you that we are on a public street." A fact which he seemed to have forgotten in the past few minutes. "As...elucidating as this conversation has been, I am expected at the theatre."

"Then I will take you," he growled, as his gaze shifted left and right, scanning the street as if he expected a threat to present itself. "My carriage is just there." With a jerky motion of his head, he indicated a carriage that was, indeed, waiting a short distance away.

"How fortunate for you. However, I won't be riding within it." Still he had not released her hand.

"Be reasonable. You haven't—" He paused, and for the first time his gaze raked over her. "You haven't even got a pelisse. *Christ*. Why haven't you got a pelisse?"

Lydia managed a tight smile. "Needs must when the devil drives. Alas, some things must be sacrificed when one lacks the funds to pay for them." Her second best dress was not yet bound for the rag heap—her good stitchery had kept it together—but it had acquired the evidence of its age. Seams that had seen better days. A hem that was slightly stained. A few fraying threads here and there.

"Lydia, that dress is at least five years old."

No one could be more aware of that than she. It had been among the few she had managed to shove into a valise, and which he had rifled through to ensure that she had not taken anything of more value than that—those things he was willing to part with only because they had no particular value to him. He had purchased this dress for her; well he *ought* to recognize it. And she—she had her pride, though he'd savaged it dreadfully. She would not flinch from that sharp gaze, so unfairly accusing.

When she had become who she was because of *him*.

"Yes," she said. "Unfortunately, being a mistress is more lucrative an arrangement for some than others."

And it was that which forced him to release her wrist, for some unimaginable reason. "You were not my mistress," he said, and the fury drained from his face in an instant, like water leaking through a sieve.

Lydia pulled a pout. "No, I suppose I was not. After all, a mistress might have expected better than I received in the end."

Something odd flickered across his face for but a fraction of a moment. "You will not inflict guilt upon me," he said. "*I* am not the villain here, Lydia. *You* betrayed *me*."

She did not dignify his assertion with a response, nor did she give him the satisfaction of her outraged dignity. Instead she simply turned on her heel and began her trek toward the theatre.

Behind her, he made a caustic sound in his throat. Then muttered a few terrible words. And at last, he began to follow behind her. She ignored him as soundly as she was capable through the short walk, and when at last they arrived at the theatre, he was once again fuming.

He caught her arm once more before she could duck in the doors. "I'll return this evening," he said. "And by God, you will get in my damned carriage of your own volition or I will shove you inside it myself."

Giles hooted with laughter, tossing his head back in delight as Lydia related her strange encounter and the bizarre threats that Marcus had issued just minutes before. "Lydia," he said on a sigh, when at last he was no longer in danger of bursting the buttons of his waistcoat with his guffaws. "Nothing you've said is in the least surprising. Sometimes a man has just got to be a *man*."

Lydia blinked, baffled. "What on earth does that mean?"

"We're quite primitive creatures, you know. Oh, we might spend an inordinate amount of time trussed up like a Christmas goose, but all the buttons and frills and polished boots can't remove the nature of man—it's only a pretty dressing. Did Newhaven never show such tendencies before?"

"No," Lydia said, sinking into the chair across from him. "Not once. He was—he was the very soul of courtesy." Right up until he had been the most wretched bastard ever to grace God's green earth.

"The *soul* of *courtesy!*" Giles slapped his palm upon the surface of his desk, chuckling anew.

"I certainly don't see the joke," Lydia groused, shifting uncomfortably.

Giles swept one palm over his mouth, smoothing away the last dregs of laughter. "Lydia, men put on a good show, but we're *none* of us as civilized as we might otherwise appear. And you've pushed Newhaven to the very end of his tether, so it would seem. He simply hasn't got the civility left in him even to give a good show of the pretense any longer. You're driving the poor man stark raving mad. I could almost feel pity for him."

"Is—" Lydia hesitated, still perplexed. "Is that meant to be a good thing?"

"You've stripped the veneer of gentility from a damned *baron* as if it were little more than old paper-hangings," he said. "*Yes*, that's good. You want him in the palm of your hand? Put your finger upon that nerve and press it until he snaps."

"What happens when he snaps?"

"Probably," Giles said, with a little flourish of his hand, "you'll be dragged off to bed by your hair."

Despite herself, Lydia shivered, unconscionably titillated by the thought. "I—well, I—"

"Oh, don't bother to protest it," Giles said. "You seemed to be enjoying yourself well enough a few nights past. Were I you, I'd take Newhaven for whatever I could while I had the opportunity. You've never judged me for my peccadilloes," he said, "for which I am profoundly grateful. I won't cast judgment upon you for yours."

"You were my friend when I had no one," she said. "I don't know where I would be without you." She reached across the desk to lay her hand over his own. "Or your sage advice in the matters of men."

"Darling, I'm an *actor*. I *live* for drama," he said. "Don't go maudlin on me now. You must scrounge up all of that delightful fury with which you arrived. I expect to see Paulina at her most scathing in no more than ten minutes."

Marcus had elected to breakfast with his family, since he did not think he could trust himself not to wring Lydia's lovely little neck if he had stayed. But he had not been able to shake the fury she had left him with, even as he stalked into the dining room. The sharp report of his boots upon the floor made Mother flinch behind the rim of her tea cup.

"Marcus." Father said, his eyes narrowed, his mustache twitching above his lip already. "Diana tells me you attended her at her dinner engagement."

"As you commanded." Marcus strode for his usual chair, surprised to find it already occupied. Rafe had come to dine? Curious. He selected the seat beside his brother and waved for a plate, which was set before him promptly.

The paper quivered in Father's fingers. "And did you happen to meet any eligible young ladies?"

"Several. None suited me." He slid a poached egg onto his plate alongside a rasher of bacon.

"*None?*" Father blustered.

"None."

"Now, Harold…" Mother had begun her typical ritual of pacification, seeking to soothe Father's temper before it could explode. "He could hardly know which girl he ought to favor on so short an acquaintance. He's hardly been out in society at all these last—" She made a tiny sound of horror, and concluded weakly, "These last five years."

"Yes, and whose fault is that?" Father's cheeks had flushed a ruddy hue, and a vein began to pulse in his head. "It's that bloody *harlot's*," he said. "And *you*." He jabbed one finger at Marcus, as if he might stab him in the chest from clear across the table. "You are falling right back beneath her spell!"

"Oh, Papa," Diana sighed as she fumbled for her fork, which she struggled to find, probably because she had left off her spectacles once again. "She's hardly an enchantress."

"She's a lightskirt," Father sneered. "A conniving she-demon who thought to finagle her way into this family—"

"One wonders why she would have wanted *that*," Marcus said, though out of the corner of his eye he could see that Rafe had gone quite still and silent. "There isn't so much to recommend it." Sometimes he wondered why he ever bothered coming to breakfast. It was never a pleasant endeavor.

Again, Mother fluttered her hands in little consoling motions. "Now, Harold," she said again, her voice just this side of shrill. "If Marcus did not favor any of those girls—"

"I'm not asking him to *favor* them," Father interjected. "I'm telling him to bloody well *marry* one of them!" He rounded on Marcus once more. "Do you think I *favored* your mother when I wed her? I did my damned duty!"

Well. There it was. Marcus had always known there had not been love between his parents, but they had generally done one another the courtesy of attempting a passing respect. Or at least *Mother* had.

This was to be his future eventually, and what a cold, depressing thing it was.

He stabbed the tines of his fork into the yolk of his egg and watched it run across his plate. A part of him, he realized, laid the blame for his unhappiness at his father's feet. Had he been wiser, he would have damned Father's approval and eloped with Lydia years ago. A *fait accompli*—Father might have raged, but it would have been a done thing.

He might have been happy.

Instead he had wasted the last years in anger and grief. He had stopped caring about Father's opinion, but it had been years too late to save himself.

Mother gave a muted sniffle into her napkin, and her trembling hands dropped once more into her lap. And Father—Father could not have given less of a damn about the humiliation he had heaped upon his wife's shoulders.

"I did my *duty*," Father hissed. "And you will damned well do yours."

Chapter Nine

Marcus' foul mood persisted, and it was not aided in the fact that his entry to the theatre had been barred. There was no performance this evening, and therefore no reason for the staff to admit him, and that—that had grated upon his very soul. That *anyone* should think to bar him from her presence, that anyone should *dare* to come between them.

So he had waited, and stewed, and reflected, and it was at last the reflection that had brought about a certain clarity of thought. Lydia had poked and prodded at him this morning, the jagged splinters of her taunts tearing at his flesh. She had thought herself so bold, and she had won more battles between them than she had had any right to do.

And he had *let* her do it.

She had proved something, after a fashion, to the both of them. And there was no turning back the wheel of time and choosing better. But she was occupied for the next several hours by the theatre, and so he had nothing but time—time in which to lay his own trap, and for once to have her at sixes and sevens.

She was going to be furious, and he…he was going to *win*.

Lydia could feel the twist and pull of every muscle in her body, and the weight of Paulina settled upon her shoulders like a funeral shroud. But at last, near enough to midnight that she could taste the yearning for sleep on her tongue, Giles had been satisfied with her performance.

At least in the interest of fairness, he had been every bit as ruthless with Clara, who would take over the role of Perdita from tomorrow until the end of their run.

She rolled her shoulders as she headed, finally, for the door of the theatre, sliding through it and out into the cold night air, which despite its icy chill felt lovely on her overheated skin.

And there, lurking in the shadows that had draped themselves over the street, was Marcus. He waited beside his carriage, his arms folded over his chest. He'd left off his hat entirely, and his lips had begun to take on a slight bluish tinge owing to the cold.

How long, precisely, had he been waiting? It had gone damned near midnight!

His breath burst from between his lips in a puff of white as he spoke at last, jerking his head to indicate his carriage. "Will you get in."

It *ought* to have been a question. It had been *phrased* like a question. But she didn't think it had been, really. Instead it was a challenge; a gauntlet he had thrown there between them, and she could almost hear it falling heavily upon the ground there at her feet.

She said, "No." And she lifted her chin to him. *So there.*

"*Good.*" And he lunged, faster than she could have imagined, faster even than she could flee, with her tired muscles spent from hours and hours of performing. He caught a fistful of her gown, and she heard the terrible rend and pull of a seam giving out somewhere. Her second best gown, victim to the fierce clench of his fingers.

"You oaf!" she hissed, struggling to seize back control of her gown—which he did not surrender. Instead he slid his arm through the flail of her own and snatched her about the waist, pulling her straight off of her feet. Her shriek sliced through the night only to be cut short by the advent of his shoulder into her stomach. Her lungs strained for air, and the whole world tilted—

No. The unmitigated arse had simple hoisted her over his shoulder like a sack of potatoes. She jabbed her fist into his side, roughly where she expected his kidney to be located. But the thick wool of his coat scarcely gave to the pressure, and she wondered if he had even felt it.

"Temper, temper," he chided, and the squeak of hinges singed her ears. The world righted itself in a dizzying blur. Her shoulders hit the plush upholstery of a carriage seat, and he shoved—*shoved!*—her within the depths of the carriage.

The breadth of his shoulders blocked out the scant light that poured through the carriage door as he climbed in after her. With one fist he pounded upon the roof, and then she was rocked again as she heard the snap of the reins and the carriage began to move.

She choked upon the fury she thought she had exhausted on the stage.

"This—this—this is *kidnapping*," she wheezed as she struggled beneath the tumbled folds of her skirt.

"Is it?" He settled across from her, blithe, unconcerned. "I suppose I should expect to be arrested presently." One knee jogged up and down, and he rested his elbow upon it as if to still the instinctive motion.

"You—you—" She had never found herself so tongue-tied in the whole of her life. "You cannot simply *abduct* women from the streets!"

"Who is going to stop me, hm?" The dark amusement that permeated his voice ought to have been a warning, but she had not the energy to heed it.

"Are you *mad?*" she hissed.

Deliberately, he misunderstood her query. "Yes. I'm fucking *furious*, Lydia."

The coarse word stung her ears. She'd heard more than her fair share of foul language—the theatre was riddled with it; with crude jests and naughty gestures. Giles had proved himself fluent in such vulgarity every time one of his employees flubbed a line or missed their cue. But she'd never heard such crudity from *Marcus*.

Her hands fisted in the skirt of her gown lest she prove herself ill-bred enough to strangle a baron in his own bloody carriage. "Take me home," she demanded.

"Ah, well, as to that…" In the tiny shreds of lamplight that drifted through the curtains, his sharp, self-satisfied smile was briefly illuminated. "You haven't got one anymore."

"I—what?" Individually, the words had made sense. Strung together, they seemed a nonsense jumble of syllables. Perhaps her brain simply did not *want* to make sense of them. "What is that meant to mean?"

"It means that while you were"—he gave a disdainful little flick of his fingertips, consigning her whole career to perdition with that tiny gesture— "*otherwise engaged*, so was I. It occurs to me, Lydia, that you have been allowed to run free too long."

"Allowed?" She choked upon the word. "*Allowed?*"

"Someone ought to have put a leash on you years before now." The white flash of his teeth, feral, predatory, glinted in the darkness. "And do you know what? I am damn well going to be the man to do it."

Giles' words flittered through her mind, floating somewhere above the vibrant red haze of wrath. *Stark raving mad.*

"What have you done?" she whispered, and the stiffness of her spine cast her off-balance as the carriage turned and proceeded down the road right

76

past the boarding house, slowing not at all. "What the *hell* have you done?"

"I told you I would not entertain conversation," he said. "I am done with it. I told you this morning what would happen."

In fact, he had not. He had merely snarled at her like a cat with its tail caught in a trap, insisting upon—well, she was not very certain what, exactly, he had been insisting on, other than that he had taken extreme exception to her residence. "I want you to stop this carriage right now."

"Unfortunately for you, my coachman takes his orders from me alone, and I've given him his direction already." His hand dropped to his thigh, fingers squeezing like he was imagining them wrapped around her neck. "I had a lovely conversation with your landlady this afternoon," he said. "I found her most obliging."

Her breath strangled in her throat. "What have you *done?*" she repeated.

"Of course," Marcus continued, as if she had never spoken, "she was sorry to see you go. Well," he amended. "Not all *that* sorry. I told her she could keep what you had paid to her already, and so she was not too entirely put out."

Lydia had died upon the stage at least a hundred times, but tonight—*tonight* she was going to do *murder.* "She did not heed you," she heard herself say, as if from a hundred miles away. "She wouldn't. You—you're no one to her. There was no reason for her to *listen.*"

"Of course she listened. I'm a goddamned *baron.* People—*most* people—tend to listen when I give them instructions." This was accompanied by a sharp stare, as if her most extraordinary fault in this moment was that she ignored him when by all rights she ought to obey.

A horrible little laugh slipped between her lips. "You couldn't leave well enough alone, could you?" she asked, in a reedy voice. "You wretched, interfering, *despicable*—"

"Stop. Such praise will make me blush."

Her breath shuddered between her teeth. "What have you done with my things?"

"Not to worry. I had my servants pack for you. There wasn't so much; it took perhaps ten minutes to do so. You'll find them at your new residence."

A protracted silence drew out, stretching into the tense stillness between them. The worst was still to come; she knew it by the way he dangled that tight, satisfied smile. He *savored* this like he would a fine wine.

"Which is?" It was little better than a growl, like that of a rabid dog.

"With me," he said. "And that, my dear, is *checkmate.*"

Lydia had not stopped shrieking since she had had to be carried bodily out of the carriage and shunted off to the room that Marcus had had made up for her. He wasn't certain whether he ought to be infuriated or impressed.

Rafe, who had stopped round for a drink, massaged at his eyes and sighed wearily for perhaps the fourth time in the ten minutes he'd been present. "How long do you suppose she can keep up that racket?" he asked.

"Knowing Lydia? As long as she needs to." Marcus gestured for the brandy, which Rafe surrendered without argument, and poured a healthy measure into his glass.

"You can't keep her," Rafe said. "There's bound to be talk. Gossip. Haven't you been the object of enough speculation already?"

He had, but some things were worth more to him than whispers behind fans or ribald taunts tossed around a crowded club. "I beg to differ. I can keep her as long as I like."

"Yes, well, I think you're enjoying it a bit more than you ought."

On the contrary; he was enjoying it precisely as much as he had thought he would. *Excessively.* "You needn't worry for her. She'll be treated well enough." Better than she deserved, considering that the late supper he had had delivered to her had been slammed, tray and all, against the wall of her room within moments of its arrival.

"You've locked her in a room."

"A room of her own," Marcus corrected. "She'll be let out in the morning, none the worse for the wear." Excepting that which she chose to inflict upon herself. "I shall even be so kind as to escort her to the theatre tomorrow." In his carriage, which kept out the frigid winter air quite nicely.

Rafe gave a small huff of dark amusement. "And after her performance?"

Marcus managed a restrained smile. "Then I shall bring her home again."

"Father's not going to like it."

"Father can go hang."

A muted crash from somewhere above them. Probably he should have thought to have anything breakable removed from her room. Ah, well—the sooner she expended her fury, the sooner she could be reasoned with.

Rafe stared into the firelight, an inscrutable expression etched across his face. "I never asked before," he said, "because it seemed…unwise to bring up old, bad memories. But I find myself wondering now. How did you discover it?"

It, Marcus supposed that he meant, was Lydia's betrayal. Well enough he had not broached the topic before, because Marcus might have snapped his head clean off of his shoulders for it. *Still* it stung.

He swallowed a mouthful of brandy and let it burn his throat before the words could do the same. "I arrived home one day," he said, "to find a man in our bed. Naked and waiting for her."

Rafe digested that in perfect silence. "A man," he said, finally. "But not *her*?"

"Finding the man was bad enough, I assure you," Marcus said, his voice hard and clipped. If he had caught them together, he might have been driven to murder. "It was clear enough what had occurred." He could still see it all in his mind. The clothing strewn about the room, as if it had been ripped off and scattered. The man, naked as the day he'd been born, occupying the spot in bed that had rightfully belonged to Marcus. He'd been hard pressed to find it in him to allow the man to collect his scattered clothing before he'd tossed him, all but bare-arsed, straight out the door.

"Hm," Rafe said, as he sipped his drink. "I suppose she denied it?"

Marcus rolled his eyes. "Of *course* she denied it. What woman in her position would not have done?"

"But you did not *witness* it," Rafe said, and there was something more than curiosity in his voice. Something remarkably close to suspicion. "You never saw *her*."

"I saw *enough*."

Rafe lifted a hand in a quelling gesture. "I'm not saying you did not," he said. "But I wonder. I wonder if you saw what you were *meant* to see."

Marcus felt his brow furrow, a frown settle over his face. "What the devil do you mean?"

Rafe gave a mirthless laugh. "Nothing—yet," he said, as he rose to his feet. "Only that I've some inquiries to make, I think, Marcus." He reached for his hat and jammed it on his head. And then, darkly, as he strode for the door, he added, "Something is rotten in the state of Denmark."

She was going to ruin her voice, Lydia realized eventually, if she did not stop screaming. It would be all hoarse and rusty tomorrow, and Giles would be put out. *Severely* put out.

Besides, no one had paid her even the slightest bit of attention. Even the manservant who had brought to her a late meal had hardly glanced at her other than to cast her a stern glare as he had dropped off the tray, as if to wordlessly warn her against trying to escape.

She had not been so foolish as that; the man had been built like a bear. She'd have been mad to try. But the *snick* of the lock turning in the door had so enraged her that she'd hefted the tray in two hands and thrown it with all of her might at the wall. And the lovely shattering sound of the precious china cracking in to chunks had been a balm to her soul. And then she'd gone and broken a few more things besides.

It was time to face facts. She was not getting out of this room tonight. *Checkmate.*

The clock on the mantel of the fireplace, which she had spared from her wrath only because it was useful, told her it had gone past two in the morning. She ought to have been abed already. She *would* have been, had she been in her own bed.

A quick search of the dressing room told her that this was not *his* room, which made him wiser than he knew, because if he had dared that much she would have gouged his eyes out of his skull. No; he had made a prison for her, and even if it was significantly more lavish than that to which she had become accustomed, a cell was a cell.

Her clothing—the few dresses that she owned—were hung up in the dressing room, taking precious little of the vast space therein. Her underthings had been pressed, folded, and neatly placed within drawers. And there, beneath them, just as she had had it tucked away within her drawer in Mrs. Hawkins' boarding house, was the small purse filled with coin. From the weight of it in her hand, nothing had been taken from it.

Probably the staff who had packed her things had simply left everything as they had found it, or near enough to it. She supposed that Marcus must not know of the purse, since she was certain he would have had *something* to say of it. More recriminations, perhaps.

The bed mocked her with its inviting presence; the curtains drawn, the bedclothes turned down as if tempting her to crawl between those clean white sheets. The velvet counterpane looked thick enough to keep one warm against the chill, if there had been one of which to speak. But the house seemed quite well insulated, and the fire that blazed in the fireplace kept the room toasty.

Lydia was tired enough for three people. She could so easily just change into her nightclothes, slide into bed, and save her battles for tomorrow. Perversely, that intrusive thought provoked a fresh flood of fury.

Well, if shouting had not gotten her the results she had intended, then she would rouse the whole of his staff. She stomped across the room to the bell pull situated near the bed, and gave it a fierce yank.

Her call was answered none too swiftly, but eventually, yes, there was the sound of heavy footsteps in the hall, and then finally the turn of a key in the lock.

The door opened slowly, as if whoever had answered were wary of any potential weapons she might lob. Which she wished she might have thought of before now.

At last, Marcus stepped into the room. Or into the doorway, rather, where he planted himself dead center and braced his hands upon his hips. "Are you ready to be civil?"

Civil! Lydia clenched her hands, felt the blunt tips of her nails dig crescents into her palms. "You can't keep me here," she spat.

"Of course I can. Who is going to stop me?" He shifted his weight, affecting a more relaxed posture. "You'll be released in the morning. I do hope you will have recovered yourself by then, for I've had enough tantrums over breakfast to last me a lifetime already."

"I doubt I would make a pleasant breakfast companion," Lydia said. "You're as likely to end up wearing it as eating it. Kidnapping *does* tend to put a woman in a foul mood."

"So I can see. However, it was necessary."

"Necessary! By what measure?"

He gave a shrug; nonchalant, unruffled. "You would not see reason. I elected to see it for you. I will not apologize for it."

"No," Lydia said tightly. "I hadn't imagined you would." He never had before. "If I am to be held prisoner, I want a bath," she snapped. "And dinner."

Marcus flicked a glance at the ruins of the dinner that had been sent up an hour or so ago. "Dinner was delivered to you," he said. "You decided it suited the wall better than your stomach."

"*I* won't apologize for *that*."

"I thought not." Marcus turned to glance over his shoulder. "Bayberry!" he called.

Within seconds, the bear of a manservant came into view, standing just behind him. Probably he had been waiting in the wings the entire time, just in case Lydia had found herself tempted to test the bounds of her cell. "My lord?"

"Would a prisoner be granted a bath?" Marcus asked. "Or a second meal, given that she deliberately disposed of her first?"

"No, my lord."

"I thought not." Marcus let that settle over the room for perhaps five seconds, and his dark gaze settled on her face expectantly.

She was *not* going to apologize, whatever he expected. "I have been in the theatre all day," she said. "I am filthy, tired, and hungry. I will also require a needle and thread, since you've torn the seams of my second-best dress!" Right there at her waist; she shoved her hand through the hole that had been made of the split seam, turning out the fabric to show the proof of it.

"I wouldn't trust you as far as I could throw you with anything sharp at the moment," Marcus said. "You can leave your dress on the chair. One of my staff will see to it in the morning."

Lydia ground her teeth together. "And my bath? My dinner?"

Another thick silence. But his eyes had drawn down to the hole revealed there in the side of her gown, studying it with a queer expression, like he knew not what to make of it. "Bayberry," he said at last. "See that Miss Alcott gets her bath and her meal." He made a rough sound beneath his breath, drawing his gaze away at last. "And whatever else she requires, provided it cannot be used as a weapon."

Baring her teeth in a wretched facsimile of a smile, Lydia dropped an impudent curtsey. "Your generosity knows no bounds."

"Don't push your luck."

"Surely you had not expected *gratitude*."

He threw up his hands with an aggravated little mutter, and Lydia allowed herself a small smile of satisfaction. "The door *stays* locked, Bayberry," he snapped, as he began to walk away. "See that she never gets within three feet of it otherwise."

"Yes, my lord." That massive manservant turned that judgmental eye upon her once more, grasping the handle of the door to pull it closed behind them.

"Don't get comfortable," Lydia advised sweetly. "I expect to be *excessively* demanding." Perhaps, if nothing else, the staff would cast her out simply to be rid of her.

Chapter Ten

Marcus heard her before he saw her. Though to tell the truth, he'd heard her all night, ringing that blasted bell until the wee hours of the morning when, he assumed, she had finally acknowledged the futility of her situation and succumbed to sleep at last.

But she had kept his staff damned busy with her incessant demands for several hours before that—which they had dutifully, if resentfully, fulfilled. She would be lucky not to find her breakfast laced with a healthy sprinkling of arsenic.

"Well, *really*, Bayberry." Her disdainful sniff preceded her. "You needn't follow quite so closely. I daresay I can find the dining room without you."

Probably she would find the nearest exit without him, and Bayberry was right not to trust her.

"My lord's orders," Bayberry grunted, to his credit, and he followed her just a step behind the whole way into the dining room. They both looked haggard, given how the night had gone. Probably Bayberry was due a raise in his wages.

"Sit," Marcus said, taking a sip of his tea. "Eat."

No doubt determined to plague him, Lydia chided, "A gentleman stands when a lady enters the room." She lifted her chin, and the haughtiness in it belied her common birth. She might well have been a queen in a past life for it. Even in a dress that had to be third-best at most, even absent any manner of embellishments or other such feminine fripperies, still she could have been a queen.

"When a lady enters the room, I shall stand for her." Marcus gestured with his knife to the chair across from his own. "*Sit*, Lady Disdain," he said. "For all that you sent my staff running about into the early hours, you did not eat much last night."

"How thoughtful of you." She sank into the chair that Bayberry had pulled out for her, given that she had few other options at present. "Tell me, when does my jailer return me to my cell?" With a whip-fast motion, she speared the slice of sausage that he had been about to seize for himself, nipping it right out from beneath his fork, and burying it beneath a poached egg upon her plate.

Marcus bit back a sigh. "You're not a damned prisoner, Lydia. I will take you to the theatre after breakfast. It's too far to walk." He pressed his fingers to the bridge of his nose and breathed deeply, striving for patience, which remained stubbornly elusive.

"Mrs. Hawkins' wasn't." Her snide, cutting tone made it perfectly clear that she had not yet exhausted herself of her ire, and that he would quite likely bear the brunt of it for some time to come.

Which was rather unfortunate for both of them, seeing as he hadn't any intention of relaxing his guard. "This conversation grows tedious. And it is unproductive besides."

Lydia turned to Bayberry, who stood still just over her left shoulder. "If you could please send someone to pack my things—"

Marcus slapped his hand upon the table. "You are not leaving!"

"You said I could!" she flashed back.

"I *said* I would take you to the damned theatre!" Marcus yanked at the knot of his cravat, which had grown altogether too tight in the past few minutes. "I did *not* say that you would not be returning. For God's sake, Lydia. Do you know what might have happened to you in St. Giles? A woman alone?"

"Yes," she sneered. "Perhaps a madman might have kidnapped me straight off the street." She gave a mock gasp, affecting an expression of surprise. "Oh, *wait*. That *did* happen."

"Oh, yes, I am *such* a villain. All manner of evils have been visited upon you since I snatched you off the street. And you were living in the lap of luxury at Mrs. Hawkins' boarding house." He snatched up a piece of toast and slathered an egregious amount of butter upon it. "Eat your damned breakfast, Lydia. I've no desire to hear you complain of how I've starved you."

She poured herself a cup of drinking chocolate, but her silence, and the drift of her eyes away from his, with that speculative look within them, were unsettling.

"Don't mistake me," he said, his voice low and even. "If I must set a man at every damned door of the theatre, I will do it. If I must personally watch you at every moment, I will do it." Was this what it felt like to lose one's sanity? He shook his head, running his fingers through his hair and muttered to himself, "Truly. Is a civil breakfast too much to ask?"

The sharp smile she half-hid behind the rim of her cup gave the answer. He might have won the battle—but the war raged on.

"You're late," Giles snapped as Lydia arrived in the office. "Inexcusably late. So I hope you have got an extraordinary one for me."

"I beg your pardon," Lydia said, dropping into the chair in front of his desk. "I was kidnapped."

Arrested and instantly interested, Giles straightened his spine. "*Kidnapped*, you say?" he inquired, with a hint of amusement. "What, by pirates?"

"By a damned *baron*."

"You don't say." He gave a low whistle, awed. "I wouldn't have thought he had it in him. Aristocrats, well—blue their blood might run, but *hot*? I've seen little enough evidence for it."

Lydia turned her chin up to him. "It was quite a cold-blooded kidnapping," she said. "Pulled me straight off the street last evening."

"How delightful. For what purpose? Do give me every single salacious detail."

"I thought I was inexcusably late already?" Lydia snipped, slanting him a glare.

Giles sighed, "Well, it cannot be anything *too* scandalous. I'd wager you'd not be in so foul a mood otherwise." He pushed back his chair, busying himself with collecting the scattered papers upon his desk and stacking them into a neat pile, as if *that* might somehow alleviate the stress of bills coming due. "If you are bound and determined to be in a snit about it, I must request that you save that glorious anger for Paulina."

A snit! "Have you not heard a word I've said? I was *kidnapped*!"

"You seem hale enough to me," Giles said. "For a kidnapper, Newhaven is remarkably careless with his charge. I've known no kidnappers to permit their victims theatre privileges. One wonders if Newhaven hasn't got some fundamental misunderstanding of the crime. What reason were you given for this alleged kidnapping?"

"Alleged!" Lydia slammed her fist down upon the desk, upsetting the neat stack of papers once more with the force of the blow. "I tell you, he took me straight off the street! And what's more, he sent his—his *thugs* to remove my things from my boarding house!"

"Forward-thinking of him," Giles said. "One has to admire it. Has he truly got thugs?"

"Servants," Lydia said, in a thin-lipped mutter. "But they might as well be thugs. He set his manservant on me as a jailer and locked me in a bedroom!"

"A bedroom!" Giles gasped, pantomiming horror as he clasped one hand to his chest. "Good heavens, you *have* been woefully mistreated!"

"Giles…"

"*Lydia*," he returned. "Let us observe the facts. You are in good health, are you not? You have been neither beaten nor starved? Newhaven did not take liberties with your person which you did not permit? You appear before me now, without chains or shackles, none the worse for the wear excepting a certain righteous indignation about you—which, I might add, can only improve your performance? Tell me why I ought to be concerned."

"You are supposed to be my *friend*," she accused. "You're meant to be morally outraged on my behalf!"

"Ah, well. Moral outrage has no place in the theatre, I'm afraid." He gave a shrug, unconcerned. "I do wonder, though, what you have left out."

"Nothing which matters."

Giles laughed; a short, rueful sound. "Come off it, Lydia. You're not *that* good an actress. If you want moral outrage, you will have to prove yourself blameless. What could have provoked him to kidnapping, then?"

Lydia made a sound of irritation deep in her throat. "He set his brother upon me," she said. "To discover my address. The wretch must have followed me home."

"Ah," Giles said. "And where, then, is home?"

"St. Giles," she muttered.

"*Lydia*. Have you no sense at all?"

"It was a respectable boarding house!" Lydia protested. "It is a very short walk from the theatre—"

"A walk!"

"For God's sake, Giles, don't *you* start in on me." She massaged at her temples, rubbing away the tension that had settled there. "I am a grown woman, capable of making my own decisions—"

"Foolish ones," Giles said, his voice clipped. "I expect Newhaven took exception to your choice in lodging?"

Violently. "Well, he told my landlady I would not be returning, had my things packed and delivered to his him, and then took me off the street last evening," she said. "So I suppose one might leap to such a conclusion."

Giles shook his head in consternation. "Sorry to disappoint, pet. I'm with Newhaven on this." Beneath his breath he muttered something that sounded recriminatory. "But he took you to *his* home," he said finally. "That's something."

It was a damned inconvenience, is what it was. "How do you mean?"

"He's keeping you close," he said. "Think of the scandal in it. There's bound to be all sorts of talk, and yet—" He paused, eyeing her speculatively. "I don't think it matters to him at all. He'd rather you be close despite the scandal of it. What moves a man to throw caution—*reputation*—to the very wind like that?"

Astonished, Lydia could only stare.

"He thinks he's got you," Giles said. "*Let* him think that. Give him every inch of rope he seizes, and *then*, Lydia—let him hang himself upon it."

Lydia's Paulina was worlds away better than her Perdita. Marcus wondered that she had not told him that she had taken up a new role, that he had had to discover it only when she blazed across the stage, all outraged femininity and solidarity with her cruelly maligned queen.

She played the livid noblewoman perhaps *too* well. Her clean, crisp voice rang out, fire and scorn dripping from every incensed syllable. And what was the power of Leontes, in all his kingly might, when weighed against the fury of Paulina? None at all—she made him appear weak; an unworthy worm writhing upon the ground at her feet.

The shame she delivered to him and set upon his head like a crown of coals was excoriating, the sort of condemnation that Marcus could taste in his mouth, as if she had spoon-fed it to him. As if *he* had earned it.

Probably every man in the theatre felt the spirit of Leontes within him this evening, paying for sins both major and minor as the lash of her anger spilled out like a pot bubbling over. The glow of the gaslights could not compete with the incandescence of Lydia herself, and Marcus—Marcus scratched at the back of his neck, which felt flushed and prickly, as if her rage had been directed solely at him.

As if, without even once glancing in his direction, she had cast *him* into the role of Leontes, and poured boiling oil upon his head with only the heat of her words. As if she had any right at all to the venom that dripped from her lips, when they both knew she did not.

The relief that swept over him at the conclusion of the third act was a palpable thing. She would not appear again until the fifth, and the passage of sixteen years in the interim surely would blunt the sharpness of her tongue.

He could not go to her now. Not while the heat of her indignation still blistered his skin.

"A fine performance, wouldn't you say?"

Marcus half-turned, wondering at the intruder in his box, only to find Leontes there, his golden crown still perched upon his head. Giles Montgomery, the company owner, by another name.

"I hadn't realized you were playing Leontes," he said inanely.

"No," Montgomery said, and closed the distance between them. "You have eyes only for Lydia, I expect. And just occasionally Florizel." A sly smile curled the edges of his lips as he took up the chair beside Marcus. "What, my lord—are you not enjoying the play?"

Not particularly. "I hadn't realized you had given her a new role."

Montgomery shrugged. "She's played them all from time to time," he said. "Some better than others, I'll own. She's not played Hermione in some time. Hasn't got the stomach for it any longer."

Marcus issued a sharp laugh. "The character for it, more like." *Hermione.* The honorable queen wrongly accused of infidelity by her suspicious and jealous king, Leontes.

Montgomery chuckled, shaking his head as if he had found Marcus' suggestion vastly amusing. "And therein lies your mistake. She never once acted Hermione, my lord. She *was* Hermione." Something heavy dropped into Marcus' lap. "Leontes' crown," Montgomery said blandly. "I thought you might wish to keep it. You wear it better than ever I did."

Marcus stared at the crown in his hands. The weight of it felt accusatory; a mockery of his anguish. "You know nothing," he rasped, anger churning in his gut. "You know *nothing* of me."

"I know enough, my lord," Montgomery said, and the silky thread of suggestion wove through his voice. "Pity that you've sat through so many performances and learned nothing yourself." He picked himself up off of his chair and flicked a bit of lint off his sleeve. "If Leontes had any sense, he would have thrown himself upon his queen's mercy and humbly begged her pardon," he said.

Marcus reared back as if the words had been accompanied by a blow. "*I am not Leontes*," he said fiercely.

"Most certainly you are not," Montgomery said, as he turned to go. "For Leontes did acknowledge the truth in the end. Unfortunately for you, my lord, I doubt you will find Lydia quite so forgiving as Hermione."

"You didn't tell me you were playing Paulina."

Lydia could not manage to drum up any surprise at Marcus' appearance in the dressing room. In fact, she could not manage to dredge up even the slightest bit of emotion at all. Paulina had relieved her of the sum of it, it seemed. It had felt *good*, even, to rid herself of it. But it had left her with a peculiar emptiness inside, and after she had felt deflated, like she had let out a huge breath that had stagnated too long in her lungs.

And she had had to acknowledge that swimming there beneath the rage and wrath, was always, *always* grief. She could feel it lurking there beneath the surface of her skin even as he came up beside her, and she disguised the minute tremble of her lips by swabbing over them with a wet cloth to remove the powder that stubbornly clung to her skin.

"Most of the company can play multiple roles," she said with a shrug. "An unfortunate accident or a bout of sickness could ravage a company if there were not ready replacements. Why should it have mattered?"

"I don't know," he said, but his jaw clenched on the words. "I don't know. But it does." His hand curled over her shoulder, a remarkably tender touch. His thumb swept across the skin revealed above the neckline of her dressing gown. A long moment passed in silence—or as much silence as there could possibly be, given that actors trickled in and out of the room in the meantime, unheeded by either of them.

His jaw worked, as if he were chewing on whole paragraphs and swallowing them back down again before they could, unwisely, escape. At length, he said, "Will you be difficult this evening?"

"Is it your intention to lock me away?" The words sounded sour on her lips, resentful. "I won't play Hermione to your Leontes, languishing away in prison."

"Ah, yes, how you have languished." A grim smile tugged at his lips, and he bent his head, his lips brushing her ear. "Do you know, Lydia, I'd quite like to lock you away. For all that you would no doubt cast Paulina at me, it would suit me very well to have you at my mercy." His warm breath stirred her unbound hair. "But I haven't the restraint of Leontes, I'm afraid. I enjoy sparring with you too much to throw you in a dungeon and forget about you. I'd visit you daily. Hourly. Perhaps I would lock myself in with you."

She gnashed her teeth. "You would find me a poor companion."

"I'd find Paulina a poor companion, to be certain. Too much wrath in her."

Lydia shrugged. "If you saw too much of yourself in Leontes, then that is only your responsibility."

"Rather, I think I saw too much of Lydia in Paulina. Why do I feel as though you meant that performance for me?" he mused, and by the frown that creased his brow, however briefly, Lydia guess that he had not much liked it.

"If you don't like my Paulina, my lord, you need not attend the theatre," she suggested. But they both knew that it would not happen.

"I liked less your Perdita," he said. "Florizel is too free with his hands."

Lydia choked on a laugh. "They are in love! Of course he touches her."

"He touches *you*." That was *jealousy* searing upon his face; a dark cloud of violent anger. "I don't like it." His hand cupped her cheek, slid along her jaw to her chin. "I don't like it," he repeated, and the ripple of warning in his voice took her breath away.

"You gave me up," she whispered. "You threw me away. You haven't any right at all to dislike it."

His hand fell away from her face, curling into a fist as he straightened once more. There was the tight snap of anger in the straightness of his shoulders, the flare of it behind his dark eyes. Gradually he relaxed the clench of his jaw, shook himself free of his intemperate emotions. "Let us make an agreement," he said finally, as if it were the most magnanimous of concessions, "to leave the past where it lies."

It could never be possible. Had he not sworn to *own* her? Was he now *unswearing* it? Even if he were, she would not so easily relinquish her own pledge.

The shame that he had given to her had never been hers to bear, but…she had burned up the anger in tonight's performance, and all that was left in this moment was the grief that had never left her. For all that he would claim to forget the past, still they could have no future. Any hope of that hand died years ago.

Chapter Eleven

Something had to give, and Marcus knew, with a horrible sense of resignation, that that thing would have to be him.

Let us leave the past where it lies, he had told her, and the worst of it had been that there was a part of him—the part that had always, *always* loved her, the part he had thought he had buried so far down that it would never see the light of day again—that wanted it to be so. He would have to concede something to keep her, and now, in the darkness of the carriage as it rattled along the streets toward his house, he knew that the only chance of that would be to surrender his desire for revenge.

He wanted her still. He had never stopped, though it had ravaged his very soul to admit it even to himself. And he could not have her with this discord still between them, when every conversation was just one battle amidst a war. A victory could not be secured with commands and volleys of harsh words slung back and forth between them.

And she had the right of it; he *didn't* have any right to like or to dislike the false love betwixt the actors upon the stage. He had surrendered any rights over her he once might have claimed.

He was going to keep her anyway, but she had to *want* to be kept. And even though he would never be so foolish as to let her learn of those emotions that still lurked within him, even if she could never be trusted with his heart, there could be peace between them. Pleasantness; ease. He had long given up the dream of her as his wife, but if he could turn the tide of this battle, he could have her for his mistress.

And he would only have to cede this battle of wills to do it. To give her that tiny victory in truth, which she already knew in her heart, in service of a larger one of his own, eventually.

She *could* have him. Because she wanted him every bit as much. But he would never give her the sort of power she had once had over him again.

Bayberry stood at the ready just inside the foyer, no doubt waiting to be called to escort her to her room, and Lydia dug her heels into the floor in rejection of it.

"I won't be locked in," she declared fiercely, turning her head away from him.

Marcus, who had been handing his hat and coat over to a footman waiting by the door, turned at the advent of her sudden flash of anger. "Leave us," he said. "We'll have coffee in the drawing room in a quarter of an hour. And something to eat, I think. Miss Alcott has been at the theatre all day."

"I don't want something to eat," Lydia hissed. "I *want* not to be locked within my room!"

"Hm." Marcus held his silence until his staff had wisely vacated the foyer. "*I* want the surety that you won't act recklessly. So what do you propose we do about this situation?" He stripped off his gloves, shoving them within the pocket of his trousers, and busked her upper arms, which had taken a bit of a chill in the walk from the carriage to the house. "You really do need a pelisse," he muttered.

"Marcus."

He smiled like he'd won something from her, and she realized abruptly that she had used his given name rather than his title.

Shifting uncomfortably, she said, "I cannot *stay* here. Do you know what people will say of me? What they will say of *you*?"

"I can make some reasonable guesses. I don't particularly care."

"I do!"

He shrugged. "I'd advise against it, but do as you will. You want your door to remain unlocked? Then give me your promise."

"My…what?"

"Your *promise*, Lydia. That you will not behave so recklessly again. That you will depart here each day in my carriage and arrive back again each night just the same. Make me that promise, and your door will remain unlocked." He had eased closer, his hand settling at the small of her back, where the heat of it seared her straight through her gown.

"I will make you no promises. You have no right at all to keep me here."

94

It came out shakier than she had hoped, unsettled by his nearness, his odd, changeable mood.

"I have every right in the world." His nose brushed hers. "I think you will make that promise, Lydia."

"I won't!" She jumped when his other hand found the nape of her neck, and the corner of his lips quirked up in amusement. The gentle pressure of his hand sent a shiver sliding down her back.

"Not tonight, then? Pity." His lips touched her cheek, her temple. "You once claimed, if I am not misremembering, that you could have me whenever you wanted me."

"Yes." That wasn't *her* voice, surely? So high, so unsteady? "I could."

"With only a snap of your fingers," he said, and there was the lightest brush of his lips across hers, barely even a whisper. She shoved down the mad desire to lift herself into that caress.

"Less even than that," she said in a fierce whisper.

A low laugh whisked across her lips. "I concede the point. Do you want me?"

Her eyes opened. When had she closed them? "This is some trickery."

"No. No trickery; no deceit." Another kiss, and another—tiny sips that sizzled across her mouth for a fraction of a second at a time. "I don't want to be at odds with you any longer, Lydia. I thought I wanted it, but it brings me no peace, no satisfaction." His thumb tipped her chin higher; his mouth slid across hers once more. "*This* is what I want."

It had been so long, and he *had* conceded. A win, by any measure. No one could claim otherwise. He had *yielded*. "Yes," she said. "Yes—I will have you." *Her* victory. Not his.

His chuckle at the phrasing was lost into her mouth. "Good," he said, his voice deep and resonant. "Good." And he stepped away, though his hands clung a moment longer as if he had had to force himself to release her. "Tomorrow. I will come to you at the theatre."

Shock splashed over her as if he'd cast a pitcher full of icy water straight into her face. "No!"

"Act four," he said. "I'll hear your promise then." He raised his voice. "*Bayberry!*"

"My lord?" Bayberry's swift appearance suggested that they had had only the illusion of privacy; no doubt a fact of which Marcus had been very much aware.

"There's been a change in plans. Miss Alcott will be dining in her room

this evening. Under lock and key, since she will not yet have it otherwise."
His hands flexed at his sides, but they still trembled faintly.

And though she cast him a killing glare as Bayberry ushered her up the
stairs, there was at least the slightest flicker of relief that she had not been the
only one so affected. He had denied himself, too.

"Lydia."

Her lids flickered, then closed immediately as the bright morning sun
poured across her face. She had forgotten—the key that kept her *in* did not
keep *him* out. "Damn you, get out of my room," she muttered, jamming a
pillow over her head and pounding one fist into the mattress.

A chuckle, closer even than his voice had been before. "I take it your
temper has not improved?" His boot crunched on the floor. Probably across
the shards of a vase she had smashed evening last, when Bayberry had locked
her once more within her room. It hadn't been precious, but it *had* made quite
a satisfying crash. "You'll miss breakfast."

Her voice was muffled through the well-stuffed feather pillow. "Then I
shall ring for fresh."

"You *are* putting my servants through their paces," he allowed.

The bed depressed beneath his weight, somewhere near her right hip.
"Get *out*." Her fingers slid across the smooth sheets until they brushed the
edge of another pillow. Seizing it in her fist, she lobbed it in his direction.
There was a soft *pop*, suggesting she had hit her target, but he tossed the pillow back into its place without comment.

"If you hadn't spent quite so much of your evening caterwauling and
carrying on," he said, "you'd be better rested."

"If you hadn't been such an arse, perhaps I would not have felt the need
to *carry on*."

"I liked it no better than you." His hand found the curve of her hip
through the thick counterpane. "If that's any consolation."

"It is not. And I don't care, besides. I won't have you now."

"Well, of course not *now*. There's hardly time enough for breakfast, lazy-
bones." His fingertips slid up, up to the very edge of the counterpane, pinching it between them. She curled her own around it, turning her back upon

him to anchor it beneath one arm. "I never knew you to be such a grouch in the mornings," he said.

"I never knew you to be so bloody *juvenile*." The counterpane slipped from beneath her arm, inching downward in tiny increments beneath the pressure of his fingers. "And stop stealing my blankets!"

He stole her pillow instead, plucking it from atop her head while she had been distracted in wrestling the bedclothes away from him. "Come, now," he cajoled, brushing her hair away from the nape of her neck and laying a kiss just there, above the neckline of her nightgown. "You'll be in a better humor once you've had breakfast. I had Cook prepare some drinking chocolate for you."

"I don't want it."

"Liar. Don't cut off your nose to spite your face." He had got the counterpane at last, and his hand came up with a fistful of the aging lace lining the cuffs of her nightgown. "In that vein," he added, "I will be having some new things made up for you. It seems you're in need of a new nightdress, in addition to a pelisse." He waited, fingertips rubbing the scratchy lace, until it became clear that she would not break her silence. "No arguments?"

"No. It's the least of which you owe me. I'll take you for all I can get." And she would feel no shame for it.

She had *meant* to offend, since his kind were ever concerned with wealth, and suspicious of those they thought might attempt to wrest it from them, but it didn't matter what he thought of her. He already thought her faithless; there was no reason she ought not throw *mercenary* into the mix and let him think what he will, provided she benefitted from it.

"You *are* prideful," he said slowly. "I thought surely you would snap at me again."

"There is pride, and then there is stupidity." And the convergence of the two was particularly ruinous. "There. I'm awake," she said, shoving herself upright, fixing him with a glare. "Will you now *go*?"

He snickered, his dark eyes assessing her face. "You sleep like an angel," he said. "All curled up in your lonely bed, buried beneath the covers. So sweet and peaceful," he mused, and his warm fingers stroked her cheek. "I hated to disturb you."

"Now who is the liar?"

"All right, I *did* enjoy it." He leaned closer, until she could smell the starch upon his collar, the shaving soap on his skin. "But I would have preferred to wake you differently, had you given me the option. One measly promise," he whispered against her lips. "It's not so very much to ask."

"I owe you nothing." But she listed toward him anyway, content enough to pit her will against his. Whatever the inducement, he would not extract such a promise from her.

The tiniest kiss, there just at the corner of her mouth. "Perhaps we owe each other," he said softly, and the words felt as though they had seeped into her skin along with the heat of his breath. And then the cold air swept over her as he stood, withdrawing once again, leaving Lydia momentarily stunned. "Don't forget. Act four," he said, as he crossed the threshold, and the lock turned once again.

Lydia buried her shriek into her pillow.

Rafe thumbed through the selection of clothes that had begun arriving in the early afternoon. "How the devil did you get all of this so quickly?" he asked.

Marcus gave a dismissive wave. "Nicked a gown from her dressing room and had a modiste pick it apart for her measurements," he said. The most ragged of the bunch had been sacrificed to this venture. "There were only four. Can you imagine?" Four dresses, which had been mended over and over again.

"I suppose she must travel light," Rafe said. "She's been all over England in the last few years, has she not? It must be taxing to take anything more than a valise."

"I suppose," Marcus echoed, but the thought did not console him. "Every seamstress has got a selection of some ready-made gowns. It was simple enough to find a few"—*several*—"who had things in her measurements, or at least close enough to them." And those that had had to be altered would be soon enough.

"A tad excessive," Rafe said, pushing a stack of frivolous silk handkerchiefs aside in favor of the delicate shifts folded up beneath them. "It must have cost a fortune."

It had, but then he had the fortune to bear it out.

I'll take you for all I can get. The words had been meant to be provoking, he was certain, but they had sounded *vengeful*, not avaricious. "You said it yourself," Marcus said. "She hasn't even got a pelisse."

Rafe scratched at the back of his neck, his eyes drifting to the pile of them laid over the back of the couch. "And now she's got…how many is that? Six? Seven?"

Marcus shrugged. He hadn't counted. It hadn't seemed particularly relevant, except that there had been enough of them that it had eased the ache in his chest.

"She'll be hard-pressed to take it all with her when she leaves. I doubt a valise would accommodate a tenth of it all."

"She won't be leaving." Marcus thought it best not to mince words. Not with Rafe, who would almost certainly see through them at once.

"Oh?" It sounded like mild interest at best, but Rafe had turned toward him once more, abandoning the haphazardly-scattered clothing in favor of conversation. "Does she know that?"

"She will. Eventually." But for the moment? No. It was better that she did not. "She is currently indulging in a fit of pique. I doubt she would take any suggestion of it particularly well."

"So you've decided, then, for the both of you." Rafe's face expressed doubt, and perhaps a little wonder at Marcus' temerity. "Had you considered that perhaps she would not be quite so eager to keep company with a man who wishes her ill?"

Keep company. A polite way to phrase it. Marcus lifted his cup to his lips. "As to that—I've had time to reconsider," he said.

"Days," Rafe said. "You have had *days* to reconsider."

"Days, then. It doesn't matter. I want her more than I want revenge." He could have one or the other, but not *both*. Something had had to be sacrificed. The anger, the hurt—they had been cold comfort to him these past years. But Lydia—Lydia was warm. He was *owed* her, after so many years spent in the freezing agony of his resentment.

"Will you marry her, then?"

Marcus managed a cold laugh. "No," he said. He would never be so foolish as to *forgive* the past. It shaped him even today. But he could make the choice to put it from his mind, and to forge on ahead in spite of it. Perhaps there would come a time when it would be robbed of its power to hurt as deeply as it once had. "No; I will never give her another opportunity to claw my heart out of my chest," he said. "I'll have her as she is, knowing what I know of her." And that would be enough. She would never have the power to hurt him again. And he would have *her*. It was a fair enough trade.

Rafe sank into a chair, brushing away the lacy underthings that had slipped over his shoulder. "I've asked around about her," he said. "Here and there, where people would likely have known of her. There's many a man to find a mistress—or even a brief liaison—at the theatre."

Christ. He didn't want to hear this. "I'm not interested in her dalliances."

"The hundred pounds you paid to her employer would suggest otherwise," Rafe said baldly. "It was…an interesting endeavor, to say the least. It's not uncommon for men to brag of their conquests, so it seemed the most expedient method to draw out those who would do the same. I suggested that I had had her to see who would rise to the bait."

"You did *what?*"

Rafe slanted him a scowl. "Strangely, I found myself the subject of much envy. It seems she's had more than her fair share of men who have made offers—generous ones—only to be refused."

Marcus flexed his fingers, uncurling them from their clench. He'd never been quite so tempted to strike Rafe in his life. "Yes, well, I *have* paid her employer quite well to ensure such offers are refused before they ever reach her."

"Offers stretching back *years*, Rafe, from men who had seen her perform in Bath, or Brighton, or—well, I suppose it doesn't truly matter. But it was all well before she had returned to London. Tell me, what is the purpose in that?"

"I cannot possibly know what is in her mind. Perhaps she simply did not favor any of them."

Rafe made low sound in his throat, a sort of scathing dismissal, as if he thought that Marcus were being deliberately obtuse. "In the end, I found only three men that claimed they had been among her lovers as well."

"*Claimed?*"

"I doubt very much whether any of them were telling the truth. Probably they wanted only to enhance their own consequence." Rafe shrugged. "I made some allusion to a mark upon her body which could not have been visible except when unclothed, and each of them—every damned one—told me that they, too, had seen such a mark. An entirely invented heart-shaped beauty mark beneath her bosom, and each of them confirmed it. *Has* she such a mark?"

"No." Marcus muttered a foul word beneath his breath. "Why are you telling me this? It proves nothing."

"Proves it? No. But do you not mark it as suspicious?" Rafe threaded his fingers through his hair, tugging them through the dark strands. "What reason

100

had she to be unfaithful, when it was not to her benefit? And then again, what reason has she *not* to take a protector when it *is*?"

Marcus closed his eyes, scrubbing at his face with one hand. *Four dresses.* Four dresses, taking up scant space within the massive confines of her dressing room, and each of them in sad condition. Each of them years old and mended and re-mended over again, so that they would sustain her through more seasons than they had been meant to do.

The ugliness of suspicion warred with the odd, futile hope that Rafe had judged correctly. And still he heard himself saying, "It doesn't matter whether or not she took lovers. The theatre doesn't pay so well as it ought. I cannot hold her survival over her head." He had let her go, after all.

You threw me away.

Strange, now, that he could hear the accusation in the words, as if she had had any right to it at all. Stranger still how they evoked a low, clenching pain in his gut.

"Perhaps she has now learned the value of fidelity," he said, hearing the acid note in his voice. The resentment that lingered just there at the back of his throat.

"Perhaps," Rafe repeated. "But perhaps it is worth your consideration, Marcus, that it was never lost upon her at all."

Marcus watched once more as Paulina railed at Leontes, subjecting him to every bit of the ridicule which he was due, and quite a bit more besides.

So. Lydia was still angry, then.

He didn't know why the thought pleased him so well. Perhaps because his head had been stuffed with little more than thoughts of her all day, and it seemed fair that she should be the same. Had she also been counting down the hours until the appointed time? There seemed a strange urgency in her; her lines delivered with both the fury that was expected and with the quick, sharp inflection of someone boldly rushing ahead in an effort to turn minutes into seconds.

How much of that sharp tongue would she save for him, once the third act concluded? Paulina named Leontes *tyrant*, but for the fact that Lydia restrained her gaze to only the stage, he would swear the words had been intended for his ears alone.

She wasn't wrong, and Marcus knew by the scornful curl of her lip that he would not have the promise he had demanded of her tonight.

But he would have *her*. There was still one scene left to play out, but Paulina's role had done for the third act, and Marcus had had enough of it besides. He hadn't the stomach for the farcical turn of the play, and better things to which to attend. He had left his box before the infant princess Perdita had been cast to the wilds of Bohemia, and the next sixteen years would play out much the same as they had any other night—this time without his attention.

He waded through throngs of people, most of whom had come in late, since the price of a seat was drastically reduced as half the performance had elapsed already, and made his way toward the doors leading to the area behind the stage, tugging at the knot of his cravat as he went.

Already his presence had become ordinary enough that few of the actors paid him any attention at all. At the most he had merited a brief glance as they attended to their costumes, or patted powder upon faces that had grown too shiny with sweat.

Lydia had made it to the dressing room before him. She sat at her vanity, tidying the little flyaway strands of her blond hair that had come loose during her tempestuous performance.

She needn't have bothered. He was going to make a wreck of it again anyway.

"Out." The word was a low growl, and it succeeded only in attracting curious stares—but not so much as a glance from Lydia, who continued on as if he had not spoken at all. The bits and trickles of conversation that had floated about the room were quelled to silence. No one moved. No one breathed.

Except him. His heart beat at the cage of his ribs like a hammer striking an anvil. "*Out*," he roared, and this time it achieved the intended effect. Amidst scurrilous whisperings and shocked exclamations, the few who occupied the dressing room snatched for their belongings and scattered like roaches.

Lydia said, "Giles will be displeased."

"I don't give a damn what does or does not please *Giles*." His cravat came loose at last and he cast it aside. The linen sailed through the air and landed somewhere on the floor near Lydia's feet. "Does that gown have buttons or laces?"

"Does it matter?"

It didn't, really. Regrettably, there likely wasn't time to divest her of it *and* get her back into it again before she was next due on stage. He shrugged out of his coat and tossed it over the back of a chair. "No. Come here, Lydia."

She rose with a sigh, graceful and elegant, giving the impression of following his order, however begrudgingly. Her shoulders rose and fell in a taunting shrug, her head canted to an impudent angle. "I won't promise," she said.

She could have her impudence if it pleased her. "You will. Eventually." And still she remained where she was, the tiny lift of her lips suggesting she would demand further concessions still. She would not be commanded.

He didn't care. She had driven him beyond caring. He didn't even care if she *knew* it. Which she did, if the satisfied gleam in her green eyes were anything by which to judge. He crossed the space between them, and let her have her minor victory.

She ducked the hand he outstretched toward her hair. "It will never pin up so well again if you muss it," she chided. "There isn't time."

Then she would go on stage looking like she'd just been thoroughly tumbled. He sank his hands into her hair, shaking loose the pins until the whole mass of it tumbled down her back. His breath pulled at his lungs. "You are going to return to the stage feeling me between your thighs," he said. "You'll hardly notice your hair."

His mouth crushed hers, raw and hungry, and she answered the same. He could taste the pleasure on her tongue, the delight of having cut him clean to the bone, revealing something primal and real. The starched collar of her costume scratched his skin, and the voluminous skirts pushed against his legs, but her hands slid up his chest, curving over his shoulders to grip and pull herself closer.

For all the tartness of her tongue, all the studied nonchalance she exhibited, she wanted this too. Every bit as much. It wasn't the most convenient of locations—distantly, he heard the chatter of voices in the hall, the sound of footsteps, the raucous cacophony of the audience as a low drone of background noise. Somehow, he managed to maneuver the both of them toward the thin slice of wall carved out between two tables, wedging them within the empty space there. It was a tight fit; the width of her skirts only just permitting.

Her teeth nipped his lower lip; a maddening bit of ferocity. "Do *not* wrinkle my gown, you louse."

He made a sound that was not quite a laugh, freeing up one hand to rifle through skirts and petticoats, peeling back the layers and casting them adrift. A tiny tinkling sound—the careless manipulation of her skirts had overset a bottle on a neighboring vanity. His hand found the soft skin of her thigh, smooth and warm.

Her hips canted to his, and she gasped into his mouth, sinking into the touch with a shudder that transmitted itself to him, singing along every long-ignored nerve.

There would be no interruption this time. His fingers found her at last, all melting wet heat, delicate tissues yielding to the blunt pressure. She made a soft, sweet sound, trembling in his arms, her fingers sliding into his hair and gripping tightly.

"Marcus," she whispered plaintively.

Yes. He damned the tight truss of her stays and the heavy fabric of the gown over it, but for now—this would be enough. There would be time later for more.

She managed to wrench one arm free, fumbling with the buttons of his trousers, each brush of her fingers a fresh agony, until at last she had freed him from the confines of the fabric, curled her small hand around the length of him, and stroked.

"*Enough*," he rasped against her temple, his breath rattling in his lungs. Christ, he was going to spend in the soft palm of her hand. "Enough." He seized her thigh, urging it about his waist as he braced her against the wall, holding her in place. "My God, you madden me."

She released him, grabbed instead for a fresh handful of his hair to drag his mouth to hers as she squeezed his hips within the clasp of her thighs. His cock notched there, where her hot, slick flesh welcomed him, and plunged.

She squeaked into his mouth, the tiniest sound of distress. Her thighs trembled; her hands clutched him a hair too tightly for a long moment.

No. His mind rejected the spurious thought that spun through it. She wasn't a virgin; he'd relieved her of that years ago. But she was so small, so tight, that his entry had not been an easy one. Almost as if—

Almost as if she hadn't had a lover in quite a long time.

Almost as if she was so long unaccustomed to such activity that it had been a struggle to accommodate him once again. And he had forged ahead without sufficient preparation.

Good God. Rafe had been *right*.

He stared at her as if she were some strange manner of creature which he had never before encountered, horrified and alarmed at the realization. And she, vexing woman that she was, sank her teeth into his lower lip and demanded tersely, "Marcus. *Move.*"

He didn't want to hurt her. God, he didn't want to hurt her. But whatever discomfort she had suffered had passed, and she wriggled like an eel, attempting to take what she could of him, for all that he held her too tightly to manage much.

Her silky inner muscles clenched around him, and he gritted his teeth against the fire that licked down his spine. A careful thrust; she keened her pleasure against the seam of his lips. Another, and her back arched even through the thick material of the stays concealed beneath her gown. She met him stroke for stroke, and he sipped the sighs that spilled from her lips, staved off the climax that hovered just in the wings, waiting to pounce the moment his control slipped.

A hard stroke, shoving himself deeper yet. "Will you promise now?"

"No," she sighed languidly into his mouth, those vivid green eyes glazed with pleasure.

Somehow, he managed something that might have approximated a laugh. "Perhaps I shall have to keep a closer eye on you, then," he said. "Perhaps I will lock you in *my* room."

"If you must." She did not sound too put out by the prospect, but she nonetheless repaid his attempt at manipulation with the score of her teeth along the skin of his throat. That had quite nearly been the end of him.

"*Christ.*" His chest heaved. He was sure his fingers would leave bruises upon the tender skin of her thighs. He was equally sure she didn't care if he did.

Her nails scratched at his shoulders, the sound of them raking over the cloth tearing through the air. "*Hurry,*" she urged, her frantic breaths beating against his chin. "It won't be long before Giles notices something amiss, if he hasn't already."

Hurry? He had been holding back in consideration for *her.* And she demanded he *hurry*! Marcus readjusted his grip to support her with the strength of one arm, wound her hair around his freed hand and slammed his mouth down over hers, muffling her whimper. She had stripped away any pretentions of gentility to which he might have laid claim, made him more animal than man in just a few short minutes. He drove into her, once, again, and— there. The hitch of her breath, the tiny flutters of her intimate flesh. Her muscles locked, frozen as her climax crashed over her, whatever sounds she might have made lost to the pressure of his mouth over hers.

He should have pulled out. The last thing either of them needed was a bastard child shared between them.

He didn't. In the moment, he justified to himself with reassurances that she'd not conceived before, and they'd been less than careful then. Probably later, when cold rationality returned, he would self-flagellate over so reckless an action. But just for now—euphoria. A bliss he'd not experienced in half a decade. An ecstasy he had never expected to know again.

She let her head drift to his shoulder, holding very still as she struggled to recover herself, to calm her disordered breathing. And he, fool that he was, swept her disheveled hair away from her face, curled his palm around the nape of her neck, and kissed the top of her head. Like a lover might do.

Exactly as he *had* done five years ago.

"You have to go," she said, her voice muted. Stunned, he thought. Just as he had been.

"I know." Still he could not make himself release her, and neither did she reiterate her command. Instead he thought he felt the brush of her lips to the underside of his jaw.

Something had changed in her. In *him*. Something he could not bear to examine too closely.

Chapter Twelve

Marcus caught Montgomery hovering about as he left Lydia to repair herself for the final act, which, given the state of her hair and the powder and rouge that had come free of her face, he imagined would take most of the time remaining to her.

The bastard had found a new crown; a replacement for the one he'd tossed to Marcus. "Run of the theatre, my lord," Montgomery sniffed, his icy blue eyes condemning, "does *not* include making free with my dressing room between acts. I've already threatened to cut Clara loose for a similar transgression. I'd hate to cut Lydia for the same."

"You won't," Marcus said. "You damned well *owe* me."

Montgomery's brows lifted. "*Owe* you?"

"One hundred pounds. You had a hundred pounds from me to run off her lovers." Marcus pinched the bridge of his nose, frustrated beyond belief.

"Ah, yes," Montgomery agreed, pleasantly enough. "I do seem to recall something to that effect."

"She *had* no damned lovers!" The virulent snarl seemed to coalesce in his throat, distilling itself into something pure and lethal, something that ought to have eviscerated its victim on impact.

Montgomery only blinked, utterly unaffected. "I never said she had. What you assumed is only your responsibility."

"And you took my money anyway." Marcus could not understand it; any of it. Lydia was a beautiful woman. *Surely* there would have been interest. "If you had some designs upon her yourself, Montgomery, then you've frittered away your chance."

Montgomery chuckled, genuine amusement sliding across his face. "If only you knew how ludicrous that accusation is." He gave a flippant gesture; the sort that was meant to convey mild mockery. "In fact, I took only some of your money. Most of it I gave to Lydia. It seemed fitting, my lord, that you should pay for your poor opinion of her. A little like a slice of justice, delivered cold." Montgomery's shoulders touched the wall behind him, and he folded his arms over his chest.

Justice. The bubble of ire that had expanded in his chest deflated just as abruptly as it had arisen. Yes; probably it had felt like that at the time, when they had both been snapping at each other like rabid animals, neither willing to give an inch. Probably they had been laughing at him, then. Probably he had merited it, with his overreaching, with his flagrant suspicion, which he had had no right to. It *hadn't* been his business, but he had claimed it anyway.

Montgomery had taken Marcus' desire for vengeance, to strip away the security of what additional income she might have been earning, and twisted it into largesse instead. An income she'd earned *because* of his distrust. She had profited at his expense. Could he truly blame her for that?

"She ought to have told me." He'd *hurt* her, however briefly.

"Why should she have done? You wouldn't have believed her if she had." Montgomery gave a one-shouldered shrug. "The truth is, my lord, that I don't think she cared enough *to* tell you. It doesn't matter what you think of her any longer. If she chooses to amuse herself with you, then that is her affair. But you won't keep her."

A chill crawled down Marcus' spine. "What the devil do you mean by that?"

"I mean you've thrown her over once," Montgomery said. "She'd have to be a fool to trust you again, and whatever else she is, Lydia is no fool." He gave a mocking, courtly bow, and the slice of his smile cut like a knife. "Enjoy your crown, my lord," he said as he turned to leave. "I do hope it fits."

"Marcus," Lydia said patiently, as he shoved yet another pelisse into her hands. "This is all very lovely. But I would like a bath." Still, her fingers stroked the wool of the pelisse, which felt thick and soft as a cloud.

He ignored her. "There's more," he said. "Gowns, shifts, stays— stockings, I think, somewhere." His dark hair fell over his forehead as he began to paw through drawers. "Don't you *care?*"

Not particularly. She'd lived too long with only four gowns to her name to fawn over such things. She wouldn't even be here long enough to wear half of it, unless she planned to change her clothing four times a day. "You can't buy me," she said. "Though you're welcome to try. I won't complain of it."

She set aside the pelisse, letting the folds of it drape over the edge of the bed, and yanked the bell pull.

"Garters," Marcus said absently. "Ribbons. Petticoats. Cloaks."

There was a scratch at the door, which Marcus seemed not even to have heard. Bayberry appeared there, his brow furrowed.

"A bath, please, Bayberry," Lydia said. "And supper, even if it is cold." Probably the water was heated already. She had sent the staff scurrying enough in the first few days that they had likely anticipated such a request.

"Gloves," Marcus continued. "Nightdresses, and—I have no idea what these are meant to be." He held up the garment for her inspection.

"Drawers," Lydia supplied. "They're rather risqué. Proper ladies won't wear them." But she was not a proper lady.

Her prediction proved correct; Bayberry returned with a large copper tub, which he set behind a privacy screen. Almost as if he had had it waiting somewhere just out of sight. He removed himself once more, but Lydia did not doubt that he would return shortly with cans of water.

As Marcus shoved the garment back into the drawer from which he had removed them, his hands stilled abruptly. There was the soft *clink* of coins as he withdrew a purse.

Lydia sat heavily at the edge of the bed, crushing the beautiful navy blue pelisse beneath her.

"What is this?" he asked, his voice light, reasonable. Deceptively so.

She licked her dry, bloodless lips. "I think you know already."

"I want to hear it from you." He brought the purse with him to stand before her at the edge of the bed. "I gave this to Montgomery."

"He gave it to me." Her fingers clenched on the counterpane. Behind Marcus, servants filed into the room, and there was the splash of water filling the tub and laying out lengths of toweling. Tiny bars of soap. A comb. Bottles of various scented oils.

"It's a bit light, I think," Marcus said, weighing the purse in his palm.

"Extortionist's fee. Twenty percent." She disguised her discomfiture with a shrug.

Marcus sighed, letting the purse slip free of his fingers to land heavily in her lap. The purse tipped onto its side, overweighted by the coins within, but the drawstring mouth remained tightly closed. "You *must* know that you could have found yourself a much more comfortable living situation with that," he said.

Of course she could have. She could have had the rent of a house of her own for a fraction of what remained within that purse, and in a better part of town.

"What did you plan for it, then?" he asked. "If not a better place to live?"

"I—" Her hands curled around the purse in her lap. "I meant to send it on to my family," she said. "I just hadn't worked out how to do it yet." He had watched her so closely. And she wouldn't have risked smuggling it into the theatre. He had been bound to hear the coins rattling around, and everyone was always in everybody else's business at the theatre; there was every chance that someone might have helped themselves to it.

"Your family," he echoed. "In Whitechapel?"

She nodded.

A brief hesitation, as if he knew not what to say. As if he had not considered that she had had a family in years. At last, he offered awkwardly, "You could visit them. While you are in London."

She said nothing. She would not discuss such things with him, when it was because of him that she had not visited. That she *could* not visit.

With a sigh, Marcus retrieved the purse, prying her fingers free of it. "Bayberry," he said, and handed it over to the dour-faced manservant. "See that this gets to Miss Alcott's family tomorrow. She will give you their direction in the morning."

"Thank you." Lydia felt her spine curve into a slouch, as if the weight of the world had abruptly tumbled straight down upon her shoulders. "Still, I won't promise you anything." She didn't owe him that, even if he hadn't elected to steal back her ill-gotten funds. Even if he would send them on to her family.

She hadn't asked him for anything, and she would not be manipulated into gratitude for what he had provided. She would not be *beholden* to him for any of it. And if he imagined she would, well, then, she—

"I want you to stay," he admitted. "I want you to *want* to stay. We're not done, you and I."

She might have laughed, if she could have scooped one out of the pit of her stomach. They had been *done* for years and years. The lingering resentment could not be exorcised so easily. He had already cracked her heart in two; she would not hand him the pieces of it to crumble in his hands.

But there was a part of her, however small, that...enjoyed this strange, exasperating *something* they now shared. As if it filed away at the jagged edges of their shared past and made it something less sharp, less perilous than it had been. She could laugh at herself again. She could laugh at *him*. Instead of the harsh, unexpected ending, it was the slow-unfurling conclusion of the brief chapter of their lives together. And when it did come, she would turn the page without having been left wanting. Perhaps she would finally be able to move past it all. She would live again. *Love* again.

"Lydia."

She didn't want to hear the tenderness in his voice, knowing it was so temporary a thing. She closed her eyes against the fierce surge of nostalgia that had swept over her. "Leave me be, Marcus. My bath is growing cold."

They *were* done. He simply had not accepted it yet. But perhaps she had not quite accepted it yet, either.

It was torture to hear her at her bath, to know that she was so close, concealed just behind the privacy screen settled in the corner. Once, he would have been permitted to join her. To help her wash her hair, to scrub her back. To cradle her against his chest and laze in the water until it had grown too cold for comfort.

Now he lay flat on his back in her bed, staring at the ceiling as the soft sound of the water sluicing over her body threatened to drive him mad.

"I could help you," he said.

"No." Another short splash. The scent of jasmine perfumed the air, subtle and delicate. "I prefer bathing alone. It gives me time to think."

"Can you not think *outside* of the bath?" Preferably where he could see her. Touch her. Feel the heat of her skin on his own. Stroke his fingers through the silk of her hair.

The water rippled in tandem with her gentle laugh. "There is such a dearth of privacy in the theatre," she said. "If I did not seize such moments wherever I could, I'd go mad. *Quiet*, Marcus."

She commanded him in his own home, and he—he *let* her do it. He let her do it because there was no other alternative. Whatever demands he might have made upon her were worse than worthless. She would simply smile that enigmatic, faintly chiding smile, and do as she would anyway.

You cannot buy me, she had said, and damned if it had not felt like the truth. There was so little that did not come easily to him, and yet Lydia remained stubbornly out of reach. Existing just past the tips of his fingers. He could lock her in her room—in *his*—and still he would not own her.

He could no more possess her than he could hold the wind in his hand.

An eternity later, he heard another splash, saw her hand beneath the border of the privacy screen reaching for the toweling that had been left out for her. She hummed softly to herself as she stepped out of the bathing tub, and he heard the faint whisk of the towel skimming over her skin, blotting away the water.

"So," she said, crisply, as at last she stepped out from behind the screen. The towel was tucked tightly around her, and her hair, wetted to liquid gold, dripped over her shoulders in shining, damp tendrils. "Here is how it is going to be."

Interested, Marcus levered himself up onto his elbows. "You are *telling* me?"

"I am," she said, her voice at once light and firm as she meandered toward her dresser, where she began to rifle through the drawers. At last she selected a nightdress made of a soft, gauzy material, and let fall the towel long enough to slip it over her head. For all too brief a moment he was treated to the sight of golden candlelight flickering over her bare skin. "I quite like having pretty things, and to not worry about pinching pence to make rent," she said. "So I will stay. For the time being."

For the time being. Unacceptable. Marcus opened his mouth to argue—

"That can change at any moment," she said, as if she had scented the advent of an argument in the very air, and the words curdled and died in his throat.

He swept one hand through his hair, ruffling the dark strands. "What, then, do you intend? To live in my house, eat my food, enjoy my hospitality?"

"Yes," she said simply. "All that, and more." The nightdress, sheerer than was proper, revealed tiny hints of smooth skin as she climbed onto the bed beside him. "I will also require the use of your carriage to conduct me to the theatre."

"Mercenary," he chided.

"Practical," she returned with a shrug. "I won't be your mistress, however," she said. "Rather, I will permit you to be my lover."

"You will, will you?"

"So long as you please me." Those green eyes sparkled with mirth, with a sort of wild delight as she bent over him. "And not otherwise. If you are very, very good"—she drew one fingertip down his chest, and he felt the

112

stroke even through the fabric of his waistcoat—"I will grant you what time remains until our production concludes its run."

That was hardly a fortnight more! "I'll want you longer than that."

"Pity." Her voice dropped to a disappointed murmur. "This is all I am offering to you."

He caught her wrist in his hand before she could withdraw. "You want pretty things? I'll buy you more. Clothing. Jewels."

"If you like. Certainly, I will have to decide what I would like to take with me when I go." She didn't even blink, utterly unmoved by the plea in his voice. "I have told you my terms, Marcus."

Her terms, not his. She would *permit* him to be *her* lover; an indulgence bestowed upon a lowly, unworthy supplicant. Granting him the gift of her favor only so long as it pleased her to do so, only so long as he *pleased* her.

His thumb drifted over the flutter of her pulse in her wrist. "Have you any other conditions I must know of?"

She nodded. "I won't be caged," she said. "I won't be controlled. If you would expect that same simpering obeisance"—her breath came quickly through her teeth in a huff of irritation—"then I would implore you to look elsewhere. I don't have it in me, and I would not give it to you if I did."

"You'll use me, then," he said. "For comfort. Security."

"Yes."

"You will make me no promises, and you will leave me when you please." His fingers caught in the fine lace at the cuff of her sleeve.

"A fool makes such promises as you've asked for." She shrugged. "If I am to stay, I do not intend to continue paying for the past, Marcus. I will have no unpleasantness, no strife. When you cease to please me, I will have done with you—whether that comes one minute from now, or whether this draws to its natural conclusion is your decision."

It wasn't enough. It could never have been enough. But it was an offer she had given freely, and he would have been a fool not to seize it while she dangled it before him. "I'll change your mind," he said.

"You won't." Her laugh broke high as he wrapped his arm about her waist and turned her so that she was trapped beneath him. "You won't," she repeated with a sigh as her arms hooked about his neck and her eyes fluttered closed. "But you are welcome to try."

Chapter Thirteen

It wasn't the low rumble of thunder that woke her—it was the heated brush of lips at the nape of her neck. Lydia's eyes opened to a dreary world. Whatever morning sunshine that might have slipped through the curtains had been smothered by the clouds that hung thick in the sky, painting the world in grey. But then, that was London more often than not, it seemed.

The fire had died hours ago, most likely, given the chill in the air. Lydia snuggled deeper into the covers, pressing her back against Marcus' warm chest, letting his heat soak into her skin. A light patter of rain fell upon the windows as he trailed his fingertips up and down her arm.

"It's a perfectly wretched day," he murmured against her shoulder. "Wonderful weather for staying in bed."

She smiled, tucking her head back against the pillow. "Is it?" she asked. "Haven't you anything to do?"

"Nothing more pressing than this." His warm breath coasted by her ear. "And you haven't, either. It's Sunday."

So it was, already. Days had passed in perfect bliss, like moments stolen from another time. There had been no arguments, no fuss, no conflict. Only pleasure.

"Stay with me today," he said, pressing a kiss to her neck. "Right here. All day."

"How indolent I should be then," she mused, turning in the circle of his arms and letting the covers settle once more around them; a lovely, comfortable froth of fabric secluding them away from the world.

His hand found her thigh beneath the blankets, wandering slowly upward toward her hip; a burning brand upon her flesh. "We'll watch the rain," he said. "Have breakfast in bed."

"Is that all?" She let her leg slide up his hair-roughened thigh, an action which provoked a swift in-drawn breath.

"Mm," he murmured into the hair at her temple. "What else would you like to do? Cards?"

114

Lydia laughed lightly, sliding her hands into his hair to bring his face down to hers. "No," she said, nibbling at his lower lip. "You know I haven't the head for them. Besides," she added, "I have got an umbrella and several new pelisses that merit wearing."

"Another day." His lips rubbed hers as his palm curled over her hip possessively before sliding around to the small of her back. "Tell me how I ought to convince you to stay."

His fingertips trailed up her spine in light, delicate strokes. "More of that," she said on a sigh. A waking dream, this—as if time itself had slowed to a standstill, minutes and hours holding their breaths, reluctant to pass. She had missed this most of all; the reverence that she could feel in every stroke of his hands, each hushed breath and whisper.

It wouldn't last, but nothing good ever did. He was hers again for these quiet moments they shared between the slip and rustle of clean white sheets. And that would be enough. She would *make* it be enough.

"You are so beautiful," he crooned against her throat, his mouth drifting lower until he repeated the words into the soft curve of her breast, and she relished them because they had been given freely, without expectation. Her hands cradled his head, raking her nails through the cool, dark strands of his hair as his tongue caressed her nipple. He teased with such gentle pressure until it tightened to a peak beneath his ministrations. "I would keep you here forever."

But she would not be *kept*. She murmured something noncommittal, arched beneath him to the slight tickle of his tongue swirling about her navel. His hands splayed over her thighs, turning the sinuous motion to his benefit. He kissed her hip, sliding lower, and held her open there, disappearing beneath the covers.

Wild titillation swelled up within her chest, and her fingers splayed over the surface of the counterpane that concealed him.

"I'll make you stay," he promised, with a kiss to the soft skin of her inner thigh. She pressed her lips together to hold in the strange, needy sound that had wanted to emerge.

"Will you?" Her voice sounded strained even to her own ears.

His shoulders wedged between her splayed legs. With a gentle stroke, he opened her, bathing his fingers in the moisture of her body. Her head fell back upon the pillow with the first touch of his tongue, her toes curling. He toyed with her, promising satisfaction in sweet kisses and mind-scrambling caresses by turn, and then dangling it just out of reach.

Sweat beaded on her skin as she strained toward it, but she found her restless movements hampered by the splay of his hand across her stomach.

"Marcus," she whimpered, clenching her fingers into the pillow behind her head. Her nails scratched at the fabric, the sound deafening to her ears.

He soothed her—and aggravated—with the rub of his cheek to her thigh. "Have I convinced you?"

"No!" It was a petulant denial, seething with her frustration. Her hips bucked, and his low laugh stirred the private curls between her thighs.

Another tiny lick, too brief and light to accomplish anything other than stoking the fires of her irritation. She muffled a short shriek behind one hand, kicked out at him with her foot. Barely brushed his side. "*Marcus.*"

"*Lydia,*" he chided. "Say you will stay in bed with me today, and I'll let you come."

She gritted her teeth against the temptation. "And if I do not?"

"I'll keep you here anyway. On the very edge. For hours. For *ever.*" The gentle abrasion of his unshaved cheek upon her skin drove her an inch closer to madness.

"That is *cruel.*"

"Is it?" He teased her again with just the very tip of his tongue; a slow, lingering stroke. "You know how to end it."

Every muscle in her body quivered with unrelieved tension, strung as tightly as a bow. There was a scream somewhere deep in her throat, waiting to burst free, and she strangled on it for a long moment. "Fine!" she cast at him at last, half-venom, half-plea. "I will stay!"

"Good girl." It was only when he fell upon her once more, voraciously, that she realized he had denied himself as well. Like a starving man he devoured her, greedy, seeking her pleasure and his own.

She sparkled like the hidden sun. She soared into it, became a flare of golden sunlight kissing the clouds. And then, too quickly, she floated back down to earth once more, replete and satiated.

With a sigh, she held out her arms to him. He slipped into them, curled her against him. His hand cupped her cheek, turned her face to his. Bussed a kiss to her forehead, her lips.

"I have missed you," he admitted, his voice pitched low, as if loath to wake the world that existed outside of his bed. "God, how I have missed you."

A tiny skirl of anxiety pitched in her stomach at this, the very first suggestion of discord. "Marcus—"

116

"No," he said, soothing it away with the touch of his lips to hers. "No, I know it already."

There was no room, here, in this bed, for the past.

"You shouldn't have come," Diana whispered as Marcus leaned down to embrace her. "Father is in a *terrible* temper."

"So an average Tuesday, then," Marcus said as he released her.

"I'm serious, Marcus. He knows you're keeping Lydia in your townhouse. He's livid."

For God's sake—did *everyone* know *everything* there was to know in the world? Was nothing private, nothing sacred? "Lydia is my business. He's welcome to his opinion, provided he keeps it to himself."

"Oh, Marcus." She slanted him a pitying look. "When has *that* ever happened?"

There was a rustle of newspaper, and Marcus could practically sense Father's glare, burning into the back of his neck. "Sit down, Marcus. Breakfast is growing cold."

Mother gave a nervous little titter. "Cook has quite outdone herself with the plum cake this morning," she said, her hands moving in a jerky little gesture toward it.

Marcus took up his seat and served himself a slice. It tasted the same as it ever had. He washed it down with a sip of tea.

"You will escort your sister to the Framingham musicale this evening," Father said, his mustache twitching. "Bound to be a number of eligible ladies present. *Pick* one."

"Framingham," Marcus muttered, turning his gaze on Diana. "Was she the short one?"

"No. Too blond, I think you said." The light laugh died on her lips when Father turned his icy eyes upon her, and she averted her gaze to her plate and subsided into silence.

Father was going to beat the spirit out of her, too. Just the same as he had with Mother. Just the same as he would have his sons, if he could have managed it. Regrettably for him, they had proved too stubborn, too rebellious to control with the lash of his tongue. But poor Diana—she hadn't the choice to remove herself from the household, to return to it only as it suited her to do.

"Would you prefer my company?" he asked of her.

She sent him an apologetic, pleading glance. "I truly would," she said. "That is to say, if you could spare the time—"

"If you can pry yourself away from the arms of your whore for a few hours," Father snarled.

"Harold, *please*," Mother cried.

"Get rid of her, Marcus," Father demanded, slamming his fist down upon the table, rattling the dishes. "Do you think you'll be able to find a wife when it is common knowledge that that harlot resides within your household?"

Marcus gave a careless shrug. "If I wished to find a wife, I might concern myself with such things. As I do not—"

"You had damned well better! I will not stand for this nonsense any longer, Marcus. You have a responsibility, and you'll meet it, just as I did." Father's face had flushed a vivid red with rage.

Tears glittered in Mother's eyes. Marcus wished she had it in her to disregard Father in the selfsame manner as he disregarded her. "Harold," she said, in that simpering sweet tone that had never gained her anything more than Father's disgust. "Perhaps it is better to let these things run their course. You know it cannot last."

Marcus stabbed his fork into his plum cake and gave it a vicious twist. Of *course* it could not last. Lydia would not stay. For all his efforts, he could not sway her. Each day she slipped a little more from between his fingers. Each hour was one closer to the end, as she had determined it to be.

"You're a fool," Father spat at him. "A fool, cradling a viper to your chest. She'll help herself to aught she thinks she can get of you, and when she is through, she'll sink her fangs into you as would any of her kind. It's in her nature."

Marcus felt his brow furrow. He would swear it wasn't. For all that she did not cleave to him as he would have liked, she was neither cruel nor avaricious. *If you like,* she said, with an indifferent shrug, whenever he suggested the purchase of something for her. She wore the clothes, drank the wine, ate the food. But she did not *covet* them like someone truly mercenary would have done. Neither did she thank him for these things, because she had never asked for them. The days when she might have fawned over him in a breathless cloud of love and adoration had truly gone.

118

He hadn't so keenly felt the loss of them in years.

Lydia stirred as Marcus settled at the edge of the bed, leaning over her to kiss her cheek. He had left early to have breakfast with his family, and she had lazed abed for another few hours in the meantime, since she was not expected at the theatre until the early afternoon today.

"Welcome home," she mumbled, turning onto her back and wiping the sleep from her eyes. "I hope you had a pleasant breakfast."

"I didn't," he said. "I never do." His hand slipped beneath her head, cupping the nape of her neck to lift her for his kiss. "I would rather have been here with you."

"Then why do you go?"

"Diana," he said. "She has to sit through Father's bluster every morning. It seems only fair that I should deflect a bit of it from time to time. I think half of Father's satisfaction in life comes from scolding his children. We are scapegraces, all."

"I'm sorry for all of you, then. What a terrible burden to bear."

Marcus shrugged. "One grows accustomed to it. I've long since ceased to care for his opinion." He hesitated. "I'll see you to the theatre this afternoon, but I'm afraid I must miss your performance," he said. "Diana has an engagement for which she desires my company."

"Does she? How lovely. I'm certain you'll both have a splendid time." Why was he telling her this? She was not his wife, to be informed of his comings and goings.

"It's possible that it will let out early enough that I will be able to make it back to you before you are done," he said. "But if not, I'll send the carriage round for you." His fingers sank into her hair, rubbing the strands between them. "I will miss you."

"Oh," she said, nonplussed. Silence settled over them, less comfortable than it had been only moments before.

His chest rose and fell in a sigh. "Will you not give me even that much?"

"Marcus, it is a few hours at most. I will be on stage; I will hardly have the time." Under the guise of a stretch, she extracted herself from his arms. Muffling the yawn that lingered at the back of her throat, she cast off the covers, reaching for the nightdress that had been abandoned somewhere on the floor during the night.

He braced his hands upon his knees, and the knuckles whitened. There was the clench of his jaw, the muscle jumping beneath the otherwise smooth surface of his skin. His mouth opened—

"Don't," she advised lightly as she pulled the nightdress over her head and twitched it into place. "Or we shall quarrel. I truly don't want to quarrel, Marcus." And he was doomed to failure if he tried.

His shoulders slumped just then, and his head dipped as his hand came up to massage at his forehead as if it pained him. Impotent to do anything but acquiesce, at last he sighed and rose to his feet.

"Have breakfast with me," he said, as she pulled a dressing gown over the thin fabric of her nightdress, and combed her hair over her shoulder.

She pursed her lips, biting back a little flutter of laughter. "You've had breakfast already."

"Yes, but I would like a pleasant one instead," he said, and crossed the room to take her once more into his arms. "No quarreling. I promise."

"How goes the tawdry little affair with your very own Leontes?" Giles inquired. "Has he asked you to be his mistress in truth?"

Lydia looked up from the pot of rouge she held in one hand and spared him a small glare in the mirror. "No," she said, "and he knows better than to do so."

"Darling, if you think that, you are truly ignorant of men. Idiots, all, I assure you—though sometimes we are blessed with bouts of competence, and the very occasional profundity."

"He knows my terms well enough," Lydia said with a shrug. "Besides, we will soon be moving on." Too soon for her taste, perhaps, but it had always had to end. She was not going to allow herself to nurture any illusions to the contrary.

"And he'll be feeling the pinch of it, no doubt. Probably he has made some sort of oblique comment. A hint, a suggestion." Giles flicked a bit of lint off of his shirt, continuing the pretense that his interest was an idle one at best. "I think he is not a man to take being denied so easily. Perhaps he thinks he can tempt you to stay."

Lydia rubbed a spot of rouge over her lips. "I won't," she said, but her stomach clenched. Because those few comments he had made, and which she had swiftly shut down before they could bloom into arguments which might have forced her to reconsider their arrangement—they had spoken to something inside her. That broken part which he had left behind years ago.

Giles had known her too many years to take that simple comment at face value. "If he offered you more? If he offered marriage?"

"He won't." Once, she had dreamed of becoming his wife. But that dream had died a traumatic death. To let the ashes of it reconstitute themselves? Unthinkable. "Giles, what is the purpose in this?"

"If I am to replace you, I'd like to know as soon as possible. I'd not hold it against you, of course. Even being a mistress would be a more lucrative career." He glanced upward, exhaling through his nose. "You're a better actress than you are a liar."

Lydia paused, her red-stained fingers pressed to her cheeks. "I've told you no lies," she said, but the words wobbled, as if they had skated unsteadily through the icy chill that swept over her. *Fear*, she thought. That was *fear* skittering inside her chest, freezing her with its frigid tendrils.

Giles sent her a reproachful glance. "Worse yet, you're lying to yourself. You'd take him, if he offered for you."

I wouldn't. Her lips formed the words; she was certain of it. Soundlessly.

His lips twitched, a queer kind of prescience lining his face. "You would," he said again, unnecessarily ruthless. "I don't blame you for it. You'd make a fine baroness, if truth be told." His keen gaze raked her costume. "You play the noblewoman well enough."

She found her voice at last. "I don't want a man who doesn't love me. Who doesn't *trust* me." And he would never offer marriage without those things. His pride would not allow it. And she—*she* would not accept anything less.

She closed her eyes, a ragged sob shuddering in her throat. And there it was—the *truth* which she had buried, and which Giles had dug out of her raw, aching chest. She *would* accept him, if he offered for her, if it came complete with his love, his trust. Unattainable things, useless to hope for.

It could never happen. It *would* never happen, even if he might have rediscovered some shred of honest emotion for her. She swiped at her eyes with the back of her hand, conscious of the rouge still staining her fingertips.

Giles made a sympathetic sound, his arms falling to his sides. "I'm sorry,

Lydia. Truly."

"Don't be." He had merely forced her to acknowledge reality. She drew in a deep breath and let it out, willing the inconvenient grief to subside. All things passed, in time. "You needn't worry. In a few days, Marcus will be only a memory."

Chapter Fourteen

Y ou look dreadfully bored," Diana whispered, though she needn't have done so—it would have been all but impossible for anyone to have overheard her, given that they had selected seats at the very back of the room, and the discordant wail of the pianoforte, which was being terribly abused by the woman performing, would have precluded such a thing, besides.

Marcus resisted the childish urge to put his fingers in his ears and hoped that the ruckus had done no permanent damage to his hearing. "If I appear bored, it is only because it is the politest expression of which I am currently capable," he muttered back. "I confess, I can't even tell which composer is currently being butchered."

Diana coughed into her hand to cover a laugh, which might have attracted undue attention. "Mozart, I think."

"Good God," Marcus said, and dropped his head back just slightly. "What has he ever done that would merit such disrespect? Let the poor man rest in peace."

"Yes, well, I'm afraid you'll likely have to sit through a good deal more of it," Diana sighed, as she squinted toward the front of the room. "Who is playing?"

Marcus felt his lips quirk up. "You would know, if—"

"If I wore my spectacles," Diana finished glumly. "Yes, yes, I can see you are bound and determined to be utterly wretched about it." She pulled the drawstring of her reticule, shoved her hand inside, retrieved the small silver spectacles, and settled them on the bridge of her nose. "Lady Felton," she said. "I might have guessed."

"How so?"

Diana lifted one shoulder in a shrug. "She's been nattering on and on about how her music instructor says she has got *such* an ear for music," she said. "But I've heard her sing before, and it was clear to everyone present that she couldn't carry a tune if she had a bucket to put it in."

"She might have an ear for something," Marcus allowed, "but it is most certainly not music."

They both breathed a muted sigh of relief as the woman finished her piece at last to a smattering of unenthusiastic applause, and her place was taken up by someone at least moderately more competent.

Diana adjusted her spectacles, and Marcus realized that the frames of them were just a little crooked. Probably they had been in use a few years too long. "When did you last replace your spectacles?" he asked. "It's likely time for a new pair."

Diana gave a little laugh. "These will have to do, I'm afraid. Father would never permit it. He hates them. Says they make me look too bookish."

"They don't. They're rather pretty, really." Marcus shifted uncomfortably as the new player hit a wrong note, and the resulting chord shrilled across the room. "I wonder that he allowed you those, then."

"Oh, well," Diana said. "He really didn't have much of a choice, there." She looked down at her hands in her lap. "In fact, Lydia got them for me."

Marcus froze. "Lydia? When?"

"Years and years ago." She gave a tiny gesture of her hand. "When she was a seamstress. I suppose she must have noticed that I squinted altogether too much, and when you brought me in once for a fitting, she took me to the back room to pin my hems—and I found that she had an oculist from a nearby shop waiting for me." She ducked her head, a tiny smile clinging to the corners of her lips. "Of course, I was a bit put out at the time. I did not *want* spectacles, you see, but she made me try on several ready-made pairs, and when I put these on"—she touched her fingers gently to the earpiece—"I could *see*. Properly see, for the first time. Textures, lines. Individual leaves on tree branches outside of the window. I took them home, of course, in my reticule. The cost of them was added to the bill. Father never knew the difference."

"She never told me."

Diana shrugged. "Perhaps she did not think it worth mentioning." Hesitantly, she ventured, "Are you going to marry her?"

Marcus made a rough sound in his throat. "Diana—"

"You could, Marcus. You might be scandalous for a little while, but you *could.*"

"It's not about the scandal." Marcus pinched the bridge of his nose. "It's not the sort of thing one discusses with one's sister."

"But you love her," Diana persisted. "I should hate to see you throw that away. To resign yourself to a marriage like our parents. To become a man

124

like Father."

Marcus stilled, growing rigid in his seat. "I'm not like Father."

She gave a sort of half-smile, hardly conciliatory. "You have grown so cold, Marcus, when you were once so happy. What will you have, in twenty years, if you have surrendered every possibility of happiness? What manner of man will you be then?"

Lydia shouldn't have missed Marcus. She had resolved to herself—and to him—that she would not. But she felt his absence anyway, in that barren box that remained stubbornly empty through the performance. Was this to be the rest of her life, after they had left London once more? Catching herself sneaking glances in the futile hope of seeing him in places he would never be?

It was all so very unfair.

She dusted her shiny nose with powder as she struggled to shove down the obnoxious hope that Marcus would, by some chance, make it back to the theatre in time. She had grown accustomed to his presence, to that intense stare that followed her about the stage, as if he had eyes for nothing and no one else. She had grown accustomed to his comings and goings, making free with the theatre as if it were his own.

These few moments of peace while the fourth act played out on the stage felt strangely oppressive instead, like the weight of her cold and lonely future had settled upon her shoulders. She was left alone in the dressing room to ponder it dispassionately, as if she were forced to watch a tragedy play out before her eyes, helpless to stop events from unfolding as they would. Like the very play in which she performed each night and from which there could be no deviation: Leontes would always repudiate his innocent wife; Hermione would always fall to the magnificent cruelty of her husband; Perdita would always be lost to the wilds of Bohemia.

She was only the player, dancing to whichever strings were pulled.

The hinges of the door creaked as they opened behind her, and she averted her eyes, wiping away the last traces of that queer melancholy that had etched itself into the lines of her face. "Leave me be, Giles. I only need a few more moments."

A caustic sound, rough and angry, had her turning in her chair. "So you are the witch who has ensnared my son a second time."

The overweening arrogance in the words sent a shiver down her spine. The gentleman who had stepped through the door had the look of Marcus, that was certain enough. The same dark hair, cut into a severe style, though his was threaded through with streaks of silver. A neatly-trimmed mustache over his lip twitched in blatant disapproval. His high cheekbones were ruddy, as if he had been angry even before he had stepped through the door.

What was she meant to say to that? This man had judged her with only a look. Less even than that—he had judged her years before now by his own words.

Anything she might say, any defense she might give, would be an exercise in futility.

"Sir." Her voice wobbled over the words, cracking high, her fingers clenching upon the back of the chair. "My lord. It was never my intention to—"

"To hell with your damned *intentions*." His lip curled with disdain, drawing back from his teeth, which were bared in a scowl. "I know your sort well enough, never content with your lot. Reaching above your station. Did you truly think you could snare a lord? You aren't fit to shine his shoes, much less to mingle blood."

Lydia's throat had gone so very dry. "I know what you must think of me," she said.

"You couldn't *possibly* imagine what I think of you. If you had one iota of sense residing within that pretty, empty head, you would never have returned." His lordship sneered; as chilling an expression of hate as she had ever seen. "I will give you this warning only once. *Leave*."

Her breath whistled through her teeth. "My lord, whatever you have been told of me, it is a lie. I loved your son. I never would have—"

A malicious laugh cut straight through her denial. "My God," he said. "You *are* a fool. Don't you think I know that? It was so *easy* to be rid of you. I simply never imagined my own son would prove stupid enough to embroil himself with you again. Once a whore, always a whore, after all."

An eerie lightheadedness assailed her, as if all of the blood had rushed from her head. As if his words had sliced straight through her, and she was bleeding out slowly upon the floor. "You," she whispered. "It is because of *you* that Marcus thought me unfaithful?"

"He was *wasted* upon you."

"I loved him!" That wasn't *her* voice; it was the pitiful wail of the girl she had once been stretching out across all the wasted years, crying out her anguish, her grief. So much pain, so much misery—because this man, this wretched, awful man, had deemed her unworthy.

Because *Marcus* had so easily allowed himself to be fooled.

"I loved him," she repeated, in a thin, toneless voice. "And you—you destroyed me for it." He had killed her heart as surely as if he had run her through with a sword.

"He will never wed you," his lordship said, in a voice oozing with malevolent satisfaction. "It will be easier, still, to be rid of you a second time. Are you foolish enough to think he would ever believe you? You proved yourself faithless once."

He had made her appear faithless, though she had never been. And he would do it again. "Why are you telling me this?" she asked. "What purpose can be served in it?"

"Women of your stamp have a remarkable tendency to rear their heads from time to time, never having learned a lesson from the past. I want you to *know*," he said. "I want you to *remember* what was done to you. How easily it was accomplished. How simple a matter it would be to rout you again. And the next time you think to return to London, to sink your filthy little claws into my son—think *again*."

Lydia closed her eyes, drew in a sharp, shuddering breath. The agony there in her chest was new; a fresh wound cut deep—but it would mellow. It would scar over. It always did. At length she opened her eyes and blanked her face of any manner of emotion. His lordship was not a man to be moved by it. "You have made your point, my lord," she said.

"I hope I have. He will never wed you. I will make certain of that." He touched his fingers to his head; a mocking parody of civility. "Good evening, Miss Alcott."

Lydia waited for the sound of his footsteps in the hall to fade, and once they had she allowed herself a moment—little more than a minute, at most—to wallow in the freshly-inflicted misery. And then she dried her face, reapplied her cosmetics, and began to make her way to the stage.

What did any of it matter? Marcus would never believe her, even if she told him. His father had made certain of that already.

Marcus handed his coat and hat to the footman as he walked in the door, his ears still ringing faintly from the torment that had been inflicted upon them. It had gone past eleven already. He wished he had not missed Lydia at the theatre, but the musical performances had seemed to stretch on and on into eternity, the hours crawling by, torturously slow.

When at last they had been mercifully released, the coachman had indicated that he had already conducted Lydia home again, and Marcus had been obliged to return Diana to their parents' residence before making his way home himself.

"Good evening, my lord," Bayberry said, as he arrived in the foyer.

"Ah, Bayberry. I trust Miss Alcott has arrived safely?"

"Yes, my lord. And your brother, Lord Rafe, came round an hour or two ago. He left a note for you." Bayberry patted at his pockets for it, but Marcus waved it off.

"I'll attend to it tomorrow, Bayberry. Rafe can keep until then."

"He *did* say it was quite urgent, my lord," Bayberry tried again.

"*Later,*" Marcus said, waving the insistence away once again. "Has Miss Alcott eaten yet?"

Bayberry hesitated. "No, my lord."

Had she been waiting for him, then? She had to be starving. "Bring up some supper, then, Bayberry, for both of us." He had managed to cram a few tiny slices of cake down his throat at the musicale, but it had been light, tasteless stuff, eaten quickly between performances.

Bayberry cleared his throat as Marcus headed for the stairs. "I believe you'll find Miss Alcott in her room this evening," he said.

"*Her* room?" Marcus hesitated, one hand wrapped round the newel post at the base of the stairs. She'd shared his room—his *bed*—for well over a week now. Why the sudden change?

"Yes, my lord." A slight crease marred Bayberry's forehead. "If you don't mind my saying so, she seemed in poor spirits this evening. She refused supper when she arrived home, and didn't even ring for a bath." Something of sympathy had settled over his face; a baffling expression on the usually placid man.

"Bring up some supper anyway, Bayberry. I'll see if I can't coax her to eat something," Marcus said. He took the stairs two at a time, turning down the hall that led to the room in which he'd first placed her.

As he eased the door open, it was clear to see that she had not been waiting upon him, engaged in some pleasant diversion that would pass the

128

time while he was out. There wasn't a hint of candlelight; no more than the faint glimmer of the moon through the heavy curtains to push through the all-encompassing darkness pervading her room. "Lydia?" he asked quietly, reluctant to disturb her slumber if indeed she was sleeping.

"Not tonight, Marcus." It was the tiniest shred of a whisper, emerging from somewhere deep within the cover of shadow, hardly reaching his ears before it was swallowed into the silence.

A strange feeling of foreboding swept over him. She sounded so faint, so distant—as if she were already thousands of miles away from him. Slipping through his fingers, ephemeral as smoke, even while she was within reach. "What troubles you?" he asked softly, moving toward the bed. His hand touched the space where her hip ought to be, but came up empty.

"Nothing," she said, still in that ghostly little voice. "Nothing worth speaking of."

He didn't believe that for a moment. *Something* had happened. "Tell me anyway," he said, sliding across the bed in the direction her voice had come from. He found her there, at the very opposite edge of the bed, curled into a ball and buried beneath the rumpled bedclothes.

"What would be the point?" she asked. "Please, Marcus, just let it alone."

The hopelessness in her voice scored him. He slipped his hand beneath the counterpane, found her shoulder, her arm. The icy chill of her skin even through the fabric of her nightdress was shocking, worrisome.

"Lydia," he said. "Come here." He caught her shoulder in one hand, turning her toward him, and she came like dead weight, as if she lacked the strength to resist, listless and resigned. She ended up resting against him, half-buried beneath her tousled hair, which he scraped carefully out of her face, since she could not be bothered.

What the hell had happened while he had been out with Diana? What was so terrible that she would not speak of it?

She would balk if he pressed her further, and she was in no condition to quarrel this evening, besides. Instead he tucked her head beneath his chin, cradling the back of her head in his hand. "I missed you this evening," he said.

He felt the hitch of her breath, the soft, shuddering exhale. Her hands wedged themselves between them, grabbed for his lapels. "I missed you," she said, in a plaintive, disconsolate little voice. "*I missed you.*"

It should have felt like a victory, but he could take no pleasure in it. He could only hold her close to his chest as she broke down into heart-wrenching sobs, and at last cried herself to sleep.

Chapter Fifteen

M arcus."

The sultry whisper pierced the thick veil of sleep that lay over him still. He was distantly aware of a warm body pressed to his back, the smooth glide of soft skin against his own. Wakefulness remained distant, but the bare leg that wedged itself between his lay against the backdrop of his semi-conscious mind like a sweet dream.

A lock of soft, jasmine-scented hair drifted over his shoulder. Delicate fingertips grazed his chest, blunt nails raking lightly through crisp whorls of hair there. They moved slowly down, in a lazy, meandering path, trickling over muscles that twitched at the brief, tickling sensation, caressing his side, his hip, his—

He was awake. *Instantly.*

Lydia made a soft sound of disappointment as he dislodged her clinging fingers and rolled her to her back. In the soft, wintery glow of the morning light, she seemed much improved from last evening. Perhaps there was a tiny, lingering puffiness about her eyes. He swiped his thumb across her cheek, but it came away clean, without having encountered the gritty, salty tear-tracks he might have expected.

She shook her face free of his clasp, shooting him an aggravated little glance. A silent warning that she would not be entertaining any of his ill-advised inquiries. She had made her own plans for the morning, which she made obvious with the tangle of her fingers in his disheveled hair, the bold thrust of her tongue into his mouth.

Her body moved in a sinuous arch, all lithe sensuality as she cradled him there in the lee of her thighs, pressed her breasts against his chest. "For God's sake, Marcus," she chided, half earthy carnality, half exasperation, "don't ruin the moment."

He might've laughed, if she had not chosen that moment to shove at his shoulder and pitch him to his back instead, not content to be restrained beneath him. The frosty dawn played over her smooth skin in shots of silver, but there was nothing of ice in the hands she laid upon his chest as she eased herself over his hips.

She had ridden him before, but never with quite so much ferocity. A wild woman, untamed, she used the whole of her body to stroke the whole of his, her smooth skin sliding over him like warm velvet. Had he not tensed his thighs and bitten the inside of his cheek, he might've spilled himself against the soft flesh of her stomach.

She knew it, the witch. It lurked in the sly smile that tilted the very corners of her lips. He could taste the satisfaction on her tongue when she framed his head in her hands and kissed him. But she didn't linger longer than a moment—a taste, and nothing more.

Instead she endeavored to drive him out of his head, balancing herself with her hands upon his chest as she worked herself over him, the lush heat of her sex drenching his cock. Her straightened arms bracketed her breasts, pushing those lovely, coral-tipped globes together, and for a moment he merely enjoyed the glorious display of them, like a work of art meant for his eyes alone.

"Good God." His voice sounded guttural and raspy at once, dying in his throat before it could reach his lips, awed and worshipful. Like a mortal man who had been, however briefly, permitted to gaze upon a goddess. She moved like sin personified, tossing her head back as she drew nearer to her peak, the sunlight playing through the blond silk of her hair as it trickled down her back, teasing his thighs.

He'd never seen anything more beautiful in his life. Probably he never would again.

Her color was high, a flush pinking her cheeks, and as at last she lifted one hand to curl her small fingers around his cock, she made a small sound of approval, a cheeky smile sliding across her face. One stroke of her palm, another—smooth and slick, using the nectar in which she had laved him to torture him.

He gritted his teeth, his hands clenching on her hips. "Lydia. Now. Take me inside you *now*." Or she would wring his seed from him with nothing more than the stroke of her hand.

A teasing flutter of her lashes, shading vivid green eyes full of mischief and cunning. "Mm. You can bear a little more," she said lightly.

He *really* could not. "Dear God, Lydia, *please*."

She hummed her delight, gave him another vicious stroke that made his breath back up into his lungs. "And what will you do if I do not?" She tilted her chin up in haughty superiority. Here and now she reveled in her power, and it had gone to her head, rich and heady. She tortured him for the sheer pleasure of it, merciless woman that she was.

"I will make you scream," he promised, and he had to force the words out of lungs that wanted only to deflate. "I swear I will make you scream so loudly that you won't be able to look a single person in this household in the face for a month."

That passion-flush ripened, spreading down her throat, her breasts. She bent her elbow, leaned down, and touched her nose to his. "Do it, then," she challenged.

Every muscle strained in an agony of pleasure, but he wrapped his fist into her hair and turned the both of them, throwing her to her back once more. Sank into her body; a hard, unyielding plunge.

She would have screamed, if he hadn't swallowed it down with the crush of his lips to hers. The smothered sound trickled down his throat like warm honey, and deep within her, her inner muscles clenched around him in the rhythmic flutters of instant climax.

He couldn't have restrained himself if he had tried. She had stripped away every tiny filament of moderation, of civility. His teeth grazed her neck where he had once left his mark and would again; he pounded between her thighs like a madman, half-crazed with lust.

And she welcomed his intemperance with soft arms draped around his neck, soft lips pressed to his chin, his cheek. Perhaps a half-dozen thrusts he'd managed, and then he shoved himself so deep that she shuddered with it, and poured himself into her, shaking through a climax so intense that his vision briefly went white.

It seemed a long while later that he remembered himself, easing to the side to spare her the bulk of his weight. She had gone lax and pliant, whatever lunacy that had held her in its grip vanquished to sweet, quiescent softness. In this moment of utter vulnerability, there was no artifice to her at all, and she looked—

Tired. A little sad. As he touched her cheek and traced the pale shadows beneath her eyes, he wondered if she had slept at all last night except in fits and starts. How early she had risen before him to swab the remnants of tears from her cheeks before he could feel the evidence of them in the cold light of dawn.

"Don't, Marcus." A gentle scolding, smoothly spoken, but with a distinct warning to it. Still waters masking a dangerous current beneath their surface.

He suppressed a sigh and settled in behind her as she turned onto her side, tossing his arm about her waist. "Sleep a little longer," he said, into the silky strands of her hair that splayed across the pillow. She needed it. Perhaps they both did.

The low scrape of wood against wood pulled him from slumber once more, and he scrubbed at his face in confusion, turning his head to gauge how far the day had advanced. Impossible to say with the sun hidden behind a thick cover of clouds, but by the faint pangs of hunger at his stomach, he suspected they'd missed breakfast.

The space beside him where Lydia ought to have been had gone cold, and Marcus shook off the last dregs of sleep, stretched out his arms in search of her, stretched out his legs—

His foot touched something hard just there at the foot of the bed. Something that had made an odd, hollow thump as he had connected with it.

"Do be careful," Lydia said softly. "I have only the one valise."

Valise? Marcus shoved himself up onto his elbows, swiping at his face. That strange sound he had heard—it had been the opening of her drawers. Lydia had dressed already, in a gown of frigid blue, complete with soft kidskin gloves. Her hair had been pinned atop her head in perfect blond ringlets. As he watched, she carefully selected a few pairs of stockings, folded them in clean, even lines, and turned to tuck them within the valise.

"Lydia." It had come out hoarse; a plea. "What is going on?"

Not even an eyelash twitched, as if she had smothered herself so deeply beneath that veneer of tranquility that even an earthquake could not have shaken her from it. "I would think it is quite clear, Marcus."

It wasn't. It *wasn't*. Hadn't he pleased her? Hadn't he held up his end of their bargain? He curled his hand into the softness of the counterpane, wringing it in his fingers. "You can't mean to *leave*."

"I have always meant to leave. I told you I would." How could she sound so calm, so collected? "Did I not say as much?" She retrieved a shift, folding it into a neat square, and it, too, vanished into the valise.

"Not yet. There's time, still." Time to sway her resolve. Time to convince her to leave behind the theatre. He had only needed more *time*.

"A *day*, Marcus." Her cheeks hollowed as she pursed her lips. "What difference would a day make? Honestly." The heels of her walking boots clicked upon the floor as she disappeared briefly into the dressing room and returned a moment later with a small armful of gowns and a pelisse.

"How can you leave like this? When just hours ago, you were—" Wild in his arms. Uninhibited, adoring. "What the hell do you *call* that, Lydia?"

"I call it goodbye," she said. "One last hurrah before the final curtain closes. Let's not pretend that this was ever going to be anything but what it was."

What it *was*. She had already tucked him away into the past, folded up as neatly as the clothing she had carefully selected and hidden out of sight within her valise. "Lydia, I want you to stay."

She paused as she dropped a gown into the valise, but that remote expression never wavered. "As what, Marcus?" she asked, so very softly. "I've told you I will not be your mistress. What, then, are you proposing?"

He could not help but think that the choice of words had been deliberate, a poke to his pride. "Lydia—"

"It's quite a simple question, Marcus. It merits an answer."

"Is that what would make you stay?" he asked, and he heard the hard surge of anger, of resentment threaded through his voice. "It's not *enough* to have been forgiven for the past. You must always have *more*."

Her eyes closed. Her head bowed, like a lily bending toward the earth. "Yes," she admitted. "Yes, I must have more. I must have your love. Your trust. I could never accept anything less than that."

"You *know* why I cannot give you that." Why he *would* not.

"I do," she acknowledged, and a tiny, cold laugh wrenched itself from her lungs. "I do," she repeated. "But *you* don't, Marcus. Not really." Another gown, tossed haphazardly within the valise, as if she had lost patience with the process. "Do you know, I think I could have forgiven you," she said, and the words sounded empty, devoid of emotion. "I could have forgiven you the past. I could have wiped the slate clean between us and started afresh."

"How generous of you."

She did not flinch to the sound of the sneer in his voice, but she turned her face to his at last, and he saw the glitter of tears there in the brightness of her eyes. "You will never know how generous. For your own sake—" Her voice faltered, breaking across the syllables with a sort of quiet anguish. "For your own sake, I hope you never learn."

With both hands she closed the valise and latched it, caught up the handle and turned to go. Without another word, she quit the room, his home, his life. There was only the soft, even sound of her footsteps down the hall, the stairs, until eventually they faded altogether.

He hadn't even merited a farewell.

It shouldn't have hurt as much as it had. They had both known that the end was drawing near, and she—she had known the inevitable result. Their roles had been assigned to them so many years ago. There had never been any hope of rewriting the script.

And still Lydia had humbled herself to offer him that opportunity. Still she had not taken to heart the lessons of the past.

This time, she had broken her own heart.

She hoped she had managed to carve off even the tiniest slice of his in the process. Like a token she could keep in her pocket. It would have been fair, she thought. A sliver of justice in a cruel world.

At last, the carriage arrived at the theatre; a journey that had taken longer than it ought to have, owing to the iciness of the streets. She had had to suffer a torturously long trip amidst upholstery that smelled like him, as if it had soaked in the heady scent of his soap. But it was the *last* journey—the very last one.

The coachman handed her down, and Lydia sucked in a deep breath of the cold winter air, clenching the handle of her valise in one hand. Done, then. *Finally* done. Not as clean an ending as she would have preferred. But they had always been meant to be a tragedy.

Tomorrow afternoon the company would move along to Brighton, and she—she would never return to London. There was nothing here for her any longer.

Only a few actors had arrived thus far, and she wended her way through them as she walked the halls, heading for the office that Giles had commandeered in the very back of the theatre.

He was bent over his desk as she strolled in, but he glanced up briefly. "Good," he said, absently. "For once you are early."

"Yes," she said. "I'm very sorry. I won't be late again in the future."

Something in her voice must have piqued his interest. He glanced up once more, but his gaze settled on her with the weight of a blow, seizing first on her face, and then at last sliding down to land upon the valise held in her hand.

"Ah, hell," he sighed, and rose to his feet, his face scrawled over with sympathy as he strode for her. "You're Hermione all over again, aren't you?"

Lydia smothered a wrenching sob in one hand, her shoulders shaking with the force of it.

"Damn Newhaven," Giles said, as he pulled her head to his shoulder. "You'll show him, then, do you hear me? If he wants to play Leontes, he can damned well suffer for it. You will *make* him suffer, Lydia."

"It's over," she whimpered into the collar of his shirt. "He won't come."

"Oh, he'll come," Giles replied darkly. "I promise you he will."

"Marcus, what the hell are you doing?"

Marcus pressed his fingers to his eyes with a low groan of annoyance. "Getting drunk," he said, lifting his glass in a mocking salute. "What does it look like?" He heaved a sigh as Rafe dropped into the chair across from him. "I told my staff I was to be left alone."

"Yes, well, just occasionally your judgment is not what anyone would call ideal," Rafe replied. "I called for you last evening," he said. "I left a damned note!"

Right. So he had. Marcus had let it slip his mind completely. "I was out with Diana," he said, rubbing his jaw. "I truly am in no mood presently, Rafe. Can it not wait?"

"No," Rafe said. "It truly cannot. Where is Lydia? Can you call her down?"

Marcus let his head fall back, a hoarse laugh rumbling in his chest. "She's already been down," he said. "Off to the theatre, I expect." A sip of brandy wasn't enough, couldn't have burned away the lingering hurt in his chest. He cast back the remainder of his glass.

Rafe made a rough sound in his throat. "It's still early," he said. "We could catch her before she must be on stage."

"What would be the point? She's left me already." His shoulders lifted and fell in a shrug too jerky, too unnatural, to evoke the carelessness he'd intended.

"Marcus. Tell me you didn't do anything foolish." Rafe's fingers tightened upon the arms of his chair.

"Of course not," Marcus said. "*She* was the foolish one, to ask for things she knows well enough I cannot give her. She *knows* why I will not marry her."

"*Christ.*" Rafe swept one hand across his mouth. "I do not envy you the amends you shall have to make, Marcus. You need to go to her. Now." He rose to his feet, shouting for Bayberry to ready the carriage.

"For God's sake," Marcus said, slouching in his chair, shading his eyes with his hand. "Just leave me be, Rafe. Is it too much to ask for one bloody moment of peace?"

"You haven't found that in five years, Marcus, and I'm sick and tired of watching you rot. I won't watch you waste away for the next five, especially when—"

Marcus waved his hand in apathetic encouragement. Acidly he said, "No, *do* go on, then. If I cannot be rid of you, you might as well."

"When it's not merited in the least," Rafe concluded, in a succession of sharp and biting syllables. "She never betrayed you, Marcus."

A pure and perfect anger wrenched Marcus upright. "If you had seen what I had—"

"What you *thought* you had," Rafe corrected. "I've had my suspicions. At first it was nothing that could not be disregarded or explained away. There's myriad reasons why a woman in her position might choose not to take a protector. I wasn't in England at the time, so it was necessary to pry information from beneath whichever rock it might have lurked."

A tiny pit of anguish formed somewhere deep in Marcus' gut. "You're basing your opinion on gossip and hearsay," he said.

"Give me more credit than that," Rafe snapped. "I had suspicions only, as I said. She had told Diana that she had not betrayed you," he said. "So I thought—if I treated her claims as if they were true, then there would have to be an interloper somewhere. Someone who had interfered in your relationship with her, for the purpose of separating you."

That pit swelled into a yawning chasm. "Who, then?" he inquired icily.

Rafe issued a low, cynical laugh. "Can you truly think of no one?" he asked. "My God, one breakfast, and I had found the answer. Father would *never* have permitted you to marry her. He knew you had planned to, and he put an end to—what did he call it? Finagling her way into the family?"

138

"But he couldn't have stopped me." Marcus closed his eyes, touched his fingers to his temple to rub away the ache that had settled there.

"No?" Rafe bit off caustically. "But he *did*." His fingers curled into loose fists at his sides. "I followed him last evening, Marcus. To the theatre. To *Lydia*. He had gone to gloat of it. I heard it all, every awful word he spoke to her."

"*No*." The word wrenched itself from his lungs, a fervent, desperate denial. "No—she would have told me." But she hadn't. *Let it alone, Marcus.*

"Would you have believed her?" Rafe inquired. "Father didn't seem to think so. He *taunted* her with it, Marcus. How simple a thing it had been to accomplish. How easily he would separate you again. How you would never believe her, even if she told you the truth of it."

Marcus dropped his head into his hands, raking his fingers through his hair as if he would carve grooves into his skull. That agony in his chest burned anew. And once he had thought Lydia had given it to him, but no— she had been blameless. Blameless, while he had heaped scorn upon her shoulders. A wretched, ugly sound burst from him, and it sounded like the culmination of five years of misery.

"Marcus," Rafe insisted tightly. "*Would* you have believed her?"

"No," he rasped, and his heart squeezed in his chest. And that was why she had left him. Because he had withheld from her his trust, his love, and she would have needed both of them if their relationship were to survive the Sword of Damocles his father had hung above it. It might have dropped at any moment, and she—she would have found herself cast to the winds again.

But she had humbled herself enough to ask those things of him nonetheless, though he had not deserved even that much of her consideration. Though she must have known what his answer would be even as she had asked. She had been packing even before he had awoken; certain of a foregone conclusion. And she had been *correct*.

"I wouldn't have believed her," he said, and it carried the same hopelessness within it as had Lydia's voice last evening. Years of loneliness he'd suffered, and for no reason at all. Father had only given him the rope. He had strung himself up with it. "I should *always* have believed her."

Instead he had mocked the absolution she had offered for sins he had not known he'd committed. Scorned the generosity she would have extended to him. Forgiveness, when he had done nothing at all to earn it of her.

You have no idea how generous. For your own sake, I hope you never learn.

But he *had* learned it at last. Too late? No—fate would not be so cruel a

139

second time. He surged to his feet, his chest heaving with a wild, terrible fear. "She leaves tomorrow," he said raggedly. "She's going—somewhere south, I think. Brighton."

"That leaves tonight, then," Rafe said. "*Go*, Marcus. Or you will miss her."

Miss her? The phrase bounced around his head as he turned for the door. He had missed her for years already. He would never let her slip through his fingers again.

Chapter Sixteen

Luck, or fate, or some vengeful god had turned against him. The icy streets had turned hazardous, and the jumble of carriages struggling to traverse them had created a blockage that slowed his travel considerably. By the time he at last arrived at the theatre, it was too late to slip back behind the stage, where the actors congregated.

Instead he had had to take himself off to his box, where he would watch the play unfold once more. Then, as the curtain pulled, there she was—Lydia; Hermione. She was both at once, and he slammed his eyes closed against the sight of her.

No. He had made this bed for himself, and he would bear the shame that she gave back to him, for she had never earned it in the least to begin with. Now he saw himself in Leontes' creeping suspicion, in his self-righteous condemnation. He watched himself accuse her; watched her plead her innocence. Watched himself discard her, and wished he could reach into the past and shake sense into himself.

But it had all happened already, and he could only sit—silent, arrested—and watch himself name her faithless, shameless, and worse. Now he could see truly what Montgomery had meant: she *had* never acted Hermione. It was all real for her; a nightmare she had suffered through years ago and from which she had never truly awoken. And now it was to become his own.

Lydia poured her grief out upon the stage in her sackcloth and ashes, a perfect picture of debased innocence—and they wept for her, the faceless crowd below. *Marcus* wept for her, though he hadn't the right to do it. But she had agonized, and implored, and died upon the stage dozens of times before, retracing the path he had carved out for her each time. Each performance, he had killed her himself.

Only now, watching himself savage her honor, demean her and humiliate her, could he understand the rage she had carried with her onto the stage when she had acted Paulina. Only now could he understand how little Leontes deserved the happy ending he would, after all was said and done, receive.

141

Just as Hermione had done, Lydia had extended to him an unimaginable grace. And it had come to naught, because he had closed his eyes and his ears to every lesson he might have learned from these performances she had given. Every iteration, every role, had told a crucial truth he had denied.

His hands lay heavily in his lap, as if the weight of the crown that Montgomery had once given him sat upon them, and as the final curtain closed at last, he wondered if the burden of it would ever be lifted.

"Let me pass," Marcus growled at the man who guarded the door; a hulking behemoth whose shoulders nearly touched the sides of the doorway in which he stood.

"Cain't," the man snorted. "None pass tonight, not for any reason. Mr. Montgomery's orders. Gotta clear out the sets, y'see." He lifted one burly shoulder in a shrug. "Some o' your lot like to take a souvenir or two."

A regrettably-familiar blond hear poked around a corner behind the man. "Ho, Leontes!" There was a smirk within the words, and another scrawled across Montgomery's face as he approached. "How fits your crown? Rather too well, I expect." Montgomery slapped the guard on the shoulder, and the man dutifully shuffled to the side to allow Montgomery to slip into his place.

Marcus fought to unclench his jaw. "Lydia. I need to speak with her."

"Mm. I think not." Montgomery folded his arms across his chest, lifting his chin. "You had every chance in the world, my lord. If you squandered your good fortune, then that is only your own fault." Those keen, assessing eyes sharpened. "Did you see yourself in the theatre this evening, by chance? I had hoped you would."

"Please." There was a terror that burned behind his ribs which would go unrelieved until he had seen her. And yet he was only too aware of his impotence—dependent upon the mercy of a man who had no particular liking for him. "Please. I need to see her."

"You need not worry for her, my lord. She'll recover. She has before."

"Five minutes," Marcus said. "Only that."

"If you had five *years*, you could not offer her the words she deserves from you," Montgomery said snidely.

Desperation tore deep furrows through Marcus' chest. "But where will she stay? She hasn't got anywhere to go. At least send her home this evening—"

Montgomery issued a mocking laugh. "And have her suffer your company? I think not. Don't concern yourself, my lord, she's perfectly safe. I have her back in my office. She'll sleep upon the couch tonight—a preferable bed, I think, to the one you would have given her." His voice fell to a vindictive hiss. "You would have made a mistress of a good and honorable lady, who should have been your *wife*."

"She *will* be." If he could only reach her.

"If you think that, then Leontes ill fits you—you're *too* mad for the role," Montgomery said on an aggrieved sigh. "I'm grateful to you, after a fashion, my lord. I'd hate to lose her. She's been a credit to my company, for all that her heart's not in it."

Marcus nearly stumbled back a step. "How can you say such a thing? Her heart was in every word." Every breath. Every step.

Montgomery shook his head in disappointment. "No, my lord. For all that she plays her parts well enough, she will never be great. She can never inhabit a role; she can only bare the pieces of herself. And you—you made her Hermione, my lord. You turned her into the tragedy you saw tonight."

Marcus' breath hitched in his chest, like a fist had closed round his lungs and squeezed the air from them.

Montgomery sneered into his face. "What you saw on stage this evening wasn't her *heart*, my lord. It was her bloody *soul*."

"I told you he would come."

Lydia turned her face into the rough upholstery of the couch. "I hadn't noticed."

"Liar," Giles accused gently. "You had to have seen him."

"It doesn't matter." She pillowed her head upon one arm and burrowed deeper into the blanket that she had wrapped around her.

"He came to the door," Giles said. "Asked for you. I sent him away."

"Thank you."

There was the squeak of the chair as he sat behind the desk. "You could probably catch him, if you wanted."

"I don't."

"I'm not certain I believe you," Giles said, and his fingertips tapped out a maddening rhythm upon the worn surface of the desk. "You were brilliant this evening, by the way."

She hadn't felt brilliant. She'd felt overburdened. As if it had stripped something from her soul to do it, ripped away some intrinsic part of her. "I don't want to play Hermione again," she whispered. She didn't want to *be* Hermione again. Ever.

"Oh?" Giles half-turned, the chair's legs squeaking beneath him. "Perhaps something more comedic next time."

It would be a lovely change, she imagined. She'd had enough of tragedy to last a lifetime. Though *The Winter's Tale* was classified as a comedy, Lydia had often wondered *why*. No one seemed to care much for the consequences of Leontes' faithlessness. Sixteen years of strife were glossed over between acts—deaths and grief and struggle ignored by a thoughtless pen, banishing years of it as if it had not been worth mentioning. The tonal shift from trage-dy to farce had always perplexed her.

And while innocents had suffered for it all, Leontes had blundered into a happy ending he did not deserve. The injustice of it scored her.

"He looked like Leontes this evening," Giles mused. "Really, I ought to have committed that expression to memory. The desperation was *delicious*. It seems only fair that I should have something of him, when he has shaken the foundations of my company."

"Kitty never wanted to play Hermione," Lydia said. "She was happy to be Paulina." It wasn't so much a disturbance, anyway. Most of their actors could perform multiple roles; a necessity when even something as common as a cold could cripple a production had there not been someone to take up a part.

"Yes, but—" Giles sighed, and she heard the sound of his fingers raking through his hair. "I never wanted you to be Hermione again," he admitted. "I know what it costs you."

He didn't, really. He *couldn't*. No one could. "It doesn't matter. I won't be her any longer."

"If it's any consolation," Giles said. "Your revenge? I believe you've won it beautifully. It hurt him, Lydia, to see you this evening. The man *cried*."

She felt her brows draw down into a frown. "He didn't."

"Like a babe. I'm surprised you didn't mark it." There was the *plunk* of his boots hitting the desk, the strain of the chair as he leaned himself back. "Tongues will wag tomorrow, you'll see. You should feel proud."

In truth, she felt nothing at all. She'd spent every bit of herself upon the stage, and there was nothing left of her but a bone-deep exhaustion. "What tomorrow brings to London is no concern of mine. We're for Brighton."

"Yes," Giles said. "I wonder."

"Be a dear and keep your wonderings to yourself."

Giles laughed. "You ask the impossible," he said. "But Newhaven has got a whole morning before we must leave. I wonder what he will do with it."

"*That* is no concern of mine, either," she said.

"Do you know, I'm not certain that Newhaven would agree," Giles said as he stood once more and snuffed out the candle that had been left burning upon the desk. "Get some sleep, Lydia. I have a feeling you shall need it." The hinges of the door creaked as he pulled it open. "I sincerely doubt we've seen the last of Newhaven."

Marcus did not sleep. Instead he spent a cold, unpleasant evening in Lydia's room, clutching Leontes' crown in his hand, surrounded by everything she had left behind. And there was so much of it—she had had to limit herself to what could fit in her valise, and there were bits of her strewn everywhere, as if she had stepped out for only a moment.

A discarded nightdress, hung around the bedpost. A pelisse she had left upon the chair. A vial of jasmine-scented perfume. Her dressing room was stuffed to the gills with gowns and bordered by a little row of boots and slippers. A single stocking hung half out of one drawer, and a fur-lined muff rested atop the dresser.

His mind kept drifting back to that last brutal conversation. Replaying it over and over again, as if he might somehow change the outcome. Turning things over in his head, absent the lens of anger, of betrayal, through which he had seen for so long.

How cruel it was that certain crucial things could be understood only in retrospect. How unfair that he had been so blind to the strings by which he had been pulled until they had been snipped free of his limbs at last. And Lydia—

Lydia had never been blind. She might not have known from which direction had come the perfidy visited upon her, but she had always been blameless of every terrible accusation he had slung at her. He had driven her from the home they had shared twice over. He had driven her from *London*.

When she might have been here beside him, if only he had trusted in her. If only he had honored what he had *known* of her to be true. *His* faithlessness, not hers, had cost him everything that he had ever held dear, every ounce of happiness he had ever held within the palm of it hand.

The ghostly image of her head, bowed in resignation, burned behind his eyes with every blink. If only he had swallowed his pride, admitted that he loved her still, perhaps he *could* have won her back. Instead he had expected her to swallow down her own pride as if it had no value, as if her desires ought always to come secondary to his own. To accept so much less than she was worth, and to be grateful for it besides.

What weapons had she had against such cruelty? All of the power would have been his. Only a fool would have thrown herself upon his dubious mercy. She had been *right* to go, *wise* to turn her back on a man who had offered her nothing but a dishonorable position in society; a mistress, when she should have been a wife.

Every move he had made had been the wrong one, every moment he had antagonized her had been another mark against him, another stain upon his soul. He hadn't protected her against the malice that had been directed toward her. He had inflicted the largest portion of it himself.

He had sworn to *own* her, when she had always owned *him*.

How did one make amends for so many wrongs? How was he meant to atone? Probably she had experienced things he could not even conceive of, and even if he had not directly caused them, still the blame for them could be laid at his door. Five years of struggle, which she would never have suffered if not for him.

The past haunted him with its unknowable tortures; the magnitude of his sins weighing more heavily than the crown in his hand. He *ached* with it, as if that knowledge had settled into his bones, burning in his very marrow. An intrinsic part of him, inseparable now.

With one hand he shoved himself upright, planted his boots upon the floor, and stalked toward the cheval glass in the corner. The mirror taunted him with the shadows beneath his eyes, his haggard appearance, as if he had aged a decade in hours.

He lifted it above his head, that crown he had earned, and in a corona-

146

tion he had not wanted, he set it upon his head.

It fit. Perfectly. As if it had been fashioned only for him to wear. Because he had always been Leontes.

Chapter Seventeen

In just a few hours, Lydia would leave London for the last time. She wasn't sad, exactly, to go—there was nothing left for her here now—but she had decided on a clean break. That off-handed comment that Marcus had made of visiting her family had stewed in her brain for too many days, and now— now she knew she would never have another opportunity. It would be best, she thought, to sever those last remaining threads that kept her, however weakly, tethered to London. To say a *proper* goodbye; the one she should have got years ago, and then to leave and begin again as she meant to go on. And if that door *was* slammed in her face, well, then, what was one more slice of heartbreak when piled atop the rest?

The butcher's shop was all but deserted when she arrived, but then it was still quite early in the day. She had used what little money she had saved to pay the fare required for a hack to conduct her here, but when she had arrived, she had hesitated, too full of indecision to do anything more than stay out of sight of the windows.

Papa was likely in the back of the shop already, preparing cuts of meat. Mama would no doubt be bustling about in the front, cleaning or organizing, or some such busy work meant to make the shop run smoother. It looked— different than she had remembered. The sign had faded from its once vibrant hues. Probably sun and time had weathered it, and the smoke generated from coal fires did tend to stick to such things.

The whole street looked more weathered and ragged than she recalled, in fact. Lavinia had, in her infrequent letters, complained that rising rents had forced out shopkeepers that had been here for decades, that the shop scarcely brought in more than it took to run. That her silk mill job supplemented their meager income only just.

Gathering her courage, Lydia peeked in the nearest window, and, oh— there was Mama, her back turned as she swabbed something behind a counter with a damp rag. Her hair had gone greyer than Lydia remembered, bound into a bun that was not quite so neat as it once had been. The dress she wore had once been blue, but the color had faded. Weathered, just like everything else.

Had the money she'd sent even made a dent in their situation? In profile now, Mama's face had acquired new lines, new grooves of worry and strain.

Somewhere in the distance, a bell tolled the hour, and Lydia jerked at the sound. She had so little time, after all, and it would march on without her. Soon enough she would have to be back to Giles, and off to Brighton. Her coin would be wasted on the fare for a hack if she did nothing.

Mustering up her resolve, she firmed her shoulders and pushed open the door—and hesitated, uncertain of her welcome.

"One moment," Mama said, her back turned still, her voice a good deal less steady that Lydia recalled.

"Hello, Mama," Lydia said, and Mama jerked, the cloth flailing with her as she swiveled so abruptly that she nearly lost her balance. Her eyes rounded as her mouth fell open, and she gave a long, shuddering gasp.

"Lydia!" she cried, and pressed the hand that held the cloth to her chest, resulting in a wet splotch staining the front of her gown. Her voice lifted still further. "Oh, Edwin! It's Lydia!" And then she was dashing out from behind the counter, and Lydia found herself enfolded into a ferocious embrace, nearly wrenching the air from her lungs.

Shock held her still as a statue. And then Papa emerged from the back of the shop, fumbling with the strings of the apron he'd tied about his waist. He let it fall to the floor unheeded, and his blue eyes glistened with unshed tears.

He squeezed her cheeks in his hands. "My girl. My darling girl."

The sob that erupted from her mouth surprised her. "I came—I only came to tell you—you needn't worry. I've done with London. I won't be returning again." The carefully-rehearsed speech she had composed in the hack came out in bits and pieces, as if it had gotten smudged along the way and had become largely unreadable. "I came to say goodbye."

"Oh, *don't*," Mama pleaded, stroking her hair. "Don't say goodbye. I was so wrong. I let my pride control my head. I wished so many times that I could take it all back—"

"We may not have agreed with your choices, but they were yours to make," Papa said, pressing his forehead to hers. "I wish we had told you instead that you could always come home. You *can* always come home, Lydia."

"Oh," she said, sniffling. "I've made so many wretched choices."

"So have we," Papa said. "So have we." And he pinched her cheek just as he had done so many times when she had been a very small child.

"We came to see you," Mama said, in a faltering voice, as she swabbed at her eyes. "Of course, we could only afford the price of admittance after the third act, but you—you were wonderful. I was so proud."

High praise, considering actresses were not well thought of. She hadn't even known that they were aware of the direction her career had taken. "I wish I had known," she said. "I wish you had stayed to talk to me."

"We thought you would not want to see us," Papa said. "Our last meeting was…not ideal."

No, it hadn't been. There had been so many angry words, so much hurt pride shared between them. She had not been innocent in it herself. Lydia swabbed at her face with the sleeve of her pelisse. "I suppose we have all said things we might have cause to regret."

"Yes, but you were so young. It was our responsibility to guide you, and to protect you, and not to let petty resentments deepen into such chasms. Five years is too long to go without seeing a beloved daughter." Another embrace, a tight squeeze with only the tiniest bit less desperation. "You don't have to leave. You never have to leave."

Lydia managed half a laugh. "I do," she said. "I'm sorry. I do—the company is expected in Brighton. I only came—"

"Then don't say goodbye," Papa implored, squeezing her just as tightly. "Write. *Visit*. You'll be welcome."

"I can't." Lydia blinked back the tears that threatened anew. "I can't. I've made enemies, Papa. Powerful ones. There is nothing for me in London any longer." She had no idea exactly how deep Marcus' father's antipathy ran. Whether it would spread to her family if she allowed it. There was no hope of her defeating so influential a foe.

Marcus would never have believed her, anyway. Even if her performance had, by some strange happenstance, moved him, she would always be suspect in his mind.

"That damned baron," Papa snarled, his face flushing. "I ought to have—"

"Edwin, remember your poor heart," Mama chided, laying one hand upon his chest. "Think of the expense if we must call for a doctor."

Lydia's own heart wrenched. "I'm afraid I've sent you all the money I can spare at the moment," she said. "But I'll send you every bit I can. I swear it."

"You've done enough." Papa squeezed her shoulder. "More than we would ever have expected."

150

"Eighty pounds," Mama whispered, and Lydia found a sliver of relief that Marcus had at least proved honorable in that regard. "It was enough to pay back the worst of the rent we had outstanding. And business will improve closer to the holidays, surely. At least enough to tuck something away for a rainy day." But the slight tremble of her voice suggested that this was more hope—a foolish fancy—than reason.

Papa gave a little huff of annoyance. "Mary, this is London. They're *all* rainy."

Despite herself, Lydia found a shred of genuine laughter somewhere inside her. "I know what is said of women in the theatre, but the money—it didn't come from *that*." Other things had, in a roundabout fashion, but they didn't need to know the provenance of her gown, her stockings. "It did come from his lordship, in a way, but it wasn't…payment for services rendered." And then, as Mama and Papa exchanged baffled glances, she added, "It's a rather long story."

Mama curled her fingers around Lydia's. "Then stay for tea, and tell it. We'll close down the shop for an hour."

"Oh, but—" Lydia hesitated, wavering. "I'm expected back at the theatre."

"Just one cup. Surely your employer could not begrudge you something so small?"

Giles would begrudge her every second late she returned, and if she was very lucky, he would not dock her wages for it. "One cup," she said. One cup—because it would likely be the last time she would ever see them. Even Giles could not be so heartless as to penalize her for that.

Marcus knew he must look like death or something very like it. He had not slept; he had not shaved. He had not bothered to take a bath, nor even had he troubled himself with changing his clothes, and so he arrived at his parents' townhouse in the very same—dreadfully wrinkled—clothing which he had donned yesterday.

Breakfast had always been a miserable affair. He had grown accustomed to those tiny miseries he had let his father inflict upon him, upon Rafe and Diana and Mother. There was a point at which one stopped hoping for different, because it would have been as futile an act as attempt to catch a breeze in the clasp of one's hand.

Father had, in one fashion or another, crushed the hope out of *all* of them. Marcus suspected he delighted in the doing of it, in delivering cruelty for cruelty's sake. So of course *every* breakfast had been horrible—but this one? This one he was going to *enjoy.*

The heels of his boots snapped out rapid, sharp clicks that seemed to set every servant he passed on edge, and they scurried out of his way lest he barrel them down on his passage to the dining room.

Father did not even glance up as he appeared in the room. "Marcus, don't loom. It's unbecoming."

It wasn't; Father simply did not like anyone else to perceive themselves as more powerful than he. He had always had to cut them down to size—or at least the size he thought they ought to be. Which was so small as to be insignificant. A mere insect in the presence of a king.

Marcus snarled, "*Stand up.*"

"Don't be ridiculous," Father said, snapping the pages of his paper.

"Stand up," Marcus repeated. "I should hate to knock you out of your chair when I strike you. It might cause something of a mess."

"*Strike* me?" Father echoed on a chortle. "You always did have a flair for dramatics. Got that from your mother, I'd wager." The contempt in his voice scored Marcus to the soles of his feet. And Father—Father idly turned pages, utterly secure in his conviction that he had cowed his son. That he had *won.*

Marcus could see them so clearly now, the strings that Father had woven around him. Connecting muscle and joint and bone, he had only to twitch his fingers, and the whole world moved at his command. Mother became deathly silent, as if she were only a doll perched upon her chair. Diana stilled, curling in on herself as if it would spare her Father's notice. And Marcus—

Marcus stomped to the head of the table, curled his fingers into the perfectly-starched linen of Father's cravat, hauled him bodily out of his seat, and planted his fist squarely in Father's shocked face. A vicious strike, followed by a satisfying *crunch* of bone.

Mother screamed. Diana fumbled for the reticule on her lap and fished out the silver-rimmed spectacles within, setting them on her nose and blinking behind them, utterly fascinated.

Father slumped to the floor—or at least as much as Marcus' hand, still clenching a fistful of cravat would allow. He made some gurgling sound in his throat, one hand groping for his face, coming away with a smear of the blood

152

that had begun to drip from the ruin of his nose.

There. *Perfect*. Breakfast had gone from wretched to wonderful in the space of a breath.

"*Marcus*," Mother said, in a frantic warble. "Whatever has come over you?"

Father wrenched at Marcus' grip, and accomplished nothing but to strangle himself with his own cravat. "It must be that *whore*," he wheezed, slanting a glare toward Mother and Diana, who did nothing. Even the footmen had quietly removed themselves from the room. Assistance was coming from nowhere.

Marcus wrenched at Father's cravat, and Father's knees slid along the carpet. The blood that ran down his face had begun to drip onto the rug beneath him, staining the pristine ivory fibers. "Don't you *ever* call her that," Marcus hissed. "Don't speak of her. You haven't even the fucking right to *think* of her."

For an instant, Father's expression of outraged dignity wavered. As if somewhere in the deepest reaches of his mind, the thought had occurred to him, if only for the briefest of moments, that he had, somewhere along the way, made a critical error. Just as quickly, it seemed that his ego papered over that wound. His fingers clawed at Marcus', scoring a gouge upon his wrist. "*Release* me, you ungrateful—"

"For what ought I be grateful, Father?" Marcus hissed. "For your interference in my life? For vilifying the only woman I have ever loved?"

Diana gasped, her hands flying to her mouth. Mother's eyes dropped to her plate, the blood bleaching from her face. So she had *known*, then. She might not have been exactly complicit with Father's schemes—but at the very least she had *known* of them. And she had done nothing, *said* nothing. Too beaten down to find even a shred of her own voice any longer.

At last, Father managed to wrest free the fabric of his cravat, and he fell away onto his back as his chest heaved, his lungs starved for air. "Get out of this house," he said, in a nasally whine. "You know *nothing*—"

"You were *followed*, Father. To the theatre. To *Lydia*."

Father froze, his face going slack. Marcus could almost see the cogs turning in his mind, attempting to uncover a way out of his situation, a new plan of attack which would restore the natural order that Marcus had upset. To claw back the power that had been torn from him. His eyes narrowed, sly, shifty. "I don't know what you think you've heard, but—"

"I think you know exactly what I've heard," Marcus countered, as he placed the toe of his boots upon the fingers of Father's right hand, trapping them beneath the sole. "How did you do it, Father?" And he *pressed*. Just enough pressure to make Father whimper in pain, his mouth twisting with it. "Tell me. *How*?"

For a long moment, Father suffered in silence. His free hand caught Marcus' shoe in a desperate bid to relieve the pressure, though the blood coating his fingers ensured that he could find no true purchase. "All right! All right, damn you," he snarled, and his shoulders shook with a wild, mad laugh as Marcus eased the pressure of his foot fractionally. "It wasn't even *difficult*," he said. "Would that all things were so simple. You thought yourself so discreet," he sneered.

Marcus closed his eyes, his breath stagnating in his lungs. *Everyone knew.* Even Diana had said as much. Had he not closed his eyes and ears to it, he might have noticed years ago.

"You are a creature of habit, Marcus. It was so easy to learn your comings and goings, to choose an opportune moment. There are always enterprising actors looking for a bit of ready cash. I had only to pay one a modest sum for a few minutes of work." He laughed again, the vindictive, gleeful laugh of a man who had gotten precisely what he had wanted.

Until Marcus pressed again, feeling the rub of bones and joints beneath the sole of his boot. "You destroyed me," he said, in a furious, seething growl. "You destroyed *her*."

"I saved you!" Father screamed, his body trembling with rage and pain. "For God's sake, you had purchased a bloody ring and met with the Archbishop! You were going to throw yourself away on that—that *nobody*. She was *nothing*!"

"She is *everything*!" The roar shook the house to its very foundation. "She is everything," he repeated, and suddenly the world seemed to go cold and grey, as if all color had faded from it in an instant. Exhaustion weighed on him like a stone settled upon his shoulders. For all that Father had deserved what he had received here this morning, still it was only small consolation.

Father might have set him up, but *he* had taken the bait. Like a prize fish, he had swallowed that hook and his responsibility was the greater for it.

The moment Marcus lifted his foot, Father crawled away, like a snake on its belly. Only when he was safely distant did he drag himself back onto his feet, steadying himself with his hands planted upon the back of a chair. "Get out of this house," Father repeated. "You're no son of mine."

Marcus shrugged. English laws of primogeniture would say otherwise, and there was nothing at all that Father could do for that. He could be disinherited monetarily, perhaps, but he was not dependent upon his father for funds. For all of Father's threats, he had no teeth with which to apply them. "You may go to the devil, Father," he invited, as he turned upon his heel. "And I—I will go to Brighton."

"Lydia!" The shout split straight through the chaos and clamor of the departing company, through the furor of voices and bodies and baggage shuffling about. "Lydia!"

Oh, lord. Lydia turned away from the direction from whence the shout had come, sliding through the actors and stage hands working to load up their belongings, toward the carriage she would be sharing with several others on the journey to Brighton.

"Well, well," Giles said, as she shouldered past him, his gaze fixed into the distance. "Right again. Newhaven's not done with you yet, I see."

"*I* am done with *him*," Lydia gritted out over her shoulder. Luckily, her tardiness had hardly been marked. Giles had been in a surly mood anyway, owing to some mishap with one of the carriages, which had resulted in a great deal of shouting. It was certainly not the first time they had encountered such difficulties, but Giles had never been a man of great patience.

With any luck, he would expend the worst of his foul mood upon Marcus, and she could find her place in her carriage in peace.

"*Lydia!*"

God save her from the unearned arrogance of *men*. Lydia did not bother to dignify Marcus' untoward caterwauling with a response. She reached the carriage at last, and pulled open the door. A succession of hatboxes and a valise tumbled out, and Lydia leapt back to avoid having her feet crushed beneath them.

"Oi! Watch it!" Kitty scowled at her from her seat, where she had been crammed between two other actors. The opposite seat was piled high with luggage, both personal and professional. She recognized the set of trunks which contained the company's costumes, and another that belonged to Giles. Probably her own valise had been packed elsewhere. In the cart containing the scenery, sets, and props, no doubt.

"Full up," another actor said. "You'll have to find another place."

"But I was promised this one!" Lydia said. "The luggage will have to be moved—"

"Bite your tongue," Kitty said. "Sybil would have your head if she heard you suggest her precious costumes ride without. Just look at the sky"—this, with a delicate flourish of her wrist—"it's going to rain at any moment."

The sky overhead gave an ominous crackle, as if to lend credence to Kitty's words. Lydia chewed the inside of her cheek and struggled to rein in the flare of temper that wanted to burst free. "Where am I meant to ride, then?"

Kitty shrugged. "Wherever you can find the space."

"There *isn't* any."

"Then you ought to have arrived in time to secure your own," Kitty sniffed. "Perhaps you can ride topside, with the coachman."

With the coachman! In *this* weather? She'd be soaked to the skin before they made it out of London. Lydia slammed the door of the carriage closed just as a drop of rain fell upon her forehead.

Never mind making it out of London; she'd be soaked to the skin before she found a place in another carriage. With a scathing little sound of exasperation, she turned—

Straight into Marcus, who grasped her shoulders when she would have retreated. "Lydia," he said, and there was something wild and reckless in his voice. "Thank God. I thought I would have to chase you all the way to Brighton."

"I can't imagine why you would bother." She gave a shrug, but could not shake his tight grip. "My lord, I must insist that you release me at once."

He flinched at the distancing address, at the reserved chilliness of her voice, and his face—already a few shades too pale—whitened still further. "Give me only a few moments of your time," he said, his voice dropping to the low, humble tones of a plea. "I would very much like to explain myself to you."

He asked now for that which he had never allowed her, and the hypocrisy of it all only deepened her offense. She shoved back the rage that bubbled up beneath the veil of her indifference, allowed not even the tiniest bit of it to color her voice. "I haven't got a few minutes, and I would not give them to you even if I had." She wrenched one shoulder free, and this time—this time he let her go, as if he knew that to hold her would only provoke her further.

Marcus held his hands out, a placating gesture. "I know I haven't the right to ask," he said. "I know that I have—blundered so terribly." The words

156

seemed to catch in his throat, scratching at it like knives. "Lydia, I know what my father did."

She should have been shocked, or at the very least *surprised*. But the truth was that it didn't matter any longer what he had learned or how he had learned it. The part of her that might have cared had died yesterday. He had squeezed the very life out of it with the weight of his condescension, his disrespect.

She canted her head to one side speculatively. "And what, precisely, am I meant to say to that?"

"I—" He hesitated, and his hands dropped to his sides, fingers curling. "I don't know what you mean."

"I mean to ask for what reason you have told me this. It doesn't matter any longer."

"How can it not matter? Of course it *matters*." A muscle jumped in his jaw, and he swallowed, hard and heavy. "Given how I behaved yesterday, I know that you must think me arrogant," he said. "Patronizing, perhaps." His dark eyes shied away from meeting her own. "Even cruel."

"I don't *think* you those things. You simply *are* those things. There is a difference between the two, my lord." Lydia made a vague, dismissive gesture with one hand, and felt a few drops of rain fall into her hair as the sky gave another threatening murmur overhead. "If you are quite through, my lord—"

"I'm not."

"If you *aren't*, then," she said, with a roll of her eyes. "I have no time for you, nor any inclination to humor your changeable moods. I have a carriage to catch."

"At this particular moment, no, you haven't," Giles snapped as he strode into view. "The damned thing has broken an axle. I've had no success in sourcing another." He slapped his hat against his thigh, scowling into the sky. "And this weather, besides! Some wretched luck, it is."

"But—but we've an engagement," Lydia said, inanely, at a loss for anything else to say. "How else are we to make our way to Brighton?"

"I haven't the faintest," Giles growled.

"There is no one to make the repair?"

"Not in *this* damned weather, and the cold besides. We certainly can't afford replacement—or even a stage coach." Giles ran his fingers through his hair, tugging the strands in exasperation as he slanted a speaking look at her—a warning, she thought, not to cast before him the fact that she had many times told him that the company required a wealthy patron particularly for such circumstances as these. *I told you so* would accomplish nothing at this juncture. "There is the mail coach," he said, "but we've too much luggage leftover for it."

"Out of the damned question," Marcus snarled.

Lydia thrust out her chin. "This doesn't concern you, my lord."

"It bloody well *does* concern me if you will be traveling by mail coach! For God's sake, even if you haven't missed the route today, I doubt you could secure better than an outside seat. Passengers have frozen to death before!" Marcus threw up his hands in a gesture of agitation.

"I've taken them often enough without incident," Lydia said snidely.

"That knowledge does *not* comfort me." Marcus turned on Giles. "You require a carriage?" he asked, and there was a crafty sort of inflection to his voice, a cold calculation that took Lydia aback.

Giles was no fool; his eyes narrowed in suspicion. "The *company* requires a carriage," he said.

"In good condition," Marcus added. "Comfortable. Capable of traversing the roads in inclement weather."

"No," Lydia said, though no one listened.

"I have got such a carriage," Marcus said. "It could carry four comfortably—up to six, less so."

"No!" Lydia repeated. "Giles—"

Giles silenced her with only a wave of his hand. "What are you asking for the use of it?" he inquired. "And how soon can it be readied?"

"It *is* readied." Marcus jerked his head to indicate a position down the street. "I have only to give the coachman the order. You could be on your way in ten minutes."

"We don't want it," Lydia said, squaring her shoulders. "Giles? *Tell* him."

"We *don't* want it," Giles acknowledged, but the weight in the words made her stomach clench and sink, as if a ball of lead had been dropped into it. "But we damned well *need* it, Lydia." He scrubbed at his forehead with his palm, casting a censorious glance toward the sky when it had the audacity to flick a few stray droplets into his eyes. "We haven't got a choice," he said in a low voice. "It's not personal; it's *business*."

But Marcus would make it personal. She had no doubt at all of that.

"What do you want for it?" Giles asked again, his patience waning.

Marcus hesitated. Long enough to provoke another flutter of anxiety. Long enough for the storm clouds to overtake the sky entirely. Long enough, she thought, to truly drive home the reality of their predicament, and while he hesitated, he stared at *her*. As if he might read something in her face, some proclivity toward mercy, or some hint of love which might be lurking somewhere deep down.

He could look as long as he liked. She would have only a blank impassivity for him.

"I want you to hire me on," he said at last, and Lydia gasped in outrage.

Giles laughed, startled and unwillingly amused. "As what? An actor? A stage hand?"

"If you like. I don't care what."

A moment of silence followed, thick and tense. "My God," Giles said at last. "You're *serious*."

Marcus' jaw clenched. "You want the use of my damned carriage? I come with it. Those are my terms."

"I can't pay you," Giles said. "No, allow me to rephrase: I *won't* pay you."

"I'm not in want of funds." A muscle twitched beneath Marcus' right eye, as if he found the conversation both unnecessary and tedious to endure.

"You'll have all the worst jobs," Giles warned. "Every low thing I can conceive of. Every chore that anyone else would complain of. It will all fall to you."

"Giles, *no*," Lydia hissed.

"You will *work*, from dawn until midnight if necessary," Giles continued. "You will follow orders without complaint or argument. You will leave your title in London, *my lord*, for no one will bother to address you by it. You will be lower in rank even than your coachman."

"Agreed," Marcus said, though he pressed his fingertips to his temples, as if a headache had settled in there. "Whatever your damned conditions, I will agree to them. If we might to the carriage, then?"

"May it be on your head, then," Giles said. "You may begin with loading our luggage." And he waved Marcus on to lead the way to the carriage. Lydia fumed silently, unwilling to give Marcus the satisfaction of more of a reaction than she had already revealed. What did she care what he did? Only a day's work in the theatre would send him running back to London with his tail tucked between his legs. And until he realized the futility of his reckless decision, at least she would have a comfortable seat in a spacious carriage.

As Marcus spoke to the coachman and arranged the loading of their things, Giles handed Lydia into the carriage, and she slid onto her seat, crossing her arms over her chest. "We are going to have *words*," she whispered to him, casting him a poisonous glance.

"I suspected we would," Giles acknowledged. "Don't work yourself into a snit. I can be a man of business *and* a friend, on occasion. I have got *plans* for Newhaven," he said.

A moment later, Marcus appeared at the door, ready to climb into the carriage. Giles stayed him with a gesture of his hand and a pleasant, if mildly caustic, smile. "Oh, no," he said. "I'm afraid you'll be riding topside."

And he snapped the door shut straight in Marcus' face.

Chapter Eighteen

I can't believe you did that," Lydia said as the carriage began, at last, to move. "I can't believe he *let* you do that!"

"What other choice has he got?" Giles said, stretching his arms over the back of the seat. "Probably it was rude of me, but I thought you might enjoy that much at least. We *did* need the carriage, Lydia."

She had known that. Of course she had, but it hadn't made it any easier to bear. "I don't want to be near him," she said, and heard the odd, husky wobble in her voice. "I can't—I *can't*—"

Giles shrugged. "You needn't be," he said. "I'll tell him, if you like. That he's not to be near you. Although I suspect it would do you some good to be above *him* for a change. Possibly it would do *him* some good."

Lydia let her head fall back against the seat and closed her eyes. "I am just so tired, Giles. I thought—I *truly* thought—that I could simply move past it all. I thought he couldn't hurt me again."

"Do you know, Lydia, there's a fatal flaw that actors seem to possess well above ordinary folk. We never know ourselves as well as we think we do." He sighed, resting his hands upon his knees. "I suppose it's because we spend so much of our time being someone else."

For all the good it had done her. "Do you think I have been very foolish?" she asked.

"No more so than usual," he said, and laughed as he dodged the foot she swiped out at him. "In truth, I think you feel more foolish than you ought," he said. "And for whatever it may be worth to you, I also think Newhaven feels just about as foolish as he should."

Too late. Too damned late for *that*. "Probably more so, now that he's stuck with the coachman," she said dryly, as the rain pattered away at the carriage. "He'll be soaked to the bone when we arrive."

"Yes. That should put you in a better temper, at least," Giles said, flicking back one of the curtains to peer out into the rainy London streets. "Did you happen to see his hands?"

His hands? She hadn't been looking at his hands. Why would she have done? "What do you mean?"

"I mean your erstwhile paramour has engaged in some sort of fisticuffs just recently," he said. "You didn't notice? His knuckles are ruined and the cuff of his sleeve was stained with blood. I'd wager he broke some fool's nose."

"That's barbaric," she said.

"That is *man*," Giles replied. "At his most primal. What do you suppose set him off? Could it be the very same thing that brought him to you humbled, and induced him to make a devil's bargain like the one he's gotten?"

Lydia averted her gaze, smoothing at her skirts. "It doesn't matter," she said, in a voice as cold as the weather without the carriage.

"I think it mattered to him," Giles said. "Lydia. What has happened?"

Lydia offered a one-shouldered shrug. "I suppose he must have discovered the truth somehow," she said lightly.

"And that doesn't matter to you?"

"No," she said, and only that. She had no words to explain it to him, the frothing rage that it evoked in her chest, the humiliation he had caused—not once, but *twice* now. It was a private sort of pain, one that bled like a suppurating wound, and poisoned everything it touched. "No," she said again. "It doesn't matter to me at all."

Only minutes into the journey, Marcus had been forced to concede that perhaps he had bitten off more than he could handle. The cold rain stung his face like pellets of ice. The wind burned his cheeks and chapped his lips. Far from the insulated warmth and the comfortably-stuffed seats the interior passengers enjoyed, the topside seat beside the coachman was little more than a hard, varnished wood surface, and though it hadn't proved too terrible upon London's well-maintained roads, as they had proceeded out of the city, the ride had grown noticeably less comfortable.

His backside would be bruised black and blue by the time they arrived from the bouncing over the nearly washed out roads. If he didn't succumb to exhaustion and find himself flung straight off the carriage first.

To his credit, the coachman had not protested the change of plans. But though he had an oiled leather greatcoat to ward off the worst of the weather, still the man's lips had taken on a noticeable blue tinge.

Over the howl of the wind and the clatter of the carriage wheels as they rolled across the road, Marcus could hear, distantly, the muted sound of voices within the carriage below. No words reached his ears though he strained to hear them. He wished they had; he was certain they would have proven elucidating.

Grey afternoon descended into greyer evening, and as the roads worsened still in the dark and the rain, Marcus was forced to curl his fingers into the seat to keep his balance, when every motion of the carriage threatened to tip him off. Hours passed like eons, one miserable moment stretching out into the next. He clenched his jaw against the chatter of his teeth. His coat was ruined and worse than useless now; it had been made for warmth but notably *not* to withstand such a heavy rain. Even the tight knit of the wool was saturated now, keeping the chilly water tight against his skin, and the cold seemed to have seeped straight through to his bones.

The only thing that kept him held in his seat was the knowledge that eventually they would have to stop for the night. The weather and the hour had deepened to the point that he could hardly keep sight of the procession of carriages and carts ahead of them—only the faint, distant glow of the lanterns upon the closest provided evidence that they existed at all.

But the coachman's eyes were sharper than his own, and his hands steady upon the reins. Eventually—after hours, days, *weeks*, perhaps—the carriage began to slow, following the one ahead off of the road proper and into the yard of what looked to be a coaching inn.

Thank God. It was an effort to unclench his stiff fingers, to find the strength to move his limbs, which felt like they creaked with every tiny motion. He hadn't realized just how much of him had gone utterly numb during the journey, but the slightest movement brought about a stinging pain in every digit, every limb. Numbness gave way to aches and pains in places he hadn't even been aware that he possessed.

The coachman—a hardier man than himself, it would seem—had jumped down already, and Marcus could only watch as Lydia at last alighted from the carriage and, without a single backward glance, made her way into the inn. And then there was Giles, still looking remarkably fresh, if a bit wrinkled.

Marcus was left to crawl from his seat by inches, on legs that felt as if they would collapse beneath him at the tiniest movement. Still the rain

dripped down his face, adding insult to injury. The commotion in the yard
had died to a murmur by the time he had made it onto solid ground once
more, and he felt himself sway on his feet, every frozen bit of him yearning
for the interior of the inn, which surely promised fire, food, drink, and rest—
and yet he held his feet by only a prayer.

There was no one coming to rescue him, he realized. Even the coachman had deserted him, to take the horses to be stabled and bedded down for
the evening. It was a Sisyphean labor only to cross the short distance from the
yard to the door, and he did it like a drunken man weaving through his paces,
his knees wobbling with exertion, exhaustion. The door seemed to stretch
away from him as he reached for it, and it was only on the third swipe that he
caught the handle and pressed it open.

The comfortable cacophony of voices that had washed up around him
initially faded to nothingness as he entered. He didn't know how long, precisely, the simple act of descending the carriage and entering the inn had tak-
en him in his wretched state, but it was instantly clear that it had been long
enough for Montgomery to have imparted some manner of information to
the rest of the company. The only one who was *not* staring at him as if he
were some strange, exotic, potentially dangerous creature was Lydia, who
could not have made her lack of interest in his presence plainer.

Marcus' gaze swept the main room, two long tables stretching practically
from one side to the other, all crammed with members of the theatre company. Some had received drinks already, or simple tavern fare served upon steel
plates. There had not been a place left for him among them, either by happenstance or design, he supposed it didn't truly matter.

Lydia sat, half-hidden, at the table in the back, carving off neat bites of
what looked to be steak and kidney pie.

"Ah," Montgomery said. "I was just telling the company about our newest employee."

Marcus would just bet he had been, and in no uncertain terms.

"Well?" Montgomery said. "You're dripping all over the floor, which I
doubt the proprietress will much appreciate. I would advise that you change
your clothing and then get yourself some supper. If we haven't eaten the lot
already."

Marcus managed something that might, on some level, have drawn near
a shrug. "I haven't got any clothing," he managed to say, through lips that felt
as if they had been frozen shut.

Montgomery's brows lifted. "No?"

"Do you imagine I keep a trunk packed in my carriage?" Marcus inquired. He'd left London with nothing but the clothes on his back and whatever coin was within his pockets.

"Mind the tone of your voice," Montgomery warned. "You'll find sympathy in short supply for you here." But his eyes fell to the puddle swiftly forming beneath Marcus' feet, and he heaved a beleaguered sigh. "Sybil," he called down the table. "Have we got anything going spare?"

A woman of middling years who had half her face buried in a tankard of ale came up briefly from it with a cough. "What?" she asked. "A costume?"

"Something plain," Montgomery said. "*Very* plain. Don't waste our best."

The woman turned an assessing eye on Marcus, looking him up and down, no doubt measuring him to within an inch. "Aye," she said. "I could dredge something up."

"Do, then," Montgomery said. "In the meantime," he added to Marcus, gesturing to the hearth some distance away, "do sit by the fire. You look like death warmed over."

There was some small satisfaction to be had, Lydia thought, in the knowledge that all that Sybil had been able to source—or, perhaps, all that Giles had been willing to spare—from the costumes packed neatly away in their trunks, was a plain linen shirt and a pair of knee breeches. Of course, Marcus had long been accustomed to only the best quality garments. His clothes had been tailor-made exclusively for him, and of the finest materials. Probably his valet took excellent care of them.

Sybil's costumes, however sturdy, were common and coarse, designed to hold up well but categorically *not* for comfort. Probably the coarse linen of them would scratch his skin raw before the night was through.

Probably the clothing he had arrived in was ruined besides. Certainly the coat—which likely cost more than all of the company's costumes put together—had not survived the journey. Though it had been hung up to dry near the fire along with the rest of his things, after so hard a beating and without the tender care of a valet to clean and dry it properly, it would most likely be utterly unwearable come the morning.

Even his boots had come away rough. Likely they'd remain waterlogged for weeks, the leather stiffened and ruined, at least aesthetically.

No one had budged up to make a place for him at either table, and so Marcus had been consigned to a place on the floor by the hearth, and he looked, for perhaps the first time in his life, *common*. Even the patrician features which would otherwise have attested to his noble bloodlines had been overwhelmed by his dishevelment, by his bare feet and his simple clothing. He looked like a farmhand who had wandered in for warmth on a nasty evening, and he ate the simple meal that had been served to him at last—a bowl of stew and a crust of bread—listlessly, as if even the process of chewing had proved too taxing for him.

Half-hidden in the shadows and mostly obscured by those seated opposite her, Lydia watched him discreetly, through lowered lashes. Minute by minute, more of their numbers concluded their meals and took themselves off to bed, since they would be once more underway shortly after dawn. Just occasionally, whenever someone stood and left their position at a table, Marcus glanced at the newly-vacated seat and seemed to take stock of himself, as if weighing the merits of attempting to rise.

Each time he had decided against it, and each time his shoulders sank lower, as if a heavy shroud of futility had settled over him.

"Careful," Giles warned in a low voice beside her. "He'll catch you staring."

"I'm not staring," Lydia whispered back. "I am *savoring*."

"Ah, yes. He does have a general air of misery about him, does he not?" Giles kissed the tips of his fingers. "Delicious. What say you I pile on a bit more of it?"

Lydia shrugged, affecting a nonchalant air. "As you please," she said. "What did you have in mind?"

"Well, I doubt he'll be well-pleased to learn that all the rooms are taken," Giles said. "In fact, I've had to house two of our number in his carriage— though, in all honesty, it's a comfortable enough conveyance that I suspect they were pleased not to be stuffed three to a bed."

"Oh?" Lydia asked. "Where did you intend for him to sleep, then?"

"The stables, naturally."

Lydia choked on a mouthful of ale. "The stables!"

"Fitting, don't you think? Of course, there's work to be done before he'll be permitted to find his bed. Anyone else would balk at this juncture, but— Newhaven hasn't got that privilege, now, has he?" Giles issued the question in a canny tone, suggesting he was enjoying himself perhaps a touch too much. "He can have no complaints, no arguments. By his own agreement."

From the surly clench of his jaw revealed in the flickering firelight, Lydia suspected that Marcus had a great number of complaints already. What remained to be seen was whether or not he would *voice* them.

"Don't look so conflicted," Giles chided, and Lydia had to resist the urge to touch her face. *Did* she look conflicted? "Perhaps we'll be rid of Newhaven by Brighton after all. This could well be his breaking point."

Marcus chose that moment to glance up, his gaze landing upon her with the weight of a blow. Through the mantle of exhaustion, through even the offended dignity at having been brought so low so swiftly, still there was the burn of determination in the depths of his dark gaze.

Any lesser man would have cried off already. Any *lord* would have protested his treatment, rescinded such a reckless bargain as he had made. But Marcus only notched his chin higher, as if in silent challenge.

Do your worst, that look seemed to convey without words. *You will not be rid of me so easily.*

A long sit by the side of the fire had restored most of the feeling in Marcus' feet. Still, he continued to suffer that terrible pins-and-needles sensation throughout his limbs, little pricks of pain that persisted despite his efforts to get himself warm and dry.

Lydia had disappeared some time ago, making for the stairs that Marcus was reasonably certain led to the rooms that the company had taken. He couldn't be certain, but while Montgomery and Lydia had had their heads bent together, speaking quietly to one another at the table, a suspicion had grown within him that a few hours in the freezing rain atop a carriage was not the last of the torture that Montgomery intended to inflict upon him this evening.

And finally, when it seemed that the largest part of the company had departed for their rooms, Montgomery made his way toward the fire, a bundle of fabric stuffed beneath his arm. Without preamble, he extended his arm and let the cloth fall into Marcus' lap.

"What the hell is this?" Marcus asked.

"Your first assignment," Montgomery replied evenly. "Since you have partaken in this company's costumes—and thus caused Sybil the inconvenience of having first to find them for you and eventually to *wash* them on your account—you'll have the mending of these."

"The—" Marcus struggled to modulate his tone as disbelief warred with horror. "I beg your pardon. Did you say the *mending?*"

The dying firelight cast upon Montgomery's face lent him a diabolical air, like some demon cast up from the very bowels of Hell for the sole purpose of tormenting humanity. Or perhaps Marcus in particular. "There is not a single member of my company," he said, "who cannot sew a button or stitch a seam. What use is there in having you about if you cannot do the same?"

Marcus considered the clothing in his lap and reflected upon this. He had, perhaps, at some point or another, once *seen* a needle. He'd never wielded one in his life; that much was equally certain. "I don't know how to sew," he said, and it sounded less defensive than baffled.

"No time like the present to learn. I have a feeling you'll be doing rather a lot of the mending. Sybil's interests lie in the *composition* of costumes, you understand. Mending is far beneath her talents, and yet it commands a not-insignificant portion of her time out of necessity."

Well, it was far above his own talents—and that, he imagined, was rather the point of it all. "I'm afraid I wouldn't know how to begin."

"Not to worry. Sybil will show you." Montgomery let his fingers drift casually toward the woman who had, however resentfully, sourced dry clothing for him perhaps an hour earlier. "She'll also be good enough to point out what, exactly, requires mending. You'll have it done before you bed down for the night."

That sounded more ominous still—*bed down*. Barons did not *bed down*. They *retired for the evening*. "And where will I be *bedding down?*" he asked.

"In the stables, provided you can make yourself room."

Ah. Well. That explained that, then.

"No complaints?" Montgomery inquired, altogether too sweetly, his mouth stretched into a macabre example of a grin.

"Not any I'll issue in your hearing," Marcus muttered, and resigned himself to a long, most likely sleepless, night. "Give me the damned needle."

Chapter Nineteen

It felt as though Marcus had scarcely blinked his eyes before someone was rudely waking him once again with a judiciously-applied nudge to the ribs. There was not a single part of him that didn't ache, and he hadn't the strength to do anything more than turn his face into the packed straw beneath him and hope that whoever had decided to rouse him would either go away or put him out of his damned misery.

"Up you get, Leontes. You've missed breakfast already."

Montgomery. Of *course* it would have to be Montgomery.

"How can I have missed breakfast?" he asked, slitting his eyes open. "It can't be much past dawn."

"The theatre is a cruel mistress. She waits for no man, and we're leaving for Brighton shortly—with or without you." There was the rustle of hay and a low, satisfied laugh as the arse began to head back in the direction he had come. "Your choice, of course."

Marcus allowed himself half a minute to find the wherewithal to open his eyes and the fortitude to drag himself upright. His hands stung as he braced himself on the packed hay—he'd probably pricked himself with the needle a dozen times last evening. If he hadn't bled all over the clothing he'd been attempting to mend, it would be a damned miracle.

But he had *done* it, that impossible task that had been laid out before him. Even if it had taken hours, squinting by the dying firelight. And he would not be defeated today.

He hefted himself to his feet at last, clutching at the bundle of yesterday's discarded clothing, and staggering from the stables to the yard, where his carriage awaited in the early dawn light. Too much to ask, probably, that he be permitted to ride within the carriage today.

Instead he climbed, painstakingly, up into the seat beside the coachman, who looked fresh as a damned daisy. "And where did *you* sleep evening last?" Marcus inquired.

Blinking in surprise, the coachman turned to address him. "Mr.

Montgomery kindly offered me a bed," he said. "He said a coachman ought to have a good rest before being at the reins."

Of course he had.

The coachman gave a delicate little sniff, rubbing at his nose as if he'd caught a whiff of something foul. Marcus could not blame him; the smell of the stables was pungent this morning. Far more so than it had been last evening when they had arrived, though perhaps the rain had mitigated the smell somewhat—

He caught the sidelong glance that the coachman threw toward him, and realization struck like a slap to the face. It wasn't the *stables* that reeked. It was *him*. He smelled of hay and horse and worse. Sybil was going to have his head if he'd soiled even her plainest costume beyond repair. *And* he was going to be forced to endure a long ride marinating in his own filth.

As a fist pounded against the roof of the carriage, signaling to the coachman to proceed, a flicker of lightning twisted through the clouds not too very far into the distance.

"Wonderful," Marcus muttered beneath his breath. "It's going to rain. Again."

And as the carriage began to move, he thought he heard the coachman mutter back, *"Thank God."*

Marcus grasped his seat with both hands as the carriage wheels on the washed-out road threatened to jounce him clean off his perch. A bath was a bath, he supposed. However he had to get it.

The rain shower had been mercifully brief, though it had left Marcus once again chilled to the bone. He had fished his coat from beneath the seat, but it had suffered from its rough treatment the previous day, and there was little to do with it but to drape it over himself as best he could to protect against the rain.

But all miseries had to end eventually, and by shortly after noon, there had been a noticeable hint of salt sailing in on the cold breeze. They had arrived at last, and Marcus found himself breathing a sigh of abject relief.

The procession of carriages and carts wound through the quaint, pretty streets, toward what Marcus assumed must be the theatre. He'd been to

Brighton often enough, though he could not recall having partaken much of the theatre when he had.

Perhaps if he had, he would have encountered Lydia sooner. Perhaps he wouldn't have let five years pass the both of them by. Perhaps he would have been a different person then; less inured in his own particular brand of unhappiness, or more willing to give it up.

Perhaps the outcome might have been a different one altogether, and he would not now be *here*, swaying in the topside seat, all too conscious that he had made too many mistakes to wipe the slate clean.

The theatre was a good deal smaller than the one in London from which they had come—but then, Brighton had not even a quarter of the population of London. Probably the productions would seem grander here, or more immersive, to the patrons who would have a much better view in a theatre that could accommodate at most a third of what the Drury Lane Theatre could.

It was startling that everyone else seemed to know precisely what they were meant to do; a revelation of a whole world full of moving parts that he had never before considered. Of course there would be things happening out of his sight to produce these things that he had so often taken for granted— his role had always been to arrive at the theatre, find his box, and sit through the production. It had simply never occurred to him that the effort that went into putting on that production, which had only ever cost him a few hours of an evening, had in fact represented *weeks* of work for someone else.

Lydia had seamlessly performed three separate roles in the time their company had been in London. How long had it taken her to learn the lines? To learn where to find her place upon the stage? How many roles and lines were stuffed into her head, and how many rehearsals had it taken for her to be able to draw upon them at a moment's notice?

He had struggled hours last evening only to reinforce a few seams, to sew buttons that had become a bit too loose. And that was the very *least* of the effort that anyone else present could offer.

The carriage jostled as the coachman climbed down to help the occupants out, and Marcus took the opportunity to climb down himself. The wind whisked through his hair, through the coarse linen of his clothing as if it were little more than cheesecloth, provoking a shiver and the rise of gooseflesh upon his arms, his legs.

It was too damned cold to be out in this weather without a serviceable coat—and his most certainly was no longer that. But at least Lydia looked none the worse for the wear, neatly buttoned into the soft wool pelisse that he had purchased for her, and that was some small consolation.

"Is it too much to ask, Leontes, that you at least *endeavor* to make yourself useful?" Montgomery's snide comment stung, but less so than the frigid pricks of the ocean breeze.

"I'm a hair away from being frozen solid," Marcus said irritably. "What would you have me do?"

With an idle flourish of his hand, Montgomery indicated the people bustling about, moving things from carts into the theatre. "Anything that needs doing," he said. "Not to worry; the cold won't last long. You'll work up a sweat soon enough, I expect."

Lydia did love the madness of theatre. Even now, when they all labored together to unpack props and sets and scenery, when it was impossible to hear oneself think over the sounds of hammers and the scurry of harried footsteps running about onto the stage. There was a kind of subtle magic in it, in how the disparate pieces of the production rebuilt themselves once more. In the airing out of costumes and the neat assemblage of props which would once more descend into chaos the moment that the play was underway.

Everyone worked for it without exception. The actors might be spared the bulk of the manual labor during the production itself, but just now when there was no audience to entertain, even they were expected to get their hands dirty. She had busied herself with the unpacking of costumes, hanging them neatly upon a rack in deference to Sybil's meticulous standards, brushing the wrinkles from them as she went as best she could.

She had thankfully seen little of Marcus, who seemed to have been pressed into set assembly, though it had satisfied a tiny, vengeful corner of her heart to briefly see him wielding a hammer alongside the rest of the crew as they had begun the heavy work of reassembling the sets that had had to be dismantled for transport. He had looked *lost* beside the rest of them, uncertain of what he was meant to be doing or why, following the orders that the other men had cast out at him with an expression upon his face that suggested he was well aware of how mediocre his skills were in comparison.

"Damned fool baron," Sybil hissed beneath her breath as she thumbed through the costumes that Lydia had sorted already, making minor adjustments here and there as she went.

Lydia's brows lifted. "Oh? And what has he done?"

Sybil snatched a shirt off the rack, waving it before Lydia's eyes. "Couldn't stitch a seam if his life depended upon it. Just look at this!" She jammed one hand down the neck of the shirt, cramming her arm into a sleeve, and tugged. "He was meant to mend a seam. He stitched the sleeve to the side of the shirt!"

Despite herself, a queer little laugh bubbled up in her chest. And so he had—there at the elbow, the fabric had been stitched straight to the waist of the shirt.

"Take me twice as much work to fix it," Sybil muttered, her chin quivering with the indignity of it all.

"Don't," Lydia said, prying the shirt from her hands. "It's his mistake. Let him be the one to repair it." No mercy, no quarter given. He could not be permitted to make a wreck of their production as he had ruined so many other things. Still, as she slung the shirt over her arm and began to assist Sybil in assessing his work for other such mistakes before they could make themselves known at an inopportune time, she experienced the tiniest sliver of regret that those other things he had ruined could not be repaired so easily as a shirt.

Montgomery had been correct. By the time the company had been dismissed for the evening, Marcus had been soaked in his own sweat, his hair plastered to his head with it. He was filthier than he had ever been in his life, more exhausted than he could ever remember being, and he'd endured the taunts and jibes of the crew, who knew him now to be a useless lackwit.

Worse still, *he* knew himself to be a useless lackwit.

At long last, he had been permitted to lay down his hammer for the evening, and he had all but stumbled toward the office in the rear of the theatre, which he hoped would not be yet abandoned. Of the myriad conversations upon which he had eavesdropped—none of which had made even the slightest attempt to include him—he had learned that most of the crew would be taking up lodgings at various local inns or boarding houses, and he had seen in his head only a terrible repetition of the same scene which had all too recently played out in London.

memory, trying to divine the various neighborhoods that made up Brighton, whether Lydia would be subjecting herself to the equivalent of St. Giles, parting with the least coin possible from her meager wages.

Montgomery spared little attention for him as he entered the office. "You're dismissed for the evening," he said, his voice disinterested. "I'll expect you back at dawn."

"Understood," Marcus said. "Is Lydia still here?"

Montgomery twitched a brow, his cheeks hollowing. "What should that matter?"

"Where does she intend to stay?"

"None of your damned business," Montgomery growled.

Lydia and Montgomery both had made it clear enough that it was not his concern. That *she* was not his concern—except she was, and always would be, and they were both of them fools if they thought otherwise. "Make it *yours*," Marcus said, as he pulled his purse from his pocket and dumped out its contents upon the desk at which Montgomery sat. "Wherever she intends to say, it must be clean. Quality. *Safe*."

Montgomery considered the coins that had spilled across the desk. "That's probably—what? Twenty pounds?"

"It's all I've got at the moment," Marcus said. Minus what little he would need to eat. "At least until I can send away for more." Probably Rafe would come to his rescue, but it would take time to send a letter, and more time still for Rafe to arrive in Brighton. "I don't want her compromising her safety."

"You *do* recall that I am not paying you," Montgomery said. "Where do *you* intend to sleep?"

"In my damned carriage, if I must," Marcus said. "But *she* sleeps safely. Do you understand?"

Montgomery steepled his fingers, resting his elbows upon the desk, and for a long moment he merely squinted up at Marcus, as if to judge his sincerity. "The company carries costs only while traveling. If you choose to sleep in your carriage and suffer for it, then that is on *your* head," he said. "Know that you'll be sacrificing your comfort for hers."

"I would sacrifice everything for Lydia," Marcus replied. "Just see that this is put to proper use." And he shoved the pile coins across the desk toward Montgomery.

"*Liar.*" The hoarse whisper startled both of them. Marcus turned slowly, and though he knew what he would find, still he was not prepared for the sight of her there, her chin thrust out in fervent denial, the sharp green of her

174

eyes acidic in the severity of their judgment. "Liar!" she accused once more, and she stepped forward as if to throw her weight behind the words. "You know nothing of sacrifice. You, in your ivory tower, insulated with your title, your wealth, your power. What could you possibly know of *sacrifice*?"

Marcus opened his mouth, but not a single word emerged. The uncomfortable sting of truth pricked at his skin, slid into his veins like poison. Nothing she had said had been untrue, nor even unfair in its assessment.

"*I* sacrificed," she said fiercely, her breath whistling through her teeth on the force of her outrage. "I sacrificed everything for you. And you—" She choked on what might have been a sob, dashing her hand across her eyes. "You sacrificed *me*. So easily."

In truth, it had been the most difficult, painful thing he had ever done in his life. But he did not think she would appreciate that knowledge—the end result had been the same. *She* had suffered for sins she had not committed. It would never matter what *his* feelings had been.

"Don't *ever* speak of sacrifice, my lord. You haven't the right." Lydia slammed an armload of clothing at his chest in a magnificent crash of fury, so volatile, so indignant, that the strength of it forced him to stumble back a pace. For a moment she stood utterly still, collecting every bit of herself that had slipped the tight leash on which she had kept her emotions, and shoving them back down where they belonged. In the darkest, seething depths of her, where they could only congeal and coagulate, simmering beneath her placid surface.

At last she marshalled herself enough to wave a careless hand toward the garments in his arms. "Your seams are crooked, and your buttons are weak," she said. "Do them again." And she turned on her heel, dismissing him in a flutter of crimson skirts as she retreated once more.

Silence reigned, think and tense. Presently, Montgomery issued a low laugh, more resigned than amused. "Well, Leontes? You have your orders."

Right. The same work he'd done already, only to more exacting specifications this time. "I'll do them," he said. "How long does the company intend to remain in Brighton?"

"Through Christmas," Montgomery answered. "Though, of course, you're free to leave whenever you please."

Long enough, then, for it to be a worthwhile endeavor to send off to Rafe for assistance. "And where will the company move to thereafter?" he asked.

"Southampton," Montgomery said, though his tone suggested that his attention given was absent at best. "Should be time sufficient for the company to source another carriage. No one will miss you if you decide you have had enough." Montgomery waved him away, shooing him out the door.

As he stopped near the theatre door, Marcus considered the bundle of clothing in his hands, the shoddy work he'd performed today for want of skill. No, he decided—no one would miss him, and probably most would celebrate his absence. Most especially Lydia.

Christmas was a bit less than two weeks away. The company might have determined him to be as good as useless—and they were not *wrong* to believe so, given the circumstances. But he had resources beyond their ken.

Lydia had been more correct than even she knew. He *had* always enjoyed the fruits of his position in society; the wealth, the power, the influence. But he had not, as such, made good use of them. Rather they had been a cushion of sorts. Protection against the myriad cruelties that the world offered to those less privileged than himself.

Lydia *had* sacrificed everything. He had driven her from her home and her family. Left her with nothing. But she had found a new home here; friends who had embraced her, who would protect her—even against him.

These people, they struggled and sacrificed and strove to the best of their abilities to produce something great. The entertainment that he had so often taken for granted—purchased for the price of a private box; a drop in the bucket when weighed against his considerable fortune—was both livelihood and passion for them.

They merited his respect, his consideration. For in those five years that Lydia had been lost to him, they had found her. Given her back the pride he had stripped her of. And that deserved both the sweat of his brow and all of the power and influence he could wield on their behalf.

Chapter Twenty

M*arcus?* Good God, what the hell has become of you?"

Marcus glanced up, letting his feet fall from the surface of the table upon which he'd perched them. "Ah, Rafe," he said. "Good of you to come. *Finally.*" He set aside the tools with which had been working as he rose to his feet and scraped his hair away from his face. "You got my letter, then?"

"I did," Rafe said, and his brows drew together in a curious blend of interest and confusion. "What the devil are you doing in Brighton? And looking like"—he gave a gesture of his hand to indicate Marcus in his entirety—"*that.*"

Probably Rafe meant to insinuate that Marcus was dressed more like a street beggar than a baron, and that he was sweaty, dirty, covered in a great deal of paint, and looked as if he'd gone wanting a good shave for some time. Most likely because all of those things were true.

"It's quite a long story," Marcus said.

"Is it." The bland, pithy reply grated upon Marcus' nerves.

"Very well, then," he said. "It's a short, rather humiliating one. Suffice it to say I found it necessary to leave London in a bit of a rush."

"Considering you did so shortly after beating Father to a pulp, I should think it's a story which I have a vested interest in knowing," Rafe said.

"*Hardly* a pulp, more's the pity," Marcus said, and gestured to an unoccupied chair that Rafe should sit. "Is that what he told you?"

"No," Rafe said, sinking into his seat. "He's telling everyone he took an inconvenient fall from a horse. But I know well enough what a man's face looks like when he's been struck straight in the nose, and I could think of no one with more cause to do it. Then there was your convenient absence—"

"Not quite so convenient for me," Marcus interjected, raking his fingers through his hair. "Have you brought what I asked for?"

"Of course. Though why you would require so much—"

"I have plans," Marcus said. "In all honesty, you'll likely find them quite foolish." He spread his hands out in a vaguely apologetic manner. "I've joined the theatre company," he said.

A long moment of silence drew out between them, and for the duration of it, Rafe stared at him as if he had suddenly begun speaking some foreign language, every word utterly unintelligible.

"I'm sorry," Rafe said, at length. "I must have misheard you."

"I doubt it. And do you know, I think I *like* it?" Marcus shrugged, settling back into his own chair. "At least as much as I loathe it."

"What the hell are you thinking?" Rafe inquired, and there was a wealth of wonder in his voice. "You certainly don't need the money, and the theatre hardly pays a pittance besides."

"Ah, well, as to that," Marcus said with a sigh. "I'm not being paid at all. Call it penance, of a sort."

"Lydia," Rafe said, understanding settling over him at last. "You're here because of Lydia. You didn't exactly specify in your letter, you know. It was all quite vague. I thought you'd gone half-mad when I received it."

"No," Marcus said. "Perhaps half-*dead* from exhaustion. But not mad." He couldn't even recall much of what he had written to Rafe, in fact. Just that he'd required clothing and money—a great deal of it. It had been a week since he'd sent it, and he'd begun to give up the hope of it reaching Rafe in time. "I've been sleeping in my carriage," he said. "I have what clothing I last wore in London, and what Sybil is willing to spare of the costumes, ergo"—he flicked his fingers to his shirt, stained with paint and worse—"this."

"Your penance, is it working?"

Marcus lifted one shoulder, just slightly. "Yes and no," he said. "They've got me doing anything that needs doing, really. Painting scenery. Manning the curtain. Changing sets between scenes. Mending costumes."

"And Lydia?"

Marcus managed something approximating a rueful smile. "I count myself lucky if she deigns even to glance in my general direction. I am, in fact, forbidden to speak to her unless she should choose to speak to me first."

"And does she?"

"Rarely, and only to cast out orders," Marcus said. "Or criticism. She doesn't want me here."

"Then why do you stay?"

"Because I need to be here." Marcus let his gaze slide back to the table, settling on the tools with which he had been tinkering. "For so long—*years*—I believed her to be untrustworthy, when all along *I* was the one who could not be trusted."

178

Rafe settled his elbows upon the table and linked his hands before him, sympathy sliding over his features. "Marcus, you weren't to know. Father lied to you."

"He did," Marcus said. "But I believed it. I believed it when I *knew* Lydia. I knew her character, knew her heart." He splayed out his hands, a gesture of helplessness. "All the power was mine," he said. "And once, she trusted me with it. But then I used it to hurt her. I abandoned her, when I knew she had sacrificed everything for me." Now he had so exhausted her of any goodwill toward him that it would be a perpetual upward climb to prove himself anew. She had taken him at his word once before, but she would never make such a mistake again.

She had *expected* him to fail. Each time she cast him a shirt with a sharp instruction to sew a straighter seam, or turned her head away when he entered a room she happened to be within, she *expected* that he would give up and run back to London. She had expected his horror and fury to be deprived of the creature comforts which he had heretofore enjoyed.

Probably she had not expected him to last more than a day or two on the outside, and yet—he'd remained. Through whatever nastiness she chose to inflict upon him, because *his* offense would always, *always* be the worse. Once, he had held every bit of power within the palm of his hand. Now, he had surrendered it to her, and he could only let her wield it as she saw fit.

"So—what? You mean to show her you won't abandon her again?" Rafe inquired.

"Something like that," Marcus admitted. "Probably won't work. But at least I will have done my damnedest to make amends. And," he said slowly, "if I cannot earn her forgiveness, then I would ensure her security."

It was the very least of what he owed to her. And still, the distinct possibility of failure tore at his chest, made his stomach clench with worry. He had been half a man without her; less even than that. He had wanted her, *loved* her, even when he had thought he had hated her. And she—she *truly* had reason to hate him. The only tiny sliver of hope that remained to him was the fact that she had all but admitted she *could* have forgiven him.

Once. Before he had crushed her heart in his fist all over again.

"Well," Rafe said. "This ought to be interesting. Perhaps I ought to stay. For a few days, at least."

"I was hoping you would. In fact," Marcus said, leaning closer, "I could use your help."

"I would hope you are not shirking your duties."

Montgomery's voice jerked Marcus from his task, and he lifted his head, wincing as the muscles in his neck tightened and pulled. He'd spent too long bent over the table, it would seem. "What duties?" he asked. "Everyone else has left for the evening. There's no one left to command me."

"And yet, here you remain."

"I haven't anything better to do." Yet. "My carriage will keep until I'm ready for it."

"It's near to midnight," Montgomery said. "What could possibly keep you here so late?"

Marcus sighed, tunneling his fingers through his hair. "Tinkering," he admitted at last, almost guiltily.

Surprise etched itself into the crease of Montgomery's brow, his jaw dropping open just slightly. "*Tinkering*? Has your mind got an inventive bent, then?"

"I doubt it," Marcus said. "But I just thought—well, look here." He spread out his tools upon the table, displaying the two pieces of wood he'd whittled to form separate halves of the hilt of a dagger. They were crude, still, and hollowed out where the pieces would meet to form the whole. "I'll wrap this," he said, "when it's ready. Sybil said she had some leather strips going spare somewhere."

"I see," Montgomery said, sliding into the chair. "What is it for?"

"It's *meant* to be a dagger," Marcus said. "I haven't quite got it figured out yet, but when I have—you see these springs?" He picked up a couple of bits of fine wire he'd twisted himself into tiny coils, squeezing them between his fingers to demonstrate their purpose. "They'll fit down into the hilt, when I've carved it out enough. I'll have to secure them inside. And then this bit of metal, here. It will be fashioned into the shape of a blade—blunted, naturally—and set atop the springs." Marcus clasped the halves of the hilt together and slid the piece of metal between them. "The idea is that when the blade is held normally, the springs provide the tension to keep the blade in place," he said. "But apply pressure"—he pressed the edge of the metal with his palm, and it slid down, obscured between the two halves of the hilt—"and the blade disappears."

"A trick dagger," Montgomery mused. "That's quite clever, really."

"Careful," Marcus said wryly. "That's dangerously close to praise."

The very corner of Montgomery's mouth lifted. "As it happens, I've got no current complaints with the quality of your work. I wouldn't have expected it from a baron, but here we are."

"No? Only Lydia, then."

"Lydia is angry with you," Montgomery said. "Justifiably, I might add."

Marcus hesitated, his fist tightening around the prop hilt in his hand. "Is she *only* angry?" he asked. "Or does she truly hate me?"

Montgomery pressed his lips together, hesitating long enough that Marcus felt his stomach drop. "I'm not certain Lydia knows what she feels at the moment," he said, finally. "Or at least—she's trying not to."

"What the hell does that mean?"

With a rough sound, Montgomery cast himself back in his seat. "Have you not noticed how wooden her performance has been of late?" he asked.

"In all honesty, no," Marcus said. She was back to playing Perdita, but he'd lost his taste for *The Winter's Tale* altogether—and he was kept so busy during the performance anyway, with everything that had to be done between acts and scenes, that he simply hadn't had the time to observe.

"She's locked herself up so tightly that she's foundering," Montgomery said, tapping his fingers upon the table, the sound sharp and rife with annoyance. "If she can't pull herself out of it, I may need to resort to drastic measures."

"I don't think I like the sound of that," Marcus said.

"Nor do I," said Montgomery. "But there may be nothing else for it." He gave an uncomfortable shrug of his shoulders, as if it didn't bear much consideration at present. "Did I hear a voice other than yours here perhaps an hour ago?"

"My brother," Marcus said. "He's come down from London. I asked him to bring me some things."

"I suppose you'll be relieved of sleeping in your carriage soon, then," Montgomery said, with a roll of his eyes, as if Marcus had violated some unspoken agreement betwixt them—if not in truth, then in spirit.

"You said you didn't care where I slept, since you weren't paying me," Marcus reminded him. "Incidentally, how many are we as a company?"

"In total? Twenty."

"Only twenty? I had expected more." Perhaps it was just that everyone was so damned *busy* that they gave the impression of more.

"You're plotting something," Montgomery said cannily. "Don't think you can pull the wool over my eyes. Out with it, then."

"I'd be a fool to share half-made plans," Marcus said. "You'll know when I have got something concrete to show for them."

Montgomery smothered a laugh behind his hand. "Do you know, I think I could like you—at least a little. You're made of stronger stuff than I would have credited you with."

"I'm not," he said. "Not really. It is only that—" It was only that he had failed Lydia twice already, and he did not intend to do so again. "It is only that I have to be better than I have been." A sort of *better* in which she could believe again. One that would never give her cause to doubt, one that would never again disappoint her.

"Hm." Montgomery glanced down once more at the separate pieces of the trick dagger. "Why did you choose to make this?" he asked.

Marcus shrugged. "Sybil said you've done Romeo and Juliet before," he said. "That you likely will again in the future."

"That's three months away at least," Montgomery replied. "Surely she told you that, too?" At Marcus' short nod, he asked, "Why are you creating props for a play so far in the future? Do you intend to be with us then still?"

Marcus hadn't much considered it—at least, he had tried *not* to consider it—but he answered honestly anyway. "If that is what it takes, yes."

"Ah," said Montgomery. "I suppose that means you're made of stronger stuff even than *you* expected."

For the first night since London, Marcus had enjoyed a decent night of sleep, a hot meal, and a bath that had been more than cold water in a bucket sourced from a local pump and used to rinse himself as best he could with only that and a spare rag.

It had been too late, of course, by the time Rafe had arrived yesterday in Brighton to make any arrangements aside from taking up the room that Rafe had secured for him at an inn within walking distance of the theatre, but he'd had his own clothing again—though he had opted for the plainer garments out of necessity, since anything he chose to wear would no doubt find itself ruined by paint and worse in short order—and he had had quite an informative chat with the owner over breakfast.

He had known, in an abstract sort of way, that Brighton was a popular destination for the aristocracy in the late spring and summer months, when the weather had warmed enough for tourists to indulge in sea bathing. But the lucrative summer months then ran into the lean winter, which sent the majority of visitors scurrying back to their homes. Hotels, inns, and the like all suffered for want of customers in the spare season, operating at less than half of what they would have expected otherwise.

Of course, Marcus was necessarily limited at the moment by the demands placed upon him by the theatre company. But that, he supposed, was what brothers were for. So he had left negotiations within Rafe's capable hands.

By noon Rafe had delivered to him a proposal outlined in clear, contractual terms, and Marcus had set aside the mending he had been laboring over—since there had been an unfortunate mishap with one of the costumes earlier in the morning, which he was not altogether certain had not been purposefully undertaken—and took himself off to the office.

Montgomery, he had learned, was nearly always fretting about funds. It seemed that one could have all the passion for the theatre that one pleased, but turning it into a lucrative enterprise was a difficult task. The company was foundering for want of a wealthy patron, and, unfortunately for all of them, Montgomery was a seething mass of artistic integrity, which would win him little with those from whom he might have solicited funding.

Which was why he expected something of a fight, if not an outright dismissal.

Montgomery did not disappoint. His head lifted for perhaps a second at the very most as Marcus entered the office—long enough to see who had invaded his sanctuary, long enough to glance down at the papers held in Marcus' right hand, and long enough to issue a single word in a bland, bored tone of voice. "No."

"You *did* say," Marcus replied, striding into the office and closing the door behind him, "that you wished to know what I was plotting."

"Only," Montgomery said, massaging at his temples, "because I wanted the opportunity to crush your scheme out of hand, lest you plague me with it later. Which you have elected to do anyway." With a low sound of irritation, he gave an over-exaggerated roll of his eyes. "What could you possibly have done so quickly? Only last night you pleaded for patience."

He had. But then, he had also grown, however briefly, uncomfortably accustomed to the necessity of it when he had been absent any other options. "As it happens, the liberal application of funds greases many wheels which might otherwise remain stuck." And that seemed—somehow unjust to him now. That pouring money into a problem could erase it as if it had never existed, when others should struggle so fiercely against the tide that he had parted with so little effort. Only with the clatter of coins across a table. "What could it cost you, Montgomery, but a few moments of your time?"

"What could it gain me but a puppet master I'd not trust with the charge of my coat, much less my company?"

Marcus sputtered out a laugh. "That's a lie, and you damned well know it." In fact, Montgomery's coat had ended up in the mending pile only days ago, after a cuff had frayed at the seam, and he had personally be charged with its repair. "You've trusted me with your coat and beyond already." Because he had *earned* it. Maybe not completely; not yet. But Marcus had been privileged to see a side of the theatre that few of his station had, and already he understood it better than most of his stamp. He understood the labors they had all undertaken, because they had become his own. Though his tenure with them had not been long, and would not be forever, still he *understood* what it meant to them. Far better than any other patron could have done.

A moment of silence, and then—begrudgingly, Montgomery threw up his hands in acquiescence. "Give it here, then." He stretched out his hand for the papers, snapping his fingers like claws.

Marcus handed them over and watched as Montgomery idly flipped through them, a muscle jumping in his cheek. "Well?"

"Wonderful," Montgomery responded, though the blue of his eyes seemed particularly cutting. "I can't fucking afford it, so it means nothing."

"*I* can afford it."

"Jolly good for you, then. I won't sell you my damned company." Montgomery slid the papers back across the desk.

"I haven't asked you to."

"But you will." Montgomery said, as if he could see straight through to Marcus' soul. "They all do, eventually. Men like you love to call themselves patrons of the arts, but what they truly crave is *control*."

"I will never ask you to sell your company to *me*," Marcus said. "I might…ask you to consider a partnership of a different variety, however. In exchange for enough funds in perpetuity to allow you to operate as you please, free from the control of—let's say a wealthy benefactor who might

184

demand more than you are prepared to bear."

Montgomery settled his elbows on the table, clasping his hands. "Lydia," he said. "You want me to make Lydia my partner."

It didn't seem a point that there was much use in arguing, and so Marcus shrugged.

"Why?" Montgomery inquired. "If you succeed in marrying her, she'll be a baroness. She'll hardly need the theatre any longer."

"No," Marcus said. "She won't need it, at least not to earn a living. But I think she needs it in other ways. She's been with your company a long while, hasn't she?"

"Five years," Montgomery said. "You would let her continue with acting, if she wishes?"

"If she wishes it," Marcus replied. "And if she does not, well—then you'll have a baroness well-acquainted with the theatre as a partner. I would imagine that if you had to take on a patron to keep your company solvent, you couldn't hope to find better."

Montgomery mulled that over silently for a moment. "And if she does *not* wed you?" he asked finally. "What then?"

"Then Lydia is still your partner, and she has the security that comes along with it." Notably, a company that would not be on the verge of cutting already meager wages for want of funds. She would have a steady income and a place within the company as long as she wished. "Regardless, the stake in your company will not be held by me."

Montgomery could have made a killing at the gaming tables, for he did not betray his feelings on Marcus' suggestion with even the slightest twitch of an eyelash. Instead, he let his hand drift across the table to the papers he'd abandoned. "Let's not get ahead of ourselves," he said. "Should I choose to entertain your offer, there will be time to quibble over details later." He stacked the papers into a neat pile and handed them back to Marcus. "You wish to be a patron of the arts? Begin here," he said. "And understand that I am offering nothing in exchange. Not even a reprieve from your duties here."

"I never thought you would," Marcus said, collecting the papers from Montgomery once more. "Since you find these terms amenable—"

"They're more than amenable," Montgomery admitted. "They're damned generous. But it's only your money you'll be wasting."

"I don't consider it wasted. I consider it *invested*." And there—though he'd done his best to mask it, for the briefest of seconds, Marcus was certain he'd seen a flicker of approval in Montgomery's eyes.

Chapter Twenty One

Again."

Lydia sighed, pressing her fingers to her eyes. "Giles, I *know* the lines."

"Then speak them like understand them. Like you bloody well *feel* them." From his seat in the pit, where he lazed with his legs draped over the chair before him, Giles pressed his cheek into his hand. "I feel nothing from you. I feel nothing from *Perdita*, and that is a damned *crime*, Lydia. Theatre must be evocative. If you cannot make your audience laugh with you, cry for you, and cheer for you, then you have failed."

"Has it ever occurred to you that perhaps your standards are set too highly?" Lydia inquired irritably, fisting her hands upon her hips.

"Do you know, it never has?" Giles slumped further down in his seat, casting one arm over his eyes. "*Again.*"

Lydia gritted her teeth, and extended one hand toward Daniel, who was playing Florizel, and who had done his utmost to appear as if he had not been listening overmuch to Giles' ruthless criticism. "Sir, my gracious lord—"

"For God's sake, Lydia," Giles interrupted. "Could you *attempt* to make it sound as if you might have even some middling affection for the man? He's meant to be your lover, not your damned *brother.*"

"I beg your pardon," Lydia snarled back. "Only tell me—should I molest the poor man upon the stage to lend credence to the fiction? Would *that* satisfy you?"

Daniel's eyes rounded, and he held up his hands in a gesture of surrender. "This is nothing to do with me," he said. "Pray do not drag me into it."

"I would be *satisfied*," Giles said, and his legs dropped down from the back of the chair, feet landing with a decisive *thump* upon the ground, "if you could speak with feeling. You must have been Perdita once. *Find* her, Lydia."

It was true, though there was a part of her she had buried quite deep down that ached to acknowledge it. She had played the roles of all three women in the theatre of her life. But first and silliest, she had been Perdita; young and hopeful. She and Perdita had both shared the suspicions that their

186

grand love would come to naught—but only Lydia had suffered that particular disappointment. She did not want to dredge Perdita up again, not even to perform with Giles' commanded *feeling*. She did not want to remind herself how far short Marcus had fallen of Florizel.

"*Christ.*" Giles scrubbed at his face. "We haven't got the time for this."

No, they hadn't—but Giles had insisted upon putting her through such rehearsals every damned day, as she had not performed to his satisfaction since London. But the weight of such a demand fell not only upon her, though she was the one who had failed to meet his expectations. They had all run through the last two acts more times than she could count just lately, and it wasn't fair. It wasn't fair to demand so much of them, when the failure had been her own. To force hours of rehearsal each day before the full run of the play each evening.

Lydia felt her shoulders slump in defeat. "Giles—"

He thrust his fingers into his hair, raking back the disheveled strands. "I wonder if it was ever truly in you at all," he said, with a scathing sound produced in the back of his throat, stomping toward the stage. "Once I thought you had the makings of greatness. But you are always only yourself. I've no use for that, Lydia. You do us both a disservice with it."

She had never wanted to be great; not really. "Has anyone complained of my performance?"

"No," he said, his voice clipped. "But half the people who attend are philistines who wouldn't know art of it climbed straight up their arses."

"Then why does it matter?"

"Because *I* know art." He threw up his hands; a dismissive gesture of aggravation as he climbed onto the stage. "Assemble the company," he said. "I've got an announcement to make before this evening's performance."

"An announcement?" A queer feeling of unease settled in the pit of Lydia's stomach. "Of what nature?"

"Not to worry," Giles said, with a weary laugh. "I'm not replacing you. *Yet.*" This he delivered with a glare, as if she had deliberately contrived to ruin his production. "Go on, then," he said, pinching the bridge of his nose and tilting his head back. "We've precious little time before this evening's performance as it is."

Somehow, Lydia knew in her heart that whatever it was that Giles intended to announce had *something* to do with Marcus. Though he had not approached her, she had noticed in the fleeting glances that she had gotten of him today that his appearance, which had suffered of late due in no small part to being consigned to sleeping in his carriage, had quite suddenly improved itself. She had, after a fashion, grown accustomed to his rather slovenly appearance, which had been a satisfying change from what he once had been. Humbling, she had thought—he had never looked *less* noble, with flecks of paint clinging to his hair, or bandages wrapped round his hands, the consequences of some bit of clumsiness or other.

The bandages might linger, but gone was the unkempt dishevelment which she had secretly savored. True, he was not exactly dressed as she would have expected of a baron. But he had affected *some* change, somewhere. And now, with Giles—well, it could not be a coincidence.

Briskly, she breezed about the theatre, ducking her head in the various rooms and hallways where the company tended to gather during rare moments of leisure, and by the time she had made it back to Giles, it was to find that they had largely preceded her, collecting about the stage as they waited for the last of their numbers to arrive. Marcus arrived after, with the last of the stragglers, whom she had caught in the midst of a last-minute repair of a rickety table leg.

"You will all no doubt be pleased to learn," Giles said, his hands on his hips, "that arrangements have been made to house you henceforth at the company's expense."

At the company's expense? Not hardly. Lydia suppressed a snort of disbelief. She'd seen Giles fret often enough about wages and repairs and all manner of other expenses often enough to know that the company could by no means afford to be so extravagant. It was hanging by a thread and a prayer, fraying at its seams.

"House us?" This, from Arthur, whose bushy brows pinched inward with confusion. "House us where, exactly?"

Fleetingly, Giles' eyes slid to Marcus, who Lydia saw give a nearly-imperceptible nod in return. "The details will necessarily differ depending upon our location," Giles said, "but while we are in Brighton, you'll find your accommodations at the Crown and Thistle, just a short walk down the road."

A soft murmur went up through the company, and Lydia ground her teeth together.

"What's more," Giles said, "you'll each have a room of your own, and breakfast and supper as well." He gave a careless shrug. "Don't expect much in the way of a hot supper, given our hours."

"If it's only bread and cheese, and the cost of it don't come from my pocket, I still say that's a good bargain," Sybil said. A rumble of laughter slid around the room in response, the atmosphere turning jovial.

Oh, *come now*! Surely they had to know that some mischief had gone on—Giles had never stuffed them less than three to a bed when it was possible. They *had* to know.

Arthur slapped Marcus on the back and nudged him with his shoulder. And then Sybil turned a beaming grin on him, and then Alfie—and Daniel—and Kitty—

They *did* know, Lydia realized with a strange, shocked realization. They knew that the money had not come from Giles, or from the company. They simply didn't *care*. He had done it, and—and he had *let* Giles take the credit for it. Let the *company* take the credit for it.

Somehow, someway, whilst she had been doing her damnedest to give him not even the tiniest sliver of her attention, Marcus had turned enemies into friends. Or, at the very least, he had gained a better opinion than that with which he had begun.

Lydia fumed to herself as the company began to disperse once more, talking animatedly amongst themselves, and she found herself conflicted on whom she meant to confront—Giles or Marcus. Clearly they were conspiring with one another, and she couldn't even sort out inside of her own head which was the larger betrayal.

She found herself stalking off after Marcus, who had begun to retreat back behind the stage once more. "*You*," she said, and the word snapped out of her mouth like a gunshot as she jabbed one finger in his direction.

Marcus paused, turning, momentary surprise quickly overwritten by guarded wariness. His whole face changed in an instant, as if he had closed his features off from her, fortified his defenses against the assault of her fury.

"You did this!" she accused.

He swiped one hand across his mouth, as if to wipe away any lingering traces of emotion from it. "You're angry."

"Observant of you." She was surprised that the words had not scorched her tongue.

"Why?" he asked. "The company is struggling, Lydia. Don't tell me you haven't noticed. I won't believe it."

Of *course* she had noticed. It would have been impossible for her not to notice. She simply hadn't expected that *he* would. "It's not your concern," she said fiercely. "*I* am not your concern!"

His jaw went taut, teeth clenching behind the grim line of his lips. "Of course you are my concern," he said. "I will not pretend otherwise, however much you might prefer it. You have every right to be angry with me, Lydia, but not about *this*."

Lydia reared back, startled by the heat in his voice. "What did you receive from Giles in exchange?" she asked, balling her hands into fists.

"Nothing."

"I don't believe you!"

"Not a damned thing!" he insisted, his voice rising to meet hers. "Except, perhaps, the comfort of knowing you will be *safe*, damn you. That you will not be pinching pence until they scream in the service of sparing as much from your wages as you can!" He made an aggravated gesture with his hands, as if she had driven him to the very limits of his tightly-leashed control. "Ask him yourself, if you cannot believe me," he said. "I am working myself to the bloody bone—"

"No one asked you to!"

"—because you were *right*!"

The sharp rejoinder died on her tongue, and unwittingly she swallowed it back down to settle sourly within her stomach.

"You were right," he said again, and his shoulders slumped, reactive anger siphoning away in the absence of her ire. "I have been insulated from hardship, from sacrifice. All my life. I've never known any different. But I am learning," he said. "Once, I turned my resources into a weapon. Now I would use them differently.

"When Montgomery allowed me to join the company," he said, "it was with the agreement that my rank would be the lowest amongst you. Well, I have learned how to wield a needle and a hammer both, how to paint, how to assemble and dismantle sets. I slept in my carriage for a solid week; I wore clothing that marked me the lowest. And still the worst of my discomfort was temporary, for once Rafe arrived to bring me the things I'd left behind in London, I had the means to buy myself far beyond what the rest of the company could afford. How is it right, how is it *fair*, that I should be better housed and fed than people who have thrice my mediocre skill? Your company, on the whole, has been kinder to me than I deserved. They work for a pittance, and they do it out of love and passion for the art."

"*You* don't love it."

"No," he said. "But you do. And that is enough, I think. It is enough for me that you love it."

It wasn't. Or, at least, it shouldn't have been. By all rights, he should have turned tail and run back to London days ago. He had no reason to be

190

here still, no right to be ingratiating himself with her colleagues.

"The company as a whole deserves better," he said. "Yes, you are a part of it. And yes, I will admit that I want you housed somewhere comfortable, with decent meals, in a safe part of town. But it's no better or worse than the rest of the company as a whole has got. No better or worse that I have taken for myself, which *is* fair. Can we not agree at least upon that much?"

Perhaps the question was fair, but Lydia did not feel very much like being fair herself, and so she deflected instead. "You've learned nothing at all," she said, and she dashed the back of her hand across eyes that had grown unaccountably damp. "You cannot *buy* forgiveness."

"No," he acknowledged. "But I had hoped I might earn it. Could I, Lydia?"

Through the tight clamp of her throat, she couldn't manage to eke out an answer. There was too much anger clawing at the inside of her chest, as if it might shear straight through the cage of her ribs and free itself. It was an effort in and of itself to shove it all back down once again, and to lock it up tight within the pit of her stomach, and to bury it beneath the mountain of indifference she had erected.

Still she could not make the words come. Perhaps she had buried them, too.

He said nothing more as she turned her back on him and fled, but she knew his eyes had followed her the whole way.

In truth, nothing much had changed for Lydia. She had, in fact, already been residing at the Crown and Thistle, at Giles' insistence, since Marcus had provided the funds for it. More than enough, though she had taken only the smallest, sparest room available and sent the majority of the remaining funds on to her family in London.

She had been among the last to arrive back to the inn, once the evening's performance had concluded. It hadn't been her best. Likely, given the furious looks that Giles had sent her way, it had been one of her worst. In no mood to endure a lecture—or worse—she had dawdled until most everyone else had left for the evening, hoping to make her way back to her room unnoticed.

But the sound that crashed to her ears as she approached the inn at last informed her that she had miscalculated. Rather than finding their beds, the company had assembled as a group in the common room, and she hadn't a prayer of slipping by unseen.

"Oi, Lydia!" Sybil gave a jaunty little wave, beckoning her in.

She cringed at the address, at the generally celebratory air that seemed to seep from the common room in an effort to swallow her up within it. They were all gathered round a table that stretched the length of the room, and which had been set with a great number of platters filled with wedges of cheese, hunks of bread, cured meats, and what looked to be a selection of nuts and preserves. Of course not a *hot* supper, owing to the lateness of the hour—but a feast nonetheless.

And there, wedged between Daniel and Giles, toward the rear of the room, sat Marcus, his hand wrapped around a tankard of ale, the joviality slowly slipping from his face as he spotted her. He looked like a pirate, with his shirt half-unbuttoned and his sleeves rolled up to just beneath his elbows.

"Come," Giles said, in an icy sort of voice that drew a frown from Marcus. "Eat."

"I'm not particularly hungry," she lied, trying for an apologetic smile. "I thought I would go up to bed—"

"I insist." The cold snap of his voice stung her pride, but she was not so foolish as to interpret it as anything other than the command that it had been. Her feet moved of their own accord, trudging to the table like one led to the gallows. Giles' mood had soured the atmosphere, and though there was still the clink of plates and the shuffle of bodies as they created a space for her there, toward the end of the table, the propensity for cheerful chatter that had existed prior to her arrival had died a rather ignominious death.

Lydia slid onto the bench, ducking her head over the plate that had been produced before her, selecting bits of food at random with the futile hope lingering in her breast that Giles would give her just one blasted evening of peace.

To her left, within the narrow field of view that she had carved out for herself with the hunch of her shoulders and the bow of her head, a sleeved arm nipped by to snatch up a cut of meat from the platter placed in the center of the table. Too fine a sleeve by half to belong to anyone of the company, and she followed it up to a shoulder, and then to a face that too closely resembled Marcus'.

"You!" she said, her voice shrill with astonishment, and to her right, Alfie grumbled a chastisement when the pitch of her elbow as she leaned away from Rafe nearly upended his tankard.

Some distance away, Marcus cleared his throat. "I invited my brother to dine with the company this evening," he said, by way of explanation, "since his assistance in securing better accommodations has proved invaluable. Lydia, you had not occasion to meet my brother, Rafe, but—"

"We've met," she interrupted acidly, feeling the burn of remembered humiliation come into her cheeks.

"Not…as such," Rafe demurred, though even in the low light of the fire she could see the answering heat tinting his own. "That is to say, there was never a formal introduction."

"Oh, by all means, let us be formal," Lydia said, and she punctuated the caustic slice of her words with the snap of her teeth through the firm flesh of an olive. "It would be *such* a refreshing change from sullying my reputation to my landlady."

"That was not well done of me, I admit," Rafe said, and his throat worked in a long, hard swallow. "My only defense is that I acted based on what little I knew of you. I do regret that."

Lydia blinked back the sting of tears that threatened, and the rasp of her voice cut through the heavy silence that had settled over the room. "Do not, I beg you, speak to *me* of regrets, my lord. You have no right to them, for they were given entirely to me years ago. How selfish, how *cruel*, that you—*either* of you—should attempt to lay claim to them now."

It was not only Rafe who had caught the lash of her ire; Marcus, too, directed a shamed gaze toward his plate, for which he seemed to have quite suddenly lost any enthusiasm.

And Giles laughed, damn him. He slapped one hand upon the table, startling the company as a whole out of the pall that had fallen over them. "*Yes*," he said, vile mood erased as if it had never existed. "At *last* some damned emotion from you."

Too much of it, in fact—and now he knew how to get it from her. She shoved herself away from the table, unwilling to endure the spectacle of his satisfaction a moment longer, unwilling to subject herself to the pitying stares of the company, to the remorse scrawled across Marcus' face, or that of his blasted brother. Instead she sought the solitude of her room, where no one could intrude upon her.

But as she turned the lock and stepped inside, she found the peace she had sought an impossibility to find even here—her room had, at some point today, been stuffed to the gills with everything she had left behind at Marcus' home in London, delivered and unpacked by careful hands, the trunks which must have once contained them stacked neatly by the door.

She didn't want them, these unpleasant reminders of what she had left behind. Tomorrow she would take them to the theatre and deliver them to Sybil to see which could be scavenged for costume pieces or otherwise repurposed. But tonight they haunted her, as if the ghosts of what might have been prowled her silent room in soft furls of silk and frills of lace and ribbon, until she turned her back on them at last and fell into a restless sleep.

Chapter Twenty Two

Marcus stood horrified upon the stage, as Montgomery's instruction clattered around inside his head. "You want me to do *what*?"

"*Read*, Leontes. Have I not made myself clear?" Montgomery stretched his arms over his head, affecting a bored expression.

The script in Marcus' hands felt as though it had suddenly gained a stone, weighing down his arms. "I'm not an actor," he said.

"No," Montgomery acknowledged. "I have little hope of achieving excellence from you. But I will *use* you to get it from Lydia, if such a thing is possible."

"I can't." Marcus swallowed heavily, his throat dry and aching.

"I wasn't asking," Montgomery said. "You can read, or you can leave." He shrugged, as if it mattered not much to him one way or the other which Marcus chose. "We are going to unwind the clock, Leontes—and *you* are going to play the part you gave to yourself."

But Lydia would suffer for it. They would *both* suffer. "I have hurt her enough already," he said. "This—this is *cruel*."

"Cruel to be kind," Montgomery said, philosophically. "That wound has never healed, and make no mistake—Lydia not the mistress of her emotions; she is the *victim* of them. You made her into that, and you can damn well do what you must to purge her of the poison you fed to her." He stretched his lips into a macabre grin. "Not to worry. It's the anger that is easiest to reach at the moment. I suspect you'll have to do little more than stand in your place and take what you are due."

"I—I—" He had no time to form any further arguments, for the click of heels just in the wings signaled Lydia's arrival, and she whisked at last onto the stage in lovely gown of deep blue.

The annoyance that had been writ across her face—no doubt to be subjected to yet another rehearsal when she had already memorized her lines—faltered as she caught sight of Marcus at last. He watched her expression become guarded, the lovely lines of her face smoothing to perfect blankness.

195

Even her eyes seemed to lose their brightness, and she slid her gaze toward Montgomery, suspicion coloring her voice.

"What is this, Giles?" she asked. "Where is Daniel?"

"Daniel won't be joining us this afternoon," Montgomery replied evenly. "You'll be reading Paulina. And here is your Leontes," he said, with an idle flip of his wrist toward Marcus.

Her cheeks hollowed, but there—in the tiniest quiver of her chin, the fire that kindled itself behind her eyes—that was *fury*. "No," she said, but it was a guttural denial, tendered in a voice that crackled with restrained rage.

"*Yes*," Giles insisted. "Here is your very own Leontes, Lydia. You know what I want from you, but more even than that, you know what he *deserves*. So give it to him. Every last bit of that which he has earned."

She didn't want to; he could see that much in the clench of her fists at her sides. But perhaps she *needed* to, in the way that savaged innocence deserved to avenge itself. To rightly place the blame for what she had suffered back where it belonged.

The flicker of her lashes ought to have been a warning, like the sharp slice of her chin as she cut it toward Montgomery. "Which scene?"

"Don't be obtuse," Montgomery laughed. "You know the one. Act three, scene two."

And still, Marcus was not prepared as the stomp of her heels cracked across the stage like lightning had erupted beneath her feet. The flash of her arm as she gestured to him was like a whip; even though it did not come close to connecting, still he felt the strike. "What studied torments, tyrant, hast for me? What wheels, racks, fires?"

Her words singed and stung, as if she had spat embers along with them that had landed upon his skin, and Marcus struggled to find his place, the script unwieldy in his hands. But he needn't have bothered; Lydia could carry the scene on her own—and she did, vibrantly, scornfully.

"What flaying? Boiling in leads or oils? What old or newer torture must I receive, whose every word deserves to taste of thy most worst?"

She had deserved none of it at all, and this was her revenge made real at last for what she had suffered at his careless hands. Her moment to tear at *his* pride as he had shredded hers.

"*Thy tyranny*," she seethed, "together working with thy jealousies, fancies too weak for boys, too green and idle for girls of *nine!*"

He had heard this all before, of course, for he had watched her play Paulina before—and at last he recognized what he had not seen *then*, when she had vented her fury upon the stage. These words had always been meant for him. It was the lingering shadow that he had cast over her life to which she had spoken them before, only now—now he had taken up the place he had once occupied only in her imagination. Now, at last, her righteous rage found its proper target, and she cast the lot of it upon his head where it rightly belonged.

He let the script fall with his hand to his side, and realized he had never truly been meant to read it—his role was only to *exist*. To feel the lash of her anger, and to accept it. This was not for him to console, nor to comfort. It was only for him to endure.

And so he did—and he did not turn away his face in shame, and he did not bow his head in remorse. Her hot gaze burned directly into his eyes, and he could do her no less honor than to meet them.

It felt like hours had passed, though it couldn't have been much more than a few minutes—but at last, she had reached the end of her speech, the end of her tether, and it seemed that she had flagged just there at the end, struggling to scrounge up the very last dregs of unrelieved wrath that she had carried so long inside of her. Surrendered, at last, to him.

A great purging of it, all that which had congealed so long inside of her. And he had *heard* her at last, those words that she had never been able to give him.

Once she had run out of words to snarl at him, she panted in the aftermath of it, pressing one hand to her cheek and wiping away the light sheen of sweat that glistened there.

Still her eyes did not drift from his. "Does that satisfy you?" she inquired of Montgomery, her voice raw.

"Greatly," Montgomery replied. "You're dismissed. Give me a performance with half as much passion tonight, will you not?"

Without another word, Lydia turned and left, and Marcus could only feel relief that even the sound of her footsteps had softened. Whatever it had cost them both, Montgomery had not been wrong. She *had* needed this.

"I need a damned drink," Marcus said, as he tossed the script aside.

"Get it while you can," Montgomery advised. "Because that was only Paulina. When I found her, she was all Hermione."

Marcus felt himself wince. He had seen her Hermione already, for just a few hours upon the stage, and that—that had been devastating. *She* had been devastating, in the grief that he had given to her. More ruinous still was the knowledge that once, so many years ago, she had been Perdita. So bright and hopeful, so full of love and secure in the certainty of his own. Right up until he had torn that from her hands, wrenching every security along with it. Right up until he had ruined her. And she had spent the last years eating the same bitterness as had he, knowing all along that *she* had been the one betrayed.

Lydia routed Giles after the evening's performance, waiting for him at the door of the theatre as he prepared to depart. "Never do that again," she said, apropos of nothing, as he fell into step beside her.

Giles' breath puffed out in a cloud of white on a low laugh. "Why not? It worked well enough. Your performance this evening approached credible, at the very least."

Credible! "You don't get a *credible* performance at my expense, Giles. It wasn't your business. It wasn't your *place*." She shoved her hands into the pockets of her pelisse, wishing she had saved at least one muff from amongst those she had dumped upon Sybil this morning. Her fingers ached with the cold.

"And was it at your expense?" Giles inquired. "Truly, I had considered it to be at Newhaven's. Did you not see his face? You wrecked him, darling, and it was glorious."

She had. She knew she had. And there had even been a measure of satisfaction in it, to see that at last he had thoroughly understood his position, the villainy in which he had been cast. It had even been *freeing*, in a sense, to loose those wild words that had simmered so long within her chest. As if at last she were no longer in danger of boiling over, losing bits of herself with each bubbling heave. If she had not achieved *peace*, then at last she had achieved *stability*.

But that anger, that volatility that had been so much a part of her had masked everything else that had lurked beneath it. She did not want to be the vulnerable, wounded woman she once had been. And what was left of her now but that?

"Just once, Lydia," Giles said, reflectively, "I would like to see you act."

"What do you mean by that?" Lydia asked, baffled. "I act! I act every evening—"

"You don't. You never have." Giles threw his head back, heaving a sigh.

"You're just *you*. Always yourself. There is nothing inherently wrong with that, Lydia, but it keeps you stuck just as you are. You can never grow, never change, never improve. When I found you," he said, "I *needed* a Hermione, and you were so deliciously tragic, I knew you would be perfect. And you were. My perfect Hermione. And that is why we always come back to *The Winter's Tale*. Because you haven't got much more in you."

Lydia gave a little start to realize that he was right—they *did* always come back to it. She might have the lines to half a dozen plays stuffed inside her head, but there were none they performed as regularly as this. Because of her? Because it was the only one she could perform with any competence?

"I don't just need a Hermione," Giles said. "Or a Paulina, or Perdita. I need Juliet and Ophelia. I need Rosalind, Beatrice, Hero, Desdemona. I need Viola, Portia, Cordelia—and you can't give them to me, Lydia. Not as you are."

"You don't think I'm a good enough actress?"

"I don't think you're an actress at all. You can love the theatre, Lydia, and not have the talent for it. It's not a moral failing." He laid one hand upon her shoulder and squeezed. "I know that I am a difficult taskmaster," he said. "But when it comes down to it, I would rather be your friend than your employer. As your friend, I would advise you to have this out with Newhaven."

Her stomach churned at the very thought. "And as my employer?"

"Ah," he said. "As your employer, I am *ordering* you to do so. I need to see what remains of you without that wretched miasma that hangs over you like a funeral shroud. And do you know what, Lydia? I think you do, too."

Lydia swabbed at her eyes with the corner of her sleeve, frustration lending her voice a petulant tone. "It's hardly fair of you," she said, "to manipulate me in such a cruel fashion."

"Darling, I manipulate everyone. Why should you be the exception?" He paused to jerk open the door of the inn. "I'm doing you a kindness. One day, provided Newhaven cooperates, you might even appreciate it. Because I imagine that he has learned, as I have long suspected, that you were never meant for the stage. You were always meant to be his baroness."

Marcus watched Lydia and Montgomery part company in the foyer, watched Lydia make for the stairs without even the slightest consideration for the company gathered in the common room around the table once more.

She had to be hungry. If her day had proceeded in the same vein as his own, whatever of breakfast she had managed to choke down before she had been due at the theatre had been the only meal she had eaten. But none of the company had called to her as she had passed the common room on her way to the stairs, and even if he had known that none of them—the company, nor Lydia herself—had been eager for a repetition of last night's uncomfortable scene, still he thought it was a shame.

That *he* was here, and she wasn't.

As if he had stolen something new from her; the camaraderie she might have enjoyed with the company that had been more a family than her own for the last several years.

Giles shook his head as he entered the room, unwinding his scarf and rubbing his hands together as he prowled across the room toward the table, and the steadiness of his steps left no doubt to where he was headed. Beside Marcus, Colin—the fresh-faced young man still small and youthful enough to play the role of Mamillius, the young son of Leontes—shoved his plate and tankard further down the table, creating a space for Giles, who claimed it at once, stretching his hand out for a clean plate that someone further down the table passed to him.

"She'll speak to you, eventually," Giles said, and the wash of other voices around them rendered the words largely inaudible to anyone but Marcus. "I told her she had to do it. She might not like it, but she'll do it. Eventually."

Christ. Marcus could not decide if a forced conversation was better or worse than none at all. "And what am I meant to say?" he asked. He had no defenses, no pretty excuses which would lessen the magnitude of his offenses against her.

Giles chuckled over his plate, picking apart a crust of bread with his fingers. "Ideally? Not much," he said. "In matters of love, you should always endeavor to listen more than you talk, but this, I think, will be more akin to a hostage situation."

Marcus swore beneath his breath, scrubbing at his face, appetite suddenly vanished. "I don't want to hold her hostage," he said. "How would *that* aid me?"

"You've misunderstood," Giles said. "Lydia is *my* hostage in this, so let her resent me for my meddling. You—you must be *her* hostage in exchange.

200

Do you now understand my meaning?"

It meant he had to make himself helpless, vulnerable. He hadn't ever been, not really. Not in any meaningful way. There were not many ways for a man of his station, of his influence, of his wealth to *be* helpless. But he had to be, because he had once made *her* helpless. He would have to peel up the armor that had guarded his heart so long and show it to her. And if she chose to take up weapons and strike out at it, to thank her for the privilege of even that much of her effort, her attention.

Because even the rage she had showed him, the anguish that Montgomery professed that she suffered still, were preferable to indifference. It had festered so long within her already. She deserved to be free of it, whatever the cost.

"She has to get out the rest of it," he said. "The same as the anger. And it must find its proper target. Because she can use it upon the stage, but it is never *spent*, until—" Until he accepted it. Until it was acknowledged by the one who had given it all to her. Until he had to *confront* it, in all of its devastation, that ruin he had made of her.

Giles issued a small nod, perhaps the tiniest sliver of approval. "I do not envy you," he said. "But you need to hear it. As much as she needs to say it, *you* need to hear it." He gave a sigh, tossing a handful of walnuts into his mouth and chewing. "You're sending your brother on to Southampton, are you not?"

Marcus nodded. "He'll need the direction of the theatre," he said. "To find some likely inns nearby with which the company can come to a similar arrangement. I expect he'll have something sorted before we arrive."

"Good," Giles said. "Good. So before your brother departs—as I suspect you will require his assistance with some of the particularities—you and I will discuss business."

"Business?" Marcus felt a queer prickle of anticipation shiver along his spine. "You mean to say—"

"I mean to say that if you had given me any other answer regarding Lydia but the one you had, we would not now be having this conversation," he said. "But unless I am much mistaken, I don't believe Lydia will be upon the stage much longer. Her time as an actress is coming to an end." He rubbed his thumb across his chin. "But the company needs the money, and Lydia…"

Lydia needed a place to belong, for her own security. A company that was not slowly collapsing for want of funds. Even if she surrendered those things that had made her so ideal for a few particular roles, then she would still have a role in the management of the company. "Yes," he said. "Whatever your terms, I will agree to them."

"Careful," Giles warned. "That's how you ended up painting scenery and sleeping in your carriage."

Marcus managed a rueful chuckle. "Do you know," he said, "as penance goes, it's been—less wretched than I might have expected."

"Yes, well, I suppose I never expected a damned baron to have a talent for prop design," Giles admitted. "You *do* realize that if Lydia, by some miracle or grace heretofore undiscovered amidst humanity, should somehow deign to forgive you your trespasses, you shall be obliged to tolerate the demands of the theatre?"

"Could I still design the occasional prop, if there's call for it?"

Giles threw his head back and laughed. "I suppose I could tolerate that," he said. "Provided you remember your place." Grabbing up his plate, he slid himself off the bench once more. "The office, tomorrow morning," he said. "We'll get this business done in time for Christmas."

Which was only a few days off now, Marcus reflected. Soon enough the company would move on to Southampton, and from there God only knew where. Probably Lydia had traveled the length and breadth of England in the years since they had parted, and he—he knew *none* of it. Where she had been, what she had done, what she had experienced along the way. There had surely been struggles she had endured that he could not imagine. Places she had resided that had been less than safe. Nights that she had gone to bed hungry.

As she had this evening.

Person by person, the company began to trickle out of the common room to find their beds for the evening, and no one noticed as he collected a clean plate and filled it from the platters still arranged upon the table. No one marked his exit as he walked silently from the room and headed for the stairs, plate in hand.

He paused for a moment before Lydia's door, considering the silence within. And at last he set the plate down upon the floor, knocked upon the door, and left before she could answer.

Chapter Twenty Three

Christmas day. It ought to have been a celebratory occasion, and Giles had always been generous with the company for holidays. There was no performance tonight, nor would there be tomorrow, since it was Sunday. By Monday they would be working to tear down and vacate the theatre, and by Tuesday they would be on their way to Southampton, but for now—two days of nothing.

It left Lydia in rather foul spirits, if truth be told. In her childhood, Mama and Papa would have closed the butcher's shop for the day, and they would have spent it as a family. Mama would have prepared a roast. Papa would have kept the fire in the hearth stoked, until the blustery wind that tended to seep through the seams of the house had been vanquished, and perhaps grumbled over the cost of coal. Lavinia would have slaved over the cider she insisted upon making each Christmas, the recipe for which she had claimed was a closely guarded family secret—and which Lydia had suspected was simply an excess of whichever liquors they had happened to have on hand.

As evening descended, they would greet whichever groups of carolers had come wassailing with whatever coin they could spare, and once that had been exhausted, with whatever remained of Lavinia's cider, or portions of plum cake and pudding. There had been a peculiar magic in it all; in the sweet strains of *God Rest Ye Merry, Gentlemen* eventually devolving into drunken disharmony as the carolers indulged their stomachs more so than their pockets, in a day of rest surrounded by family, trading pauper's gifts bound in brown paper and string. Two Christmases in a row, Lavinia had given her knitted gloves that had had no thumbs, because Lavinia had never had any particular talent for knitting. And still Lydia had loved them, unwearable as they had been.

Once, she had spent a Christmas with Marcus. She had had such high hopes, then, so full of the certainty that by the next, they would be married. She hadn't known, then, that it would be the last Christmas she would have cause to enjoy. Every Christmas since had been more unendurable than the last.

She had spent the majority of the day out in Brighton, since it had seemed a better use of her time than to mope about in the silence of her room, but in the end there had simply not been much to do, since she had little enough money of her own and most shops had been closed besides. Add to that the families that had been milling about the streets, the happy couples linked arm in arm as they passed—it had been enough to drive her back to the inn even before sunset.

The common room had been bustling since breakfast, the company coming and going in bits and parts, wine and ale flowing freely in the spirit of the day, and she might have joined them but for the desire not to let her own dour mood spoil their fun. Someone had brought out a deck of cards, and they seemed to be wagering handfuls of roasted chestnuts, and the atmosphere was merry and jovial, things that had not lived within her for years now.

She would have made it to her room unheeded, had Giles not caught her upon the stair, as if he had been lying in wait for her.

"Ah, Lydia," he said. "I had wondered what you had got up to today. Here; I have got a gift for you."

A gift? Giles had never given her a gift—for Christmas or otherwise—in all the years of their acquaintanceship. But it was not a beribboned package that he slapped into her hand. It was a sheaf of papers, the neatly-printed content of them uncertain, written in what appeared to be oblique legal terms.

"What is this?" she asked, perplexed by the documents.

"Ownership," he said. "Congratulations, Lydia. Come the new year, the company will belong to both of us in equal measure."

For a moment, it was as if every word had deserted her. There was nothing in her head but a strange, tinny ringing, bouncing about the inside of her skull, coalescing into a deafening cacophony that blotted out every other noise in the vicinity. At last—minutes later, maybe days for all she could guess—she sucked in a great lungful of air and said, "Have you gone *completely* mad?"

Giles shrugged. "You've long said I required a patron," he said. "That the company has been bleeding funds."

It was true, and it had been for years, but *still*. "You refused!" she snapped, and waved the papers about until they snapped beneath the force of the breeze they created. "Do you think me a fool? That I cannot see what this is? How could *I* be your damned patron, Giles? I haven't got any more money than you!"

"You're not my *patron*," Giles said. "You're my partner. There is the tiniest difference, there."

"Why would you let him do this!" It was impossible to keep the note of betrayal from her voice, and she hadn't particularly wished to try, anyway. "How could you make us beholden to him? How could you make *me* beholden to him?"

Giles shook his head in exasperation. "Good God, Lydia—give me more credit than that, at least." He flicked his fingers to the papers, which trembled in the hard clasp of her hand. "You have got the details there," he said. "Before you go slinging such slanderous accusations at my head, you ought to at least be certain you know what it is you're speaking of. So *read* them."

She didn't want to read them, she wanted to—to cram them down his bloody throat!

"Newhaven *is* an idiot, I grant you," Giles said. "He asked me to keep the details between the two of us. I suppose that men in his position who never have to think about money can't truly consider how often the rest of us do. And you—you're more suspicious than most. Any attempt at secrecy or obfuscation was doomed to begin with, however little he wanted to acknowledge it."

Of course it would have been. Where *else* would a sudden influx of funds have come from—most especially when Giles had been adamant on the matter of retaining control of his company for years. And she had simply been meant to accept that he had suddenly changed his mind?

"How could I *not* know?" she asked. But how could *he* have done it?

"I suppose," Giles said, "it was really the only gift he could have gotten for you for Christmas, when one considers that he's hardly left the theatre, except to sleep. Where would he have found the time? We have been working him like a dog."

She reared back, as if the words had hit her like a blow. "I would not have accepted a Christmas gift from him," she whispered.

"Do you know," Giles said, "I'm certain he knows that well enough. Why else do you think he wished it to remain a secret?"

Marcus hesitated outside Lydia's door, plate in hand. She had not come down for Christmas dinner with the company—which he had paid a premium to ensure would be a proper one—but then, he supposed that he had not truly expected her to do so. She hadn't in days.

Still he had brought her dinner each evening on his way back to his room, though there was no way to know whether or not she had eaten it. Possibly the inn's staff simply removed it each morning—but it had comforted him at least a little to leave it at her door, just in case she *had* taken it.

And so he left the plate, which was stacked with thick slices of roast beef doused in gravy along with assorted vegetables, right at the seam of the door as he always did. And just as he had every night for the last several, he gave a single, firm rap upon the door and turned to go.

He hadn't gotten more than a step from her door before it flew open, hinges groaning at the rough treatment. He had hardly managed to turn back around before Lydia, clad in a deep violet dressing gown, slapped a fistful of papers to his chest. Perhaps half of them connected, whilst the rest, puffed about by the violence of the action, fluttered from the stack.

"What the hell is *this*?" she asked, in a low hiss.

Marcus snatched for the papers that had gone flying about, though from the careless handling they had received—both his and hers—he knew they would never lie flat again. "Where did you get these?" he asked. "They're not—you weren't—" She had never been meant to have them. He thought he'd made that clear enough to Montgomery. "You weren't meant to know this," he said at last. Not *this* part of it all. Not the carefully-worded details of it.

Something like a laugh eked out of her throat; a miserable little sound that held only the mockery of humor within it. "Do you think me foolish enough to believe that Giles would simply *give* me such a thing? What, out of the kindness of his heart?"

"I thought him a decent enough actor to have concocted something convincing, yes." But she seemed to sag at the words, as if the very suggestion had taken something more from her, something he could never have anticipated.

And it wasn't *anger* in her voice when next she spoke. It wasn't annoyance, or indignation—it was resignation. As if she had suffered the last shattering blow that she could bear, and had broken at last beneath the strength of it. "Why would you ever think I would wish to be dependent upon you again?" she whispered, and her arms drifted over her chest as if to protect

206

herself from a mortal blow.

Dependent? The papers gave a vicious crunch in his hands as his fingers clenched around them. "You didn't read these," he said. She couldn't have—she *couldn't* have, and still think that. "Lydia, there is nothing in them that would make you dependent upon me."

"How could I *not* be? How, when the company depends upon your money!" Her shoulders shook, her lips trembled. "Have you not taken enough from me already?" Listlessly, like a forlorn little ghost, she drifted away from the door. And there it was—all of the grief she carried around with her, bubbling up to the surface in queer little jerks. The odd pitch of her breath, the draw of her brows.

She didn't even make it the bed tucked away in the corner near the window. Instead she wilted halfway into the room, as if her knees had collapsed beneath her. Marcus could only linger in the doorway, conscious of the fact that he had no right at all to enter.

He braced one hand upon the door frame, drawing a deep breath into lungs that felt as if they had been squeezed in a vise. "They're not my funds," he said. "At least—they won't be, in a few days more. It takes time, of course, to arrange such things. But the contract is valid, and it will be carried out." There seemed to be an invisible line there, just at the entrance of her room, which he knew he ought not to breach. Tentatively, he set just the toe of his boot across it anyway. "The money," he said, "will be in an annuity. In your name, and Montgomery's. It will pay out four percent each year, more than enough to continue to run the company without outside influence of any kind. Should you choose to dissolve the company at any point, you'll each own equal shares of the principal balance. And when—*if*—you choose to marry, your share will be held in trust as your sole and separate property."

Another tentative step, and he hadn't yet burst into flames, nor had she cast even the smallest glance in his direction. "No one can take it from you. Not even me. It's not a string I hold in my hand with which to control you," he said. "Nor a reward to be dangled and withdrawn as I please. That is the point of the annuity. You don't have to take me at my word, or extend trust I haven't earned. The law itself protects your interests."

She gave a fierce sniffle, and her shoulders slumped as if the weight of the world had settled upon them. She croaked, "Why?"

And there were so many answers to that simple question, so many thoughts clogging up his head. Already he had violated Montgomery's instructions to listen more than he talked, but—Montgomery had thrust this

mess into his hands, and he had never wanted her to know the details for precisely this reason. Because she had too often accused him of attempting to
buy her affections. Because she thought he had more money than sense, and
probably he did. Because he had *known* she would not appreciate it if she
knew from whence the funds had come. Because she could not trust his intentions, and it was only his own fault.

"Because I have broken so many promises I made to you," he said.
"You once told me I *owed* you. And you were right in that, and so many other
things. So I thought…that the very least that you were owed was the security
I stole from you. I can't give you back everything I have taken, but this—this
I can return." Somehow his face had grown damp, and he swabbed his sleeve
across his cheeks. "I don't want you to lose the theatre, unless it is by your
own choice. And Giles—he was willing to sell part of it, under certain conditions."

"The annuity." It came out husky, with a lingering trace of bitterness.
The thickness of tears there, and he hadn't the right to comfort her.

"Creative control," Marcus corrected. "That's what he wants; it's what
he's always wanted. You own half, but he still chooses his actors, his productions." The plate—he'd left it at the door. He turned to grab it up, and it was
the excuse he needed to approach her. "In fact, the annuity was my condition.
The money needed to be wholly separate from me. And, Lydia…I never
meant for you to know from whom it had come."

She turned her head from the plate he set upon the nightstand near her
side, and Marcus was left with the terrible suspicion that he had ruined even
the simple pleasure of a good, hot meal for her this evening. The air in the
room felt stifling and heavy, dense with the cloud of words hanging there
unspoken, like he had only to reach out and pluck the excoriating epithets
from the air itself—*liar, fool, traitor.* Words that ought to have been said years
ago. Words she had never been permitted to speak, words which he had
smothered with his condescension, his scorn.

He had stolen even her voice from her. And so he gently closed the
door, and sunk down to rest his back against it, and waited. Minutes stretched
out in a silence so taut that it could have been plucked like the strings of a
harp.

Her hands fell into her lap, cradled atop the violet fabric of her dressing
gown that flowed around her in a cascade of silk. Her blond hair slid over her
shoulders, coming loose from its pins. "The last words you spoke to me five
years ago," she said stiffly. "Do you remember them?"

"Yes," he said, pressing his fingers to his eyes. As clearly as if they had just been spoken. *Leave London. Should you ever return, I will make you regret it.* "Yes."

"I do regret it," she said, and her shoulders sank, defeated. "I do regret it. So I suppose you've won after all."

His head dropped back against the door as his eyes burned with helpless tears. He'd won nothing—nothing at all. They had *both* lost.

Chapter Twenty Four

The ragged sound—like a suppressed sob—that reached Lydia's ears surprised her. And when she turned to glance over her shoulder, it was to see Marcus struggling to compose himself once more.

"A moment," he said in a thick, choked voice when he caught her looking. He took a few deep breaths and scrubbed one sleeve across his face; a flagrant violation of everything he must have been taught from the cradle. As if, in a few short weeks, he had become something anathema to the lord he had once been. "Go on," he said at last, and if his voice had quavered, at least it was not so rough as it had been moments before.

Go on?

Something of her confusion must have shown on her face, for he gave a brief, tremulous gesture of his hand. "All of it," he said, though a muscle flexed in his jaw. "Everything. Every wretched thing." He drew up his knees as if he were bracing himself for something, and draped his arms over them, linking his hands. "Tell me everything I was too blind to see. Tell me everything I should always have known. Tell me everything for which I am responsible. Be brutal, Lydia. I need to hear all of it."

Her hands fisted in the folds of her dressing gown, but there was so little strength in it. Once she might have carved divots into her palms with the motion, but that white hot fury had been exhausted, and now there was just— grief. Layers and layers of it, misfortune piled on top of catastrophe piled on top of ruin.

"I lost everything to you," she said, and her fingers twitched; the tiniest little motion, peeling up those layers one at a time to reveal everything she had kept buried for so long. It had been self-preservation. She had had to do it only to survive. "I lost my reputation, my family. My self-respect. My future."

He made a small sound, neither assent nor dissent, but from the corner of her eye she saw his head dip briefly.

Her hands shifted in her lap, curling around a memory to hold it within them—the worst one of them all. "Can you imagine," she said, "how very frightened I was that day?" The *last* day, she meant to say, five years ago. But she was certain he knew that already. "I had just come home, and you were there, and you were so *angry*. You made such a dreadful scene, Marcus. You threw me out onto the street, in the cold, and I—I didn't know why. I had no idea what I had done to displease you."

"Nothing." It was a terrible rasp. "You had done nothing."

Her head tilted back, and the weight of the memory in the palms of her hands felt like tons, pulling her back down into it. "You said—such terrible things to me. *Of* me," she whispered. "And—I suppose I had known even then what is said of mistresses. But it seemed so cruel to sling them at me, when I was only what you had made me. And I didn't know *why*." There was the warmth of tears sliding down her cheeks, the slow drip of them off of her chin. "It seemed so impossible for everything between us to have changed in a moment. I didn't know what I had done to merit such treatment. And you—you were so cold to me."

"Cruel," he said. "I was cruel. It's neither untrue nor unfair, Lydia. You're permitted to say it."

Cruel. Yes. He had been that. The memory crumbled to nothing in her hands, collapsing beneath its own weight. "I gave up everything for you. Foolishly, I believed in the promises you had made to me. And so I had nowhere to go, no one to turn to."

His breath hitched. "Your family?"

"Until a few weeks ago, I hadn't seen them in five years. They had known all along what I was too stupid to grasp. That you had never intended to wed me. That men like you prey upon pretty young girls. They chew them up and spit them out, and they don't even bother to turn and see what wreckage they have left behind." A little choked sound eked out of her throat, and she stilled her trembling lips with the tips of her fingers. "I had thrown my reputation away upon you," she said, "And I had nothing at all to show for it. I was turned away from my former employer—too sullied, then, for my fingers to touch gowns meant for proper ladies. I had what few gowns I managed to pack before you threw me out, no money, no prospects. Despite your threat, I could not have left London. I had no money for passage elsewhere."

"Where did you go?"

"Near the docks," she said. "It was such a long walk, since I could not afford even the price of a hack. But I knew I would be only one face amongst hundreds, and no one would notice me, and I—I wanted to fade. I felt as if I had already died. I was only waiting for someone to notice and pitch me into a grave at last. There was no one to miss me."

A raw sound from behind her, as if it had been pulled from him without his consent.

"I had begged a job from the owner of a tavern, who didn't care who I was or from where I had come, provided I could serve ale and tolerate the dockworkers pinching me in unmentionable places." She swept back the hair that had fallen into her eyes. "Giles found me there," she said. "He said I was tragedy personified. Not *tragic*. Tragedy itself." An ugly little laugh wound through the room on the wake of those words. "He asked me to join his company."

"Thank God," Marcus said, and his hands clasped themselves as if in prayer. "Thank *God*."

"And still, I wasted so much of my life on you," she said, rife with self-censure. "*Years* before I moved from heartbreak to anger. I suppose I didn't know how to reconcile the loss of a love that had just—ended. You had torn yourself free of me, and I—I went on loving you anyway. I didn't know how to simply *stop,* as you had."

"I never stopped loving you." It was muffled, thick with tears, and she turned once more to see that he had buried his face in his arms. "I never stopped loving you," he repeated. "Not for one moment. And there was a time—when I was still blind to the truth—that I hated myself for that. And yet, despite it, I have loved you, and *missed* you, every minute, every hour, every day since."

Finally he managed to lift his head, and his eyes were red, bloodshot, his face damp with the tears that still streamed from them. "There has never been anyone else for me," he said. "There never *could* be. And whatever else you must think of me, I always intended to marry you. That is why Father tore us apart. He'd discovered that I'd applied for a license and purchased a ring for you."

"How could you expect me to believe that?" Lydia asked. "I have long learned, my lord, the cost of trusting in you."

Marcus gave a hoarse laugh, full of self-recrimination. "I deserve that, and more," he said. "I was so stupid, Lydia, and selfish, and, yes, cruel. Every evil thing you could name me, I would deserve. I convinced myself that it didn't matter if you were first my mistress so long as we were discreet about it; I could restore your respectability in a moment only by giving you my name. In my arrogance, I thought myself untouchable."

In her naïveté, she had thought the same. That there was nothing in the world that could have parted them, though she could feel it even now; that great, gaping tear that had opened up between them. The frayed edges of the threads that had once bound them drifting off into nothingness, unmoored.

She pressed her lips together, wondering at her own reticence to hurt him. Why, when he had hurt her without compunction? "I was going to revenge myself upon you," she admitted, knitting her fingers in her lap. "Giles suggested the possibility that you had some…lingering emotions. I meant to use them, and to crush your heart the way you had shattered mine. And in the end—I could not do it. I broke my own heart instead."

"As it happens, you had your revenge years ago and every day since," Marcus said. "I have not known a moment's happiness in years. You were all the happiness I had ever known." His eyes squeezed shut, his shoulders dropping as his legs slid down to the floor. He looked like the victim of a stabbing, left for dead in an alley, and still she could find no satisfaction in it. The anger had gone, and there were no flames left for his misery to feed. "You were everything I had ever wanted. Without you, there was no light in my life. No joy. No pleasure."

"You threw me away," she said, but the accusation had turned into a plaintive little wail of grief.

"Yes."

"Twice!"

"Yes." His shaking hand covered his mouth. "I still loved you, and I knew I could never let you know it. That the only way I could *keep* you was to keep you beneath my thumb so that you could never hurt me again. But you had never hurt me to begin with. And by the time I learned it, it was too late." His breath snarled, came in strange, jerky heaves. "Lydia, I wish I had answered you differently before you left. I wish that I had swallowed my pride. You offered me a gift beyond price, and I offered you only scorn in return."

She bent her head, feeling the burn of shame there at the back of her neck. "Don't," she said. "I have been humiliated enough already."

"The humiliation is mine," he said. "You should never have had to bear the weight of it; you were always blameless in this. As much as I would like to cast the lion's share of the blame upon my father, I can't. I knew you. I knew your heart. And still I let my faith in you shatter so easily. There is no defense for that. There is no recompense that I could offer that would equal the value of what you lost at my hands."

Her brows drew together at the hopelessness that had threaded through his words. They had sounded—not like an apology, per se. But like responsibility. Spoken not to seek forgiveness or absolution, but to take accountability. To acknowledge his part in the wrongs that had been done her, and shoulder the burden of what they represented. The consequences that until now had only ever been hers.

"I kept you once, and I should never have done it," he said, and she could hear the self-flagellation within it. The revulsion that he had once directed toward her had found its proper target at last. "I should have married you and presented my father with a *fait accompli* rather than risking your reputation. I *used* you, even though I loved you, in ways that were neither right nor fair. I held every bit of power in my hands, and I proved myself both a coward and a villain. I used it against you."

"I don't know what you want of me," she said, and she was suddenly so tired. Of him; of herself. Of the world in its entirety. She had become, all at once, a very old woman. Like every year she had lived had become a dozen, and she was old and wizened and grey, heavy with an exhaustion that went straight to her soul. "What do you expect me to say to that?"

"I expect nothing of you," he said. "But you—you should expect everything of me." His knees popped as he dragged himself to his feet, and he stumbled like a sleepwalker across the floor toward her, and dropped into a crouch at her feet. "You told me once that you would use me," he said. "So use me, Lydia."

The wretched, broken part of her heart clenched, like shards of glass crunching in on one another until she was again bleeding inside. "Marcus—"

"I love you," he said. "I have always loved you. And that is yours without expectation or obligation. Even if you don't want it. Even if you throw me away." His fingers touched her cheek, a tentative, gentle brush, his thumb rubbing away the tracks of salt her tears had left behind. "I love you," he said again. "I would give everything I own just to see you happy. And I won't ever expect you to love me in return. Just let me love you. Because I—I could spent the next fifty years of my life paying for my transgressions in whichever way you deem appropriate, and still I would be happier than I have ever been without you."

The heat of his fingers seared her cold skin, and she turned her face away, rubbing at the spot he'd touched as if to scrub away the sensation. "My God," she muttered to herself, discomfited. "You'd have me keep you like a dog on a lead? Have you no pride?"

"None. Of what use has it ever been to me?" His arm settled across his bent knee. "Please, Lydia. I will make no demands of you. If all you will ever have for me is bitter recriminations, then I will take them and be thankful to have earned even that much of your attention. Everything I have is yours. Only let me give it to you."

"You would have to be a fool to make such a poor bargain," she said, thrusting out her chin to lay down the challenge. "I could so easily make a beggar of you. Humiliate you."

"You could make no more a fool of me than I have made of myself."

Oh, that terrible ache in her chest. Her eyes burned anew, and she swallowed back a fresh rush of tears. "You—you should go back to London," she said, hearing the precarious wobble of her voice, as if he had shaken even that. "There is nothing to be gained in this."

"Do you want me to go?" The question drew her up short, and she stared at him, disturbed and perplexed. "If you tell me to go, I will go," he said, "But I hope you will not."

She tried for a glare and came up woefully short. "I will make you miserable if you stay," she said, though it hadn't come out sounding as much of a threat as she would have hoped. "I will give you back every bit of pain you gave to me and more again."

"That's fair. And *just*."

"I will have you working until your back breaks in service of me," she said, and she tried desperately for the ferocity she had possessed only days ago that had somehow deserted her. There was a wealth of disorder in her mind; every ugly thing that she had buried down deep coming up again and out and filling her with a wretched jumble of conflicted emotions. "I'll have you begging to be free of me within the week."

"I will beg, if it so pleases you. But not for that." There was a stark sort of relief there in his dark eyes, and he collected her cold hands in his, warming them in the clasp of his fingers. "Thank you," he breathed, and his lips brushed over her knuckles. "I don't want to leave you. I never want to leave you again."

The sob caught her unawares; such a horrible sound that had sneaked up from that wounded place inside of her. And then there was another, and her shoulders shook with the force of them, and she could not even reclaim her fingers to stifle them as they poured out in succession, one after the other, until she could not breathe around them. As if he had *dug* them out of her with his foolishness, and once the pressure under which they had been placed had been relieved, there had been no stopping them.

Distantly she was aware that he had tucked her head against his shoulder, that his fingers were massaging the nape of her neck—that he carried her through her storm with soothing, nonsense murmurs that were unintelligible even so close to her ear as they were. Her tears had drenched his collar, and her breath came in shuddering hiccoughs.

"Why couldn't I say it?" she whispered miserably. "Why couldn't I just be rid of you?"

"I don't know. Perhaps you should have done," he said against the top of her head. "But I am so grateful for it."

Chapter Twenty Five

Lydia set about proving herself a tyrant almost immediately. It was in the interests of self-preservation, really, so that she could produce her own evidence of his veracity or his deceit. He had either meant exactly the words he had said, or he was again a liar and a coward, but at least she would *know*.

She had had a full day Sunday, keeping him at his paces, nudging every limit of which she could conceive, pressing her finger down upon every nerve she suspected would send him fleeing. She had done her best to be demanding, contrary, exacting, and merciless, and if she had expected an untoward reaction, she had been doomed to disappointment.

He had not balked even once.

He had brought her countless cups of tea and a mid-afternoon meal which had sent him to no less than three different places to compile its separate elements and at which she had picked without much enthusiasm. He had sourced drinking chocolate for the whole of the company at her direction, though it had been something of an exercise in futility, since the company at large much preferred the ale and cider provided by the inn even to the rare indulgence of drinking chocolate.

She had torn a seam deliberately and then cast her pelisse into his hands with the demand of a quick repair, and he had not so much as twitched an eyelash at the outrageousness of it. In fact he had been startlingly quick about it; so quick that she suspected he had done it during the fruitless, unnecessary errands upon which she had sent him.

She worked him like a scullery drudge, and he—he completed every task she set before him in a spirit of contrition, as if he were collecting fragments of her favor, which she doled out sparingly. He brought her things she had not asked for, and for which she had been obliged to, however begrudgingly, thank him. But even her foul mood did not dampen his good humor, and from dawn until nearly midnight he labored, while the remainder of the company rested.

Come the morning, the company would begin the arduous process of tearing down sets and neatly packing away costumes and props; a ritual that had been delayed by the Christmas holiday, and which had been delayed still by the additional day of rest that they had been granted on account of the Sunday that had followed it. And while everyone else lazed or dozed or nursed the inevitable aftereffects of cider that had been too liberally laced with liquor, Marcus worked instead.

It was, she thought, a delicate handling of the sharp edges that comprised her, threatening a nasty cut from every angle. Only time and care could blunt them, and she—she had come by her sharpness honestly, and she did not know what would be left of her if he succeeded.

Perhaps worse still, she did not know what would be left of her if he failed.

She was trying to drive him away, just as she had promised she would do. Just because she had not been able to make herself say the words that would send him away, it did not mean she would not try to affect it anyway. There was nothing of subtlety in it, nothing of subterfuge or deception. Each demand had been delivered with an upturned chin; a challenge of its own. She did not understand, yet, that he was just so damned grateful only to have been permitted to remain that he would have done anything she asked of him without argument.

It had *wrecked* her, that unspoken admission which he had gotten of her only because he had asked a question whose answer he had feared more than death. She could have killed his every hope with a weapon he had handed her himself, and in so few words: *Yes, I want you to go.*

But she had not been able to make herself *say* them. So perhaps there was some hope which lived within her too. Probably just the smallest sliver of it, hidden down so deep in the dark that its very existence had surprised even her.

The tempestuous storm of emotions that had followed had embarrassed her, he thought. She held him responsible for them, and it was for that reason that she punished him now—or thought she did. Probably she did not realize that he had spent more time in her company in the last day than he had in the last two weeks, and that was its own reward, regardless of the sharpness of her tongue or the spitefully-issued orders she cast at him.

It had not surprised him that, come Tuesday morning, his carriage had been commandeered once more for the journey to Southampton, once they had got the whole of the set taken down and packed away, but it *had* surprised him that he had at last merited a place of his own out of the elements, since the weather had turned a dreary and dour grey once more. Not within his own carriage, of course, but rather crammed in with several other members of the company, which had made the journey a good deal less comfortable than he might have preferred. Still, it was eminently better than riding topside where he would no doubt have suffered under the deluge that had begun perhaps half an hour into the drive.

They had left Brighton early in the morning and had stopped only briefly along the way at a coaching inn to change horses and for whatever meal could be gotten swiftly, but despite the rain they had made good time and they arrived in Southampton by late afternoon.

Marcus had snatched only a brief reprieve to stretch his legs from the long hours stuffed into the carriage before Montgomery had ordered him on to assist with the unloading of the sets, which promised to be hours of labor in itself. The rough roads had inflicted no small amount of damage upon the sets, rattling nails from their moorings and chipping paint here and there.

"You grow accustomed to it," Alfie had said, as they hefted wedges of scenery into the theatre together. "There's always something due for repair. And these—well, we've not built new in some time now. It's only a matter of time before they crumble completely."

Probably it was. Though he'd not been about it long enough to judge so well as most of them, he could spot the problem areas now with a competency he'd lacked before; the damaged wood ravaged by more and more nails only to hold it together, the flaking paint that did not lay as flat as it once had, weathering beneath layers and layers of the same. To the audience, somewhat distant from the stage, these flaws would not be particularly noticeable. But to these people, who took such pride in their work, they were hallmarks of a company in decline.

But that would improve itself soon enough, he suspected. Sybil would not have to stitch and re-stitch again lace that had begun to fray years ago, or to cull what she could from the wardrobe that Lydia had surrendered to her. There would be time—and funds—for the company to become what it had been meant to be.

It was hours before they had at last reassembled most of the set, repairing what they could as they went. By the time Marcus was able to leave the theatre and walk to the inn which they had taken up rooms within, it was to find what had been left out for supper largely picked over and Rafe all but asleep in a chair near the fire, ostensibly having been kept waiting all this time.

He had expected Lydia to have gone up to bed already, but instead she was still within the common room, embroiled in an argument with Montgomery, quiet and fierce. Marcus piled the cuts of cured meat and tiny wedges of cheese that had been meant for supper onto a plate, collected a tankard of ale, and finally allowed himself the pleasure of stretching his legs out beneath the table that Rafe had commandeered.

Rafe jerked from his half-doze, scrubbing at his face with both hands to rub the sleep from his eyes. "Good God," he said, in a sleep-roughened slur. "They do keep you busy, don't they?"

"You've no idea." Marcus abandoned the table etiquette that had long been ingrained in him in favor of filling his stomach swiftly. "Are you staying much longer?"

"I suppose that depends," Rafe said. "Am I no longer needed?"

Marcus shrugged. "We're here three weeks," he said. "That's time enough to engage my solicitor to find us an inn in Bath before we leave— provided you are willing to carry a letter back with you to London to deliver to the man."

"I might as well do," Rafe said, stretching his arms over his head with a massive yawn. "Since I've got to pass along the instructions for the company's investments, besides." His eyes scanned the common room, lighting upon Montgomery and Lydia some distance away. "Any luck there?" he asked, with a subtle inclination of his head.

"Some," Marcus said. "Less than I'd like. More than I had hoped." He sighed, leaning back in an ungainly slouch that would have given their mother a fit of the vapors. "I have squandered so much trust that even the truth is suspect," he said. "But—it might be possible to earn it back."

"Is that what you are doing here?"

"After a fashion." Marcus dropped his voice, lest the sound carry. "Lydia has been running me ragged. She's trying to drive me away. Menial tasks, pointless errands, anything she thinks might offend me. It's all quite transparent, really."

"And you do it anyway."

Marcus closed his eyes. "Twice I savaged her pride to protect my own," he said. "*Twice*, Rafe. I don't think I would have forgiven myself even once. If this salvages hers? Yes; I will do it." He picked a hunk of bread apart between his fingers. "A few nights' past, we talked. And I listened. As I ought to have done before. It was…difficult to hear," he said.

"I can imagine," Rafe replied.

"You really can't, and I hope you never do. It was dreadful, all of it dreadful. To hear from her lips the sort of villain I had made of myself…" Marcus took a deep drink of his ale and came up for air with a tiny gasp. "She thinks I never meant to marry her at all. I told her otherwise, but—" *How could you expect me to believe that*? "My truth means nothing. I have been branded a liar by my own actions."

Rafe sighed, settling his palms upon the table. "Can you truly blame her for that?"

"You mistake my meaning," Marcus said. "I don't blame her in the slightest. I know well enough, now, with whom the blame truly lies." But it had taken five years to achieve that knowledge. Five long years wasted in a sort of misery that had never *had* to happen, but that he had *let* happen.

"Do you know," Rafe said, reflectively, "you look better than you have in recent years. You *sound* better. I mean to say, you look utterly wretched. Like you've been run through a box mangle"—here, Marcus smothered a laugh in his palm, because it was entirely honest and the rest of the company had fared little better—"but still, you look *better*. Lighter, I think."

"I am better," Marcus said, and knew it for the truth. "And I will be better still." A little more, every day. Just so long as Lydia did not ask him to leave.

"Miss Alcott. Might I have a word?"

Lydia looked up from the glass of wine she had been nursing for the majority of the evening, already annoyed to have been pulled from the bowels of a perfectly serviceable sulk. "Lord Rafe," she said sullenly. "I thought you would have gone already."

"I thought I would have as well," he said, "but it seems that the demands of the theatre have kept my brother quite busy." He gestured to the chair that Giles had vacated perhaps half an hour earlier. "Do you mind?"

She didn't see how she could stop him, considering that he was just as entitled to the use of the common room as any other guest. "By all means." She flicked a glance around the room to find that Marcus, too, had left. Probably some time ago. "And where has your brother gone off to?"

"Bed, I think. I think he made some mention of getting an early start on some repairs tomorrow morning. It seems your company's cart is not in the best of condition. There were damages to some of the scenery."

Nothing was really in the best of condition any longer, but that was simply one of the many travails of the theatre. "Industrious of him, I suppose," she said.

"And of you, to keep him at it. Amongst other things, I hear." He leaned across to a nearby table and snagged up the remainder of a bottle of wine that had been deserted at some point in the evening, pouring the dregs into his own glass. "I realize, Miss Alcott, that you have got some just cause to be…we'll say *less than trusting*, when it comes to Marcus."

"More cause than most," Lydia sniffed. "I'm not certain what this has got to do with you, my lord."

"Probably nothing," Rafe said. "But he is my brother, and so I feel I can be forgiven for a bit of brotherly meddling."

"I wouldn't know. I have only got a sister."

"*Hah*," he said, as if he had won some battle in which she had not known they had been involved. "No one meddles quite like a brother. You may take my word on that." He hesitated a moment, swirling his wine in his glass. "It is…good to see him again," he said.

Lydia felt her brows draw down into a frown. "Have you been away so long, then?" Though he had been away when last she had known Marcus, that had been years ago.

"No," he said. "In fact, I returned only months after the two of you parted. It is only that the man he was when I returned was not the brother I had known. I hated you for that," he admitted, "back when I thought I had cause for it. Because once you had made him so happy—and then he was only a decaying ruin of who he had once been. And I missed him."

Lydia said nothing, though she chafed at the blame he would have assigned her.

"I have no cause to lie to you, Miss Alcott," he said. "So perhaps you can believe *me* when I tell you that he always meant to wed you. His letters were filled with every one of your virtues he could find the words to espouse, and I was certain that by the time the I returned home, I would find that I had acquired a new sister by marriage. I have got the letters at home somewhere, I'm certain, should you care to see the proof of them." He managed a low laugh over the rim of his glass. "In one of them, he had even included a sketch of the ring—very poorly done, mind you; Marcus has never been much of an artist—but he was so eager to show me that he attempted it anyway. I suspect that, were you to ask, he would be able to produce that ring. Likely it's in his house somewhere still. He was never able to let go of you."

Lydia cast her gaze down into her glass, shifting uncomfortably in her chair. "I cannot see what business that is of mine," she said.

"Can't you?" Rafe asked, and his eyes seemed to bore into her. "Undoubtedly you've numerous other sins to lay at his feet, but that—that is not one of them. I thought it might be worth something to you to know. From someone who has no reason to lie."

"It doesn't matter," she said. "It doesn't matter what he intended. Not anymore." But the whispered words had the tenor of a lie, and she clenched her hands beneath the table.

"I think it does, at least a little. At least *enough*. And I think—if ever again he had the opportunity, he would not hesitate to see it through." Rafe's fingertips drummed atop the scarred surface of the table. "He was never happy without you," he said. "Not for one moment. I doubt he ever could be. But you—you could make him happy again. You do already."

Did she? With all of the snide disdain she could summon to the point of her tongue? It seemed doubtful. "I don't see how he could be. I have been trying to be rid of him."

"Not well enough, it seems. And you would only have to tell him that, besides. Why haven't you, then?"

Lydia gritted her teeth, praying for patience. Perhaps the blasted man was right, and brothers were indeed prime meddlers. "*That* is no concern of *yours*, my lord."

"Rafe is well enough," he said, waving off the formal, stilted address. "Since I suspect you will indeed be my sister by marriage sooner or later."

"*My lord.*"

Rafe gave a sigh, and an exaggerated roll of his eyes. "Later, then, I suppose."

"How blithely men do tender their opinions," Lydia said. "Especially those unasked for."

"*Someone* had to tell you," he said, and he polished off the last of his wine and pushed back his chair. "Well, I'm to bed, since I intend to be on my way back to London in the morning. But do think on it, won't you, Miss Alcott? I

223

think you must know, even if you cannot yet acknowledge it even to yourself, that the only way Marcus would leave you is if you asked it of him. Because you could be as miserable, as wretched, as demanding and contrary as it pleases you to be—and still, he would be happy just to be near you."

Chapter Twenty Six

Marcus was not, in his lowly position within the company, privy to the majority of its workings. But he hadn't had to be to have sorted out relatively quickly that something had happened that had left Lydia out of sorts and more snappish than she might otherwise have been.

In the few performances they had given in Southampton since they had arrived, Lydia had performed at only one. And it had not taken much speculation to understand that she had not been well pleased by this turn of events.

Marcus had resisted remarking upon it, since he assumed it was a matter of some sensitivity, but eventually it had become unavoidable. When she had not returned to the inn far too late into the evening for comfort—not even to bypass the common room to go straight to her room—he had risked going in search of her.

The theatre had been locked up tight for the evening, but she could not have wandered far, and eventually he found her overlooking the water of the River Itchen, staring aimlessly out into the night. Though she was underdressed for the weather, which was frigid, she seemed not to feel the cold that certainly must be seeping through her gown absent the thick wool of a pelisse.

Marcus cleared his throat to announce his presence, though she glanced only briefly—dismissively—over her shoulder. "You've missed supper," he said, although that was not precisely true. There was still plenty left for her. It was just that she hadn't come for it.

Her shoulders lifted, fell; a listless shrug, without much enthusiasm. "I'm not particularly hungry this evening."

"No?" He tugged at the buttons of his coat, shrugging out of it. "I'll fetch some for you, if you like." He draped his discarded coat over her shoulders, stepping into place beside her. Close—but not so close that she might protest.

"No, thank you." She mumbled the words into the collar of his coat, which she turned up against the chill.

"Will you not come back to the inn?" he asked. "It's quite late."

"Is Giles still in the common room?"

"Last I saw, yes." Which had been probably at least a half an hour, now.

Her head dipped, and the breeze that slid down the street brushed a few stray strands of hair across her cheeks. "I'd rather not, then."

Trouble there, then. But then he had known something was amiss—and he recalled that the evening they had arrived in Southampton, he had seen them in the common room together, and the nature of their conversation, though he had not heard it himself, had seemed contentious enough even at a glance. "Have you quarreled?" he asked.

Lydia pulled a scowl, and he knew he had hit upon the crux of the issue. "I did not come here," she said, in scathing tones, "for conversation. I came here to be alone!"

She could have managed that more comfortably in her room, but the point did not seem worth arguing given her present humor. Quite possibly she had simply wanted to escape attention altogether, and she had been bound to attract at least a little at the inn.

"I beg your pardon," he said. "Would you like me to go?"

"*Yes*," she snapped, turning her face away from him.

"All right. I'll leave you my coat, then." She had not wandered too far, even if it was too late for her to be out on her own. She had weathered places less safe than this. "When you care to return, you should eat something. I'll see that a plate is left out for you."

He'd made it perhaps a half dozen steps before her voice split through the silent night. "Giles—Giles says I'm not an actress at all," she said, her voice quavering across the syllables.

Marcus turned, keeping the distance he'd gained from her. "Is that why you have not been on the stage?"

Her expression crumpled; she could maintain it no longer—not the reserve, not the anger that she had cast at him in lieu of casting at Montgomery. "He won't give me even Perdita," she said in a ragged whisper. "I don't have it in me. Perhaps I never really did."

She hadn't had to tell him. She could have let him walk straight back to the inn on his own. But she *had*, and that felt—somehow significant. Like the slow ebb and flow of a tide turning on itself. Marcus risked a step closer. Just one; just in case more would press his luck. And he didn't know what to say to it all, except, perhaps: "I'm sorry. I know you loved it."

She seemed to startle at that, swallowed into the folds of the coat he'd draped over her shoulders. "I didn't," she said, and she swiped at her eyes with just the tips of her fingers before she folded her arms over her chest. "I didn't *love* it. The acting."

Another step, and she hadn't even noticed. Or if she had, she'd said nothing, done nothing to suggest that encroaching on the distance that she had initially demanded had offended her in any way.

"I just—I thought I would always have it," she whispered. "Even if the audience is dreadful, and the hours are mad—I thought it was still *mine*. I thought I had *earned* my place in the theatre."

"But you have," he said. "And it's still yours. Half yours, in fact."

She gave a derisive sniff. "Apparently, a man's half is always greater than a woman's." But the contemptuous tone wobbled off into sorrow, and she ducked her head once more. "I was never acting," she said, like she had been admitting to some heinous crime. "Not really."

Marcus had known that, eventually. Montgomery, it seemed, had known it—or at least suspected—from the beginning. And she didn't have it in her any longer; all those terrible emotions that had made her so convincing in the roles he had given to her. She had memorized the lines, and delivered them with all of the passion they had deserved. But it had always been *her* pain, *her* grief, *her* anger coming out there upon the stage. Never an invention; never a pretense. "I know," he said. "I do know that, now."

She made a ragged, tearful sound deep in her throat, sounding shaken. "Will you—will you hold me? Just for a moment?"

Christ. Marcus crossed the remaining distance between them in only a second, and she gave a harsh, shuddering gasp against his shoulder when he pulled her into his arms. "Yes," he said into the puff of her hair that had spilled over the collar of his coat. "Whenever you need."

"It hurts," she said, in just a shred of a whisper. "Even if it wasn't my dream, it still hurts to lose it." A tiny, broken sound—like her very voice had shattered. "Tighter," she mumbled.

His arms encased her, and he had the vague sense that she was using him to hold herself together. *Using* him, but this time for comfort. To keep the pieces of her that threatened to scatter into the icy breeze held into some shape that approximated human, until she could do it for herself.

"It's still yours, Lydia. Even if you take on a different role within it, it's still your theatre, your company." His palm found the small of her back beneath the wool of his coat and pressed. "You don't love acting," he said, repeating back to her her own admission. "But to have stayed so long, you must

227

have loved other parts."

He felt the smallest rise and fall of her shoulders. "The people," she said. "The company itself. I love the satisfaction of having produced something. The chaos of the theatre. Working for something together."

Because they had found her when she had been lost. It had given her a purpose when she had had nothing and no one. "You have that still," he said.

"Do I?" There was a wet-sounding sniffle, and she searched the pockets of his coat, eventually coming up with a handkerchief that had been stuffed into one of them. "I feel like I'm losing myself in pieces. A bit at a time."

"I think you're finding yourself again," he said. "For whatever my opinion might be worth to you. What was it to you—the stage—if not your dream?"

Stark silence settled over them, and the wind that twined through her hair lifted a few strands to tickle his chin. "A holding space," she said at last, in a distant voice, as if she were looking into the past. "A place to be exactly as wretched as I felt. Where I was expected to be so, and there was no one to cast judgment upon me for it."

She had needed that at the time, he thought. And Montgomery had let her have it; a mutually beneficial arrangement for the both of them. Her misery turned into his gain. "You can still be wretched if and when it pleases you. Perhaps you simply don't need an audience of hundreds for it any longer."

"I suppose I can." Her breath no longer came in distressed puffs that whitened the air around them. "Perhaps I don't need it anymore," she said slowly, and he thought there was the tiniest bit of understanding in her voice at last. That she had lost more than just the acting—that she had lost the pain and the grief that had made it possible to begin with. That in the doing, she might have gained things as well. Peace. Hope. The chance to dream again.

"It's still your company," he said. "You haven't lost that. All the rest of it—the things you *do* love—they are still there for you." Her hair was so soft beneath his hand, and she pressed her cheek against his shoulder while he stroked it. "Without the stage itself taking up so much of your time, I think you'll be a wonder at the management of it."

Somehow, she managed a rusty sort of laugh, as if she had had to search for one deep down inside herself and had sourced only that pitiful example of humor. "Probably," she said. "Giles is rubbish at business. And so disorganized."

And there; that was something. Just enough, he thought, that she could mourn what was lost to her without being mired in the pain of that loss. Her breath feathered out on a long, low sigh. Acceptance, he thought. Choosing to look forward instead of back.

With one hand she balled up the handkerchief and blotted away the last of her tears. Gradually she shifted, and he was forced to relinquish his hold upon her as she collected herself once more. But she did not press for more space than that. "We're moving on to Bath in a few weeks," she said. "How long do you intend to stay with the company?"

Marcus shrugged, unconcerned. "Until you tell me to go."

She blinked, clutching his coat tighter around herself to ward off the chill of the air. "We won't be back to London for some time," she said. "Probably not until midsummer. You're a *lord*; you can't just—"

"Lydia. You asked me a question. I gave you an answer." He caught an icy blond curl that had been tossed about on the breeze and rubbed it between his fingertips. "Until you tell me to go."

The hard-won composure that she had managed to cobble together slipped from her grasp once again. An odd, strangled sob clawed at her throat, and she ducked her head, violently blotting at her eyes once again. "Don't go," she said, and there was a ferocity in her voice that surprised him. "Don't go."

She trembled, suddenly, possibly from the cold, but more likely from the weight of what she had asked of him, and what it might mean for both of them. And she let him hold her together once more.

"Am I in imminent danger of murder?" Montgomery inquired as Marcus entered the otherwise deserted common room at last, late into the following evening. "Lydia's hardly spoken more than a word or two to me just lately."

"What, since you told her she hadn't got a lick of talent and you didn't want her as an actress if she wasn't perfectly miserable?" Marcus returned lightly as he assembled a plate. "Why should she have taken that poorly?"

Montgomery scowled over his ale. "I didn't say *that*," he said sullenly.

Marcus sent him a glance over his shoulder—just a single, hard look, and Montgomery slouched his shoulders.

"In so many words, at least," Montgomery grumbled. "It is true, though, you know."

"She's still permitted to be hurt," Marcus said. "You have to *let* her be hurt. And she will come through it in her own time, in her own way." A loss was still a loss, even if that lost thing had not been truly beloved.

Montgomery heaved a sigh and extended his legs beneath the table, sprawling out. "I suppose you would know," he said. "She is still running you ragged?"

Marcus managed a chuckle, and gave an exasperated shake of his head as he approached Montgomery's table and dropped into the chair across from him. "Between her demands and those of the theatre, I've little time for anything but the occasional meal and perhaps a few hours of sleep, if I am very lucky."

"I suppose we've both earned our positions in Lydia's disfavor, eh?" Montgomery snagged an olive from Marcus' plate and devoured it, and would have reached for another had Marcus not slapped at his hand.

"But you, at least, she will forgive. Deep down, she knows you were right, even if she resents it presently." Marcus wrapped his arm around his plate to fend off any further untoward advances. "She didn't love the acting, but she did need it, for a time. Hard to let go of, I think."

Giles hesitated a long moment, and his lips pursed as if to contain words best not spoken. At last he sighed and let them out anyway. "She'll forgive you as well," he said. "She might well make you suffer the rest of your natural life"—he glared as Marcus choked out a laugh—"but she'll forgive you. She loves you. She always has."

Between bites of a hunk of bread that had gone half-stale already, owing to the lateness of the hour, Marcus said, "Would that I could be so certain."

Montgomery chuckled. "I'll grant you that I might be a right arse at times, but I'm no liar—and Lydia is the closest thing to a friend I've got." Clearing his throat, he added, "And I *do* mean *friend*, Newhaven. There was never anything more between us. There never could have been."

Marcus had wondered, of course. It would have been impossible not to entertain such thoughts. "Even if there had been," he said, "it would not be my business. I lost all right to such concerns years ago." But it was still, however, a relief to know that he was not in competition for Lydia's affections, especially with the man who was now her business partner.

"Enlightened of you." Montgomery hesitated, his fingers tapping out an unsteady rhythm upon his tankard. "But I *do* mean that there never *could* have been," he said, finally, his voice drifting lower, in the cadence of secrets shared. "It's…known, within the company, of course. But you're bound to

230

discover it eventually, and I should like to deal with the inevitable fallout sooner rather than later."

Confused, Marcus could only nod along, hoping that at some point that Montgomery would begin to make some sort of sense.

"I'm discreet, naturally," Montgomery said. "Haven't heard so much as a whisper, and no one here would ever betray me. But you—you are still something of an unknown quantity."

"Montgomery, what the hell are you talking about?"

"I don't prefer women," Montgomery said. "I never have. Infrequently—due largely to the nature of my profession—I enjoy the company of men. Intimately."

"Oh." Marcus had heard, of course, about such men, though he had not, to his knowledge, ever met one. "*Discreet*," he mused. "Hell of a way to have to live." Discretion had been of little service to him, in the past. But to have to live one's whole *life* beneath the cover of it?

"I hope I have not misjudged you," Montgomery said. "In fact, it is one of the reasons, I think, that Lydia and I have been friends all these years. After you, she could never bring herself to trust the intentions of men—"

"But you didn't want anything from her," Marcus said, with a sudden clap of understanding. Montgomery, at least, had made himself worthy of her trust when it had been badly damaged.

"Not intimately, at least," Montgomery said. "So, you see, there was never that between us. There could never have been. But we *are* friends, and I suspect that we ever shall be, and so I thought—in the interests of honesty, you should know. And I think she would take it ill if you were to denounce me—"

"I'm not going to denounce you." Even if Marcus could not quite wrap his mind around the concept, still it did not change the core of who Montgomery was—which was to say, a friend to Lydia when she had desperately needed one. "I can't say I understand it, but it seems that that is your business, not my own." In the spirit of rapport, he lifted his arm from around his plate and slid it toward Montgomery, who hesitated only a fraction of a moment before he snatched up another olive. "It's been at least two weeks since last you called me Leontes," Marcus said.

"I suppose it has," Montgomery murmured reflectively. "You've not much *been* Leontes just lately."

"All right, then." Marcus extended his hand across the table. "Suppose we call ourselves friends?"

"Good God. I *had* hoped to avoid that," Montgomery groaned, but at last he put his hand in Marcus' with a beleaguered sigh. "But I suppose we must."

Chapter Twenty Seven

A scratch at her door forced Lydia from the contents of the letter she had been reading, and she rubbed at the headache that was forming at her temples and called, "Enter."

The door hinges creaked for want of a good oiling, and Marcus poked his head through the door. "I've brought you a cup of hot cider," he said. "It's been freezing all day."

She had not asked for it, but then he'd brought her quite a lot of things she'd not asked for lately. Just because he could, or because he thought she would like them. "I'd not thought the kitchen staff was awake so late," she said.

"For you, they are awake at all hours." He tipped his head, a subtle request for entry.

Lydia nodded, holding out her hand for the cup that he slid into it. Just this side of scalding; redolent of cinnamon and apples, with the sharp bite of whatever liquor had been mixed into it carried in the scent. "Thank you," she said, because somehow she had fallen back into the habit of it—like there was a part of her that had tallied up marks of his debt to her, and found it relieved enough for civility. "You needn't have. But thank you."

Marcus shrugged, as if the effort that he had gone to for the cider had not been worth the effort to which she had gone to thank him for it. "You are troubled," he observed, and his eyes lit on the letter in her hand. "Bad news?"

"Trouble at home," she said, and managed perhaps the shade of a woeful smile. "Lavinia has written to me again. Her wages at the silk mill are not ideal, and my father's shop is not as busy as once it was. Prices just keep rising, and they owe rent that had gone unpaid too long as it is. They're struggling." And she had already given them what she had to spare.

"Eighty pounds was not enough?" he asked, but it was only curiosity, not judgment. He took a seat just there at the edge of the bed, settling his hands on his thighs.

"It was enough to pay off the worst of their debts, I think. But there were more even than I knew." More even than she could hope to make up with her wages. There was still that shame there, not too very deep down. She set aside the cider and drew up her knees, laying the letter across them. "I ruined them," she said. "When I left. My wages as a seamstress kept us above water, and I didn't know it. It's been five years without them, and they have suffered."

"You have been choosing the lowest places to stay," he said. "The cheapest?"

Lydia nodded, and she had not even realized she had been crying until he reached out and swiped a tear off of her cheek with his thumb.

"You send the rest home," he said. "Anything you can spare. That's why you had gowns years out of date."

"I had to. They could have lost everything." A terrible burst of near-hysterical laughter burst from her lips, and she smothered it with her palm. "They will anyway, I'm afraid."

"They won't," he said, and then caught her hand up in his, squeezing it tightly. "Lydia, I promise you they won't. And even if, by some terrible twist of fate, they *did*—I would see them taken care of. This is also my responsibility."

It would have been so easy to cling to her pride and to refuse. But the consequences were beyond what she could bear alone, and he—he *had* been trying to right his wrongs. Without excuse or expectation. And with a sense of surety she'd not thought she would ever feel again, she found that she knew that if she *did* lay it into his hands, he would do exactly as he had said. Trust, she thought. She *trusted* that he had meant those words. And he had earned it, perversely, because with the annuity that now belonged to her and to the company, he had made it so she had not *had* to trust him. That simple acceptance of the judgment he had earned had won him much. It had taken time to see it for what it had been intended to be: a gift, without strings, without the intent of manipulation. A security that no one could take from her. And so she ducked her head and whispered, "All right."

"May I see the letter?" He held out his hand to her.

She laid the pages within it, and watched as he arranged them to read. The dim candlelight flickered across his brow, which seemed to grow more dour and forbidding by the moment.

"I think I sense my father's hand in this," he said roughly.

"What?" she said, her shoulders going rigid. "But how?"

"My own fault, most likely." Marcus dragged one hand through his hair, ruffling the dark strands. "Lately, Father has proved himself more devious, more underhanded, than I would ever have suspected him capable of being," he said. "I told him I was going, you see, after I"—he flexed his fingers, though the bruising on his once-ruined knuckles had long faded—"after I made myself clear to him. I told him I was going to Brighton. To you. In fact, he has no hold over me *except* you. I would not put it past him to strike out in any way he could to bring me running home again. At least, I cannot discount the possibility."

"You think he is contriving to ruin my family?" she whispered.

"I think my father would seize at control, at power, any way he had to." His fingers grasped the letter anew, and the pages trembled in his hand—a testament to his fury. "He has been pressuring me to marry for years," he said. "And I was only amenable to it when it was—"

"Me."

"Yes." He sighed. "For a time—once he had got you out of the way—he stopped pressing quite so fiercely. And then you were back, and he started it all up again, because I had only ever wanted you, and he—he could not accept that." His voice dropped to a hushed murmur. "You were acceptable as a mistress," he said. "Many men have mistresses. Father's had several himself. But—"

But men didn't marry their mistresses, and she had become expendable the moment Marcus had taken concrete action to make her into something more. Somehow, she had let herself push that nasty fact to the very back of her mind. That there were so many more obstacles than *trust*. That they had been ruined before they had ever begun. Ruined *years* ago.

Lydia dashed at her eyes and tried to shake her hand free of Marcus', though he only tightened his grip upon it, reluctant to surrender her. "He never would have let you wed me," she said, the words abrading her throat like a rasp. "He never will."

"Lydia, I have bowed to Father's dictates for too many years already. I will not do so again. The choice is not his to make," Marcus said, and his fingers squeezed hers. "It is yours."

But it wasn't. It hadn't ever been, really. The choice had been made for her already. And yet it felt like ceding the last tiny bit of hope that had dwelt within her to acknowledge the reality of it. "Marcus," she said softly. "You must know it's impossible."

There was the minute loosening of his fingers upon hers. Those fingers, which had crossed such a vast distance to connect with hers once more, yielding—however reluctantly—all that he had gained. His head bowed, his lids lowering over his eyes. "Because you can never forgive me?" he asked, and though he had made a distinct effort to modulate his voice, to inflect it with neither hurt nor accusation, still she could see what it had cost him to ask that last, crucial question. The hope that it had burned through, like a fragile scrap of parchment kissed by a flame.

And honesty was the least she could offer in return. "Marcus, I would ruin you if I married you," she said.

"You will ruin me if you do not. I'm already ruined, Lydia. I have been for years." The pages of the letter drifted to the floor unheeded as he turned toward her to scrub at her cheeks with the sleeve of his shirt. "Don't cry. I truly can't bear it."

How could she not? It was a death all over again, and she had been denied the chance to mourn it appropriately the first time. And so with nothing left to cling to, she clung instead to him, crawling across the bed to twine her arms about his neck and bury her face in his shoulder. One last, fierce embrace before she would have to let him go.

His arms came around her, cradling her like a child across his lap, and she thought she felt the terrible hitch of his breath in his chest. "Why?" he asked, his voice muffled in the plait of her hair that had draped over her shoulder.

"You have to marry within your class," she said miserably. "A proper lady. Someone without a hint of scandal attached to her name." And she had ever so much more than a *hint*.

His hand cupped the back of her head. "The scandal was never your fault."

No, it hadn't been. She had been only a young and silly girl, too idealistic, too naïve to have expected the treachery that had laid in store for her. But that was the way of such scandals—they never seemed to attach themselves to men in the same manner that they adhered stubbornly to women. It would never matter how innocent she had been in it; it was indelible still. And if Marcus committed the unpardonable sin of binding himself to her permanently—it would be his as well.

"I would never have been acceptable even as a seamstress," she said, the tinny pitch of her voice quavering through the air. "And I have been so much worse since." A mistress. An actress. The stain of those things could never be washed away. "Your father was right," she said, though the words seemed to

236

tear at her very soul. "You cannot throw yourself away on me."

"That's not true." His lips touched her temple. "Lydia, I will never marry elsewhere. You will only be consigning me to a lifetime of loneliness."

"Don't say that," she whispered. "You owe it to yourself—you owe it to *me*—to be better than that."

"It's only the truth. I have been at most half a man without you. How could you ask me to go on like that?" He pressed a kiss to the top of her head. "Even if you will not marry me," he said, "let me stay with you."

"You would lose everything," she said. Every ounce of respectability, every pound of friendship. Every door which had once been flung open wide to him would slam itself closed. Every opportunity and privilege to which he had been entitled on the basis of birth alone would evaporate as if they had never existed at all. "And to be—what? My kept man?"

"If you like. If that is all you would have of me." He whispered the words into the shell of her ear. "Would you keep me on a lead and command me to sleep at the foot of your bed?"

Lydia managed a rueful laugh that seemed to trickle out into a smothered sob. "Be serious."

"I am. Lydia, I would gain everything that matters to me and lose nothing I value." He turned her face to his and laid a kiss just at the corner of her lips. "I have still got the ring I purchased for you," he said. "I could never give up what it represented to me. It has always been yours, even if you don't want it any longer."

Lydia squeezed her eyes shut, surprised by the stabbing ache of her heart. "You must know I would never be accepted," she said. "What sort of life would we lead, Marcus, with your father contriving to hurt us at every step? With the dark cloud of scandal hanging over us? My reputation is worse than ruined. So far past the point where it could be repaired by marriage." The scandal that had precipitated their parting had been made so very public. She would always be thought a faithless opportunist.

A strange stillness settled over him, and a tense silence stretched out. His fingers played in her hair, stroking the smooth strands. "Perhaps not repaired," he said slowly, lingering over the words with a peculiar, wondering intonation. "But…perhaps it could be corrected."

"Corrected?"

"Suffice it to say, for now, that I've learned from my time with the company that people love a good drama," he said obliquely. "I have had quite a lot of time to think, and to contrive revenge fantasies of my own, and I think

I might have…something of an idea. And it may well come to nothing at all, but even if it does not—Lydia, I would sacrifice everything for you. Can you believe in me at least that far?"

He was asking for her trust. For a leap of faith. For the clasp of her hand within his, with the certainty that this time, he would not let it go. And she gave it to him at last, the twine of his fingers through hers felt like a promise. A pledge, five years removed from when it had first been offered—but now it was every bit as real as his hand in hers. "Tell me your idea, then," she said.

"Father is proud," he said. "His reputation is everything to him, and he will spew his venom without shame or remorse to protect it. To silence him, to thoroughly enact the revenge he so richly deserves and to ensure that he'll have no recourse in the future, we must reveal him for what he is. Publicly."

"How?"

"Give him a slight he cannot possibly allow to pass unheeded. We'll tell him we plan to marry."

Lydia shivered, remembering the cold, ruthless demeanor of the man who had come to the theatre only to threaten her. Yes, she thought. That would be an unforgiveable sin to such a man.

"Of course," Marcus said, lightly, tentatively, "fiction plays best when it is presented as fact. We might have to marry in truth."

Despite herself, Lydia laughed—and it sounded cleaner, softer. Like a great weight had at last been removed from her chest, where it had settled so long ago. "Don't be ridiculous," she said. "I won't marry you to revenge myself upon your father." She tucked her head against his shoulder, breathed in the clean scent of his shaving soap, and felt the last icy shards that had pierced her heart so many years ago melt away to nothing. "But I will marry you because I love you."

Marcus shuddered with relief, his arms holding her so tightly for a moment that she thought the air might be wrenched from her lungs. "You can't take it back," he said fiercely, and his lips caught at hers in a desperate kiss.

"I won't," she said, turning her face to his. They had gotten lost for a while, but this—this felt like coming home. A long journey of diverging roads, with the twists and turns that had led them both so far astray, until at long last they had converged once again. This time, it was a choice to walk that road hand in hand, in the knowledge that whatever challenges might come would be faced together.

"We're going to be happy," he said. "I promise you that. Whatever comes, we're going to be happy."

238

"Even if this nebulous scheme of yours comes to nothing?" she asked, her voice wobbling precariously through the syllables. "I could not bear it if you were to regret—"

"Even then," he said. "*Especially* then. If I only have to share you with the company rather than with all of society, I will count myself blessed." He dropped tiny kisses on her nose, her chin, her cheeks. "All I want—all I have ever wanted—is you."

And there—that was honesty. She could hear it now that she let herself, and she was going to trust that the words he had given her had not been spoken lightly. He had had ample time to consider the consequences, and if he said that they were nothing to him, she was going to believe it.

"Tomorrow morning," he said. "We are leaving for London."

"London?" Her stomach clenched at the thought. "Why?"

"Because I am going to do what I ought to have done years ago," he said, tucking her head beneath his chin. "Marry you before you can come to your senses."

Chapter Twenty Eight

So you're going," Giles repeated, lifting his cup of tea to his lips, exhibiting a stunning lack of surprise—or concern. He'd managed to drag his attention away from the paper that lay, half-folded, upon the table before him.

"Yes," Lydia said. "Immediately. As soon as the carriage is packed." She had dreaded telling him, but it had had to be done. But there was the comforting pressure of Marcus' hand on hers, his steadying presence at her side. She fidgeted, shifting her weight from one foot to the other, bracing herself for the flurry of arguments that she assumed would soon ensue.

"I need the carriage," Giles said cannily. "Or at least, the company will, in a week."

Of course. Because they would soon be moving on to Bath, and Giles had too much enjoyed the extravagance of Marcus' carriage to have gone to the bother of hiring out another. Probably he had expected to enjoy it longer.

Marcus cleared his throat. "As to that—we hope to return before then. And failing that, I'll send one down for the company."

"Hm," Giles said, and his gaze flicked back toward the paper. "Yes, all right, then. Safe travels, and all that."

She deflated as if every word that she had held between her teeth, ready to lobby against his judgment, had been torn out unvoiced into the slow breath she exhaled. "That's it?"

Giles lifted his brows. "Lydia," he said. "You became my legal partner some days ago. You don't require my permission or approval to go where you will."

"I—" *Oh.* "I don't. That's right—I don't." How strange that was, and how freeing. She drew in a full breath, surprised by how weightless she felt with it.

"Of course you will be missed, however long you are gone," Giles said, his gaze sliding once more to his paper. "But your responsibility—such as it is—does not lie upon the stage any longer."

And that, too, was a sort of freedom. She would not be letting the company down or forcing them to scramble for a replacement with her sudden absence. And she wondered if he had known that, too—that there might come a time when her responsibilities would lie elsewhere. That by removing the stage to which she had stubbornly clung beyond the time that she perhaps ought to have done, he had also given her back the scrap—the *hope*—of a dream she had long abandoned.

Perhaps he had always seen her more clearly than she had ever seen herself. And just like that, the lingering shreds of resentment that she had been nurturing slipped from her fingers. "I shall miss you," she said, blinking back the burn of tears behind her eyes. "Wretched meddler that you are, I shall miss you dreadfully."

"Lydia," Giles chided, reaching out to grasp her shoulder. "For God's sake, it's not *goodbye*. You'll be back before you know it. Besides," he said, "Newhaven knows that he owes me new props by spring. Your husband-to-be has discovered a latent talent for tinkering, and damned if I don't intend to take the fullest advantage of it."

Swiping one hand across her eyes, Lydia managed to issue a light laugh. "I suppose so," she said. Not *goodbye*, but still the beginning of an inevitable change; the death of the past that had been—when she had needed a friend, and he had needed a tragedy—and the birth of a new relationship that would necessitate certain changes.

"He was always going to take you home," Giles said. "I knew it, even if you didn't. You were always meant to be his baroness."

Yes; she knew that now. But the company would always have a portion of her heart, even if Marcus had claimed the greatest part of it.

Marcus held his hand out to Giles. "We'll have business, I expect," he said, "with theatres in London. Perhaps we can work out a more permanent situation for you there. Something that would not require quite so much travel." Something, Lydia knew he meant to imply, that would let her keep it closer to home.

"I wouldn't say no," Giles said. "We only got the engagement we had there by chance. But it would be—agreeable, I think, to have a bit of stability. Easier to grow the company when it stays in one place." He clapped Marcus' hand in his. "And if you manage, by some miracle, to accomplish your little scheme, I imagine we'll be in higher demand. But you're due for a miracle, I think."

Lydia caught her breath. "Do you think it will work?"

"I think I'd love to be a fly on the wall even if it doesn't," Giles said.

"But then I do love a good drama."

"But you said I wasn't an actress."

"Darling," Giles laughed, "You're not. But the difference is that you will be playing yourself. And that, I think, is the role which suits you best." With one hand he collected his paper again, and used it to shoo at them. "Get you gone, then," he said. "One can stomach only so much maudlin sentimentality in the morning, and I've hit my limit. I'd wish you happy—but I can see you already are."

Nerves settled in shortly after the carriage had got underway, clattering through the icy streets of Southampton toward London. It would be a long journey; plenty of time to worry and stress and wind herself into knots imagining anything and everything that could possibly go wrong. Which was rather a lot, when one got right down to it.

But Marcus was there beside her, and as if he had sensed her working herself into a tizzy, he tucked away whatever it was he had been fiddling with beside her and wrapped her arm around her shoulders, drawing her closer to his side.

"Don't fret," he said softly, into her hair, which had already begun coming loose from its pins.

"But we're going back to London," she said. "What if—what if—"

"We're going to be married," he said firmly. "Immediately. The very first thing."

A nervous laugh trickled from her throat. "But how? Even a common license—"

"Ah." He turned her face to his and kissed away the frown that had settled between her brows. "I'm afraid you'll have to endure the dreadful scandal of being married by special license."

A tiny fraction of her nerves drifted away beneath the heat of his hand. "But they're so dear. And what if you can't obtain one?"

"I promise you I can." He smoothed a stray lock of hair away from her face. "But if I can't, we'll detour to Scotland. It'll take longer than I'd like, and assuredly I'd have to send a new carriage to take the company on to Bath, but—"

242

"What if we are discovered?" Lydia cuddled closer still, tucking her head against his shoulder. "What if someone stops us?"

"How?" Marcus laughed. "We are both of age, and there is no other impediment to our marriage. Lydia," he said, as he took her cold hand in his and pressed his lips to her knuckles, "there is nothing that could be done. Even in the worst case scenario, we'll be married in three days."

"In the best?"

"Ten hours, if the weather holds." He stretched out his legs, propping his feet upon the opposite seat. "First thing," he promised. "Straight to the archbishop to secure a license. By late this evening, we'll be safe at home in our own bed—husband and wife."

Somehow his certainty quelled the flurry of anxiety that had bubbled up within her. "Husband and wife," she whispered, drawing her fingertips across the expanse of his chest, toying with the white linen of the cravat tied about his throat. "At last."

"Yes," he said. "At last. So put your worries aside, just for a few hours, hm?" That arm that he had slung around her held her closer. "By this evening—God and weather willing—you won't need them any longer."

She had lived a life too plagued by uncertainty to surrender such fears easily. But it was…easier than she had expected to lay her head against his shoulder and take a few deep breaths, releasing what she could of them into the warm air of the carriage.

"I am always going to be involved with the theatre," she said. "In one fashion or another."

"I never expected otherwise." His fingers stroked her cheek, brushing a stray lock of hair away from her face. "I would not ask you to give it up."

No, she supposed he would not. Not when he had gone to such lengths to secure it for her in perpetuity. "Did you mean it, then? Finding a theatre in London?"

"If I can. I can't make any promises, but I shall certainly try. And if it comes to nothing, well…" He shrugged. "I suppose we'll do a great deal of traveling."

Traveling. Yes, they would have to. "But your home is in London," she said. "You would—you would have to be away from it a great deal."

"My home is wherever you are. London would be convenient, since we would have a fine house fully staffed already, but I've no objection to traveling if it is necessary." He gave a soft huff of chagrin. "Giles can have his own carriage. He's monopolized mine too much as it is already."

Incredibly, she laughed. Just the tiniest little sound of amusement, but God, it had felt good. And that nasty knot of tension that spent so many years tangled in her chest began, at last, to unwind.

Just two words, spoken before a reverend, had changed the course of her whole life: *I will.* Such a tiny nothing of a sentence, and yet it had changed Lydia into a wife, as if by magic. She hadn't quite been able to make herself believe that it would happen; not when Marcus had been to see the archbishop and had returned with license in hand and dangled it before her eyes, full of satisfaction. Not when Marcus had directed the coachman to his townhouse and had sent Bayberry out in search of a reverend who could be enticed into performing an impromptu wedding irrespective of the lateness of the hour. Not when the requested reverend at last arrived, and Marcus had produced a ring—*the* ring—and a glass of mulled wine, which he had pressed upon her in an effort to relieve her of her jitters.

Not until they had at last spoken those magic words which would bind them together forever, and he had slipped that ring—the one that he had kept all of these years, secreted away in a drawer within his bedchamber; a perfect circle of gold with a delicate filigree of twisting vines blooming with flowers—upon her finger.

For once, everything had gone perfectly to plan. Their marriage had been witnessed, and the license signed, and—that was *it*. That last-moment interruption that she had expected had never come. They were married.

Married.

The house had grown very still as the shroud of night spread over the city, as if it had let out a last sigh of relief and settled down for the evening. Somewhere, there must be servants about, running through their paces before they would find their beds, but just now there was only quiet. Peace.

"I thought we would save proper introductions for tomorrow," Marcus said, as he plucked at the knot of his cravat, peeling the snowy linen from his neck.

Introductions. Yes. That was what was meant to happen when one became the lady of such a grand house. There was a certain order to it all; the staff was meant to be presented to her, and, ostensibly, their orders would

244

now come from her. "Yes," she said. "Tomorrow. That's best, I think."

"Of course you know them all already," Marcus said, because of course she did. It was not the first time she had stayed within this house. It was just her first night as its legal mistress. "Still, there are formalities that ought to be observed. But—not tonight." His waistcoat slid off over his shoulders, and he tossed it carelessly toward a chair situated near the fireplace. "Turn," he said, pantomiming the motion with his index finger. "You haven't got a lady's maid just yet, so I suppose I'll have to do for now."

"I can manage. I've been dressing and undressing myself for some time now," she said, twisting the ring upon her finger.

"I'm certain you can. But let me do this anyway." He brushed a cluster of curls which had long since come down from their pins over her shoulder and away from the buttons that marched down her back. "A reward," he said, "for being right. Ten hours, on the outside."

The tiniest trickle of laughter slid across her lips; a hole in the dam she had made of her emotions for the last few hours, struggling to keep that ever-present anxiety at bay. "I didn't think it would happen," she admitted.

"I know." He nudged buttons from their loops slowly, and tugged at the laces of her stays as they were revealed beneath the parted fabric. Her lungs expanded in a deep breath, which then shuddered out on a sigh. *Relief*, she thought. The scattering of all the tension that had wound her so tightly these last hours. Her shoulders fell from where they had felt hunched about her ears down to their natural slope.

"There," he said, as if he had been waiting for exactly that. "Better?"

"Yes." That was the gown gone—he'd slipped the sleeves down her arms and it had wafted to her feet in a puddle of pink silk. Her wedding gown, she realized. She hadn't given much thought to it this morning when she had put it on. If she had, she would have chosen blue instead. It seemed strange to think of this now, important only in retrospect.

The bedclothes had been turned down, she realized as her petticoats and her stays came off. While she had been fretting and pacing the drawing room in the wait for the reverend, the staff had been off making ready for them here. In this room that now belonged to her just as much as it did him. She suspected that, were she to walk into the dressing room, she would find that her clothing—what remained of it, since she had given the bulk of it to the company—had been neatly unpacked for her already.

Her chemise came off over her head, and a loosed pin dropped to the floor along with it. She was meant to be nervous, she thought—brides were meant to be nervous, weren't they? But the soft crackle of the fire was a comfort to her senses, and the temperature of the room was warm and pleasant even to her naked skin. There was the soft whisk of Marcus' fingers through her hair as he hunted for the remainder of the pins buried in it until at last the whole mass of it came down, tumbling over her shoulders.

"Perfect." It was a low murmur just at her ear, delivered with a kiss to her cheek. "Into bed with you. You'll catch your death." He patted her bottom, and she jumped at the shock of the sensation, a breathless little sound climbing from her throat.

She did as he had asked, even if there wasn't the slightest possibility of catching her death in a room already so warm, removing her stockings before she slid between cool white sheets and retreated to the side of the bed shrouded in shadow. She had been here, in this bed, with him before. It was familiar, and yet—so different than it once had been.

This time, when Marcus had finished removing the last of his clothing and came at last to bed, it would be as her husband. Beneath the smooth velvet counterpane, Lydia turned to her side, propping her head into her hand, listening to the rustle of fabric, watching firelight flicker across skin slowly revealed as Marcus peeled his shirt off over his head.

He sat at the edge of the bed to pry off his boots and stockings, and she reached across the empty space between them to drag just the tip of her finger down the length of his spine, swallowing back a laugh as his muscles flexed and pulled, imbuing his hands with a clumsy sort of urgency as he began to fumble with the fall of his trousers. And then, at last, he climbed beneath the covers, reaching for her.

Bare skin to bare skin. The steady beat of his heart beneath her hand, the light dusting of hair covering his chest tickling her palm. The smooth slide of her legs against his; the curl of his hand at the back of her neck.

"Perfect," he whispered again as she settled there against him in the sweet, soft darkness of the shadows that collected over them.

Her fingertips traced aimless patterns, stretching from his chest to his shoulder and back again. "Perfect," she whispered back. There would be chaos in the near future, she was certain, and scandal, and gossip—but for now, peace. A perfect moment. One where his hand stroked gently through her hair, and there was nothing in the world beyond the gentle flutter of the bed curtains.

Marcus laced his fingers through hers. "I thought—amongst other things, of course—we would go visit your family tomorrow."

246

Lydia smiled against the plane of his chest. "I would like that."

"Will they like me, do you think?"

An indelicate snort. "When they meet you? No." They had had their own resentments for years, and they had been no less valid than her own. It would take time and care for them to fade, though she suspected that proving himself a good husband and a charitable relation would go some way toward repairing the poor opinion he had earned. "But, eventually, yes, they will like you."

"Good," he said. "We are going to take care of them. It's a pity we have missed the chance for a family Christmas. But there is next year."

Yes. And the year after that, and so on, and so forth, stretching out into the unknowable future. A future they had claimed at last, and it promised to be a beautiful one. She could almost feel it there, sparkling at the very tips of her fingers, so bright and lovely and warm.

"Do you know," she said, sliding her leg up the length of his thigh, "marriages must be consummated?"

"Must they?" There was the warmth of a smile in the words. "I suppose you're right. But we have got a busy day ahead of us tomorrow. Probably a few busy days ahead of us."

"But not tonight." Tonight was only peace and magic. Hours and hours of it, and it belonged only to them.

"No," he said against the seam of her lips. "Not tonight." There was no hurry in the gentle caress of his hands as they slid down her back and found the curve of her hips. Only a peculiar sort of reverence; the amazement of a man who could not quite believe his good fortune. "I love you," he murmured, turning her onto her back. "I promise you, I will never give you reason to doubt it."

"I know."

"You don't." He softened the words with a brief kiss. "I always wanted to say it. Too many times to count. So you'll have to grow accustomed to that, I'm afraid."

"Will I?" She arched into the caress of his hand as he slid it down the flat plane of her stomach. "How lovely."

"Of course I will want to hear it, also." The delicate stroke of his fingers drifted across her most sensitive skin. "Often."

A chuckle faded into a sigh. "How often, do you think?"

"As often as you can manage." The stubble burnishing his jaw abraded the skin of her throat, but the touch of his lips soothed away the brief burn.

Arousal bloomed beneath the teasing touch of his fingers, the radiant glitter of it lighting every nerve. Her hips lifted and jerked as he slid his fingers inside her; a deep velvety stroke that touched the deepest part of her and left tingles in its wake.

"I love you," she gasped against the back of her hand, as she clutched at his shoulder with the other. "I love you."

"Mm. Yes; just like that." He murmured the words against her breast, and his teeth caught her nipple in a delicate pinch that made her throw her head back against the pillow.

Lydia writhed, half-mad already, her nails digging tiny divots into the flesh of his shoulder. His name trickled from her lips in a litany, descending from terse demand to plaintive plea as long minutes passed in sensual torment. The growing tension became unendurable, the arch of her hips strung by the tautness of her thighs, held wide at last to admit the width of his hips between them.

"Again," he said, poised there on the precipice of madness himself.

"I love you," she said, the words catching in her throat with a sob, as at last he slid home, burying himself within her. She embraced him with her arms about his shoulders, her legs about his hips, and he caught the kiss she offered to him, giving his own back to her.

"Lydia," he murmured into her mouth. "My wife. My love."

Yes. The heat of passion misted her skin with a fine sheen of sweat, but it was the warmth of love that held her cradled safely in its grasp, in his arms. Marcus whispered them to her, all of those love words he had long denied, every secret thing he had held within his heart now freely shared.

And then—and then words became not just unnecessary, but impossible. But the love remained there still between them, traded in soft touches and sweet kisses. In the clasp of arms and the sweeping caresses of fingertips. She met the slow plunge of his hips, reveled in the tenderness of his lips over hers.

That tenderness remained even when that honeyed adoration turned wild; when delicacy had burned away into desperation. His groan vibrated against the smooth skin of her shoulder as she lifted her hips into each thrust, bearing down upon him with silky inner muscles that strove to keep him within her. She sank her hands into the cool, dark strands of his hair and brought his mouth back to hers, swallowing the indecent sound he made as her own splintering climax forced him finally to his own.

The delicious flow of pleasure spreading out in glorious golden waves.

248

The indecipherable pattern of his fractured breaths near her ear, and the warm, heavy weight of his body over hers, two hearts beating as one. A miracle—a dream—come true at long last.

Marcus pressed his forehead to hers and interlinked their fingers; a weave that could not be broken. That vast distance closed and bound by the thread of the gold ring he had placed upon her finger, and sealed with the most solemn of vows shared between them.

"Perfect," he said, turning her into the cradle of his arms.

And it was.

Chapter Twenty Nine

Lydia's fingers had long since cramped past the point of uselessness, but there were still so many invitations left to address. Dozens at least, though she knew not how many of those who would receive them would accept. And the hours had been steadily whiling away into the depths of the evening.

But at least she had had good company. "Are you certain you won't be missed?" she asked.

Diana smiled, her pen pausing on the sheet of parchment over which she had been laboring. "No," she said. "Not really. Not by much of anyone." She dipped the nib within the inkwell situated near her elbow and continued writing in her perfect, fluid script. "It was only a ball this evening, and I'm a perpetual wallflower." Rafe had offered to escort her—a task that their Father once would have foisted off upon Marcus—only he had brought her here instead. He and Marcus had been occupied much of the day otherwise, off on their own to do their part in their grand scheme.

There had been so many plans to make, and they had needed all the assistance they could get. But Diana had always been an accommodating sort of person, and she had been pleased as punch to throw her lot in with theirs.

"I don't suppose," Lydia said, carefully, tentatively, "that, should things go to plan, you might...wish to come stay here? With us?"

Diana's lovely dark eyes widened in surprise behind the silver rims of her spectacles. "Could I?" she asked. And then, "I suppose I could, at that. It's not a bachelor household anymore, is it?"

No, though it wasn't yet common knowledge. "I'm certain Marcus would agree," Lydia said. "Though I can't say it would do your reputation any favors. But—you are welcome. If you like."

"I would," Diana said, and she stretched her hand across the table to grasp Lydia's. "I would like that very much."

Another obstacle surmounted, Lydia thought. Her first real friend within the social class she had married into. She had made just incredible mountains of them, those obstacles which she had thought would forever be between them, but one at a time they were being dismantled. Marcus had made good with her family just this morning—or at least as good as *could* be made, given that Papa had been at first forbidding, and then at most begrudgingly accepting once Lydia had made her wishes plain. That, too, would improve itself in time; especially with the liberal contribution of funds which Marcus had provided, and which would keep Mama and Papa secure and their butcher's shop in good stead with their landlord. Though they had tentatively broached the subject of closing it down for good in favor of a generous annuity which would keep them more than comfortable, her parents had not yet been ready to surrender their livelihood.

But she thought he had earned at least a grudging respect of them, for his humility. For having come to them in a spirit of contrition, and for doing all in his power to right past wrongs.

"How many more?" Lydia asked, flexing her fingers as she took up her pen once again.

"Let me see," Diana said, as she scratched through a name on the list, and scanned the lines remaining. "Only thirty or so."

Lydia barely stifled a groan.

"You married into this," Diana remarked lightly, a twist of humor lingering about her lips. "It's all letter-writing and morning calls. Occasionally, you shall have to pretend to be vastly interested in someone's mediocre skills at the pianoforte—or worse, the flute. I swear to you, I have heard notes so shrill they might have shattered glass."

Chuckling, Lydia scratched out another invitation, though her penmanship, after so many, had left something to be desired. "Do you think…do you think they'll come?" she asked.

"All?" Diana asked. "No chance of it, I'm afraid. But the very worst of the gossips? Most assuredly. They'll skip another engagement if they have got one already in order to do so. If even half of those invited choose to attend, you'll have more than you need."

As Lydia folded up another invitation, there was the sound of boots in the foyer—and then Marcus was striding into the room, Rafe on his heels. "We've secured the theatre," he said.

"Good," Diana said. "We've almost finished here." She gestured to the stack of completed invitations.

"Wonderful. I'll give them over to Bayberry once you've done with them." Marcus bent to brush a kiss high on Lydia's cheek. "How has it gone while I've been out?"

"Quietly." But then, no one knew, exactly, except Rafe and Diana now, that they had come back to town. "I've decided that Diana should come to live with us," she said.

"Have you, then? Splendid." His gaze slid to Diana. "Well, I suppose you are of age, Diana, if you're amenable. Lydia, would you call for supper?" He cast a glance over his shoulder. "Rafe, will you join us?"

"Might as well." Rafe dropped into a chair and slipped something from his pocket. "You nearly left this behind at the theatre," he said. "Why should you be carrying a knife?"

"It's meant to be a dagger, actually. Just something I've been tinkering with," Marcus said, as he collected it from Rafe's hands. "I've almost got it; I'm certain of it. Here, let me show you."

Lydia slipped from the room to find a servant and give the order for supper, grateful to have the chance to stretch her legs for a moment, and to give her aching fingers a rest. They had almost come through the worst of it, she thought. Tomorrow would tell whether their efforts would be in vain.

Lydia had not asked how Marcus had secured the use of the theatre, but she assumed that it had involved the greasing of several palms—from the owner straight down to the actors who presently had the use of it. All that mattered was that it *had* been secured for the few hours in which they would require its use.

Several of the more enterprising actors had been enticed to stay as well, in exchange for a few extra coins, just to ensure that all ran smoothly. It had been a great help indeed in ensuring that those who had come—out of curiosity or support, it was impossible to say—had found their seats swiftly, and more importantly, *silently*. It was, in fact, the exact opposite of what one could typically expect of a visit to the theatre. There were no orange girls selling their wares, no maddening thrum of conversation threatening to drown out the players. At most, there was the occasional footfall, mostly muffled by the heavy curtain that separated the audience—perhaps as many as a hundred people on the upper end—from the stage.

They had been promised a spectacle in exchange for their silence. And by God, she would give them one. A spectacle in one act; perhaps the most important role of her life.

She found Marcus there upon the stage, tinkering even now in a chair at a table that had been left over from whatever production was currently on, looking as if he hadn't a care in the world. Blithely fidgeting with his design, he didn't even notice her until she was upon him. "What are you doing?" she asked, lowering her voice to a bare whisper, conscious of their unseen audience. "You're meant to be backstage already."

Sheepishly, he set his invention aside upon the table, turning to face her. "I thought this the safest place to be," he said. "At least until Father arrives. Wouldn't want to be caught out before the show."

Reasonable, she thought. But still not ideal. "You're certain he'll come?"

"Oh, yes. Diana said he was *apoplectic*." He smothered a snicker with his palm, rising from his chair.

She could just imagine. For a man who had thought himself secure enough to threaten her as once he had, she could only guess at the depths of the rage into which he had sunk when he had received his personal invitation.

To their wedding—or so he was meant to think.

There had been no lines to memorize; this would be a performance from the heart. And even if it did not proceed precisely as they had hoped, still it would be a victory of her own. A gauntlet thrown down to put Marcus' father in his place. *We have won, and you—you have lost.*

"The acoustics are good," Marcus said as he rose to his feet. "But it wouldn't matter even if they were not. Father is very fond of shouting, and I imagine he'll do a great deal of it."

God, she hoped so. She settled into the crook of the arm he offered her, tucking her head beneath his chin. One embrace for bravery, just to hold as much as she could of him with her until it was all over. "*Go,*" she said, as she plucked her ring from her finger and dropped it into the cup of his palm for safekeeping, softening the demand with a kiss. "You can't play my part for me."

"No, but I will be the first to offer you my congratulations." He squeezed her hands in his. "Soon." Then he was gone, sliding off the stage into the shadows.

Now there was just to wait.

Father had come earlier than instructed, but then they had expected that. Of course, he would have wanted to foil a disadvantageous marriage before it could come to fruition. He had done so once already. Marcus could hear him even now, tearing through the areas behind the stage, searching for him, or for Lydia, or both. Probably the whole of the theatre could hear him in the stifling silence.

From his position in the wing, Marcus watched Lydia flinch at a massive crash that had rolled out in a cascade of sound—a temper tantrum, he thought. Absent his true targets, Father had elected to take his fury out upon some innocent prop or another.

It would not be long now. He watched Lydia compose herself, steeling herself against the rage that would soon be directed at her. She had set herself up for it after all, there, in the yawning vacancy of the stage. *Look at me*, her presence there seemed to say, clad in the armor of her lovely scarlet gown. *Look only at me.* She commanded attention with her vibrancy, and that—that was more or less the point. To drown out everything else, until she had the whole of Father's attention, with none left to be spared for anything beyond her.

It didn't take long. Father had blundered his way toward the stage at last, and the vivid hue of Lydia's gown had caught his eye; like a red flag waved before an enraged bull.

"You *whore.*" The seething hiss ricocheted about the stage, and the pound of Father's footsteps across the stage climbed high over the tiny ripple of murmurs, swiftly hushed, beyond the curtain. He hadn't noticed. To him, nothing but Lydia existed.

And she looked *bored.* "So you have said, my lord," she said in that clear, carrying voice—her stage voice, not that Father knew any better. "And it is growing rather tiresome."

Father hadn't noticed that he was being led directly to his own humiliation; that Lydia held the whole of the theatre in the clasp of her fingers. "Did you honestly believe that I would allow you to marry my son?" he asked, his fists clenching at his sides as he strode forward, one threatening step at a time.

Lydia hit her marks like the trained professional she was, subtly reorienting them, turning just slightly, a bit at a time, until she faced the audience, and Father—Father stood in the place she had intended for him, his back to the curtain. "Allow? No. But I fail to see how you could possibly stop me." Her chin notched up, challenging, without the slightest hint of trepidation. There
254

was so much strength within her, so much courage—and she let Father see it upon her face; that ungovernable spirit, the indomitable essence of her. A queen standing as tall as she could, brandishing her disdain like a saber in the face of an unworthy foe.

Marcus felt his chest—his *heart*—swell with pride.

He pulled the ropes of the curtain himself.

More people than she had expected, each watching with rapt attention. There was Diana, in the very front, and Rafe beside her, bordered by so many curious faces that Lydia did not recognize. The squeak of the wheels and strain of the ropes coupled with the sweep of the velvet had hardly registered above a whisper. She had, after all, positioned herself in the center of the stage, and the curtain, parted only halfway, framed the scene perfectly. So long as nothing else pulled his attention elsewhere, his lordship would never notice that this small slice of stage had been revealed to the audience.

And the audience—titillated, scandalized—scarcely breathed.

"No?" the marquess said, on the hoarse rasp of a malicious laugh. "Have you forgotten my warning so quickly?" Another step he took toward her, but Lydia stubbornly held her ground. "I seem to have arrived before the reverend," he said, "though God alone knows why one would have agreed to this—this *farce*, performed upon a *stage*."

"The stage has been my home these past years," she said, making an effort to ignore the audience behind him. "It seemed fitting." His nose was slightly crooked, she noticed. Good. He had deserved that, and more besides. "You won't be rid of me so easily this time, my lord."

It was bait, although he had not realized it. A snare she had cast out at his feet, and he stumbled straight into it. "You stupid, foolish girl. It was comically easy to ruin you five years ago. I could ruin you and everyone you hold dear with so little effort, and to complain of it would avail you nothing. Do you think anyone of note would ever take the word of a woman of your stamp over my own?"

"Marcus would," she said. "He loves me. He would have married me then, if not for you. If you hadn't staged that scandal."

"I *saved* him from you!" The fierce shout echoed, drowning out the small, shocked gasps the admission had garnered from the audience. "I saved him, and if he was not properly appreciative of my efforts, by God, he will be one day." Another step, drawing him further from the audience at his back. "So here we are. You think you have *won*."

She knew she had. And if she had not won back her reputation, at the very least she had won the acknowledgment that she had never committed the crime for which she had been unjustly accused. And that, she thought— that was enough. It would be enough to silence Marcus' father, if only for the fact that he had proved himself a liar and a villain upon this very stage. He had earned his own reputation, now, and it had been won honestly. Whatever he said of her, whatever the color with which he attempted to paint her pub- licly, it would be for naught.

No one would lend him credence ever again.

"I think," she said, in the gentle, crisp tones of the lady that Marcus had made her into, "that you can cast whichever stones you like into our path, and it will avail you nothing. We have weathered worse. We have—"

"You have *nothing*. Not a damned thing." His foot lashed out sending the chair in which Marcus had so recently been sitting flying across the stage with a resounding crash. "No ring, no reverend, nor even a groom. I'll be damned if you'll be married today—or any other." He braced one hand upon the small table underneath which the chair he had so ruthlessly abused had once been tucked, and his gaze fell upon his hand there, which he had inadvertently placed upon a small object. A rippling laugh began in his chest, growing in mania every second.

Lydia felt her breath stagger in her throat. Marcus had been tinkering there when she had found him and shooed him away—and he had left behind his dagger.

And as his father curled his fingers around the leather-wrapped hilt of it, she realized all at once that her play in one act had quite abruptly acquired an unanticipated death scene.

If not for the tiniest flick of Lydia's hand in his direction, Marcus would have charged out of hiding. And now he was frozen there in the shadows, watch- ing his deepest fear play out upon the stage, dread settling in the pit of his stomach.

High and shrill, tinged with terror, Lydia laughed. "Murder is beneath you, my lord."

"But expedient." This was issued in a tone of idle consideration; Father weighed the merits of such an action with the counterbalance of the dagger in his hand. "I warned you away, and you have shown yourself to be incapable of appreciating the chance I offered to you. I could be forgiven, I think, for creating a more permanent solution."

Good God, he was talking himself into murder! *Justifying* it to himself, with the sort of blind fanaticism of a man who could not be reasoned with, who could never be moved to consider any opinion that might run contrary to his own.

"You cannot hope to get away with such a thing," Lydia said. "Your presence has certainly been marked."

"By *actors*," Father sneered dismissively. "Who would believe such claims from those who make their livings with lies?" His shoulders rolled in a shrug, as if he sought to convince himself as much as her. "And even if they did, peers do not often pay for their crimes," he said. "You—you will not be missed much."

Lydia gave a resounding shriek as he lunged, her hands flying out as if to ward him off just as Father lashed out with the dagger, driving it straight toward her heart. For a long, tense moment there was only silence as that ear-piercing scream abbreviated itself into tiny, muted whimpers.

Father's face wrenched in disgust, and he drew away as Lydia staggered back one step, then another, her fingers clutching at the hilt of the dagger he had released. In a great puff of scarlet skirts, she wilted to the floor.

"*Lydia!*" Marcus cried, fear seizing in his chest as his legs unlocked themselves at last and he sprang onto the stage.

"My God, he's killed her!" came a shout from the audience.

Father gave a fierce jerk as the words assaulted his ears. Slowly, with the encroaching realization of the position in which he had placed himself, he turned to face the audience at last, there revealed in the half-drawn curtain. The florid fury that had lent a violent red tinge to his features seemed to drain from it all at once, a ghostly pallor stealing over his face instead. "I—I—"

Marcus scarcely heard the disapproving murmurs that had begun to swell. His knees collapsed beneath him as he reached Lydia's side, lifting her head into his lap with trembling fingers.

She blinked her eyes open at once. "Was that too much, do you think?"

The relief that swept over him was so pure and perfect that he shook with it. A hoarse bark of laughter slipped from his throat, and he swiped one hand at the tears that had escaped in the horror of the moments before. "A bit overdramatic," he managed to say, sweeping her hair away from her face. "My God," he whispered, bending to brush a kiss to her lips. "I thought I had killed you." Such a careless act, forgetting his dagger there upon the table. "I thought for certain I had botched it; that the mechanism had failed and he'd stabbed you in truth and it would be my fault."

"In truth, it *does* need some work," she said, and pulled the dagger away from her chest. There was the tiniest tear, there in the front of her gown. The blade had not retracted completely, it seemed; just the very tip had been exposed, and though it had been deliberately blunted, still it had caused some damage to the fragile silk of her gown. "Giles will murder you if you let this make a wreck of his costumes. But it served its purpose well enough just now."

There was yet another riffle of shock through the crowd as Marcus helped Lydia to her feet, and Father, who had been unable to offer much of an explanation for his actions to the horrified onlookers, now turned his attention back to them.

"A farce!" he exclaimed, his mouth contorting into a sneer. "I ought to have known—you set a trap for me."

"And how easily you stepped into it," Lydia said, as Marcus wrapped his arm around her.

"You *meant* for me to kill you!"

Lydia issued an incredulous laugh. "In fact, that was an accident. You *chose* murder, my lord. We meant only to allow you the opportunity to make your confession before a jury of your peers. And they *are* your peers, sir." Her chin lifted, and she gestured toward their audience with a tiny flutter of her fingers. "You have revealed yourself—and the evil of which you are capable—to them."

As whispers turned to rumbles and rumbles to scornful jeers, Father seemed to shrink in on himself, growing smaller and smaller in the abrupt turn of their once good opinions. Those whom he had once called *friend* were no longer. He had severed his respectability with the same blade with which he had meant to do murder.

"You ought to be thankful, my lord. Only think how much worse it might have been had you succeeded," Lydia said, above the rising crescendo of contempt issued by their audience. "I don't want you to hang. I only want

258

you to let us alone. We are done with you." She jerked her chin to the audience. "And so are they. Say what you will; no one will hear you now. You are proved a liar and a scoundrel by your own admission, by your own hand."

Marcus slipped his hand into his pocket and retrieved Lydia's ring. "You had lost, Father, before you had even arrived," he said. "We were married days ago."

Strangely, as Lydia slipped the ring back onto her finger, there was a scattering of applause from the crowd. They had not, in fact, expected the approval of those they had invited to witness this scene; by any measure, they would have considered Marcus to have married beneath him.

But Lydia preened beneath the endorsement, however minor. A subtle sign of changing tides, Marcus thought. She had wrested validation from those naturally reluctant to give it and secured a place for herself amongst them, garnering if not *acceptance,* then at least a begrudging respect.

Humiliated and beaten, Father had no recourse but to slink away, enduring the judgmental stares he had earned with a passive stoicism that spoke of smothered pride. Probably he would retreat for a good long while to lick his wounds and wait for this newest scandal to blow over, but—he would never again enjoy the same position in society he once had had.

"I imagine you'll find yourself quite popular," Marcus said, *sotto voce,* to Lydia. "That was a truly convincing death scene." To the point that it had given him heart palpitations and a cold wash of fear that had yet to fully relieve itself.

"Do you think?" Lydia asked.

"Oh, yes. There's nothing quite like London gossip. This little drama will be all about town by nightfall at the latest. You'll be buried under invitations." From all of those people who would want her to recount it all again and again. "Musicales. Balls. Dinner parties. I'm certain you'll have your pick."

"How lovely," Lydia mused, turning her cheek to receive a kiss. "I'm loads of fun at parties."

Epilogue

London, England
One week later

I've had a letter from Giles," Lydia flashed, storming into Marcus' office, waving the letter about as she dropped into a chair, her vibrant yellow skirts fluttering with the force of her ire. "Just listen to this: Dearest Lydia."

"It's started off well enough," Marcus interjected, earning himself a glare.

"Dearest Lydia," she repeated, in scathing tones, as she read once more from the letter clenched in her hand. "My most sincere apologies. I suppose I am forced to admit that you *can* act to save your life. But only *just.*"

Marcus disguised the burst of laughter that had risen in his throat with a cough, though he could see that he had not fooled her in the least. "It was a remarkable death scene," he said, consolingly. "Truly inspired. The talk of the town."

"I am going to *geld* him!" she seethed, folding her arms across her chest.

"No, you aren't," Marcus said. "Besides, I'm certain you can find more effective ways to make Giles miserable than that."

"Not from London I can't." She pulled a pout as she returned her attention to the letter. "He thanks you for the carriage you sent down to Bath, by the way."

"Does he?"

"Well, not in so many words," she admitted, and Marcus was willing to bet that he hadn't been thanked in *any* words. "Still, I wish—"

He knew. They had *meant* to meet the company in Bath, but life so rarely turned out as one expected. Father had removed himself from London like a thief in the night, and Mother—never the hardiest of souls—had been unable to bear the scandal that had reared its ugly head, though it had not been of her own making. She had *gone visiting*; a polite term when one wished to escape

260

such things. She had a small property in Scotland to which she had fled, and Marcus suspected it would be some time indeed, if ever, before she chose to return.

But the absence of both Mother and Father had left Diana more or less to her own devices, and she had required chaperoning. She and Lydia rubbed along well together, and they had spent much time in one another's company since Diana had moved in, but it would take time to secure an acceptable chaperone for those times that they would be absent from London, and it could not have been done in time to remove themselves to Bath with the company.

So Lydia had been working as best she could here, sending just avalanches of letters back and forth, trying to keep abreast of company news. She had taken to the business end of it like a duck to water—but he knew she missed it. The people; the chaos. The camaraderie.

And she would have it again. Probably sooner than she had thought.

Marcus reached for his desk drawer, rooting around within. "I didn't want to tell you," he said. "Not until I was certain I could manage it, you understand."

"Manage what?" Her blond brows pulled together, confusion drifting across her face.

"Well—" Marcus sighed, snatching up the letter he'd tucked away in the drawer and pulling it free. "*This*," he said, sliding it across the desk to her. "It's not a patent theatre, mind you." That would mean no Shakespeare; no serious dramas. But perhaps they were all due for a bit of comedy.

Lydia snatched up the letter, her brows lifting as she read. In a wondering tone, she said, "You found us a theatre?"

Marcus shrugged. It had taken some doing, in fact, and he had not been certain he had managed it until just this morning. "If you want it. It's not *ideal*—"

"It's *perfect*." An airy trickle of laughter floated around the room as she leapt from her chair. "You found us a theatre!"

But the decision was only hers to make. He had engaged himself with the preliminary negotiations, the inquiries, the menial work of it. But the company itself was not his own, and never would be—by design. "If you want it—if the terms are agreeable to you—I can have my solicitor draft up a contract at once."

"Yes," she said, imbued with delight. "Yes—of course I must tell Giles, but he does prefer London, so I can't imagine he will have many objections.

261

But *first*." She placed her palm right upon the smooth surface of the desk, and the sparkling glint of her smile had only the competition of the bright winter sun.

"First?"

"First, I am going to have you six ways to Sunday, right on this desk."

"*Only* six?" He managed to inflect his voice with the tiniest shred of disappointment.

"To begin with," she purred. Thank God he had kept his desk organized, with few loose papers or knickknacks strewn across it—for what little *had* been there she swept aside. A few unread bits of correspondence, a stoppered inkwell, and a wax stamp went tumbling to the floor as she crawled across his desk, both Giles' letter and the one from the owner of the theatre abandoned in the chair she had vacated.

She managed to sink back onto her knees there before him—a neat trick, considering she had had to pull her skirts out from beneath them first—and reached out to slide her hands into his hair, pulling him toward her.

"All right." Somehow he had achieved just the right amount of mock exasperation. "Have your way with me then."

Lydia nipped his lower lip, a playful little love bite that didn't even sting, and sighed as she slid from the desk into his lap. "I will have my way, won't I?" she murmured against his lips.

"Always," he said. "Always."

Six months later

"Oh, for God's sake," Giles muttered, slamming his hand over his eyes like some sort of scandalized damsel, providing precious time in which for Lydia and Marcus to frantically attempt to right clothing that had become unforgivably disheveled. "Will you *please* take your revolting connubial bliss elsewhere?"

With a guilty flush, Lydia pulled at the sleeves of her gown, sliding them back up her arms. "So what if we were christening the office?" she muttered. "You might have knocked, at least!"

Marcus had turned his back on Giles in favor of fastening the fall of his trousers, but she heard the slight wheeze of his barely-stifled laughter.

Giles gave a sigh of exasperation. "It doesn't need to be christened. It's an *office*."

"It's *my* office," Lydia shot back. It pleased Giles to be contrary about such things, but he truly didn't *want* the office. He was content enough to leave the business of *business* to her, and to spend the time that it had freed up for him trying his hand at writing his own plays. He had yet to produce a play entire, but she had faith that he would, eventually. The scenes he had, however abashedly, offered for her perusal, she had found to be vastly entertaining. "And henceforth, you will *knock*."

"You may be certain I will do so," Giles sniffed, tilting his nose in the air in a ridiculous attempt at an unearned hauteur. "If only so I might avoid the sight of your husband's bare arse in the future."

"Lydia quite likes my arse, if you must know," Marcus remarked.

"I'd rather I did not. I'd *really* rather I did not." Giles pinched the bridge of his nose. Collecting himself, he drew in a deep breath and jabbed a finger at Marcus. "*You*," he said. "You have hardly been pulling your weight around here. I've half a mind to put you back at the mending."

Marcus rounded on him, appalled. "I beg your pardon! I've perfected the dagger, haven't I?" Finally, he had got the working of it exactly right, and it hadn't left so much as the smallest of tears upon even the flimsiest costumes.

"Not a lot of murders in comedy," Giles said snidely. "It's useless to me now, and *will* be until and unless you can secure us a contract with a patent theatre." He scrubbed at his face with one hand. "Your cravat, Newhaven. It's a damned mess."

"What?" Marcus touched his hand to his throat. "Ah, hell. So it is. Lydia?"

"Perhaps if you had not decided to use the office as the site of your illicit little trysts—"

"*Hardly* illicit." Lydia waved her hand, and her ring glinted in the candlelight. But her efforts toward smoothing the neat folds of Marcus' cravat were for naught; it was hopelessly wrinkled.

"I have dismissed actors for less," Giles remarked.

"You can't dismiss me; I'm your partner."

"Newhaven, however—"

"Isn't actually an employee, and still remains our best chance at securing a patent theatre in the future." Lydia patted Marcus' chest. "I'm sorry. You'll have to do as is."

"Not to worry," Giles said. "No one of note will mark his dishevelment, given that he'll be manning the curtain this evening."

"What! Lydia—"

Lydia shrugged. "Giles runs the company every bit as much as I do," she said. "It's the curtains for you, my love."

"Ah, I see." Marcus pulled a scowl, shoving his hands in his pockets. "You cannot punish her, so you'll punish me instead."

"Why, Newhaven." Giles placed one hand over his heart. "I'd not have credited you with half so much intelligence." His gaze slid to Lydia once more. "Before I was so indecently assaulted with the sight of your husband's bare arse—"

"You can stop saying *bare arse*," Marcus muttered beneath his breath. "We're all aware."

"—I had come to tell you that your family has arrived."

"Have they?" Lydia grinned. "And how long until the performance?"

"Ten minutes," Giles said.

"Damn," Marcus sighed, dragging his hand through his ruffled hair. "Not enough time. We'll tell them after?"

"I suppose we must." Disappointing, but it would keep for just a few hours.

"Tell them what?" Giles asked, his eyes narrowing in suspicion, that icy blue that could ferret out a secret at twenty paces. "Oh, lord—you're breeding, aren't you. I *thought* you had gotten a bit thick about the waist."

"Rude!" Lydia gasped, pummeling Giles in the shoulder, and he laughed as he fended off her weak attempt at assault. "And to think we meant to ask you to be Godfather!"

"*Godfather!*" he said. "To *your* wretched little bratling?" He dodged another feeble blow. "Darling, I'd be delighted."

Lydia stifled a hiccough with her palm, her eyes watering.

Marcus patted at his pockets. "Oh, Lord," he said. "You've done it now." He found a handkerchief tucked away somewhere and passed it to Lydia. "She'll be a watering pot for the next half hour at *least*."

"I can't help it," Lydia sniffed, patting futilely at her face. "I'm just— *happy*."

"Well, you look perfectly wretched." Giles heaved a sigh, scrubbing at his eyes. "In light of this momentous occasion, I suppose I could be moved to mercy. Just this once, mind you. Take your wife, Newhaven, and go revel

264

in your joy together with your family. I shall find some other poor soul to man the curtain in your place."

"*Revel in your joy*?" Marcus echoed, laughing incredulously. "What a peculiar turn of phrase for you, Montgomery."

"Naturally, if asked, I shall deny that I have ever said any such thing. Now go—go, before you can pollute my theatre with any more of your nauseating happiness." Giles made a little shooing motion with his hands.

"What do you say?" Lydia asked of Marcus as she blotted away the last of her tears. "I think I'd quite like to watch from a box for once. Shall we?"

"Of course," he said. "Anything you like." Marcus offered her his arm, and together they left the office to make their way to the box which had been reserved for them. And it was there that Lydia experienced the true magic she had so longed for, and it wasn't on the stage at all—it was just here, in a private box, surrounded by everyone she loved, and who loved her.

She took her seat at last, as Marcus clasped her hand in his, bordered by her parents, her sister, Diana, and Rafe.

The curtains swept across the stage, and with them came a great sense of the rest of her life unfurling before her with just as much promise.

And the play began.

Author's Notes

I have taken quite a few liberties for the purposes of plot here, so I hope you will forgive them! It is true that the theatre of the time was quite a spectacle, and was not generally given the level of reverence that it commands today. During the time period this book takes place, a visit to the theatre was mostly a social event, where the rich would go to see and be seen. People would conduct business and conversations, attendees would often come in late— especially those of the lower classes, who could sometimes only afford to attend later in the evening, when theatres would reduce the price of admission because so much of the play had already passed. There would be orange girls selling their wares, possibly entertainment between acts, and often a pantomime after the conclusion of the play.

Also in the time period, it was more likely than not that if you attended the theatre regularly, you would see a different play each time. For obvious reasons, that was not ideal for my purposes, so I elected to use the more modern standard of staging productions in runs.

Until 1843, certain theatres were designated as 'patent theatres,' which is to say that these were the only theatres legally licensed to perform the works of Shakespeare and other serious dramas. The Theatre Royal Drury Lane was one of three of these in London, along with the Covent Garden Theatre and Haymarket Theatre. The first two operated in the winter months, while the latter operated in summer. There were other patent theatres across England, and by 1788, local magistrates were permitted to issue such licenses to theatres more than 20 miles outside of London. Because of these restrictions, some particularly enterprising actors employed certain methods to circumvent them in truly remarkable ways. If you're curious about that sort of thing, I would definitely recommend looking up the rise of illegitimate theatre in the era. It's fascinating.

Just a decade earlier than this book takes place, theatres would have been lit by candles. It was an arduous task to manage them, since if they were not regularly tended to, the wax would drip down upon the attendees below, and most people took hot wax falling upon them from above poorly. So many candles could also prove dangerous—the Drury Lane theatre had burned down twice already by the time this book takes place. By 1817, Drury Lane was lit by gaslight.

Actors were not particularly well thought of, and actresses in particular commanded little respect—though some did in fact marry into the aristocracy, it was more common for gentlemen with means to seek them out as mistresses. A few actresses could even lay claim to the fact that they had been the mistresses of kings.

Although I *did* look, I was unable to find any concrete information on the invention of stage knives with retractable blades, so it's quite possible that Marcus is either too early *or* too late in the game there. What information I did find suggests that they are actually dangerous and should not be used if it can be avoided, in fact. However I did want him to invest himself in the theatre, since it is such an important part of Lydia's life, and strive to make himself genuinely useful there. But then since I included it, I became a victim of *Chekhov's Gun* (which is a narrative principle that says that if a gun is introduced in act one, it should, at some point, be fired). So I had to find an actual use for it, naturally. Attempted murder seemed fitting.

And now I have to confess that this book had a title before it had much of a plot. Some of you might have recognized it as a play on one of Shakespeare's most famous stage directions—[exit, pursued by a bear]—which does in fact originate from act three of *The Winter's Tale*.

I thought it was practically *begging* to be used as a title. It was so easy to make it into one! But then—*then* I had to write a whole *book* around it. I have read quite a lot of Shakespeare, though I will absolutely admit I am a basic *Much Ado About Nothing* bitch, but I had actually never read—or seen—*The Winter's Tale*. And I don't think it would have been right to steal a title from The Bard himself without at least that much.

So I read it. And I watched it. And I *hated* it. Really! It is three acts of tragedy followed by two acts of farce, and no one seems to care terribly much that people *died* because Leontes made an ass of himself. It is entirely glossed over! And Hermione—who lost a son and sixteen years of her daughter's life—just *lets* him get away with it! Absolutely unacceptable.

You can find an absolutely beautiful production of it on YouTube, if you would like to have a deeper understanding of the play. It is in fact very well performed, and Hermione's speech at her trial moved me to tears. But I cannot say I found the play *itself* enjoyable. I wish I could!

Still, the main female players—Hermione, Paulina, and Perdita—were all perfect archetypes of Lydia at various stages of her life, and I found that much at least compelling.

The speech Lydia gives to Marcus on the stage is pulled straight from Paulina's speech in act three, scene two of *The Winter's Tale*, and it is such a good one. Paulina, in particular, is such a powerful figure in the story. It is a shame that Hermione is really only allowed to be a tragic queen; I would have liked to see her own fury on her behalf.

But instead I coiled all three women together, and gave their feelings to Lydia to manage. And I gave all of the suffering that we should have seen from Leontes to Marcus instead, because it is not fair to the reader to hand-wave sixteen years of it between acts.

People *died*, Shakespeare! *People died!*

Thank you so much for reading! There will be more to come in the future from the Beaumont family; I have nebulous plans for Diana and Rafe. If you enjoyed this book, please tell people! One of the best ways to support indie authors is through exposure, whether through ratings, reviews, or just telling friends! As always, you can keep up with me on Facebook and Instagram, or email me at aydra@aydrarichards.com.

I also have a website and a newsletter! You can sign up to receive book news and other tidbits from me at aydrarichards.com.

Love,

Aydra

To Sue

MIDDLE PIDDING

by

Val Whitehouse

Love from Val Whitehouse